## Praise for novels by DiAnn Mills

### Breach of Trust

"This masterfully crafted suspense novel immediately hooks the reader. . . . A real page-turner."

*BOOKLIST*

"Featuring a well-paced plot and an engaging protagonist, Mills's new series launch is a solid . . . suspense title."

*LIBRARY JOURNAL*

"A novel jam-packed with twists that will leave readers breathless. A must-read for any avid suspense reader."

*ROMANTIC TIMES*

"An engaging page-turner with intriguing characters facing difficult choices."

*CBA RETAILERS + RESOURCES*

"A fast-paced, character-driven thriller. . . . Readers who enjoy the works of Dee Henderson, especially her O'Malley series, will love *Breach of Trust*."

MIDWEST BOOK REVIEW

### Sworn to Protect

"Readers who like contemporary romantic suspense . . . will enjoy this intriguing page-turner."

*BOOKLIST*

NOV 1 1

"A glimpse into the dangerous world of border patrol makes for an interesting and worthwhile read."

> *ROMANTIC TIMES*

"Combines the best aspects of thriller, romance, and inspiration to offer an exciting and satisfying read."

> ASSOCIATEDCONTENT.COM

## Pursuit of Justice

"A character-driven story that is sure to keep you reading long into the night."

> *ROMANTIC TIMES*

"Mills packs this third book in the Call of Duty series with an interesting cast of suspects that keeps the reader guessing. Fans of romantic suspense will savor the pursuit of justice."

> *CBA RETAILERS + RESOURCES*

"DiAnn Mills scores another home run. . . . *Pursuit of Justice* is Christian fiction at its best, and Mills has established herself as a suspense novelist of the highest caliber."

> CHRISTIANFICTIONBOOKREVIEWS.COM

"Mills once again pulls her readers into a fast-paced, action-filled suspense story that will keep them enthralled to the very last page."

> FRESHFICTION.COM

"Characters with grit, faith, and stories with real meat on their literary bones . . . that's what you'll find in a book by DiAnn Mills."

> TITLETRAKK.COM

DiANN
MILLS

# Attracted to FIRE

Tyndale House Publishers, Inc.
Carol Stream, Illinois

Visit Tyndale online at www.tyndale.com.

Visit DiAnn Mills at www.diannmills.com.

*TYNDALE* and Tyndale's quill logo are registered trademarks of Tyndale House Publishers, Inc.

*Attracted to Fire*

Designed by Jessie McGrath

Edited by Kathryn S. Olson

Published in association with the literary agency of Janet Kobobel Grant, Books & Such, Inc., 5926 Sunhawk Drive, Santa Rosa, CA 95409.

**Library of Congress Cataloging-in-Publication Data**

Mills, DiAnn.
    Attracted to fire / DiAnn Mills.
        p. cm.
    ISBN 978-1-4143-4864-3 (sc)
        1. Secret service—United States—Fiction. 2. Teenage girls—Fiction. 3. Children of presidents—United States—Fiction. I. Title.
    PS3613.I567A93 2011
    813'.6—dc22                                                      2011023618

Printed in the United States of America

17  16  15  14  13  12  11
 7   6   5   4   3   2   1

*Dedicated to the courageous men and women of the Secret Service*

★

# Acknowledgments

MANY THANKS to all who made this book possible: Beau Egert, Cass Taylor, Dr. Dennis Hensley, Dr. Eriko Valk, Dr. Richard Mabry, Julie Garmon, Louise Gouge, Marsha Tallman, Mona Hodgson, Stephen Steeves, and Tom Morrisey.

# CHAPTER 1

"IF HE DOESN'T MUZZLE his daughter, he's going to lose the presidential nomination."

Special Agent Meghan Connors cringed at the TV anchor's analysis of Vice President Hall's campaign, even though the statement rang with validity.

"Although early popularity polls indicated Hall to be a strong contender for the presidential race, his ratings are dropping daily." The blonde reporting the news gave the camera a tilt of her head. "We are currently waiting for a statement from his office regarding Lindsay Hall's appearance on *The Barry Knight Show* last evening, where she stated, 'My father is a poor excuse for the office of president of the United States.'"

The screen flashed a clip of Lindsay Hall sporting cleavage and lots of leg.

"And she's our new assignment?" Special Agent Bob Lawson eased back in his chair and stuck his thumbs in his pants pockets. "I've heard she swears like a convict. Smacked a couple of agents in the face."

Meghan kept her opinions in check. She focused on the TV mounted in the corner of the coffee shop, not far from the White House. Thank goodness the shop was empty except for the barista moving to whatever was playing on his iPod.

The news anchor continued her report. "Take a look at Lindsay

Hall's escapade three nights ago." The screen reverted to footage taken in a local nightclub. Lindsay toasted the camera with a bottle of beer. Clearly inebriated, she sat in a booth enjoying media attention. The news anchor shook her head with a smile, an obvious display of her political preference. "Many are asking, 'If Vice President Hall cannot control his daughter, how can he effectively run our country?'"

Ouch. That nailed the situation. Meghan wrapped her fingers around the loop of her coffee cup and walked out onto a patio filled with umbrella tables and chairs. A steady mist filled the afternoon heat with humidity. She needed to focus on her new assignment—and the challenges ahead. Protecting the VP's daughter was supposed to be a promotion. If she failed, this could mean a permanent stall in her career.

Sensing Bob standing beside her, she turned to give him her views about their situation. "We're made of better stuff than the agents dismissed from Lindsay's protection team."

"I keep telling myself that."

"They let her manipulate them. Plain and simple."

"But we're not babysitters. We're special agents for the Secret Service."

Meghan didn't know the agents who'd been reassigned as a result of Lindsay's latest antics, but Bob had called them friends. She took a sip of her strong coffee, ignoring the raindrops gaining momentum. "Escorting her to the TV station and not informing the vice president was poor judgment. Her statements severely damaged the VP's image. Maybe even his chances of securing the party's nomination."

"Everything she says and does chips at his ability to lead the country. *The Barry Knight Show* and that entire TV network are out to crucify him and the party."

"So we're back to our assignment." Meghan stepped under the coffee shop's canopy to avoid the rain. "I'm committed to protecting her, and I know you are too."

"I have to be." Bob set his cup on an empty table. "Taking a bullet for her would qualify as above and beyond." He pressed his lips. "But that's what we do, right? Can't let personal opinions get in the way of duty."

"Absolutely, and I'm sure there are plans to curb her actions. In fact—" Her phone rang, and she reached inside her shoulder bag. A quick glimpse told her it was her supervisor, Tom Warrington, from the Secret Service office.

"Bob there with you?"

"Yes, sir."

"I need both of you in my office at 1400. Ash Zinders, the SAIC for this assignment, needs to brief you and the other agents assigned to the protectee."

Meghan slipped her phone back into her shoulder bag and relayed the information.

Bob whistled. "Good old A2Z isn't wasting any time."

The nickname for the special agent in charge assigned to Lindsay Hall's protection detail wasn't a title any agent would say to his face. He was known for his obsession with detail and his domineering personality. Meghan hadn't met the agent, and she didn't look forward to his browbeating.

"It really bothers me that she now has six agents protecting her when any other VP family member has three." Bob pulled a dollar from his wallet and anchored it beneath his cup. "Did I say I regret accepting this assignment? Hasn't been two hours since the call."

"There's a reason, Bob. We were chosen because the VP needed agents who can get the job done. But I question the number of us too, and what it means."

The potential to fulfill her dreams, the circumstances surrounding Lindsay Hall's unpredictable behavior, and the nightmare of working under Ash Zinders had Meghan wondering if the challenges ahead would be worth it.

★ ★ ★

Ash believed in Vice President Hall, known as the Shield by the Secret Service. He respected his commitment to his country and his devotion to his family. Books had been written about his political views, and one had been on the bestseller list for six months. How could a man of such integrity have a daughter who was a source of embarrassment for the whole country? International media laughed at her irresponsibility, and critics used her for comic relief in their opening monologues. Four years of protecting Lindsay Hall, and the situation had grown worse. Why couldn't the VP and his wife control their daughter's behavior? Ship her off to the Peace Corps, Siberia . . . anywhere but in the media's playground.

Across the desk sat his supervisor, Tom Warrington.

"Ash, I need to brief you on a few changes in protocol prior to meeting with your team." Warrington shuffled papers in front of him. "They'll be here in thirty minutes."

"Changes, sir?"

Warrington drummed his fingers. Not good. "You'll continue your role as SAIC for Lindsay's protection team, but the vice president has made a request. After last night's unfortunate incident on *The Barry Knight Show*, we've decided to bring in a woman agent."

*A woman agent?* "Why?"

"Special Agent Meghan Connors has an excellent reputation for getting the job done. And we think she'll be able to help keep Lindsay out of trouble. Possibly provide some direction with her medical issues."

"In what way? Our job is to protect her, not help her buy lipstick."

Warrington lifted a brow. "Connors will be a part of the six-agent team."

The addition of more agents, including a woman, ground at him. "Why six agents for a VP's daughter?"

4

"That will be explained in depth when the VP arrives."

"Sir, I don't understand the changes."

He cleared his throat. "Note that Agent Connors will be assigned to Lindsay seven days a week, 0800 to 1700."

A woman agent wouldn't work with the way Ash managed his team. Why was she being assigned his hours?

Warrington handed him three files. "These are the new agents. You've worked with Bob Lawson and Rick Norris before."

"With all due respect, sir, I prefer to work with men."

Warrington frowned. "The VP is desperate. We need to give her a chance for Lindsay's sake. For the VP's sake."

"I understand, but—"

"You and I go back a long way, and I know why you feel this way. I'd like to think you could get beyond judging every woman agent because of one bad experience. Agent Connors has a stellar record. She's tough, and she's dedicated to her job. Do this for the vice president, Ash. She might be the one person who could turn Lindsay around. And that would help the VP and this country."

"I'll do my best. However, I'd—"

"Deal with it, and do your job."

Resentment seeped into Ash's bones. He had a spotless record, and he'd been reduced to taking care of two women? She might be a dynamic personality, a fine person, but women had no place in the Secret Service.

"The Vice President has located a working ranch in Texas for Lindsay." He turned his computer to show a satellite image of a large ranch house, a barn, horse stables, and a couple of outbuildings.

"She can't run there."

"I agree. It's about a hundred miles west of Austin. She won't have access to a phone or computer. Just fresh country air."

"I'm assuming the VP needs her out of sight."

"There's more to the problem. A call was made to the VP about 0300 this morning. A man said he had a bullet with Lindsay's name on it if she didn't pay up. He claimed she owed him for meds."

The situation grieved him. Lindsay had so many opportunities to better herself. Maybe another woman *would* help. "She's in deep this time."

Warrington handed him another file. "Here are the details of the ranch, photos, list of employees. The VP and his wife are deciding on a doctor to treat Lindsay at the ranch."

"I knew they'd been investigating an alternative method of treatment. I saw the short list of the psychologists and psychiatrists." Ash studied Warrington's face—obviously he'd been awake since the threatening call. "So this is crisis intervention in a big way."

"And the media have to stay out of it."

"Any leads on the caller?"

"Not yet. Working on it. The transfer will be made in the next couple of days."

Lindsay did need to be out of the public's eye.

"One more thing here. President Claredon is back in the hospital. Looks like VP Hall will be taking on more responsibilities."

Ash had heard rumors that the cancer had spread. "I'll do what needs to be done, sir."

# CHAPTER 2

MEGHAN GOOGLED LINDSAY HALL on her BlackBerry, while Bob battled DC traffic in ninety-degree heat and blinding rain. The young woman's dossier read like a rap sheet. "We can only hope some of this is manufactured. Wish I'd been given her file before this meeting. I detest walking into a face-to-face unprepared."

"Zinders won't leave out a thing."

Maybe she should have googled Ash Zinders instead of Lindsay Hall. The rumors were just as intimidating. "Have you worked with him before?"

"About seven years ago on a counterfeit case. He had a reputation for being a pain in the rear. But I'll tell you this—he's one of the best agents out there."

Meghan's stomach twisted. She wanted this assignment. It was the next step of her career plan. "I heard he doesn't like women agents."

"You can drive that to the bank."

The first time she'd experienced prejudice against women Secret Service agents was in her first day of training. "Any suggestions?"

"You've proved yourself, Meghan. Do your best, and he'll have no reason to complain. It's his problem, not yours."

*Right.* "Is he married?"

"No."

Zinders's views about women agents would make her job

miserable. Meghan clenched her fist and noted the missing diamond on her left hand. That relationship had gone sour, and she had to forget him and all he'd once meant to her. Her focus zeroed in on job performance. Nothing else.

"What more did you find out about our protectee?" The square-jawed man whipped his attention to her, then back to the traffic-clogged street.

The windshield wipers swished in time to the questions pounding in her brain. She scrolled through the list of articles. "From what I see, all we've heard has been documented. Some with glossy pics. She definitely has issues—and ruining her father's career is one of them."

"Drugs and alcohol are major problems. Look at how many times she's been in and out of rehabs."

Meghan knew exactly what drugs could do to a person's mind. She continued to scan the articles. "She's had several DUIs. An arrest for striking a cop. Cocaine possession—more than once. That's the CliffsNotes version."

"We're going to be busy."

Could this get any worse? A drug addict protectee and a special agent in charge who didn't like women on his team?

Bob turned into the parking garage of the unmarked building. Meghan noted the scowl and the way he locked his hand over the steering wheel. His attitude about this assignment hadn't changed either.

★　★　★

Ash still fumed about having to deal with a woman agent. Give her a chance? He couldn't imagine dealing with a woman's emotions when logic and quick action were critical to their protectee's safety. Women agents rarely lasted long. Later he'd pore over her file and find her weaknesses. He'd heard how she saved the VP's life in Atlanta. He'd like to believe that was hype—some female reporter wanting to put another woman in the spotlight. But the VP didn't blow smoke. Agent Connors had performed well in the line of duty. Glancing at his watch, Ash shoved the situation from his mind . . . for now.

Two minutes to 1400. His people knew how he valued punctuality.

The door opened and in filed his team of special agents, all familiar faces except Meghan Connors. An off-duty agent was at the VP's home with Lindsay, while feds labored over the investigation to locate the caller threatening her.

"Take a seat." He nodded a greeting at Victor, Wade, and Rick. Seasoned agents.

Lawson stuck out his hand. "Good to see you again, sir."

Ash grasped it firmly. "Glad to have you on the team." Lawson had worked the past three years in Houston protecting Bush Sr. His reputation spoke of integrity, but how he'd manage their protectee was another matter. If Lawson hadn't been handpicked, Ash would wonder if he'd been demoted.

Connors reached out her hand, and he shook it while capturing her gaze. She didn't blink or move a muscle. He'd give her credit for not being intimidated. Not yet, anyway. The agents found a seat, but Ash remained standing. He preferred it that way.

"This briefing will be quick. Vice President Hall and Press Secretary Scottard Burnette will be joining us shortly." He pointed to the files on the table. "Each of you has an updated report on Lindsay. For those of you who aren't aware of my style, that means you memorize everything. We leave at 0500 for Texas. A temporary team will be assigned to Lindsay until she joins us in a few days. This can't leak. Additional information will be given to you in the morning en route. I'd—"

A knock at the door interrupted him, and Vice President Hall and his press secretary walked in. The agents stood, but the VP gestured for them to sit.

Ash studied the face of the Shield, the man who covered for

President Claredon while attempting to rein in his daughter. Lines deepened across the man's forehead and at the corners of his eyes, forming an oval from his nose to his chin. At fifty-two, the vice president shouldn't look so haggard and worn. Considering the president's battle with lung cancer, VP Hall could be taking over the country at a moment's notice.

The VP moved to the front of the table. "Please, sit down. I want to talk to you agents about my daughter. Protecting her is your job. Caring for her is mine. And for this assignment, we have to work together on both fronts."

Ash took a chair across from Agent Connors, the arrangement providing an opportunity to observe her. Red-gold hair was swept back from her face and anchored at her nape, professional and neat. Impassive expression, motionless body. He couldn't read a thing. Someone had trained her well.

"I don't need to explain or excuse Lindsay's behavior." The VP drew in a deep breath. "She's ill and needs extensive medical care. Her mother and I have decided to remove her from DC and place her in a remote area where no one can find her. Specifically, a working ranch west of Austin, Texas. Lindsay will be under the care of Dr. David Sanchez, a psychologist, and his nurse for an indefinite amount of time." For a moment, his shoulders slumped. Then he regained his composure. "Dr. Sanchez has experienced tremendous success in treating patients similar to Lindsay. I believe his information has been added to your files."

"It has, sir." Ash had read enough about Dr. Sanchez to understand the VP and his wife were taking a risk in finding a solution for Lindsay's problem. His unorthodox methods were unconventional, and he hoped Lindsay's health didn't take a nosedive.

"Another critical matter is that Lindsay's life has been threatened. I believe the problem will be solved soon. As quickly as arrangements can be made, Lindsay will be escorted to Texas. She's not aware of this." He glanced around the table. "Scottard, what would you like to add?"

The baby-faced press secretary poked his glasses onto his nose. "The media are going to be on this like flies on sugar once Lindsay disappears, but pacifying them is my job. I'll announce that she collapsed at her parents' home and is receiving medical treatment. I'll appease them with routine updates and lure them to other areas of the country. Except for her doctor and his assistant, no one is to have contact with her but the VP and his wife."

"And Scottard." The VP stood. "He owns the Dancin' Dust Ranch, and Lindsay knows him as an uncle figure. I understand there's a truck in the garage for your use. To your advantage, a hard room is located on the first floor. Regarding Dr. Sanchez, he uses a natural, holistic approach with extensive counseling to treat cases like hers. No drugs will be administered. Some of his methods may seem peculiar to us, but I have to trust his expertise."

Why didn't they say she had an addiction problem? They all knew it anyway. The whole country had seen her high on *The Barry Knight Show*.

The vice president's gaze swept around the table. "Take care of my little girl. Her medical condition is critical, and I'm deeply concerned that someone has threatened her."

"We'll not let you down." Ash made his way to the VP's side and shook his hand and then Burnette's before opening the door.

Once the pair left, Ash turned to the agents. "I'm giving you a ten-minute break; then we need to discuss shifts and how we'll occupy our time at the Dancin' Dust. The agents in this room are going to be your buds. Get to know them." He regretted the protocol changes with Connors, but he had no choice. "Read through the new information in your files while on break. Wade, Victor, you know Lindsay Hall as Sunshine. That will continue. You are dismissed. Connors, I need to see you alone."

She rose and faced him. Slender, medium height. Attractive. Not what he wanted to see.

"Yes, sir."

"You are to be with the protectee seven days a week, 0800 to 1700."

Agent Connors lifted her chin. Intelligence registered in her brown eyes.

"I didn't request you. Your assignment came from the VP. In my opinion, women agents are a waste of the Secret Service's time and taxpayers' money."

"Obviously someone saw my merit."

He hadn't expected a response. "Getting on my bad side isn't a good idea."

"Looks like I'm already there."

If only she'd say or do something he could use against her. Instead, she handled herself . . . like a pro. "We'll see how long you last. Lindsay Hall will tear you to shreds."

"So you want me to resign before I begin? Because it's not happening."

"Are you challenging me, Connors?"

"Do I need to? I thought we were talking about my ability to protect Lindsay Hall." She picked up the file and smiled. "Is there anything else, sir?"

# CHAPTER 3

MEGHAN LISTENED to the helicopter blades whirl as they rose into the morning sky, leaving Lindsay's protective detail at the Dancin' Dust. Texas heat and dust settled on her face. Already the temps were nearing ninety on the thousand-acre ranch. The manicured grounds and Olympic-size swimming pool indicated Scottard Burnette and guests took advantage of the remote hideaway to rest and relax. The white, two-story house with its wraparound porch seemed to be the perfect place for Lindsay to recover from the abuse she'd given her body. According to Ash, the VP and his wife had joined Burnette often, which meant Lindsay might be familiar with the property.

Sleek quarter horses flicked their tails and ignored the Secret Service agents, exhibiting not a care in the world. But all of this peacefulness could come to an abrupt halt if Lindsay's location leaked to those intent on inflicting harm. Drug dealers played for keeps, and taking out the VP's daughter would show their power.

While in the shower at 0400, Meghan's thoughts had swung from Lindsay to Ash Zinders to a possible assassin. She wondered if she could do this assignment well. Could she keep Lindsay safe and possibly influence her to fight the drug addiction and find some purpose for her life? Meghan's batting average was zero in turning around addicts. But she wasn't a quitter. She'd get back in the heat and take the punches.

She studied the ranch's terrain, familiarizing herself with the shape and size of the buildings. A creek flowed to the east of the property beside a small grove of live oaks. Other than that, the land was hilly and rocky, characteristic of West Texas.

About thirty-five feet from her, a balding man in coveralls watched the goings-on. This was probably Ethan Leonard. He gestured with his hands, pointing to the road and the agents walking toward him, reminding her of a cop at a crosswalk. The operation must look like a movie to him, one he hadn't wanted to watch. A Jack Russell terrier stood beside him, and he bent to pet the dog. A woman walked up to the man, sporting spiked, white hair—Pepper Davis, Scottard's personal chef when he spent time here. They all had their clearances, even though the chef and the ranch hands didn't need them for a VP's daughter.

"We lucked out with the two ranch hands." Bob stood beside her. "It's a father and son, and they live in the back of the stables. Burnette swears they're solid, the real goods."

"From here, the stables look to be in better shape than most houses."

Bob laughed. "I grew up in the wards of New Orleans. It is better than where I lived." He glanced at the main house. "Guess we'd better get started."

Meghan heard shouting and turned her attention to the man in coveralls.

"I want to know what this is all about." The man raised his fist at Ash. "I wake up this morning to a helicopter landing. You people act like you own the place. What do you take me for? Some redneck who doesn't have the sense to understand?"

"We're the Secret Service team assigned to this property for the next couple of months. Would you like to see our IDs, Mr. Leonard? Mr. Burnette has given us permission to use his ranch for a protectee, and we'd welcome your cooperation."

"I've seen your fancy papers, and they don't mean squat to me." His drawl added emphasis to every word. "Neither do your shiny badges. Handguns and assault rifles. What next?"

"Would you like for me to call Mr. Burnette? Set your mind at ease?"

"You bet I would. Me and my son take good care of the Dancin' Dust, and I don't 'ppreciate any of this. I take my orders from him. No one else."

"Have you tried to contact him?"

"His office says he's busy. Will get back to me. Frustratin'."

"Sir, I understand. I've been told you and your son do a fine job of taking care of Mr. Burnette's property."

"You can take that to Washington and tuck it under Lincoln's Memorial." He lowered his fist but maintained his stance.

Ash demonstrated admirable control. Ethan Leonard had almost punched him. Not that Meghan blamed the older man. He was accustomed to a quiet, orderly world. Hard to believe Scottard Burnette hadn't informed him about their arrival.

A younger man raced from the barn, same height and slender build. Must be Chip Leonard. "Dad, take it easy. These men are special agents for the Secret Service. Their IDs are legit."

"Not until I hear from Mr. Burnette, they ain't." He waved at the woman who'd be cooking for the agents. "Hey, Pepper. You in on this too?"

Pepper had been on her way to the house, but she turned and took a step his way. "Ethan, did you let the battery run down on your cell phone again? I tried calling you on my way here last night."

"I did, but it's charging now. I called Mr. Burnette on Chip's phone a few minutes ago."

That explained the miscommunication. Scottard Burnette conducted every part of his professional life with precision, and the Leonards didn't have a landline phone.

Meghan watched Ash pull his cell phone from his pocket. Hmm. What went on behind his sunglasses? Did he think through every scenario and have the answers to everything? A lot of folks thought so, but Meghan would wait to form her own opinion.

Ash whirled around at the five agents. "You men check out the inside." His tone reminded her of a drill sergeant. She hid a grin. So the pressure of being the only woman on the team continued. At least she was officially one of the guys.

"Let's get started." Bob shifted his laptop to his left hand. "A2Z will have this handled in thirty seconds."

Meghan followed Bob to the back door of the home and into a large and airy country kitchen.

"I'm home again. Would you look at this." Pepper planted her hands on bony hips and cast an admiring glance around the kitchen. Its size and equipment were a gourmet chef's dream. "I'll be whipping up my specialties in no time at all."

Wade pointed to an arched hallway in the far corner. "This way. Ash said we'd find an operation room back here."

Meghan and the other agents filed past Pepper and down the arched hallway. Alcoves on both sides displayed paintings by a renowned Texas artist. Wade opened a door to a study containing a twelve-foot table for their operation. Bookcases lined two walls, and floor-to-ceiling windows looked out onto the swimming pool. Wade and Victor slid into chairs across from computers. It all looked great, but for sure the assignment would be boring—and probably abusive if it stayed true to form. Four weeks on and two weeks off for four agents would help them keep their sanity and a connection to the real world. Meghan and Ash weren't among the lucky four. The VP had asked her and Ash to remain on duty until the assignment ended. Wonderful.

What a team they were. Wade Enders, the freckle-faced Caucasian from Ohio, passed the bar with a score of 97.8 percent. He and Ash shared the 1700 to 0100 shift. Wade's wife was due to deliver their second child in the next few weeks, and he hoped the baby would wait until his weeks off for the arrival.

Victor Lee came from LA, an Asian American whose computer expertise earned him the title of one of the agency's top hackers. He'd have the 0100 to 0900 shift with Rick Norris, a handwriting expert from Nashville.

Bob Lawson used to play linebacker for the New Orleans Saints. He had a keen mind for firearms—could take apart and put together a SIG blindfolded. He'd work with Meghan 0900 to 1700.

Meghan, the token woman, could hit a target dead on at 1,100 feet. She thought about why she'd been chosen. Possibly her stint in Atlanta when she'd brought down a shooter who had the VP as his target. The other reason she'd been selected for this assignment might not be in her records, but the VP knew.

The back door opened and creaked like an old man's bones. "Connors, I want that door fixed now, or the next time I'll rip it off its hinges."

Grunt work. She headed to the kitchen, but Ash met her in the arched hallway.

"Not until I finish saying a few things." He dropped two cell phones onto the wooden table. "Victor, run checks on Ethan and Chip Leonard and their cells. Those two are going to be a pain. Connors, before you see to that door, check on a vet. Ethan says one of their horses is foaling. The last thing we need is a local letting the media know what's going on here."

"Yes, sir." She knew her job, and she understood his condescension was just warming up. "Most mares foal between 2200 and 0400. She may be in trouble."

"If I want your opinion, I'll ask for it. Right now, take care of finding a vet. Keep the old man happy."

"I'll try to remember that." She left, making sure the door didn't bang behind her.

This would be a long, hot assignment.

★  ★  ★

Ash exited the hard room on the first floor off the living area. He was pleased with the windowless area designed to keep a protectee safe. Scottard Burnette had done an excellent job in stocking the room with food, water, ammunition, and medical supplies. Ash walked through the five-thousand-square-foot house, noting each room and its dimensions, the height and width of the windows, and fire exits. When Connors turned in her report about the home's security, he wanted to make sure she completed it to his satisfaction.

Warrington said she'd proved herself in Atlanta. Ash didn't need the reminder. Her prominence rose three months ago during a temporary assignment. Vice President Hall had been vacationing in Atlanta when a deranged man interrupted his golf game. The VP was playing the ninth hole on a Tuesday morning when a gun-wielding cab driver raced across the grounds shouting obscenities and exhibiting deadly intent. She stopped the shooter with one shot. Sure spoiled the VP's vacation, but his high regard for her fast thinking had carried over to a commendation from the director of Secret Service. After that, Meghan Connors had become the VP's first choice for Lindsay's additional team. Ash had spent the wee hours of the morning reading every detail of her file. Impressive. Even admirable.

Her marksmanship rivaled his—accuracy of 99 percent at fifty feet, and she scored in the upper 2 percent during her last qualifying.

Ash stared out the window at the pastures of grazing horses and black cattle. He couldn't rid Connors from his mind. She had a double major in communications and computer science. And she'd been a part of several sting operations while working counterfeit. Nothing but stinking glowing reports.

To aggravate him further, her good looks drew the attention of every male on the team. He'd seen it the moment she'd entered the room yesterday. That red hair could be spotted a mile away, and no disguising her hourglass figure. Great for the other agents' egos but a distraction for the job. Another reason why women agents needed to be banned from the service. Let them show their feminine power and find a husband elsewhere.

A twinge of remorse halted any more disparaging thoughts

about Agent Connors. He should give her a break and allow her to do her job. But he couldn't. She might slip and their protectee or an agent could be killed. Other critical matters battled his thoughts about Meghan Connors, including Tom Warrington's final words to him.

"Ash, VP Hall has already indicated that he wants either you or Special Agent Connors on his protective detail as soon as this assignment is completed. Agent Hawkins is retiring."

No stress there.

# CHAPTER 4

MEGHAN TOOK HER FIRST BREAK after seven hours. She rubbed her aching neck muscles and took a sip of tepid coffee. Her stomach growled, and she realized this was the second day that she'd worked without taking time to eat. This morning, she'd subsisted on black coffee and a banana after taking a four-mile run. This had to stop. Not feeding her brain meant lousy job performance. Ash would thrive on her mistakes.

Although the massive home was well built and contained every modern convenience listed in *Architect Design*, she found some of the wiring for the alarm system archaic. The rewiring coincided with Burnette's purchase and remodel of the home five years ago. Perhaps the contractor had cut a few corners. The logical side of her said the amount of work to secure housing for a VP's daughter wasn't necessary, but she needed to stay busy and avoid Ash. Plus the threats made on Lindsay's life called for heavier protective measures.

She scooted her chair back and walked down the hallway to the kitchen. Grabbing a plate, she eyed what would fill her stomach and reactivate her brain. The bottles of water were ice cold. Perfect. Pepper had filled the kitchen counter with sandwiches, various chips, salsa, fruit, and homemade oatmeal raisin cookies the size of a man's fist. Agents came and went in shifts, some returning for another round. The air-conditioning seemed to take priority over being under Ash's scrutiny. He barked a lot, but she wondered if beneath that crusty exterior was a man with a good heart. He knew his stuff, and he didn't miss a thing.

After thanking Pepper for lunch, she hurried back to the operation room. Ash sat across from her, his focus on his computer screen. Now was as good a time as ever.

"The wiring in the house needs to be updated, possibly redone. It's not adequate even for regular household needs."

He lifted a brow. "Make it happen. Burnette indicated it might need to be changed." He lifted his sandwich to his mouth, then laid it on his plate. "Is what's there dangerous, or are we okay until an electrician can complete the work?"

"We'll make do. I've already written the order."

She pulled two jalapeños from her chicken salad on whole wheat.

Ash stood and opened the door leading down the hall to the kitchen. "Pepper, can I see you a minute?"

She appeared in the doorway, wearing short shorts and a halter top. Hard for Meghan to believe her deceased husband had been an agent.

"Would you make me a sandwich without jalapeños?" He handed her his plate; he'd taken one bite from the sandwich. "I prefer a croissant."

"That's lunch." She handed the plate back to him and flashed her pearly whites. "Supper is at six thirty."

Meghan hid a grin. Oh, these two would definitely be comic relief. If they didn't kill each other first.

Ash's eyes narrowed. "You're telling me I have to eat this gut-burning sandwich or wait until tonight?"

"The other agents devoured my original recipe. Asked for seconds. You're outnumbered."

"Then they have cast-iron stomachs. I'd like a normal sandwich."

"Fix it yourself. I'm a class-A cook, not short-order."

22

"Then someone needs to give you a few lessons. Last night we had chicken tortilla soup that rivaled the Alamo massacre. This morning it was jalapeños and eggs with some white, gritty oatmeal loaded with these green things. Now this. Can't you cook like a regular person?"

*Ouch. He might get decked for that remark.*

"I'm a highly desired chef. Probably paid more than you." She saluted him and leaned against the doorjamb.

"Your conduct is going into my report." He set his plate on the table. "As well as your dress."

Pepper glanced at her attire. "I'm not wearing a dress. I'm in comfortable clothing that allows me to do my job."

His demeanor suggested he might be losing control, and his eyes shot fire. "I don't appreciate your condescending mannerisms."

"Tsk. Tsk. Do you always throw temper tantrums when you don't get your way?"

"I suppose you have a sister named Cinnamon and a brother Herb."

Pepper moistened her ruby-red lips. "How immature, Special Agent in Charge Zinders. But you tell me, A2Z. You read the background check."

"I had that coming." He anchored his hands on his hips. "So let's call a truce. I'm hungry and in a bad mood. We're adults here."

"Oh, really? You insult me, make demands, and now you want a truce?" She narrowed her eyes. "You gonna pull a gun on me?"

Ash's face flashed as red as a neon sign. "Why waste the bullet?"

He'd lost it for sure.

Pepper spit a few expletives. "I'm going outside to the stables, where the air's fresh. I prefer the company of horses." She slammed the door behind her.

"Shovel some for me, would you, Pepper, honey?"

Those two were a stitch. If Scottard Burnette hadn't recommended Pepper, she'd be in the ranks of the unemployed. Highly paid chef or not.

Ash gripped the back of his chair, as though trying to figure out his next move. He hesitated, then followed Pepper's footsteps down the hallway to the kitchen. The back door creaked open and closed.

Meghan stifled a laugh and inched his way.

"There's a snake out here." Ash's voice rose from the outside.

She rushed through the kitchen to the back porch, envisioning a six-foot rattler coiled and ready to strike.

Standing on the sidewalk leading to the stables, Pepper peered at him. "That's a king snake, Special Agent in Charge Zinders. Sometimes we call them chicken snakes. You'd better watch out. They eat rodents."

Meghan hurried back to the operation room and slid into her chair. Biting her lip to again keep from laughing, she heard him enter the house. A few moments later, Ash entered the study with a plate full of chips and salsa, a banana, and two cookies.

She studied his plate. "Watch the red stuff, sir. It's hot enough to open your sinuses."

★ ★ ★

Ash studied the satellite imagery of the Dancin' Dust Ranch, looking for ways someone could access the property. If Lindsay had been placed here simply as one more effort to rehabilitate her, he wouldn't take all these precautions. But the threats on her life kept him wary. And no one got hurt on his watch.

The latest from DC said the man threatening Lindsay had been linked to a drug dealer working out of Colombia, and she owed him $10,000. A nice chunk of change. Did she think her father's position bought her clout with those who'd just as soon blow her away if she didn't pay up? She really was in la-la land.

The front gate at the end of the half-mile-long driveway was electronically locked, and an intercom and controls for the gate were located in the kitchen and stables. A security camera panned the immediate entrance. Ash stared out the window at the pool, not seeing but thinking about how to ensure Lindsay's safety. For now he'd disconnect the controls in the stables. The Leonards might not appreciate the Secret Service taking over one more part of their life, but he felt the extra precaution was necessary.

Bob knocked on the operation door. "Ethan Leonard needs horse feed and a few other supplies from town."

Another concern about their location leaking. "All right. Go with him and make sure he gets enough to last a long time."

"He also said he and his son go to church on Wednesday nights and Sundays. He doubts if they'll go tonight because of the mare foaling."

"Must be like pulling the donkey out of the well."

"What?"

"Never mind." His conscience nudged him. How long had it been since he'd been a faithful churchgoer? But his job responsibilities meant grabbing God when he found the time. "Can't they stay home until our assignment is over?" The moment he uttered the words, he realized the Leonards' absence from church would bring the community to the ranch. "That won't work. If they are in the habit of attending services, then find someone to accompany them who'll fit in."

"I'm on it. An out-of-town friend or something."

Ash glanced up at Lawson, noting his dark skin and the broad shoulders that reflected back to his football days. "Talk to Enders. You look like a bouncer and—"

"I get it."

"In fact, have Wade go with him for feed. No point in the folks around here seeing two strange faces." Ash leaned back in his chair and appreciated how it fit every curve of his back. "I'd better talk to Ethan. Smooth things over so he won't tell anyone what we're doing to spite me."

"He has a garden."

Ash grinned. "Smart man, since I don't know a thing about

horses, and I despise Pepper's spicy cooking. Maybe I can look pitiful." He shook his head. "Some fresh vegetables sound like an icebreaker to me."

"Could be."

He pointed to the screen. "Study this for me while I talk to him. See if I've missed anything. I'm concerned about the angle of the cameras mounted at the main gate. Looks useless."

A flash of amusement crossed Bob's face. "And you want my opinion?"

"Contrary to popular belief, A2Z does have a human streak—once in a while. And I do need advice—once in a while." Ash rose from his chair and made his way to the doorway. "Don't tell anyone. Might spoil my image."

Suffocating heat met him the moment he stepped onto the porch. Pepper's comment about the snake stung. He'd get even during their next "discussion." He whirled around in case the snake had changed its mind. Who in his right mind would sit out here? The air seemed like breath from a fiery dragon. He'd never get used to this. His attention lifted to the horses grazing in the pasture. Suspicion took hold of him. Didn't horses give birth in the spring? He'd have to find out. Connors had indicated specific times, and she appeared to have information about horses.

Ash spotted Ethan filling a water trough and walked toward him. The older man took a long drink from the hose, soaking the front of his long-sleeved shirt in the process. Ash considered doing the same in the soaring temps.

"Mind sharing the hose?"

Ethan's face hardened, but he handed it to him. Ash drank deeply of the warm water and then began to fill the trough. "We got off to a bad start."

"I'm used to taking orders from Burnette."

"He's a fine man, and we're indebted to him for the use of his ranch. How's your mare?"

"Doing okay. So's the colt. Born about 1:30 this mornin'."

"Congratulations." Ash shrugged. "I don't know protocol about horses."

"I didn't pass out any cigars, but the colt's from good stock."

"I thought horses gave birth in the spring."

"That's usually the case. This mare was bred late in the year." Ethan took the hose and continued to fill the water trough. "Who's coming?"

Ash had to trust this man. He had the power to blow the assignment and possibly get Lindsay killed. "I need your word that what I'm about to tell you stays between us. High security measures are in place."

"Do I need to fetch my boy?"

"I'll tell him myself." Ash leaned on one leg. "Vice President Hall's daughter, Lindsay."

"The wild one? Humph. Saw her a few times on the news."

"Might want to keep your son from her."

Ethan narrowed his brow. "He's old enough to make his own decisions."

"No one's ever too old for a warning."

Ethan lifted a brow. "Read about some of the things she's done. Right down embarrassing for the vice president and his wife. Must be drugs."

"I understand you're a churchgoing man."

"Don't suppose you'd know anything about that."

Ash chose to keep his faith to himself. The man before him might not believe his convictions. "Enough to get by."

"Ignoring God gives man a one-way ticket to heat hotter than Texas. So don't be tellin' me I can't be goin'. Last night was different." A subtle challenge wove through Ethan's words.

"I'm not. But I will be sending an agent along. Possibly a new cousin."

Ethan nodded. "So which one of your men will be going with me to town?"

"Do you have a preference?"

"Connors is prettier than the rest."

Ash forced a laugh. So he'd noticed her too. Another reason to get Agent Connors off the assignment. "I can arrange that. But I need her expertise today. How about Wade Enders?"

"That'll work. He's a friendly guy."

Ash reached out to shake his hand. Ethan gripped it, his calluses rubbing against Ash's grind of paperwork and computer keys. "I hear you have a garden."

"Got a hankerin' for a fresh tomato?"

"I do."

"Be glad to show you, and help yourself anytime. Cucumbers and bell peppers are good this year. So are the beans and corn. Wash 'em good. I use organic gardening techniques, but I believe in giving them a good bath. We got plenty. See those flower bushes over there?" Ethan pointed toward a pink flowering bush. "Since you're a city boy, I'll give you a bit of advice. Like you said, no one's ever too old for a warning. Everything about the oleander bush is poison. Just stay away. If you want to pick flowers, choose another kind. The ones at the front end of the garden are good for impressing a lady."

"Thanks. I'll remember that."

"And watch for snakes." Ethan laughed, but Ash didn't find a single word of it amusing.

# CHAPTER 5

ONCE AGAIN LINDSAY was at her parents' home. She lay awake and listened to the gentle sound of country music flowing from her iPod. In her private moments, she often switched from hard rock to the tunes she loved—the sounds that stirred her heart and allowed her to live out her fantasies in a world where love was the most important part of a person's life.

Fortunately, the iPod had been in her purse when Daddy had his men pick her up from her apartment. He hadn't been too happy about her appearance on *The Barry Knight Show*. She'd been high and hadn't been able to string enough thoughts together about what happened in front of the cameras and later at her apartment.

The song changed to an old George Strait tune. Not at all what her crowd expected from Lindsay Hall's music preference. While the twang of a guitar soothed the emptiness, Lindsay allowed a tear to slip from her eye. Only one—that's all she could spare. Her choices had destroyed any dreams to have the life she longed to live.

Was anyone interested in understanding who Lindsay Hall was? Certainly no one who mattered. She'd done a good job of alienating those who might call her friend . . . or sister . . . or daughter.

Sleep—if only she could sleep and forget. Instead, her head pounded like the drums from last weekend's party. Had it been that long since she'd partied with her friends?

She needed to get to an ATM machine and hoped Daddy hadn't cut her off again. She couldn't go to him for money right now. Seeing the pain in his eyes brought on the guilt and disgust for her behavior. She already knew the scenario. They'd argue, and she'd let him know how much she hated him. Then he'd give in, and she'd slip back to her apartment.

What time was it anyway?

"Honey, do you want a glass of water?"

Someone touched Lindsay's arm, and her eyes popped open to see her mother in a chair next to her bed. Lindsay pulled out her earbuds and cursed. "How long have you been here?"

"About a half hour. You were asleep, and I didn't want to wake you." Mom picked up Lindsay's hand, but she jerked it back.

"I want to be left alone." She closed her eyes and fought the sickness churning her stomach.

"We don't think you should be left alone right now." Lindsay envisioned Mom's pale face and faint smile. She'd swallow to hold back the tears. Always in control. Perfectly poised for the public. Lindsay wanted to gag.

"Get a life, Mom. This is who I am." Sweat dripped into her eyes, intensifying the pain behind them, as though someone twisted an ice pick. "Are you afraid I'll do myself in and ruin Daddy's election plans?" Lindsay wanted to spout every spiteful word she could think of. "Oh, wait a minute. I've already done a good job of lowering his ratings. I'm sure you caught *The Barry Knight Show*. How did you like the part about Daddy beating me? The tears caused the show's ratings to skyrocket." She did remember that segment.

"You know he never touched you."

"The alphabet stations believe he did."

"That wasn't really you."

"*The Barry Knight Show* wants me back."

"Why do you do these things?"

"You know, a suicide would prove me right and end the spotlight for the vice prez and his lovely wife, Alexa."

"You don't really want to hurt yourself."

Lindsay licked her dry lips. "Of course I do. In case you didn't get my text, I despise both of you. If you can't give me the money I need to survive, then I have no use for either of you. I want to be taken home."

"We'll not support your addictive behaviors."

"What I need is a hit of coke or a pitcher of margaritas. You can choose. Maybe join me. Might loosen you up."

Mom gasped. "I've had enough, Lindsay. Drugs have taken over your mind. Poisoned you against your family."

Lindsay opened her eyes, hoping her glare showed her contempt. "Am I demonic? Is that what you're saying? Perhaps an exorcism would make me the obedient daughter."

"Don't you want to stop the addiction? Get clean? Feel like a normal human?"

"Whatever." Lindsay fought the pain now radiating to the base of her skull. "Why would I ever want to stop? You've read the books. I'm self-medicating to avoid my inner turmoil."

"How many trips to rehab is it going to take?"

Couldn't the woman talk without asking one miserable question after another? No wonder Lindsay's head hurt. "Stop the pathetic intervention. I'll stop when I'm dead."

"Maybe that's what it'll take. You certainly have the role models for it."

Ah, the superior tone in her voice. "Oh, now it's reverse psychology. Are you thinking an overdose will actually help Daddy's career? I admit sympathy is a good platform. You could fake your grieving—*People* magazine, *USA Today*, even *Time* would want an exclusive. Too bad I'd miss the photo shoot."

Mom stood. "Forcing our hand is not good. We love you, and—"

"Get out." What did she have to live for anyway? "Don't try another rehab. I know how to answer the questions and make all the promises. I'm a master at it."

Mom picked up Lindsay's cell phone from the nightstand.

"Hey, Alexa. You have no right to take that." Lindsay bolted upright in the bed, the pain staggering, blinding her.

"Yes, I do when your father pays for it." Mom headed to the door and turned on her heel. "I love you, but I will not stand by and watch you destroy yourself."

"You forgot the part about Daddy's future."

"We'd leave all of that behind today if we thought it would make a difference."

"Get out." She couldn't go on like this much longer. The money. The threats. They'd all be better off if she were dead.

# CHAPTER 6

SINCE TUESDAY, Meghan and the team had worked nonstop to secure the ranch. Although Lindsay Hall did not have priority status, her position had risen from a VP's rebellious daughter, needing drug intervention, to a critical situation. The security measures were in place to protect her from whoever had decided to end her life.

As dawn crept across the horizon and Meghan pushed her body into the fifth mile along the dirt road lining the Dancin' Dust, thoughts about Lindsay occupied her mind. For now, the front gate remained unlocked while she ran, but that would change once their protectee arrived.

Lindsay must be under lock and key in DC because the media were scrambling for news. Each network gave its own version of what might be happening, feeding from past reports about Lindsay's previous behavior. FOX speculated that she'd been admitted into a small rehab near Seattle. ABC reported she'd been seen at a resort in the Catskills. CBS claimed to have spotted her at a treatment center in Switzerland, and NBC still gloated over Barry Knight's interview.

Every member of the team on the Dancin' Dust had become restless. Like Meghan, they craved a change from the long, quiet days.

Rounding the path that led past the stables and to the house, she smelled ranch life—wildflowers and a downwind of manure. Ethan and Chip exited the stables, both walking quarter horses.

Right on time. They must set their clocks to when her run ended. What else had they observed while the agents prepared for Lindsay?

Close to Ethan's left heel trotted their terrier, a friendly dog with a mostly brown face and ears and a healthy white coat. He answered to the name of Chesney. Meghan cast an admiring glance at the horses. Both mares were a copper color, sleek and white-faced.

"Hey, little lady." Ethan grinned and Chip waved.

"Mornin'." She slowed to a walk, perspiration dripping from every inch of her. She pulled the earbuds from her ears.

"Need a bottle of water?" Chip's gaze swept from her head to her running shoes, a little too admiringly. The two men had sparkling green eyes and sandy-colored hair. "Got one right here." He held up a bottle.

"My drink of choice." She took it. "I finished mine on the fourth mile."

"Bet you don't have a thing on that iPod." Chip laughed.

He'd been watching too many crime shows. "Are you kidding? Run in this heat without a beat?"

"If I had your job, every part of me would be trained to the surroundings."

"Everyone needs a break." She gestured around her. "This ranch is breathtaking. A great place to relax. No wonder Mr. Burnette steals away whenever he can."

Chip nodded. "It's home. Hey, I have coffee, too. Won't take a minute to get you a cup."

"No, thanks. I need to cool off a little first."

"What's your Secret Service expertise?"

She laughed. "Running. And I'm the token woman."

"They picked the best-looking agent I've ever seen."

Poor Chip. He must be in between girlfriends. A man with those eyes and thick hair probably had the girls beating down his door. But not while the Secret Service guarded the ranch.

Lindsay would use him for sure. *Click. Store that data.*

Meghan twisted off the lid of the water bottle and drank deeply. "You're great company, guys, but I have to get cleaned up." She toasted the house with the bottle. "Coffee is about the only thing Pepper doesn't lace with jalapeños."

Ethan shook his head. "Don't I know it." She gave him her attention, a little safer on the eyes than his too-good-looking son. "God love her, but she gave me an ulcer one summer when Mr. Burnette's sister came with her daughters. That's why we do our own cooking."

"I might sneak to your place when she's not paying attention."

"But not A2Z." Ethan cocked a brow. "Can't quite figure him out yet."

"He has a job to do, and he's particular. Where did you hear his nickname?"

"Chip told me, but all you have to do is listen." Ethan nodded toward the back porch. "In about two minutes, he'll stick his head out the door and check to see if you might be late for your shift."

"Guess I shouldn't give him an opportunity to write me up." She patted Ethan's mare. What else had the Leonards heard? "I used to barrel race with a beauty like this one."

"Where you from? You got time to talk. You're earlier than other mornings, and he ain't looking yet."

"Little east of Abilene."

"I knew it." Ethan slapped his thigh. "No gal as pretty and as friendly as you could be from anywhere but Texas. Welcome home, Meggie."

How did he know her family nickname? *Click.*

★ ★ ★

While the shadows of evening enveloped the Dancin' Dust, Ash watched Meghan interact with Wade and Victor in the living room. Pepper had popped corn and joined them for a movie. Until Lindsay arrived, their schedules were flexible, which allowed the team to form a bond and build on each other's strengths and understand their weaknesses.

Meghan kept a professional stance. Not even a glance with a sexual connotation. For three days, she'd done her job. She took his hassle and appeared unaffected, and she usually had a comeback of her own. Nailed him more than once. Not bad to look at either. Maybe a hint of admiration had seeped into his concrete heart.

When had he started referring to her as Meghan?

He startled, not visibly, but enough to shake him. Women agents didn't belong in the ranks. He knew what could happen.

"I need a full report in five minutes. All of you have done more than what is needed for a VP's daughter, but we all know the potential problems if we relax."

"The installer will be here tomorrow to finish rewiring the alarm system." Meghan handed him a printout of the work order. "He'll be here at eight."

"Good. Wade, is Ethan Leonard cooperating any better?"

"He likes horses, baseball, and Jesus."

Ash's phone rang. It was Warrington.

"We need to transport Lindsay tonight. She'll be there in about six and a half hours. Dr. Sanchez and his nurse will be accompanying her, along with the vice president and his wife."

"Dr. Sanchez's nurse hasn't been cleared. Her ex is doing time."

"Deal with it, Ash. Lindsay is low on the priority list."

His eye twitched. "Yes, sir."

"The Halls will be leaving here as soon as their daughter is settled. The hospital is making sure she's all right to travel."

Hospital? *Settled* meant heavy sedation, but that was against Dr. Sanchez's convictions. "Is there a reason for bringing her here at night?"

"Suicide attempt."

That was a first. "I'm sorry. How are the VP and his wife doing?"

"Not good. Also another threat to Lindsay. Happened before the suicide episode."

Now Ash understood. "We'll see you in a few hours."

Sympathy for the Halls turned to anger. Why did God allow good people to suffer? The VP and his wife had spent years in third world countries helping women and children survive persecution, disease, hunger, and slavery. More than once, the couple had been airlifted out of places the most stalwart of people would avoid. And this is what they faced now? Possibly the greatest trial of all.

Ash studied the faces of his team. All eyes were on him. "Heads up. Lindsay will be here in about six and a half hours. We have lots to do. Pepper, that means you, too. Don't even think about going to bed."

"I'm the cook, not a techie." Pepper snatched up her Dr Pepper can.

"I want coffee for us and something for the VP and his wife when they arrive." Ash squared his resolve. "I think Mr. Burnette would want you to take care of his guests."

She paused, then disappeared into the kitchen. For once, she didn't balk.

"Connors, I need a thorough background check on Carla Bertinelli. Everything you can find. We've talked about this. She's a widow, but husband number one is doing time for extortion. See what connections both husbands might have had."

"What about the Leonards?" Wade picked up a notepad as though he already knew the answer.

"Brief them and again impress on them the gravity of the situation."

Agents flew in different directions, and Meghan was already on her laptop. With no one else in the room, he noted her intense concentration. "Lindsay can be difficult."

"I read the report."

"She has good aim."

"I'll learn how to duck."

She wouldn't back down. "You're doing a good job."

Her gaze never left the screen. "Thank you."

"But women don't belong in the agency."

She slowly lifted her head, fingers positioned on the keys. He'd never noticed her long lashes or the splattering of freckles on her nose and cheeks. "We'll see. I want to prove I'm not one of the weaker sex."

From the way his insides weakened when he looked at her, she was already on her way to proving her point.

# CHAPTER 7

AT 0300, THE DISTINCT SOUND of whirling helicopter blades captured Meghan's attention. She stood with the protective team and waited near the lighted landing pad, while the VP, his wife and daughter, Dr. David Sanchez, Carla Bertinelli, and two special agents disembarked.

The lines on Vice President Hall's face had deepened since Meghan had seen him four days ago. With agents at his side, he carried his sleeping daughter into the house. No doubt sedated, a dichotomy since Dr. Sanchez's methods opposed any prescriptions or over-the-counter drugs. Doubts bannered across her mind about the infamous psychologist and his high percentage of rehabilitating addicts who stayed clean.

Once Lindsay had been put to bed, the medical team, Pepper, and the agents met with the vice president and his wife in the kitchen. The aroma of fresh coffee filled the air, and Pepper had baked a coffee cake, but no one seemed interested in the latter. Pepper poured a fresh cup for Alexa Hall and added a dollop of cream and a spoonful of sugar, but Dr. Sanchez and Ms. Bertinelli declined any food or drink.

"We refrain from sugary baked goods and caffeine." Dr. Sanchez stiffened.

Meghan studied the man chosen to counsel and encourage Lindsay to shake her addictions. If the grim look on his face was any indication of his personality, the protective team and Lindsay were in for a long summer.

The VP eased into a chair with a cup of black coffee. "Dr. Sanchez, I'm putting my daughter into your care."

"Is that why you sedated her before you called?"

The VP's face hardened. "I had no choice."

"You could have discussed it with me first." Dr. Sanchez, a slight, blue-eyed man, ran his fingers through dark hair. "I apologize, sir. My work and my patients are my life. I thought we'd agreed on Lindsay's treatment. Every time a foreign substance enters her body, her recovery is delayed."

"My daughter is more than my life." The VP's words sounded like rumbling thunder. His wife touched his shoulder, and he gave her a tight-lipped smile before giving his attention to Dr. Sanchez. "Lindsay was hysterical and violent, outraged that the suicide attempt had failed. You saw her bandaged wrist. And you—" he aimed his finger at the doctor—"didn't find her. I was the one who forced down her apartment door and found her in a pool of blood. I phoned the ambulance while checking her pulse. I pressed a towel onto her wrist and prayed."

"Yes, sir. Again, I apologize for my outburst and my insensitivity. It won't happen again."

The VP lifted his coffee cup to his lips, as though needing time to compose himself. The red in his face faded. "Before I talk to Agent Zinders about the state of the ranch's security, I want you to explain to these fine agents your treatment plan."

Dr. Sanchez cleared his throat. "Carla and I will work closely with Lindsay during the coming hours, days, and weeks. We have no idea how long it will take for her to make a decision to leave the past behind. My method is to treat her with nutritional supplements, have her eat balanced meals, involve her in exercise and around-the-clock counseling."

"What supplements will she be taking?" Meghan had researched his approach to rehabilitation and wanted to monitor Lindsay's intake while on duty with her.

"I appreciate your interest. Lindsay will be taking vitamin B12 under the tongue to improve her nutrient uptake and enzyme action for better brain function. She will take balanced macro-nutrients to include quality proteins in medical foods for optimal blood-sugar control. This will be administered in the form of a smoothie twice daily. She will eat every three hours, which will also optimize blood-sugar control." He nodded at Pepper. "I'd like a consultation appointment with you as soon as possible."

"Also on her plan is vitamin B6 and Saint-John's-wort as a nervine tonic to balance emotions. Fish oil for cell membrane support and better hormone signaling, flax oil to help restore the lipid membrane of damaged myelin sheath from body tox-ins, magnesium for nerve transmission and a calming effect, and passionflower at night to help her sleep and encourage hormone production." He pulled several sheets of paper from his laptop case. "I have her treatment plan here for Miss Davis and for any agents who are interested."

"I'll take a hard copy and an electronic one." Ash's tone clearly indicated his skepticism. He jotted his e-mail address and gave it to Dr. Sanchez.

"I'd like both too." Meghan reached for the offered sheet of paper. "I'll give you my e-mail address in the morning."

Mrs. Hall slid into a chair beside the VP. "We believe in Dr. Sanchez's methods, and we hope all of you will encourage Lindsay to cooperate." She was pale, trembling. "There cannot be any repeats of . . ."

The VP took his wife's hand. "Special Agent Zinders, do you have questions? I forbid any alcohol consumption on this ranch while my daughter is here. Scottard gave me a key to his bar." He handed it to Ash. "Before you go to bed, lock it up."

"Yes, sir."

The VP nodded at Ash. "Need I remind you that my daughter's life is at stake?"

"Sir, I have Lindsay's best interests at heart. Always have."

The VP rubbed his face. "I know. This has been a long day. Longer night. You've never let me down. Didn't mean to bite your head off."

Dr. Sanchez gestured to the petite, middle-aged woman beside him. "My assistant will be available to answer any questions, but understand her first responsibility is to Lindsay."

"As is ours." Ash's voice fired electricity around the room.

"Thank you, Ash." The VP took another drink of coffee. "Dr. Sanchez has the ultimate word about Lindsay's treatment. However, Special Agent Zinders and his team are in charge of her security."

"I understand." Dr. Sanchez's confidence in his methods would surely rival Ash's policies. "I also have her diet and cooking instructions."

"That's for me." Pepper held out her hand and another copy went to Ash and Meghan. "We can have the consultation appointment anytime tomorrow."

"I'll leave extra copies on the kitchen counter." Dr. Sanchez lifted his chin. "Lindsay's diet is like a triangle. Each point is critical to her recovery: protein, carbohydrates, and fats and oils. This discipline—"

"Dr. Sanchez, just the basics." The VP smiled.

"Certainly." He reached inside his laptop case and pulled out a thin book, which he gave to Pepper. "I've written a book that explains the diet, what's included, and why. What's important is that she consumes natural and organic foods and nutrients."

Pepper frowned. "Am I supposed to cook separately for the agents and Lindsay?"

Dr. Sanchez continued to smile—like a Cheshire cat. "I'd like to think we all could eat nutritionally sound."

"Never mind." Pepper blew out a sigh. "I'm not going to ruin my reputation by preparing bland meals. If fresh and organic is what Lindsay needs, then she'll have it. The garden is at my fingertips."

Meghan hid her amusement. What a motley crew.

"Thanks, Pepper. Scottard said I could depend on you." The VP nodded in her direction. "Once we leave here, we'll not be returning until Dr. Sanchez assures me that Lindsay is ready to see us. He needs to have Lindsay's confidence, and my wife and I are not in that circle. Agent Connors, I hope you're able to influence her to make appropriate decisions for the future. Your past indicates success in many areas, and I hope this is one more. In addition, Dr. Sanchez is aware of the threats made on Lindsay's life."

"I believe we're all on the same page." Ash handed him a printout. "This is an up-to-date report on the security plan—much tighter than in the past."

The VP turned the sheet of paper over and folded his hands. "I've shared everything with you in the hopes that you'll better understand the seriousness of my daughter's illness. Pepper, Dr. Sanchez, Ms. Bertinelli, you are excused. Ah, Ms. Bertinelli, I understand you're sleeping in the same room with Lindsay tonight?"

"Yes, sir. I'm a registered nurse."

"She can be difficult to handle. Do not hesitate to call for assistance. An agent will be posted outside the door."

The three left the room, bidding good night to those remaining. The stairs creaked, indicating their ascent to the second story.

Meghan had used nutritional supplements, sound nutrition, and exercise for years and advocated them to family and friends. Her doubts about Dr. Sanchez subsided, and she allowed her suspicions to rest for a moment. She'd learned early on in her career to reserve her trust until a person proved worthy. It was a priceless commodity, and anyone could be bought for the right price.

"And now I want to give you the latest information about the threats." Lines deepened across the VP's forehead—a time line of agony. "The threats against Lindsay have yet to be traced. I know you're aware of the latest reports."

"Do you have a name yet?" Ash seated himself across from the VP.

"Only that his origin is Colombia. Possibly a resurgence of the Medellín Cartel."

"But that was dismantled in the early '90s."

"Some habits are hard to break. Millions of dollars flow through Colombia's drug trade. But we're on it."

Meghan studied the VP's weary face. So much responsibility filled this man's life. The president was dying, and that meant the Shield could soon be taking over the world's toughest job. She had no doubts about his leadership abilities. His life consisted of one outstanding achievement after another. Currently, his peacekeeping efforts in the Middle East were obtaining worldwide recognition.

She focused her attention on Ash. She didn't see any animosity, only a deep concern for the vice president and his plight. Perhaps his detail-oriented nature was a plus to protect all of them—a possibility she hadn't considered.

# CHAPTER 8

*WHERE AM I?* A hazy mist fogged Lindsay's mind while she struggled to remember the last several hours, or was it days? Depression. Wanting to die. The hospital. Bright lights. Muffled voices. Sterile and medicinal. This felt different. Smelled fresh.

*Oh no, not another rehab.*

Blinking, she recalled slipping into a black hole that consumed her, urging her to leave this world behind. *You're worthless. No one loves you.* She'd stumbled to her kitchen for a knife, then took it back to the bathroom. Staring at her wrist, she wanted so desperately to die and yet craved a reason to live. The veins seemed to pop up and taunt her, until she had no choice but to slice into them. The blood. Red and thicker than what she'd imagined. She forced herself to stand and write "I'm sorry" on her bathroom mirror in blood. So many other thoughts about her wasted life had flown in and out of her mind, but she couldn't concentrate on anything meaningful, much like now. The last thing she remembered was sliding to the floor, her blood-coated finger trailing the *y* in *sorry.* She tried to add that she loved them, but her strength was fading. Weakness replaced the self-condemnation, and she basked in the relief. Soon it would be over. No one wanted her, and she couldn't blame them. They were better off. She'd been a burden since the day she was born. So many mistakes . . . believed so many lies.

"Lindsay."

Who was that? Not Mom. The voice had a low pitch. Lindsay turned to a gray-haired woman seated beside her bed. Must be a nurse or a new doctor.

Her gaze swept around the room. The Texas decor—antique furniture, framed art, a huge, rusty metal star on the wall. The Dancin' Dust. Her stomach knotted at the thought. She'd stayed in this very room. Must have been Uncle Scottard's idea. How long had it been since she visited here? Oh, it was the summer she turned fifteen, when Daddy wanted her away from a loser boyfriend. Nothing had changed, except now the loser boyfriend didn't want her.

"Lindsay."

She turned to the woman. "Who are you?"

"Carla Bertinelli. I'm Dr. David Sanchez's nurse and assistant. How are you feeling?"

"Like I've been drugged." Then she recalled the nurse in the hospital saying she was giving her something to help her sleep. Daddy and Mom hovering nearby. Tears from both of them. She'd failed suicide, too. "Leave me alone."

"I will in a few moments. Dr. Sanchez is waiting to speak to you."

"Who is he? Why am I here?"

"Your parents thought this would be a good place for you to rest and recuperate."

Carla's soft voice might persuade another addict to fight for her life, but not Lindsay. "I don't have the flu. I tried to kill myself." She held up her bandaged wrist.

"We're aware of the circumstances."

"I'm sure you were given a full report. The Dancin' Dust is out in the middle of nowhere. Has it been turned into a rehab?"

"We'd prefer to call this a time of reflection and an opportunity to regain your health."

Lindsay stared at the woman, who had more laugh lines than her mother. "Are you for real?"

Carla leaned toward Lindsay. "I'm real, and I care about you. So does Dr. Sanchez."

"I hate fake compassion. Seen it all. I suppose you're going to spout Scripture, too? That's already been done by a priest who gave up."

"Forcing religious beliefs is not my style. Truth is my bandwagon, and you'll always hear it from me. Whether you want it or not."

She'd heard the truth claim before too.

Carla stood. "Dr. Sanchez is waiting to talk to you. Do you need to use the bathroom first?"

"I'd rather sleep." Weakness urged her to tune out the nurse and the doctor who awaited her. She preferred to drift away where she'd forget.

"I'll leave you two alone. I'm looking forward to working with you."

"Pardon me while I gag."

Carla opened the door and a slender, dark-haired man entered. "Good afternoon, Lindsay. I'm Dr. David Sanchez, but I prefer to be called Dave."

This sounded like so many rehabs. "Don't waste your breath. An addict has to want to be clean. What time is it?"

"Three fifteen. You've slept since around nine o'clock last night."

"You drugged me, I'm sure."

He walked to her bedside and sat in the chair his nurse had just vacated. "I don't use any kind of drugs. It's not a part of my treatment plan."

"I do. I like how they make me feel."

"And that has nearly destroyed your life. My methods are different."

"None of the other methods worked, and yours won't either. I've been through withdrawal more times than you can count."

"And you will again. Right here on this beautiful ranch. I've read your file, and I have an idea about your experiences. But this time, we're treating your body with supplements."

Had her parents lost their minds? "Vitamins? You've got to be kidding. Are they shaped like little bears?"

"I have a high success rate with conditions like—"

"Doc, I'm an addict. I snort coke and I drink."

"I'm glad you're able to admit it." He smiled. "Along with the supplements, you'll be eating fresh organic foods every three hours, and as soon as we can get you out of bed, we'll be adding exercise. I see there's a lovely pool outside, horses, and acres to walk and meditate."

"How much did you take my father for? This is priceless." Her stomach churned. The withdrawal symptoms had begun.

"My fees are not what's important. Restoring your health is."

"So I'm stuck here on this ranch, dancin' in the dust."

"The length of your stay depends on your attitude." He added a little edge to his words, but the smile remained intact. *Must be Botox.*

"Is Ash here?"

"He is, as well as five other Secret Service agents."

Panic twisted through her. Why had her father doubled the number of agents? Memories of what had happened in DC raced through her mind. She needed to sort them out and make a few decisions. "Is this also about the threats?"

Dave nodded.

Lindsay turned away from him. "They should have left me to die. Having me out of the picture would have solved everything."

"Taking your own life is never a viable solution. All problems can be worked out. Carla and I will help you talk through the issues that have sunk you into this depression."

"You mean the black hole?" She cut sarcasm into every word.

"Sufferers refer to the depression accompanying addictions by many names—the shadow, a demon, or the monster."

She whipped her attention back to the doctor, who thought his textbook responses could make her world a peaceful existence. "You have no clue about any of this. I suggest you get as far away from me as you can get. Or all of you will end up dead."

# CHAPTER 9

SATURDAY MORNING, Meghan stood at the open door of Lindsay's darkened room and watched the young woman sleep. In the shadows, she looked peaceful. So far she'd refused to eat or take the supplements. She'd been vomiting and hysterical. Meghan had seen it all before. She also had her doubts about Dr. Sanchez's methods. In her opinion, supplements and proper nutrition were better adapted to a maintenance program than the struggles through withdrawal and counseling.

Dr. Sanchez had expressed disappointment in Lindsay's refusal to move forward with her treatment plan, but the ambitious psychologist would have to be patient. Surely Lindsay was not his first reluctant addict. From what Meghan had learned about her, she held her own on the stubborn scale. The doctor said Lindsay had type O blood. According to him, her stubborn and impatient streak came naturally, along with an insistence upon having her own way. He also claimed she could have a tendency to be lazy. He planned to discover those positive things that stirred her passion and work through them to build her self-confidence.

Meghan wondered what A-positive blood meant, but she didn't think she really wanted to know.

She snapped on Lindsay's dresser lamp. The two needed to talk, and Meghan was ready for the infamous abuse.

Lindsay's eyes fluttered.

"Good morning, Lindsay. I'm Special Agent Meghan Connors, assigned to you from 8 a.m. to 5 p.m."

Lindsay stirred, and her eyes were but slits. "At least you don't talk to me in military time. Hey, that's Ash's shift. Where is he?"

"Downstairs. He'll work the late afternoon and evening shift."

"Four weeks on, two weeks off?"

"Not for Ash and me. We're here for the duration." Meghan added a bit of lightness to her voice. She needed to be a friend so she could help this girl.

"Aren't you lucky." She studied Meghan. "You brought down a shooter in Atlanta. Saved my dad's life. Received special recognition."

So Lindsay was aware of the news. "That's me."

"Were you assigned to me because of your good aim, or is Daddy hoping a woman can get me off the drugs?"

"Both." Possibly the candor would break the ice.

"I'm used to Ash. He doesn't talk much. We have a mutual hate/hate relationship."

"His shift is after mine. There's a total of six agents."

"So I've heard. Are you afraid I'll run?"

"Possibly. There's another reason I was assigned to you."

"I don't care how or why you got this assignment." Lindsay faced away from the window. "My head hurts, and I feel sick. The blinds are not keeping out the light. Do something about it."

"The blinds are already adjusted as far as they'll go."

Lindsay cursed. "The light hurts my eyes. Makes going through this even harder."

Meghan wondered if she'd begun hallucinating yet. Alcohol withdrawals could be frightening.

"Look, just get out of here. I'm getting sick."

"Do you need help to the bathroom?"

"No, thanks. That might be against the rules."

"You won't find anything sharp in there."

"Very funny. I need something to help me through this."

Lindsay swallowed hard. No doubt the nausea had teamed up with the irritability. "I've always been given meds for this in the past."

"That's not my call, and I believe Dr. Sanchez has described his treatment plan to you."

"Vitamins and fruit smoothies. Yum."

"Think about it, Lindsay. What if he's able to pull you out of the addiction? What—?"

"Not interested, Agent. I like my life just the way it is."

"What if you find purpose and meaning?"

"Leave me alone."

"What if you can get out from under your dad's thumb?"

"What if a bullet gets to me first? Or . . . ?"

"Or what? You're a smart girl. The jerk who threatened you has the US government breathing down his neck. Who is he?"

"You wouldn't understand."

"Try me. I've seen the worst of characters." Meghan regretted peppering her with questions. Hadn't worked with Shelley either, and Lindsay had tuned her out. Maybe . . . "Wouldn't you like to prove them all wrong?"

When Lindsay hesitated, Meghan knew she'd gotten through on a minuscule level. She left her alone, hoping that somewhere in Lindsay's confused state, rebellion would become her best ally.

★ ★ ★

At noon Meghan took a break and picked up a sandwich—hoping neither the ham nor the cheese was loaded with jalapeños. Lifting the top slice of whole wheat bread, she pulled off the pepper jack cheese with its little green additives. Although she was a Texas gal, the hot peppers were not a three-meals-a-day treat.

She added a spinach and strawberry salad and joined Ash in the operation room, while Dr. Sanchez counseled Lindsay and shared lunch. She longed for another agent to fill the awkward silence. Bob worked the front of the house. Victor and Rick, who had the graveyard shift, were sleeping, and Wade was in the stables with the Leonards. Mealtimes had become a battleground between Pepper and Ash. Meghan almost felt sorry for him. He had three women driving him nuts. At least today, she'd not stick around any longer than it took to finish eating.

She checked the news on her BlackBerry and caught a glimpse of the *USA Today* headline: "Lindsay Hall giving NBC a live exclusive on the evening news." She lifted a bottle of water to her lips. Did Ash know this? The announcement had been made less than ten minutes ago.

He sat across from her eating a sandwich, not really frowning but not smiling either. Why not take a chance?

"NBC is hosting Lindsay tonight. They must be running the previous show."

His forehead crinkled like an old man laboring over a checker game. "Redundancy wastes time and energy."

"Sir, calling a matter of importance about our protectee to your attention is not redundant but merely an indication of an agent who is diligent to her job."

Shock registered in his baby blues. "Good call, Connors. You don't take my junk."

Instead of biting into him, she took another bite of her sandwich. Too bad she didn't know any vampires to send his way. Maybe an exorcist would do a better job. Ah, those weren't good thoughts. She'd win him over yet.

"I need a report in two minutes about where the Leonards attend church."

"Excuse me?" Ethan and Chip aced their background checks. They were ranchers with a solid work ethic. No priors. But this was Saturday and tomorrow was church—an important day for Ethan.

"You don't like your orders, Connors?"

"My opinion or preferences are exactly that: mine. I'm on my lunch break, and my shift hours are assigned to Lindsay. Her counseling and lunch are nearly finished."

He glanced at his watch. "One minute, thirty seconds."

The news continued. She doubted the VP would respond to the latest report. He preferred not to comment on his daughter's shocking exploits. His restrained method had worked in the beginning, gathering support from those within his party and a large majority of independents. But lately the media claimed he didn't care what happened to Lindsay, and his silence proved it. Meghan remembered the day before the shooting in Atlanta, when she'd overheard Burnette advise him to ignore Lindsay's bikini-clad photo on the front of People magazine—as he'd done in the past. Emotion nearly overcame the VP.

Meghan hoped God was hearing this family's cry for help.

Realization crept over her, sending chill bumps up her arms. Why hadn't she considered this angle of Ash's resentment? When she stopped the shooter in Atlanta, the VP commended her quick thinking. Ash probably learned about the VP requesting her for the VPPD once this assignment was completed. Only one position was available on that team, and Special Agent Ash Zinders wanted that slot too.

"Fifteen seconds." Ash's gaze bored into her face.

She stared back. He wasn't a bad-looking man. What had happened in his life to make him such a miserable human being? She'd do a little asking around to see what surfaced.

Meghan stood and pressed her palms against the table, not once taking her eyes off him. "Three, two, one." She smiled. "Your report is on my screen, and I'm going back to my protectee. Have a good afternoon, sir. You have mayo on your face."

# CHAPTER 10

ASH WATCHED MEGHAN DISAPPEAR, leaving a hint of citrusy scent. That woman spent more time in his thoughts than he wanted to deliberate. She had a knack for getting in the last word that left him scrambling, and he wished he had a recording of what went on in her mind. Gutsy. Gorgeous. Good agent. He was on a roll, and it was time to stop.

He picked up his mug and walked into the kitchen for another hit of coffee. *Surly* best described him, and the caffeine would give him the punch to keep his brain charged. He had too much work to do, and thinking about Meghan was a distraction.

He hadn't talked to Lindsay yet, but Dave Sanchez and Meghan had indicated she asked about him. Odd, since Lindsay despised him. He didn't look forward to witnessing her withdrawals again, watching a beautiful young woman spiral into a helpless, pitiful human being. The hallucinations were the worst.

Victor entered the kitchen, sleep glossing his eyes. He had a cup of coffee in one hand and a sausage biscuit in the other. Sliding onto a stool at the counter, he yawned and pulled his cell phone from his pocket. He hadn't been to bed since he'd gotten off his shift at 0800, and Ash had seen him swimming laps shortly after that.

Victor studied him through half-open eyes. "Anything I can do?"

The quiet Asian seemed to sense when Ash had cratered to

new lows. Victor apparently understood he needed space to think through details.

"Thanks. I appreciate it. Is Wade still with the Leonards?"

"Yeah. They're talking weather."

"Good." Ash stared at the steadily blackening sky. "Storm's blowing this way. Should bring cooler temps."

"Or a tornado." Victor slid his finger across his phone's screen, then showed Ash a weather map. "Conditions are right. Want me to check on the storm cellar before I head to bed?"

"Thanks. Take Pepper with you. I saw her in the garden a few minutes ago. That'll keep her out of my hair until I can make my rounds outside. Hope the tornado passes by us. Not enough room in the storm cellar for all the agents. However, I do know who I'd keep out."

"Then who'd cook?"

Ash chuckled. "You, Victor. I'd take wonton soup over *pico de gallo* any day."

"Rooster's beak."

"What?"

"That's what *pico de gallo* means in Spanish."

"Figures. I'd give up my vacation for a decent meal." Sometimes Ash wondered if God was getting even for his colorful past.

"If you don't need me, then I'll check on the storm cellar."

Ash's phone rang soon after Victor left. Tom Warrington's name flashed on the caller ID.

"Are things quiet at the Dancin' Dust?"

A car horn would be a welcome sound. "It's clear. Our protectee hasn't emerged from her room yet."

"Has she started her new treatments?"

"No. But today's a new day."

"For the VP's sake, I'd sure like to see her kick a few habits. Wanted to give you a heads-up. Lindsay's Bimmer was blown up at her apartment."

He shuddered. She could have been killed. "Anyone hurt?"

"A woman was killed and a man wounded. Happened about thirty minutes ago. We're working on it. Looks like a pipe bomb."

"Any warning?"

"Nothing."

Ash's mind raced. None of this made sense. "Tom, I'm processing aloud here. How angry could Lindsay have made a drug dealer that he'd take on the US government?"

"Maybe this isn't the first time she's held out money."

"I don't recall that being the case in the past. She always found the money somewhere."

"As I said, we're on it."

Ash picked up on the vagueness. What was Tom holding back? "I'm simply exploring. Don't you find this situation strange? A drug dealer threatening the VP's daughter? Untraceable e-mails and texts sent to her? And now a bombing?"

"Hard to say at this point."

"I'm talking a conspiracy. One man from Colombia doesn't act on his own to create such havoc."

"Right."

"But you're not telling me a thing, are you?"

"Just keep Lindsay safe while we unravel this." Which told Ash that Warrington was receiving lots of heat.

"You got it. How's the VP doing?"

"Always the Shield."

"What about the media?"

Warrington swore. "They're all over it. Call me if they find Lindsay."

Ash flipped the phone shut and tucked it into his pocket. His mind continued to draw out the possibilities. Although Warrington had blown off Ash's speculation, or gave that impression, whoever was behind the bombing and threats had powerful resources. He needed to talk to Lindsay, but in her condition, she could have a meltdown. Best keep her in the dark for now.

Ash wished he could get his hands on the reports flying across the desks of Homeland Security. Realizing the ones responsible had the technology to evade DC's sophisticated trackers made Ash cringe to think of what they might do next.

★ ★ ★

Midafternoon, Ash walked into the kitchen for a Diet Coke. He'd seen Pepper step outside and stole the opportunity to get his hands on something to drink. While he was drinking the Coke, Meghan entered the kitchen. He was tempted to ignore her. After all, his thoughts weren't keyed to being congenial, and she seemed to bring out the worst in him.

"Who's with Lindsay?"

"She and Dave are in a counseling session on the front porch. Nice breeze out there. Bob is close."

Ash couldn't find a thing to criticize.

Meghan opened the refrigerator door and pulled out a bottle of water. Her jeans clung to every curve. He'd watched her run that morning—perfection beat into every stride.

"Sir, do you have a moment to discuss Lindsay?"

"Has she slapped you?" His sarcasm bit into his conscience. Why couldn't he accept the fact she did her job as well as any agent on the team?

She stiffened. "No, sir. I wondered if you could fill me in on your dealings with her."

"I already did."

Meghan wrapped her hand around her water bottle and squeezed. "Sir, she's frightened, and I'd like to know if this is normal behavior. Crack withdrawal symptoms are basically emotional, but she's experiencing nausea. The alcohol causes depression, and she's had a few hallucinations. But the fear is what bothers me the most."

Ash needed to stop the intimidation, but old habits were hard to break. "Have you talked to Dave? He has her medical records."

"He agrees with me. She's hiding something."

Ash leaned back against the refrigerator. Isolating himself from one of his agents could put their protectee at risk. "Lindsay doesn't have normal behavior. She wavers between high and hysterical. And hysterical is accompanied by lashing out at whoever is in her way."

"My conclusion is still the same. She's afraid."

"You're wrong." Ash shook his head while she studied him. A chill crept up his spine. "What are you looking at?"

"The SAIC I'm talking to." She took a step his way. Fire sparked in her eyes. "I know you've been assigned to Lindsay for the past four years. I know you hate the idea of working with a woman. I know we're both up for the same assignment with VP Hall. But Lindsay is our protectee, and besides her addiction, someone out there wants her dead. We need to work together on this."

She was right, and he'd been unprofessional. Ash pointed to the kitchen door. "Let's take a walk. How about the driveway toward the road?" He set his Coke can on the counter and reached for a bottle of water from the fridge. "The rest of the team knows what happened this morning in DC, but you were with Lindsay, so I waited to brief you."

Outside, he explained the car bombing.

"This doesn't sound like an upset drug dealer. I wonder how far it reaches."

"My thoughts too."

Under a gray sky, they neared the front gate. Where did he begin except to tell all he knew about Lindsay? The words refused to come. Or was he working harder at ignoring his attraction to Meghan than at confiding in her about their protectee? Most agents scurried into the woodwork when he approached them. But not her. She had strength and pull with the VP. Her last qualifying proved her marksmanship equaled his. And that wasn't the only area in which she rivaled him.

Meghan had moved from what he thought was an easy replacement to a worthy team member. They did need to work together on all fronts. It was time he stopped allowing his personal feelings to interfere with his responsibilities.

"I've been a real jerk, and I want to apologize."

"Thank you." She tossed him a smile that could rival the Dancin' Dust's wildflowers. "Apology accepted. There have been times when I could have walked away, but instead I said exactly what I felt."

He chuckled. "That's one of the things I admire about you."

"Pepper's pretty good at speaking her mind too, but I don't want to go there."

"Don't get me started on our spicy cook. This assignment might break the bank in antacids." He noted the change in conversation topic had helped him relax. "I did wonder if you cooked."

She laughed, an easy lilt that caused him to do the same. "A little. But it's not on my list of favorite things to do. In case you're interested, Pepper collects stamps."

"Thanks. I'll log onto the post office's site and memorize a few." He took a deep breath and stared at the steadily darkening sky. He needed to tell her what he knew about their protectee. "You've read Lindsay's file. You have the stats. What you don't know is how she got to this point. I took over this assignment four years ago. Shortly after Mr. and Mrs. Hall returned from their latest humanitarian mission, President Claredon approached the Halls about the upcoming election. The nation was ready for a change, and Jackson Hall became Claredon's running mate. About the same time, Lindsay was kicked out of boarding school, and the Halls decided to bring her home. That's when I came into the picture."

"Do you know why she's such a handful? At twenty, she's a little old for adolescent behavior. Her sister is finishing her grad work at Yale, and—" Meghan stopped and faced him. "I get it. She couldn't handle her parents' work with third world children while she sat in a boarding school. She resented their mission work, saving other people's children when she needed to be saved too."

"I think you've nailed it. Lindsay and I never got along—mostly my fault because I did my job and that was it. She needed more attention, and her parents didn't understand her behavior. She constantly reminded them about those years in boarding school."

"Holidays and summer vacations weren't enough?"

"For Lindsay, no. For her sister, Kelli, it was fine. She's older and has her career mapped out. An independent and intelligent young woman. To the best of my knowledge, she's never given her parents any problems. While the two girls were in boarding school, Kelli tried to steer her sister in the right direction. Mothered her too."

"When did Lindsay start using?"

"That's why the school removed her. Got caught smoking pot in her room."

Meghan blew out a sigh. "The VP and his wife must have explored every type of counseling and rehab out there."

"Remember what the VP said? He'd do anything to help his daughter. They've never given up. Scottard Burnette has tried for years to counsel her, but he's never been able to get through. Not so sure I'd have the same commitment. But I don't have kids."

They walked on in silence while he waited for Meghan to respond.

"I understand Lindsay much better now, and I see how the VP and his wife could blame themselves. Guilt is pretty powerful. Drives you hard."

Ash blinked. Had Meghan read his records?

"Has she ever been threatened before?"

"Nothing substantial. Upset boyfriends, and those leads have all been checked out." Ash shoved his hands into his jeans pockets. "Here's one for you. If she cares so little for life that suicide was the only way out, then why is she frightened? Looks to me like she'd welcome any method of putting herself out of misery."

"But a murder attempt is out of her control. From what little I've seen, Lindsay must be in control of everything around her. I know that doesn't make sense when she uses drugs and alcohol to escape her problems. But again, she chooses those methods."

Ash had heard a similar thought from Alexa Hall. "Then why isn't she helping the authorities track down this guy?"

"Maybe she doesn't think she's worth saving."

"You're contradicting yourself."

"Drug addicts don't make sense."

"Sounds like firsthand information." Ash stared at the navy-blue sky. Clouds had rolled in, casting an ominous aura across the sky along with decidedly lower temperatures.

"Maybe it is," Meghan said. Ash looked at her, but she was watching the sky. "What if she has no idea who this guy is?"

Ash pointed to a greenish-black area to the west of them. "Then we have more trouble than the storm headed this way."

# CHAPTER 11

EARLY SUNDAY MORNING before her shift, Meghan read Chip Leonard's background check for the third time. Although those who were trained to track down killers were working nonstop to find who had threatened Lindsay, that didn't deter her from investigating every angle.

Chip had cleared the Secret Service radar, but not to her satisfaction, and she intended to find out the source of her doubts. Something didn't ring true about a man with an MA in statistics leaving a lucrative job in Dallas to help his dad breed and train horses. He was twenty-eight years old. No wife or kids. His dad was fit, and Meghan had Ethan's latest medical checkup in front of her. That ruled out responsibility to an ailing father. Chip had never been in trouble. Had no questionable ties to any of Homeland Security's blacklisted organizations, and he was extremely intelligent. The latter picked at her like a pesky mosquito. Wasn't he bored living out in the middle of nowhere with only his father and horses for company?

Ethan Leonard swore allegiance to Jesus, Texas, and the Republican Party in that order. He'd buried his wife ten years ago after a long battle with breast cancer. Chip came to live with him about the same time the VP took office. That could be a coincidence or part of strategic planning. She'd ask Ash and the team about a possible link. If her theory proved true, Chip had the advantage of keeping an eye on Scottard Burnette and any of his high-ranking political guests. The idea Chip might have overheard some of the agents' conversations surfaced again. Did he have a listening device tucked away beneath his belt buckle?

Thunder cracked across a dark sky, and she jumped. Another storm increased the likelihood of Ash threatening to send them to the storm cellar again. He knew nothing about Texas twisters. Yesterday afternoon's light and sound show was a baby kicking its feet.

"Chip a puzzle for you, too?" She hadn't heard Ash enter the room, and now he stood behind her. Dangerously close for a woman who found him attractive.

"He's no hayseed, and he's watching every move we make."

"What do you think motivates him to live here and work so hard?"

Ash's interest in her thoughts was a rarity, but she'd play along. After all, yesterday he'd talked to her like a real human being. "Curiosity. Maybe boredom with the normal routine. But a smart man can only be stimulated for so long before he starts looking for other means to occupy his time."

"My concern too."

"I'd like to find out why he really gave up a prestigious career for mucking out stalls."

"Mucking?"

"Shoveling manure." Meghan bit back a grin. Ash needed a fast-track course in ranch life.

"According to Wade, Chip said he was finished with the fast-paced life."

"What does Wade make of it?"

"Thinks he's the real thing."

Meghan's skepticism remained intact, but she could be wrong. "He knows when I run in the mornings and my path, which I change every day. And he knows the moment you'll stick your head out the door to check on me, and he picks up on the agents' conversations."

"I wasn't exactly checking on your running status." Ash rubbed his forehead. "Give me some examples."

"Sunshine. The Shield. The status of the front gate's camera. President Claredon's current health status. And his dad calls me by a name only my dad used. Of course, that could be nothing." Meghan drummed her fingers against the tabletop. "It's as though he has all of us bugged. He could be simply perceptive, but I'd like to be sure." She omitted the time Ethan referred to Ash as A2Z. No point going there.

"I'll talk to the agents, but those men are trained to keep information confidential." He frowned. "My team doesn't step out of protocol."

"My point." Meghan scrutinized the lines on Ash's face that she'd quickly learned to interpret as the way he conducted his thought process. "I've heard stories about men abandoning their careers to get back to nature, but those men had families—a deep-rooted need to raise their kids away from city life. Chip's a statistician. I want to know why he gave up a hundred and fifty grand a year for room and board out in the middle of nowhere. I know our profession boasts of 70-percent accuracy in detecting lies, but I honestly can't tell with him, and it's driving me crazy. All I have to go on is his unusual background."

"Meghan, he talks to you as much as he does to Wade. Chip's job here doesn't offer mental stimulation, unless other things are occupying his mind. Why don't you see if he'll open up?"

"I think I will. He's expressed interest, but I don't want him to think we're using him."

"Keep on it."

"The Leonards have invited me to dinner a few times. I'll see if the invitation is still open."

"Take it slow. I know you grew up with people like this."

She laughed. "Do you mean rednecks?"

"I didn't mean you."

"They are country people—hardworking, respect traditional

values, and fiercely patriotic. But back to me talking to Chip, I'll report in tonight if I learn anything."

"Thanks. I tell you this: sticking around here with all the goings-on in DC is making me antsy."

"What happens when Lindsay discovers Chip? My guess is it will open a can of worms."

Ash paced the room. "You can count on it. I've seen her in action, and she could charm an Uzi from a terrorist. Wade's warned Chip about her. But she won't view him as off-limits. It'll take him telling her he's not interested and sticking to it."

A jagged flash of lightning broke the horizon. "They need to find this stalker so we can get back to DC. Dave can treat Lindsay there, and we can get back to real living. Last night's storms were the only excitement we've seen since we got here, and it's been a week."

Most of the time, Meghan found the ranch refreshing, a time to reconnect with her roots. But Ash acted like a caged animal. "Did you get much sleep, sir?"

He shook his head. "Between thinking about the bombing and the storms, I might have gotten three hours. By the way, I don't want Lindsay to know about her car. Dr. Sanchez actually agrees with me on that one."

At the sound of his voice's low timbre, she was drawn to him in a peculiar sort of way. "I'm going to grab a bottle of water and visit a few minutes with the Leonards."

"Be my guest. Considering my indigestion from Pepper's meals, I'd be tempted to join you."

They laughed, and she sensed the walls crumbling between them. "I hope I'm not being unrealistic by hoping Lindsay will come to her senses. She'll always struggle with addictive behaviors, but I'd like to see her come out on top."

"Hope is what keeps us alive."

"A good topic for a sermon."

He strode to the window as another jagged path lit the sky.

"Been weeks since I've been to church. God's probably erased me from the roll."

"Oh, He knows where you are."

"That, Agent Connors, is what keeps me going." He lifted a brow and grinned. "So what's your nickname?"

"Not on your life. Might be used against me." Meghan turned her attention to the computer and lowered the laptop lid. She'd ponder Ash's spiritual life later, but she did feel better knowing he acknowledged God.

"I'll find out. Nicknames are my specialty."

"You don't want to go there."

"Ouch, Agent Connors. Do you mean I have one?"

She left the room before he had another comment. Nice guy when he wanted to be.

★ ★ ★

Ash worked through to midmorning, searching restricted government sites for any clue leading to who and why the chaos in DC persisted. He resented the implication that the Secret Service was inept and hadn't been able to find those responsible for bombing Lindsay's car and sending untraceable e-mails.

He stood and gazed out at the gray sky. Matched his mood. He needed a Diet Coke to help him through the next couple of hours. Hopefully, he could sneak into the kitchen and Pepper would be gone. When he opened the operation door that led to the kitchen, silence greeted him. Normally, she had country music playing. He couldn't resist a grin, as though he'd completed a successful clandestine mission. The moment he rounded the corner, he spotted her drinking a glass of red wine. The bottle rested on the counter.

Ash struggled to contain his anger. The many times he'd seen Lindsay drunk added fuel to his fury. "Why are you drinking?"

She arched a brow and huffed. "Because I want to."

"You heard what the vice president said—no alcoholic beverages were to be consumed. I repeated the order the first morning at breakfast."

"This is medicinal, sir." Condescension dripped from her words. "It helps me endure the distasteful parts of my day."

Ash picked up the bottle and poured its contents down the drain. "It's your turn. Get rid of it. Now. Per the vice president's orders."

"I take my orders from Scottard Burnette."

Ash wished he had the authority to fire her. He'd be content to live on peanut butter and jelly for the next six months. "Scottard Burnette takes his direction from Vice President Hall. I'm going to ask you one more time to pour out that wine."

"And if I don't?"

"Why do you have to be so difficult?"

"Why do you have to use your authority to shove everybody around like you own the place? What I drink from my own supply in my room is my business."

Ash stared at her. How could one woman be so self-centered? "Lindsay is an alcoholic. She's trying to get sober and clean. The drugs and alcohol will kill her if she isn't able to beat them. If she sees you drinking, she'll search the kitchen until she finds it."

She blew out a sigh. "All right. Have it your way." She dumped the contents of her glass down the sink.

"Could we make an effort to get along?"

"Maybe." She grabbed her garden basket. "You remind me too much of my husband. He always had to have his nose in everything I did. I resented it then, and I do now."

*No wonder the man died of a heart attack.*

# CHAPTER 12

MEGHAN TOOK A SIP OF HER WATER and walked into the stables. The scent of fresh hay and horses brought back memories of a simpler time when she was living at home and her family felt normal. Those were the good days when the most traumatic event centered on taking second in a barrel race instead of first. The perfectionism still reigned.

The broken engagement bothered her, not so much for her own sake but for disappointing Mom. The dear woman had looked forward to a Christmas wedding, and she had enough grief with Shelley. Someday, Mom would have that son-in-law of her dreams and grandbabies to spoil. Probably in about a hundred years. And probably not from Meghan.

She walked across the concrete floor, swept cleaner than her mother's kitchen, and grasped the depth of the Leonards' dedication to keeping Burnette's ranch running smoothly. The thoroughbreds were exercised, trained, and groomed every day, as though the horses were on display. No matter what Ethan's and Chip's motives, their work was flawless.

"Mornin'." Chip's voice came from the back, and he walked to meet her. Dressed in jeans and a cowboy hat, he looked better than a gift package. The shadow of a beard added to his rugged appeal. But she'd been there and done the male appreciation thing too many years ago. Good looks had a way of spoiling a man's heart. At least in her experiences.

"Did the storm keep you from running?" he said.

"I'm an exercise freak, not an idiot."

"Yeah. Lightning doesn't attract me either. I run at 2 a.m. I mean 0200. Sometimes the weather is a little iffy then too."

Why did he run at such an early hour? "Do you set your alarm and then go back to bed?"

"I do. A habit I started in Dallas when work stressed me out. Weird, I know."

"Yeah, it is. I'm surprised you're here. Thought you'd have headed out for church already." She leaned against the side of a stall like she was posing for a photo shoot, which was exactly how she'd earned her way through college.

An admiring gaze bored a hole through her, but that's what she intended. "I'll be leaving soon. Too bad you're on duty. I'd ask you to tag along."

She smiled. "And I'd go. I don't like missing church."

He grinned. "So you're one of them?"

"A Christian?"

He nodded.

"Yes, and you aren't?"

"Haven't decided yet. But I promised Dad I would investigate it."

"Do you always do what your dad says?"

He pushed his hat back. "Not at my age. But I respect his wisdom."

"I like him. Reminds me of my family." She smiled and meant it. "If you're searching for God, He'll find you."

"Sounds like you've been listening to my dad."

"Is that a bad thing?"

"Not at all. He likes you. Says you're the real thing, not a Texas wannabe like most of the agents here. I imagine juggling the Bible's teachings with your job is a challenge."

She didn't think he was insulting her. More like trying to find out what made her tick. "Living up to God's standards is always a struggle, no matter what our profession. Too much junk out there designed to snatch our attention."

He shrugged. "I agree, which is why I'm still looking."

"Well, I'm glad I made the cut with you and your dad."

He lifted a brow. "Oh yeah? We both like Wade, too. A decent guy."

"We're all a good team. We have a job to do—protecting Lindsay at all costs."

"But you're after more, aren't you? You have bigger stakes than a pat on the back."

What did he mean? "Guess I have."

"Hard to be a woman in the Secret Service?"

"At times. We have to prove ourselves, just like any other agent. But the trust factor can be an issue."

Chip studied her, but she could handle his scrutiny. "I had a friend in the FBI who claimed most women jumped aboard to find a husband, or they were out to prove something to the male members of the species."

"I've known a few like that in the Secret Service. They don't last long. Obviously." For a moment, she flashed back to a few agents who were interested in something she refused to give.

"I bet you qualify just fine."

Chip's words held more meaning than she cared to tackle. "I do all right."

"I have no illusions, Meghan. You're probably out here to fish information out of me."

She laughed and took another sip of water. "Why? Do you have something to hide?"

"The last time I checked, I passed clearance."

*Not as far as I'm concerned.* "Actually, I am here for something. Is your dad's invitation to dinner still open? I can't handle one more of Pepper's jalapeño meals."

Chip leaned on one leg. Did he doubt her or was he reading her? "Dad'll love it. Sunday night is fried chicken and garlic mashed potatoes . . . and whatever needs eatin' from the garden. No church tonight. The preacher's on vacation. Come by about six thirty." He held up a finger. "Make that 1830. I might even bring out the guitar."

"A concert? You're an unusual man."

"The word's *mysterious*. That's what keeps the women chasing me."

"Please." She laughed as she studied his appeal. The broken engagement had sealed her heart on ever wading into those waters again. But this guy had charm oozing from his hat to his boots.

Lindsay might have a hard time resisting him.

# CHAPTER 13

SUNDAY AFTERNOON, Lindsay wiped the tears from her face and stared out the window. The upstairs loft also served as a game room. Today, games were not on her mind, for the room was the site of another counseling session. Gray storm clouds deepened her pensive mood, layering the terror covering her heart. As the raindrops splattered against the window, so did the reminders of threats that had accumulated over the past four years.

Staying at the Dancin' Dust gave her no comfort. She needed a place where no one could find her. But no hideaway existed except in her drug-induced fantasy world when reality spun out of control. No matter where she went, either on the run or in her mind, she couldn't escape the prison.

"Dave, I don't want to talk about why I use drugs, my child-hood, my relationship with my parents, or anything else. I have a headache."

Dave leaned back in the copper-colored leather chair. She recognized his body language from past counselors who encouraged her to spill her guts. Good gesture, but she didn't plan to fall for subtle or direct means of urging her to talk. No point in going in a direction that had *death notice* shadowing every word.

"Your headache is natural. You know the withdrawal symptoms."

She nodded and squeezed back another tear. Why couldn't the

rain stop? Why couldn't it all stop? If only there was a way out . . . other than what she'd attempted and failed.

"Let's talk about what you'd like to do with your life."

"My life is hopeless. That subject's off limits."

"Hope is a choice. You've got to work at it. Where do you feel safe?" Dave's soft tone irritated her. He'd been paid big bucks to be nice to her, and that made him like most of the other people in her life. Caution ruled her tongue. Her parents might not be the only ones depositing funds into his bank account. Oh, to have a real friend, one who didn't expect something in return.

"Lindsay, when you don't answer me, I can't help you."

Biting back a caustic remark, she tried to form an answer that would pacify him. Progress brought her closer to a discharge from the Dancin' Dust, and she had the textbook answers memorized to ensure freedom. What did that word mean anyway? If she was honest with herself, she had no clue.

Carla sat at the opposite end of the sofa with Lindsay. Dave's assistant neither smiled nor frowned. She could have been a mannequin.

Dave leaned closer. "Tell me about your sister."

She could give him a little. Maybe he'd leave her alone. "Kelli has her act together. She's smart, and I've humiliated her a bazillion times."

"I don't think she's embarrassed. She wants to visit you."

No matter how much she wanted to see Kelli, why put her in danger? "She's the last person I want to see."

"I don't believe that at all. What about when you were kids? What was it like then?"

"Do you mean at the boarding school when she tried to parent me?"

"Did you resent her? I'd like to hear about those days."

Lindsay closed her eyes. "My sister is an image of perfection. She's always been a good role model. I was the one who rejected her. I'm jealous. Got it?"

"You can do and be anything you want. Again, it's your choice."

The trim man with the serious eyes had no idea how far she'd fallen. "It's too late." Visions of their childhood danced across her mind. Kelli reading stories. Tea parties on rainy afternoons. Long walks under elm trees. Fairy tales about a handsome prince who would whisk Lindsay away to live happily ever after. "None of those days are important."

"What is? What occupies your mind? I know you're afraid of something, but what or whom? All of us here are on your side. I want to see you healthy. Your parents love you and look forward to the day when you're home with them again, and the special agents want you safe. But none of us can help you unless you take the first step."

Dave hadn't touched on her cooperating with the agents before. Ash must be pressing him. Or her father.

"You want me to change my attitude?"

He nodded. "A change of heart followed by hard work is your best ally. I'm your friend, and I'm dedicated to helping you to attain emotional stability."

She couldn't tell Dave or Ash or Meghan about her demons. Not anyone. She held his glance for a moment. Oh, she needed someone . . . desperately.

# CHAPTER 14

SUNDAY DRAGGED ON. News from DC was slow, and Ash fought boredom as though it were a worthy adversary. Looking around at the agents in the operation room, he wanted to tear into someone to add a little oomph to his life. Not exactly an ideal solution when he should be in church. He'd give ten years of his life to be in DC with the action. Maybe five. But he wanted to be a part of the team looking for who was behind the crimes in DC.

Only the thought of a new assignment with the VPPD kept him going.

He listened to Victor type with lightning speed. The agent would pause, read the screen, then take off again. But that was his style. He could hack into the best of systems, and he'd been at it for hours in an attempt to find the source of Lindsay's untraceable e-mails. If Ash hadn't insisted on his being a part of this protective detail, that amazing brain would be behind a desk in DC.

"Let's take a break." Ash glanced at those gathered around the table in the operation room. Even Meghan had joined them, while Dave and Carla counseled Lindsay upstairs. He wished Meghan could sit in on all those sessions, but the vice president wanted his daughter free to confide in the psychologist.

Victor snapped up his personal iPhone.

"Hey, man, let up. We'll find this guy." Ash scooted his chair back and walked behind Victor. "Are you running on pure adrenaline?" He saw the screen on his phone. "Oh, I see what you're doing."

Victor's attention zeroed in on his diversion. "My break, my time."

Ash clamped a hand on Victor's shoulder. "You're not even on duty. Hey, how much sleep have you had in the last twenty-four hours?"

"I'll get to it." Victor grinned. "A few priorities here, then I'll be diving beneath the sheets."

Ash pointed to the screen. "It's all about skating. Sure wish Bob wasn't outside sweating in this heat. He'd love this."

"Skating?" Meghan joined them. "What kind?"

"The only kind." Victor leaned back in his chair. "Take a look at this." He set his phone on the table. Skaters perched on their boards zoomed down and then up a concave ramp.

"Are you a spectator or a participant?" Meghan slid into a chair beside him.

Victor scowled. "I don't watch sports. I experience them."

She laughed, a light sound that was real and . . . sweet. "And you compete?"

"I don't compete. I win."

He typed in another site with the same type of skating action. This one had sound.

"That's you? Wow." Meghan studied the screen. "Didn't know you were so talented. Are they shouting 'Victor Lee' or 'victory'?"

"Oh, you're good. Take a look at the trophy." He pointed to a picture of himself on the iPhone screen holding a two-foot-tall skater figurine. "I'm Shaun White's worst enemy."

The agents roared.

"I have no clue who Shaun White is, but I'm sure you'll tell me." Meghan's response brought on more laughter.

Victor crossed his arms. Frustration creased his features, but Ash knew it was an act. "Try Olympic winner. Where have you been? On a ranch in Abilene?"

0

"Ouch. You got me there. I'm just surprised, that's all." Meghan looked closer at the screen as the video caught a skater jump and twist. "Impressive, even if I haven't heard of your hero. Makes sense, though. You're from LA, where the majority of skaters do their thing. I mean, you're a computer geek and you're Asian."

"Are you profiling me?"

Meghan hid a grin. "No. Getting even for all the times you've harassed me about being the only woman on the team."

"You picked up on that?" Victor typed in another skater site.

"Yeah, the day you handed Bob a tube of lipstick. Thought it might be my color. I should have asked where you got it."

Ash listened to the agents banter. They worked well together, and each member had a specialty for this assignment. The team needed that camaraderie to secure the ranch and ensure Lindsay's safety. They played by the rules and that kept him happy.

He studied Meghan. Odd how the one person he didn't want on the team had become his favorite.

★ ★ ★

Meghan added a dangling pair of earrings to accent her outfit and a dab of perfume to her neck. What she was about to do filled her with excitement. Maybe she should have joined the CIA and gotten involved with covert operations. But with her luck, she'd have been assigned to a desk job.

Ash met her at the bottom of the stairs. A spark of approval glistened in his blue eyes. Was it how she looked or what she attempted to do? Either way, she liked the perk.

"Looks like you're on a mission." He had his phone to his ear, and he held up a finger. "Yes, thank you, sir."

After he ended the call, she waited for him to speak. He always needed a few minutes to process data. God must have designed his brain like a hard drive. They'd all be in trouble if he ever hit Delete.

"I have a call at 2100. Do you think you'll be back by then?"

"Hard to say. I'm playing this for all it's worth."

"Okay. Catch me as soon as you walk through the door." He moistened his lips. "You look pretty good to be spending the evening with a couple of cowboys."

"Thanks." If she didn't know how he felt about women agents, she'd think he had a jealous streak.

Outside, the foul weather had passed, leaving puddles and mud in its wake. She hated gray, and the sky had mellowed to blue . . . much like Ash's eyes.

Meghan looked forward to the evening, and a bit of homesickness kicked in. Once this assignment was completed, she'd make the trek home to Abilene. Maybe this time she'd do some good with her sister. And Mom deserved to know why she'd broken her engagement.

She walked the familiar path to the stables, her thoughts darting about like fireflies on a clear night. Although she wanted the people apprehended who had threatened Lindsay and killed the agent in DC, she didn't want the Leonards to be part of a treacherous plan. But those who worked against the law were successful because they were highly intelligent and the least-likely suspects.

After all, Judas was a disciple.

She'd toyed with the idea that Chip could have encountered one of the bad guys while working in Dallas. He could have been offered a tremendous amount of money to pull off an operation, like worming his way into Scottard Burnette's confidence and finding ways to secure information about those who were guests at the ranch. But why target Lindsay? She was a drug addict and an embarrassment to her family—and the administration. If Chip was involved with a sinister operation, perhaps his issues and the drug dealers were two separate problems. Wouldn't that be a mess?

Another aspect could be someone trying to get rid of Lindsay to eliminate the dark stain in the VP's life. Meghan had considered so many scenarios that this one rang with as much validity as the others.

Meghan walked around the side of the stables to the door of the Leonards' home. Chesney greeted her on the stoop, and she bent to pat his head. Chip must have heard her one-sided conversation with the dog, because he opened the door.

"Hey, buddy. Are you turning traitor? I thought Dad and I were your best friends. Hmm. I can't say I blame you."

How interesting that Chip would begin their evening together with what she wanted to know about him. Outfitted in a white shirt and jeans, he looked very much like a contemporary cowboy. She patted the dog's head again. "He is irresistible."

"I think I just got my feelings hurt." He gave her a once-over. "You clean up like a girl who needs a night out on the town."

She laughed. "What I need is a home-cooked meal that doesn't keep me up all night."

"Come on in." Ethan's voice in the background reminded her of an uncle in Abilene. "I can take care of what ails you."

She hoped so on more than one front. The idea of either of these two men being arrested for crimes against the US government didn't sit well. She had to keep that in the forefront of her mind.

Entering the Leonards' home brought back memories of family dinners, comfy furniture, and the smells of good cooking.

Ethan stirred a pot on the stove. "Your mama raised you right."

"How's that?" The enticing aroma of fried chicken made her stomach growl.

"You're a little early, which means I can put you to work. Got a glass of iced tea with your name on it." Ethan wore a white apron with the words *I rope 'em and cook 'em* in red letters across the front. "Sweet or unsweet?"

"Unsweet. Got to watch my figure."

"I know *I* am." Chip poured a glassful and handed it to her. "Strike that last line. I've been around the ranch too long."

"Son, you got to let these agents turn you loose." Ethan laughed. "You're beginning to sound like a redneck."

Hadn't she and Ash discussed the same thing? The Dancin'

Dust was beautiful, but the desolation got to all of them after a while. She thanked Chip for the iced tea and took a long drink. "What can I do?"

Ethan pointed to the sink. "Slice those tomatoes and cucumbers. Chip, I need those potatoes mashed, but don't put in the garlic. You never add enough—like you're afraid of it."

"All right, but stay clear of my pecan pie. Yours is always runny."

"Mine's not runny. Yours is just baked into a brick." Ethan picked up a potato masher.

"Watch it, or I'll dump red pepper into your precious gravy."

For the next thirty minutes, she observed Ethan and Chip in their own private world. They worked well together, and it didn't appear to be an act for her benefit. Her suspicions about them faded.

She'd seen their home during a walk-through on the first day at the Dancin' Dust, but it was the two men's personalities that gave the rustic furnishings a homey appeal. The deer head mounted on the living room wall wasn't her style, but it fit two ranchers in West Texas. The brown sofa looked like it had seen a lot of use.

Meghan hadn't tasted food this good for a long time, and she went back for seconds on the chicken.

"How about another slice of pecan pie?" Ethan reached for her plate.

"Please, no." Meghan waved him away. "Can't eat another bite."

"Are you sure? Tomorrow you're back to Pepper's cookin'. Trust me on this. She's just getting warmed up. The more she cooks, the hotter the food. Before the summer ends, we'll be calling the volunteer fire department for all of you."

Meghan groaned. "Don't remind me. I feel indigestion thinking about it. But I'd be on Ash's gold-star list if I could bring him back a plate of this delicious dinner."

"Will do, Meggie. Poor guy probably doesn't have a clue about good country food." Ethan chuckled. "Since I gave him permission to take what he wants from my garden, I see him picking tomatoes, bell peppers, and cucumbers—washes them at the hose and eats them outside."

Something new about Ash. She missed those outings while working her shift with Lindsay.

Ethan cleared their plates from the round, wooden table. "I hope you plan to stay and visit awhile tonight. We haven't had a guest in a long time."

"I do. Haven't been home in months, and this is pretty close."

"What's your daddy do?"

"He was killed when I was still in high school."

Ethan grimaced and loaded the dishwasher. "Sorry to hear that."

*Does the death of a loved one ever stop hurting?* "It's okay, really. The tragedy caused me to think about how to keep innocent people safe." Telling them about herself helped build the trust she needed them to have in her. "Dad tried to convince a drunk not to drive, and the man shot him."

"Is that why you chose the Secret Service?" Chip's eyes were clear—not a muscle twitched.

"Yes. I looked into various law-enforcement possibilities. But the Secret Service seemed like my calling." She reached for the aluminum foil and wrapped a piece around the leftover chicken.

Ethan took the plate from her and set it in the fridge. "Brothers or sisters?"

"A sister. She and my mom live in Abilene."

"Are you all close?"

Meghan pondered her answer. "I am with my mother."

Chip's slight smile told her he understood. "Let's talk about something a little more pleasant. Where did you go to college?"

"A&M."

Chip chuckled. "I should have known. What about a boyfriend?"

"Don't have time. Most guys feel threatened by a gun-carrying woman."

"Yeah, that might stop me, too."

"But not his old man. I'd like a woman who's handy with a rifle and a sidearm."

Meghan smiled into Ethan's weathered face, then looked back to Chip. "Curiosity is driving me crazy. Why did you leave the big city with all the people, shopping, restaurants, technology—and Starbucks—for ranch life?"

He studied her as though evaluating her motives. "Honestly, I missed the quiet, open air and the satisfaction of living close to the earth. Which was exactly why I left in the first place. At seventeen and heading off to college, I thought the penthouse apartment and boardroom meetings were my destiny. And I lived that life for a few years. Got into the politics of corporate business and hated it. Got my heart broken by a woman who was headed up the ladder of success. Bought more things than I'd ever use, and none of it made me happy. I longed for the feel of a horse lunging beneath me. Wondered which mares foaled in the spring. Even missed the muscle aches after a hard day's work. Nothing beats the taste of homegrown vegetables and beef that hasn't been injected with growth hormones and chemicals." Sincerity bannered across his eyes.

"Are you ever bored?"

"Sometimes. But I like to read and play the guitar."

"And he's going to church with me." Ethan poured himself another glass of iced tea. "God's gonna get his attention for sure. Ya know, Meggie, God gave me and my sweet wife Chip when I was forty years old. We'd given up on having a family. What a surprise. While other men my age were dealing with teenagers, I was changing diapers. He's a good boy. Always has been."

"Don't you forget it either." Chip grinned. "Someday I'll make sure you have a half-dozen grandkids to spoil."

Nothing cast a doubt about either man's credibility. But she had plenty of questions.

Chip took a final swipe at cleaning off the table. "How about a concert? Nothing like good old country music to soothe a special agent's nerves."

"Who said I was nervous?"

"Didn't have to. Women just get nervous being around me. Their little hearts pound, and they lose control of everything their mama taught them."

Meghan shook her head at Ethan and grabbed the bowl of mashed potatoes. "Is he always like this?"

"Yep. Been that way since the day he was born. Could talk his mama into anything."

Chip disappeared and returned with a guitar. He swung a hip onto a stool and tuned the instrument. Soon the lyrics of a popular song woven with soft guitar music filled the room. Not bad. For a little while, she forgot about who might want Lindsay dead.

# CHAPTER 15

Ash checked his watch at 2200. Meghan must be having a good time . . . or the Leonards weren't offering any information. The reason she hadn't returned bothered him more than her not finding incriminating information against the father and son—specifically Chip.

Reality crept in like an unbidden stranger. He was losing his heart to Meghan Connors. *Lord, what are You doing to me? I'm a career man. I can't allow a woman to steal my organized life? I'm A2Z, not A4Z—Ash 4 Meghan Zinders.* He'd become downright sappy, and his last thought proved it.

He stiffened and homed in on the truth. Too much baggage plagued his life to ever be right for Meghan. Forget it. Keep moving.

Ash stood in front of the house, eyes open and alert to the darkness. Anyone could jump the fence and find Lindsay. His concerns were twofold: her stalker had a deadly inclination and Ash despised reporters as much as he detested snakes.

Wade had volunteered to keep watch inside so Ash could speak to Meghan when she returned from the Leonards. What was she doing? He'd heard music. Were they two-stepping and moving to the Cotton-Eyed Joe? Whatever those dances were. He'd been reading about favorite pastimes for Texans and any other local flavor that would help him understand the Leonards.

Strange how the night came alive with the sounds of nature. Cicadas sang louder than DC traffic. Since arriving at the ranch and taking on the afternoon and evening shift, he'd used the darkness to pray for Lindsay, each of his agents by name, the Shield and Alexa, reconciliation with his past, his aging parents . . . The list went on.

When he spotted Meghan rounding the stables, his heart sped, and he shoved away his rising interest. Granted, praying for someone made the person more of a concern. But concern was not what he was feeling. The way his pulse raced whenever she was near couldn't come from God because He wouldn't play such a cruel joke. The infamous A2Z falling for a female agent. For certain, if his heart ever took the dive, the woman would have to be someone who challenged his wit while stealing his breath.

*Stop it, Ash. Your mind focuses on Meghan at every opportunity.* She challenged his wit and stole his breath. That's why he was in serious trouble.

Meghan strolled toward the porch, and he waved. She carried something—perhaps a plate. Even in the shadows, her red-gold hair flowing around her shoulders gave him chills. The idea of Chip and Ethan having her to themselves tonight did make him jealous.

Meghan held out a foil-covered plate. "This is for you. I suggest you eat it now before Pepper finds out. I know you're on duty, so I'll get a knife and fork. Want a Diet Coke?"

Heaven had come to West Texas. "Wonderful on all counts." He brushed his fingers across her hand, and he reacted as though he'd been burned. *Great. Hot and cold at the same time.* He'd never felt like this before. Never thought a woman could make him feel like a hero and mush at the same time. Ash gritted his teeth. The Secret Service was no place for a woman. Too distracting.

"Be right back."

His emotions registered in the frazzled zone.

She returned with the utensils and drink. "How was your evening?"

"I should be asking you that." The aroma of the food made his mouth water. Good. Filling his belly would get his attention off the woman in front of him.

She leaned against the porch post. "Relaxing. Ethan is a wonderful cook. Fried chicken done to perfection with all the trimmings." She pointed. "Go ahead. You'll see."

He peeled back the foil. The fried chicken called his name.

"The pecan pie is wonderful too. Ethan served it warm with a scoop of vanilla ice cream. I think Pepper has French vanilla in the fridge."

"Thanks. Let me dive into this first. Tell me about your evening."

She glanced around. "Not out here. Is Victor in the operation room?"

"Probably. He never sleeps. Do you want to see if he'll step out here for a few minutes?"

Once Victor replaced Ash, he and Meghan entered the house. Thankfully, Pepper had retired for the evening, allowing them to sit in the kitchen alone. Was that smart? He'd have to focus on reporting the evening's latest news . . . and on the food.

"What was for dinner?" Meghan opened the fridge and took out a bottle of water.

"Stuffed poblanos."

She laughed. "Why don't you eat, and I'll brief you on the evening?"

They sat side by side on the kitchen bar stools. She was dangerously close, and her citrusy scent lingered, driving him nuts.

"What happened tonight other than eating?" He forked a bit of chicken into his mouth. It tasted better than anything he'd eaten since arriving at the Dancin' Dust.

"Chip serenaded me with his guitar, and we talked."

Why did annoyance worm its way into him? "Did you learn anything?"

She proceeded to tell him everything from the moment she entered the Leonards' home. "Chip's body language didn't give any indication of pretense, but he does hide behind his intelligence."

She paused. "I still have unanswered questions. We're going riding with Lindsay in the morning. I'll probe deeper."

"Maybe I'll come too."

"Didn't know you liked to ride."

He refused to answer, and he'd fake his lack of horsemanship. "First time for everything. The sooner we get to the bottom of this, the better off we'll be." He added gruffness to his tone. "New development while you were gone."

Meghan gave him her attention. Why couldn't she have a wart on her nose?

"They caught a man attempting to access the VP's home. A known drug dealer from Colombia by the name of Jorge Ramos. He'd been arrested previously and deported. Back again to see what he could do."

"Best news I've heard in a long time. Maybe now we'll get some answers."

Ash frowned. "Not really. He fired at the agents and was killed."

"But has it ended, Ash? Can we assume Lindsay is safe from the stalker?"

"Warrington has no proof that the man who threatened her was Ramos." He sighed. The day had been long. "There's more. An hour after the shooting, an e-mail came through for Lindsay. The sender writes as though he knows her."

"What did he say?"

"I thought you'd like to see it." He picked up his plate. "Let me show you."

They moved to the operation room and Ash's computer screen. "Take a look, Meghan. Maybe you can read something into this better than I have. Victor's already worked on it." He offered her his chair.

Hey, Lindsay,

I really do want to see you. We have a lot in common, and you know it. Both of us hate the vice

president's guts and love to party. Too bad the
shooter didn't get inside your parents' house today.
We could be celebrating now. And I'd bring the
good stuff.

I know where you're hiding, Lindsay. I could help you
get away where no one could find us. Tell me when
you're ready.

Remembering our last date.

Meghan stared into Ash's face. "He has to know we're monitoring her e-mail."

"He's playing games."

"Did you respond?"

"I thought I'd give you the honors. Figured you could sound
more like Lindsay." Ash meant every word.

Meghan hit Reply.

Hey,

Don't know who you are. I've had lots of dates with
lots of guys. Come clean with who you are and help
me get out of here. I'll make it worth your trouble. I
have a raging headache, and the withdrawals are the
pits. To make it worse, Daddy has this nutcase nutri-
tionist filling me full of vitamins. The only kind of pills
I want aren't sold in a health-food store. Let's hook
up. I need to score bad. They've taken my phone.

Lindsay

Ash read Meghan's response. "Hit Send. What do we have to
lose?"

"All right. Let the games continue."

Two minutes later, another e-mail for Lindsay slid into her in-box.

> Lindsay,
>
> We'll be together soon. Give me a little time to work out a plan. Let's be honest here. The Secret Service is reading every word, but they're stupid. Ash Zinders is getting careless, and he's bored. All he can do is follow his rule book and bark orders. His team thinks he's a joke. And that woman assigned to you? She's nothing more than a diversion for the other agents. Might give her a whirl myself. But why settle for trash when I can have you?
>
> They'll end up dead, and you'll help me do it.
>
> Soon, Lindsay. Real soon.

Meghan typed another response and sent it. "Message is undeliverable. The account's been closed."

# CHAPTER 16

MONDAY MORNING, Meghan replayed her evening at the Leonards. She'd failed to uncover a solid lead on Ethan's or Chip's possible involvement with Lindsay's stalkers. But Chip was the one who most likely had contact with them. This morning she wavered between ignoring her suspicions and her own type A personality that spurred her to investigate him further. The situation had her mind and stomach spinning with unanswered questions.

Meghan waited outside Lindsay's bedroom. Some mornings she wanted Meghan's company, as though they were best friends. Other mornings she acted as though Meghan were the enemy. Today they were to go riding, another opportunity to observe Chip. An ear-piercing scream sent Meghan into her protectee's room. Lindsay sat up in bed, face pale and eyes wide. She trembled and wrapped her arms around her waist.

"Get them out of here." Terror oozed from Lindsay's eyes. "They'll kill me."

"Who? Talk to me." But Meghan understood exactly. Lindsay was hallucinating.

"The purple monsters." She pointed toward the closet. "Can't you see them floating out from the wall? They have knives—long, jagged ones."

For a moment, Meghan considered going after Dave. But what would he do? Have her drink an extra dose of vitamin C? Instead she hurried to Lindsay's bedside and grasped her shoulders. "Look at me. Not at the purple monsters, but at me. Take deep breaths."

Lindsay hesitated. "I can't."

"Yes, you can." How many times had Meghan coaxed another young woman into focusing on reality? "You know what this is. You've been through it before. Let me help you. The hallucinations will pass."

Lindsay slowly turned to Meghan.

"Good. Now look into my eyes."

She obliged, and her body eased slightly. "I've been sober for almost a week. Why now?"

"I don't know, but we'll work through it." Meghan sat on her bed and drew Lindsay into her arms. "I imagine Dave will have answers."

"Please, stay with me." Lindsay's sobs muffled in Meghan's shoulder. "I hate being alone. They'll come back."

"I'm here for as long as you need me."

"You don't see the monsters? They spit fire, and their knives have blood on them."

Any other time, the conversation would be ridiculous, as though a child were having nightmares. But this was a young woman whose body craved alcohol and drugs to function. "Do you want to see Dave?"

"No. I just want to go back to sleep."

The clock on Lindsay's nightstand flashed 8:35. "Didn't you sleep last night?"

"No. I had nightmares."

"Close your eyes. I won't leave." *Oh, Lindsay. I want so much for you.*

"If only I could escape this horrible world."

"I know." Meghan held her until she heard even breathing. Then she laid Lindsay on the pillow. Such a pretty young woman— blonde hair, blue eyes, a face like an angel. Meghan prayed she'd find the will to fight the drugs and alcohol for good.

At 1300, Lindsay wakened, and Meghan stepped out into the hallway, where Dave and Carla waited. For certain, they had Lindsay's health and well-being as top priority. Admiration rose in her for their dedication, and she chided herself for sometimes thinking their methods of treating Lindsay were foolish.

"She's awake." Meghan closed the door behind her. "Right now, she's in the bathroom."

"Thank you for staying with her. I wanted to intervene, but I trusted your instincts. I've witnessed so many patients suffer through hallucinations, and I know they're terrifying." Compassion radiated from his eyes. "I have a call scheduled with her father in less than five minutes." He glanced at his phone, and it vibrated.

"Guess that call is now." Dave walked to the stairway and turned to face Meghan. "Good morning, Mr. Burnette. I was expecting the vice president." He moistened his lips. "I understand. She had a rough night. Nightmares and hallucinations. But I'll see if she feels like talking."

Dave nodded at Meghan, who went inside to check on her protectee and relay the message.

"I don't want to talk to him," Lindsay said on the other side of the bathroom door.

"Mr. Burnette cares about you."

Lindsay cursed. "No way."

Frustrated, Meghan responded to Dave and walked downstairs. Unfortunately, Lindsay's behavior was typical, and changes took time.

Once in the kitchen, Meghan reached for a small bowl of lettuce and added toppings from an assortment of veggies, egg salad, and roasted turkey on the kitchen counter. She joined Ash in the operation room. Not sure why she often chose to eat with him instead of in the kitchen. If she examined her motives, she'd admit this absurd attraction to him. They were so much alike, almost scary and yet challenging at the same time. Lately he'd been more congenial, but she also knew his moods could turn as quickly as Lindsay's. What demons chased him?

Again they were alone. Maybe that needed to stop. After all, he wanted the same assignment to the VP's protective team, and his kindness could be a way to find something to use against her. Today he seemed agitated. Nothing new there, and he kept sneezing. Probably allergies. She'd come to the conclusion he hid behind his gruff reputation. Wade told her he had a deep faith, and his dedication to the Secret Service sprang from his relationship to God. But God was loving and didn't push people away. Maybe someday she'd learn the reason he erected a concrete wall, and when she did, perhaps she could find a way to penetrate it.

"When you finish eating, would you mind checking on Lindsay's e-mail and texts? Our guy hasn't contacted her again. He might have a new approach."

"Any leads?"

"The man shot Sunday night was part of the Medellín Cartel—bold, mean, and gaining power. They're building a drug-trafficking empire throughout Colombia, and they're incorporating other smaller dealers by eliminating key persons."

"How did Lindsay get involved in organized drug smuggling?" Meghan shook her head. "Strike that. They probably targeted her. No surprise when you consider the crowd she runs with."

"Doesn't matter. She got sucked in, and they mean business. Unfortunately, that's all we know since Jorge Ramos is dead. Last night's e-mail has me furious and alarmed. The guy has guts." Ash pointed to her plate. "You'd better eat. After the screams we all heard this morning and the energy it must have taken to calm Lindsay, you've got to be hungry."

She stared at her salad. "How did you handle the hallucinations?"

He hesitated as though forming his words. "I tried talking to her, but any act of decency on my part was quickly tossed back. Not that I blame her. As you already know, we have a volatile relationship. Usually I prayed. Sometimes a counselor or her mother witnessed them."

"Ash, do you pray for her still?"

He studied her for a moment. "Yes, and every member of my team."

"I do too. This morning when she clung to me, I nearly lost it. I'm a driven woman, so I don't quite understand her self-destruction."

"You and I are on the same page when it comes to Lindsay." He took a deep breath. "I'm glad you're here for her. Bet you didn't expect that."

She smiled and pushed her plate back. What she'd eaten competed with her whirling thoughts. She turned to a computer.

"Meghan, you can't take the job personally."

She snapped up, understanding he wasn't aware of her past. She had her own demons. "You have no clue how I can take a job personally."

His face registered surprise, but for once, he didn't say a word.

What was she thinking? "Sorry, sir, I was out of line. No excuse."

"I understand. We both want so much for Lindsay, but she has to make the first step."

After retrieving Lindsay's text messages and finding nothing, Meghan scrolled through their protectee's e-mail. Friends questioned about the next party and whether she'd gotten a new car. Some offered sympathy because she'd obviously been whisked off to another rehab, or she'd have responded to them. No one mentioned the woman killed in the car bombing or asked if she'd been injured. Meghan reread a message from a supposed male, one that had dropped into Lindsay's in-box twenty minutes ago.

"Ash, this one reads a little strange, and it doesn't appear to be from last night's sender. Maybe it's my radar. 'Hey, Lindsay, met you two weeks ago at Dominic's party. I'm the guy who offered breakfast at my place. I thought I'd try your e-mail. Sorry to hear about your car. The media are going nuts. When can we get together? Are you living with your parents?'"

"Did he sign it?"

"No. Want a tracer sent? Maybe we'll have better luck this time."

"Yes, and I'll ask Warrington to run a background check on this Dominic fellow and see if he can get a list of the others who attended the party. I remember the guy who hosted it, the son of a congressman. Would you mind answering the e-mail? Seems to be your specialty." Ash worked his way around the table and bent over the back of her chair. The nearness of him unnerved her, his warm breath sending chills along her neck. She needed to end these reactions now.

Meghan read what she'd typed. "'I remember meeting you but not your name. What did you have in mind?'"

"Send it."

She refused to look at Ash for fear he'd comment about her reaction to him. "Wonder why he didn't leave a name, especially if he went to all the trouble of mentioning Dominic?" She glanced at the incoming messages. "Delivery failure. Let me guess . . ." She scrolled down the e-mail. "Unknown user."

"This pattern could be ego or a new strategy in the game plan."

"I've come across a few of those in my days." Her memories weren't pleasant.

"I wish we could figure out who and what are behind stalking the vice president's daughter. At this point, it still looks like a disgruntled drug dealer. But it has to be more. Drug cartels don't become powerful without money and intelligence behind them. Whoever is sending these e-mails is daring us to come after him." He walked back to his own computer. "It's cold in here. I'm going to bump the AC up a notch."

Oh, great. He noticed her chill bumps. Meghan sent the e-mail trace. She had to find a way to hide her attraction instead of responding to him like a teenager drooling over the captain of the football team.

"Odd, the temp is set at the same place. Want a cup of coffee?"

Couldn't he just leave it alone? "No, thanks. I'm cutting back to drinking it in the mornings. Dr. Sanchez's book is making me feel guilty."

"I read it too. Much too healthy for me. I hear Lindsay started taking the supplements last night. Even drank a medicine smoothie."

"I fixed the nasty thing," Pepper called. "Pink, powdery stuff that's supposed to taste like strawberries whipped up with ice and blueberries."

He walked to the door. "Pepper, are you standing in the hallway eavesdropping? This is Secret Service business. When I'm having a discussion with an agent, it doesn't include you."

"Unless it's about Lindsay's diet. That's my job. And you left the door open. What was I supposed to do?"

Ash clenched his fists. "Did she drink it all?"

"About half. I tasted it. Not bad for medicine, but it's not a taste treat either. I'd rather have mine in a margarita."

Meghan hid a grin. Glancing at her screen, she saw a response to her inquiry about the previous e-mail and waited until Ash closed the door. "Can't trace the originator."

Lindsay's phone buzzed with an incoming text. "It's the same message that just came through the e-mail. He's anxious." Ash typed in a response. "I said, 'Can't figure out who you are? Send me more.' How does that sound?"

"Good. Shows she's curious."

Ash pressed Send. A moment later he shook his head. "Message can't be sent."

"So whoever is sending the e-mails is smart enough to use a new e-mail address each time, then close out the account. And the texts didn't show the originator's number?"

"Right. Must have incoming texts disabled."

Meghan met his gaze, calculating. "Should I ask Lindsay about him?"

"Go ahead. Might sound better coming from you."

"Dr. Sanchez mentioned swimming today, since the storms have passed."

"Good call. It amazes me to see how many people can be bought." He walked to the end of the study where the wall-to-ceiling window looked out onto the pool. "Ever notice how the sun causes the water to glisten like diamonds? Like a man could reach out and pocket enough to set him up for life."

"All he'd get is a wet pocket."

"My point. But he'd try."

# CHAPTER 17

MEGHAN REACHED FOR A TOWEL and wiped the perspiration dripping from her face. A dip in the pool would cool her off, especially since her capris were soaked with liquid heat all the way through. Maybe tonight when she was off duty, she'd take a swim. The sun had erased traces of the storms of the past few days and seemed to dance off the turquoise water. Like diamonds. Ash's statement opened up another side of him, a side that demonstrated he had a philosophical way of viewing life.

She studied Lindsay flirting with Victor and Rick. Her bathing suit had less material than Ethan's red bandana. Same color, too. Every agent who had a glimpse of the pool did a double take. And Chip Leonard was no exception. What she feared with Lindsay and Chip would no doubt happen soon.

Lindsay paraded around the pool like a beauty pageant contestant, exhibiting none of the fears of this morning. Twenty minutes ago, she didn't want to walk outside her room. But now she was on stage, and her need for attention was evident to all those present. Sad, but true.

Meghan turned to Dave Sanchez. "I've got to ask Lindsay a few hard questions."

"It's too soon for her to know about the bombing. And after this morning . . . well, I can't permit it."

"It's not too soon to ask her about the origin of e-mails and texts."

He lowered his sunglasses to capture her gaze. "You don't know who sent them?"

"We're working on that."

"Are you telling me that with all the technology available to you folks, the origin of these e-mails and texts can't be found?"

Meghan swallowed her irritation. "I said we are working on it. But I need to talk to Lindsay about content and what she's willing to tell us about the sender."

"I can't allow you to upset her. She's depressed and fighting withdrawal symptoms. *Fragile* best describes her."

Lindsay's laughter rippled around them, grinding at Meghan's nerves. Granted the heat didn't help, but neither did his attitude. "Dave, Lindsay's health is your area of expertise. The six agents assigned to her are here to ensure she stays alive."

Dave watched Lindsay twirl a finger on Victor's chest. "She's trying to find a spot of happiness in her unhappy life. I can't take that away from her right now."

"I understand her history." She moistened her lips. "I respect all I've seen you do with Lindsay, but I intend to speak to her with or without your permission."

He glared at her, then inhaled. "I gave my word to the vice president that I'd work with all the agents. I'm not going to the mat over a difference of opinion unless I feel her health is threatened."

"Thank you. I'd expect nothing less. We're all on the same side."

"She might feel threatened if we're together. I'll leave you two alone." He stood from the poolside chair. "Lindsay, Agent Connors would like to talk to you."

Lindsay smiled at Victor and touched his cheek. He took a step back, and she giggled. "We're having a conversation. I'll be there in a few minutes."

Fifteen minutes later, Lindsay stretched out on a lounge chair beside Meghan. "This must be serious since you ran Dave off."

Meghan leaned back on a chair beside her. "I've been trained to be intimidating."

"Ash should have told you I rarely cooperate."

"Has your life been at stake before?"

Lindsay grasped a bottle of sunscreen. "Every time I get high."

"That's of your own choosing."

Lindsay squirted the lotion onto her hands. "You sound like Ash packaged in a sweet voice."

"We're trained by the same people."

Lindsay stared at the lotion in her palm. For a moment, Meghan saw the frightened little girl from this morning. "What do you want to know?"

"Who did you meet at a party two weeks ago at Dominic's?"

"Friends."

"Not a new guy?"

She glanced out at the pool but not at anyone. "No. I'd have remembered."

"You've received an e-mail and a text from a guy who says he met you at Dominic's party and wants to get together. Didn't leave a name, and the e-mail and text can't be traced."

Lindsay's lips quivered, and she took a deep breath. "I can't help you."

"I think you can."

"The stakes are too high."

"Lindsay, if you're concerned about the ten grand you owe for drugs, we can take care of it and get this guy behind bars."

"I wish money could take care of the problem, but it won't." Lindsay rubbed the lotion onto her leg. "I'm in too deep. Give it up."

"What are you afraid of? Look around you." Meghan gestured. "Six Secret Service agents are here with the sole purpose of keeping you safe. Have you been dealing?"

"No. Haven't gotten that low yet."

Meghan wanted to shake her. "I need for you to tell us about this guy so we can stop what's going on."

"All right, Meghan. I didn't meet anyone at Dominic's party. It's a bogus e-mail, and I have no clue why you can't trace the sender. That's all you get."

Meghan weighed telling her about the bombing. Dave would be furious, but she had to take that chance.

"Excuse me, but this is for Miss Lindsay." Pepper stood with a frosted mug in her hand. "A raspberry medicine meal with frozen raspberries." The woman had impeccable timing.

"Thank you." Lindsay reached for the mug. "Gotta do what the doc says if I'm ever to be released from this prison." She narrowed her gaze at Meghan. "I'm finished answering questions. Oh, and tell Ash I had a wonderful time spending all those silent hours with him last evening. He should have stayed for the show that you got."

"Would you like something, Meghan?" Pepper wiped the perspiration beading her forehead. "A cold bottle of water or blackberry iced tea?

Lindsay toasted Meghan and Pepper. "Never trust a skinny cook." She took a sip of the raspberry smoothie. "You know, this ranch wouldn't be such a bad place if it didn't belong to Scottard Burnette."

# CHAPTER 18

WEDNESDAY MORNING, Ash felt miserable. He reached for a tissue and sneezed. Once. Twice. Three times. He set the tissue box onto the back-porch railing. At this rate, he'd get nothing done today. He squinted at the horses grazing in the pasture and fought the urge to scratch his eyes. They burned and were swelling shut. The sinus pain coupled with the pounding in his ears made him want to crawl into bed.

Burnette had a medicine cabinet in the guest half bath filled with every allergy, sinus, and cold remedy possible, but they'd all knock him out for the next two hours, even the non-drowsy kind. But he craved relief.

Victor walked out onto the porch. "Have you taken anything yet?"

"No. Thinking about it though. Drinking lots of water, and I popped eight vitamin Cs this morning."

Victor chuckled. Over the years he'd experienced Ash's bouts with allergy problems. Dry climates made them worse. Unfortunately, Ash had never found a product that worked, prescription or over-the-counter. As a kid, he'd taken allergy shots. Hadn't helped a bit, and he had no intentions of injecting himself with the same stuff causing his problem ever again.

"Why don't you take something and sleep it off?"

"Not on your life. Besides, then I'd be groggy the rest of the day."

"If you don't feel up to it, I'll take your shift."

*What a guy.* "Thanks, but I need to carry my own weight. Even if half of it is the junk pouring from my head."

Victor shrugged and walked inside. No doubt he didn't want a taste of Ash's bad mood as the allergy symptoms persisted. They always worsened as the day wore on. By nightfall, he'd be a raving maniac, begging for anything to get him out of his misery.

A few moments later, the door opened. Who had invaded his suffering? Great, it was Dave, the nutrition expert, aka miracle worker.

"Heard you were having problems with allergies. Brought you a few things to help battle this dry air."

Ash frowned. "Name a product, and I've tried it."

Dave smiled, an irritating, confident smile, which made Ash feel like he was in grade school again. "I have a tablet here that will help open your sinus passages and clear your eyes." He opened his palm to reveal half of a gray tablet. "Let it dissolve in your mouth. You'll begin to feel the difference. And I advise taking sips of water with it. You'll need it." He handed him a bottle of water.

At least Dave warned him about the taste. Ash shook his head. "Trust me, it won't work."

"Then what do you have to lose?"

He was right. Ash popped the tablet into his mouth. "What's in it?"

"Different herbs, one of which is cayenne."

"As in the pepper?"

"The same."

Ash reached for the water. "You and Pepper must be related. Nasty. I think I've found the cayenne. And this will help? Or is your remedy a practical joke?"

He grinned. "Keep going. While you're working on it, I'll bring you a cup of tea. The taste is more pleasant."

Dave disappeared, and Ash considered spitting out the

horrible-tasting mess dissolving on his tongue. He startled. The herb was beginning to work. He sensed his head clearing.

Dave returned with the tea. "How are you doing?"

"It's potent."

"I agree. When you can't handle it any longer, swallow it. Then begin the tea." He unwrapped a soft substance that looked like a piece of candy. "Keep this in your mouth while drinking the tea. It's ginger."

Ash swallowed the tablet and took the ginger. The tea had a menthol aroma. Not bad. Reminded him of being a kid and having his mother rub his chest with Vicks VapoRub. The ginger and the hot drink were definite improvements from the tablet. "What's in the tea?"

"Different things. You'll recognize licorice, ginger, thyme."

"And this will make me feel human again?"

"I doubt if any of my remedies can help your personality. But we can always hope there is something in nature that will make you human. If all fails, we can try counseling."

"Ouch. Have a little pity on an ailing man."

"I'll try." Dave sat in a chair beside him and talked about the ranch, the garden, the horses . . .

Ash startled. "It worked."

Dave shook his head. "And you're surprised?"

Why hadn't he noted Dave's quirky sense of humor? Guess he needed it to work with mentally unstable people. Ash heard a chuckle and turned to see Victor, Wade, and Rick behind them.

"How long have you guys been there?"

Victor crossed his arms over his chest. "Since the tea. Are you a new man?"

Ash frowned but couldn't resist the grin. "Maybe. Any requests while I'm in a good mood and not blowing my nose?"

Bob raised his hand from his position on the other side of the pool. "No requests, except I'd like to be next in line for the treatment. I've never experienced problems with allergies until we got here. My eyes are killing me. If we were invaded by bad guys, I wouldn't be able to see to shoot."

"You could tackle them." Wade gave his best defense pose. "I'd run."

"Very funny. I'd still have to see who I was chasing."

Dave waved at Bob. "Sir, you and any of your cronies are welcome to follow me into Miss Pepper's kitchen for your own herbal cure. Since Wade's the football wannabe, he could relieve you for a few minutes." He picked up Ash's Diet Coke. "I'll toss this for you."

"I just opened it."

"It's not on the allergy plan."

"You have no mercy. Bob, I'll give you a break. No one should have to go through these allergies." Ash waved at them. "But it works, and you know how stubborn I can be."

None of them answered, and he laughed. Some reputations were hard to live down.

# CHAPTER 19

Thursday morning, Ash carried a pot of coffee into the operation room and set it on a small corner table with cups, creamer, and sugar. A platter of warm cinnamon buns scented the air. At last, something Pepper baked that didn't set his stomach on fire. He closed the door behind him, mindful of Pepper's tendency to overhear conversations. Not that he didn't trust her. As Scottard Burnette's private cook at the ranch, she'd overheard many discussions from high-ranking people within the government. But she had no business listening in on Secret Service conversations.

"Listen up. I called this meeting so Meghan and Bob could be here before taking over their shift. I'll talk to Victor and Rick later. I appreciate all of you and your dedication to our assignment. Yes, I agree it gets boring, but we're managing okay." Ash poured Bob a cup of coffee and handed it to him.

"Media got wind of President Claredon's medical report before an official White House statement was made. The president is stepping down. His cancer has spread to his brain, and he's been given six months. In short, the Shield is being sworn in as of 0900 ET."

Bob stirred two spoonfuls of sugar into his coffee. "Does our situation change with Lindsay? Will we be reassigned?"

"Nothing's changed at this point. I'll let you know as soon as I learn about a new plan. As you'd expect, the security here will ramp up now that our protectee is the president's daughter. Media are scrambling as usual to find her location, all the while bashing Claredon for waiting so long to step down from the presidency. They are also working overtime to discredit the VP, using Lindsay as leverage. Nothing we haven't heard before."

"How long before they discover where she is?"

Ash understood Bob was as concerned as the rest of them about Lindsay's safety. The media's interference meant more problems for all of them. "We've done all we can to keep her whereabouts secret, but we have civilians in on this too. The county sheriff has given us his support, but we have no guarantee that our position won't leak to the public. The First Lady wanted to visit Lindsay next week, but I doubt if that will happen now. I've heard Lindsay's sister, Kelli, wants to see her, but that means another risk of exposure. With the VP taking over the country, all those associated with him are high profile. They'd be followed for certain, and the Dancin' Dust would then be another hot spot on the news."

He could almost hear the wheels turning in the agents' heads.

Ash poured a cup of coffee for Wade then Meghan. "Meghan, you have more patience than I do with Lindsay, and I see you're securing her confidence. Bob, I admire the way you use humor to keep me from killing Pepper. Wade, you've done a dynamic job of showing the Leonards that we're not the enemy. I've seen you playing horseshoes and engaging them in conversation while enduring this relentless heat. Saw a good show of archery the other night too. We'd all be lost without Victor's computer skills, and Rick's a complement to the team."

Agents offered thanks, but Ash waved away their gratitude. "All of you follow the rules, and that makes us a good team. I hope we're able to stay together, but that's our new president's decision." He wondered if he'd be promoted to the president's protective detail. What if Meghan . . . ? He pushed the thought aside to continue business.

"As the Shield takes his oath of office this morning, I'd like to think our country will rally behind him." He huffed. "I'd also like to think we could get our hands on Lindsay's stalkers. Any questions or comments?"

"I'd like permission to tell Lindsay about the car bombing." Meghan reached for half a cinnamon bun. "I believe it falls under our jurisdiction as a safety issue, although Dave may not approve. I want her to know about the man killed at her parents' home too. With your permission, sir, I'd like to inform her about her father's new role. She may want to call and congratulate him. A definite step in the right direction for reconciliation with her parents."

Ash had been thinking along those same lines. "Go ahead. I'll check with you later about her response. Uh . . . don't tell Dave what you're doing. He'll probably want to fill her full of vitamin C first."

Chuckles rose from the group, easing the tension if only for a moment. Ash knew the men had varied responses about being reassigned—and most of them wanted as far away from the Dancin' Dust as possible.

Minutes later, in the empty operation room, Ash savored the coffee and a mean cinnamon bun dripping with frosting. What was he doing thinking about food when he wanted a shot at the presidential protection detail? The VPPD had been a possible step up in his career, an opportunity to eventually be a part of the presidential team, but now the Shield would be in charge.

He sighed. His responsibilities and priorities were right here on the ranch, keeping Lindsay safe. If a promotion was in his future, it would happen after he completed this assignment. He didn't want to think of the media showing up. The headaches of dealing with reporters trying to crawl all over the ranch would be miserable.

Another thought of higher priority kept his mind occupied. The threats to Lindsay had him baffled. The Shield's role in leading the country, the bombing, the shooting, and Lindsay's untraceable communications were a part of the same conspiracy. Warrington indicated he felt the same way. Ash hated sitting on a dirt ranch in West Texas while someone else worked the clues.

★ ★ ★

Once Ash dismissed the team, Meghan walked up the stairs to relieve Victor. Exhaustion circled his eyes.

"Long night?"

Victor walked to the stairs and sat. "Humor me for a moment."

Meghan handed him a cup of coffee. Black, like he preferred. "I'm fresh out of jokes. What's going on?"

"The worst. Lindsay cried for hours. Started about 0200. Said the demons were laughing at her. Begged me to help her leave the ranch. Offered me money. Stood in the doorway wearing nothing but a tear-stained face." He lifted a bruised cheek, a circle about a half inch in diameter. "Used her stiletto to make a point."

Meghan groaned. "Did Dave intervene?"

"He tried to calm her but couldn't get anywhere. Carla did her soothing routine, but Lindsay was hysterical. At one point Dave asked her if she wanted you."

"What did she say?"

"I don't want to repeat it. Dave gave her a couple of supplements called serenagen, and I think it helped."

Meghan nodded. "I'm familiar with that herb. It's used to help alleviate stress. I can't believe I didn't hear her."

"Volume wasn't the issue. I've seen her this way before. So has Ash. But I can't remember her condition ever being this . . . well, desperate and pitiful."

Like she was spooked. Meghan wanted to research withdrawal symptoms. She thought she had a working knowledge of how a body reacted when denied drugs and alcohol. But no two cases were alike. Lindsay had exhibited the confusion, inability to sleep, tremors, and it looked like tonight, she'd experienced more hallucinations.

"I'll try talking to her. At times, I've been able to get through. One minute she responds logically, and the next she's angry and refuses to talk. Everything has to be on her terms. According to Dave, she's providing all the right answers to get out of here and nothing we can use to keep her safe." Meghan didn't mention Lindsay's comment about enjoying the peacefulness of the ranch, if only it didn't belong to Scottard Burnette. Of course, everything connected to her family sent her into a tantrum.

"Good luck. She trashed her room. Thought I'd warn you. Better duck, too. She's throwing everything she can get her hands on."

"I'll be all right." She started to add she'd been through this before with another addict, but that part of her life was personal.

Victor glanced at the door. "You've gotten farther with her than Ash or I ever did. Must be the female bonding thing."

"Who knows? I just want to see her healthy and using Dave's tools to stay clean. Oh, Ash wants to see you."

"How bad?"

"Not bad. Just more for us to consider."

"You're no help at all, Meghan." He stood from the stairs and finished his coffee. "Did you hear about the guy who used to skate ten miles a day, then he found a shortcut?"

# CHAPTER 20

LINDSAY CRAVED A SLEEPING PILL, anything to help her escape the demon who posed as her friend. As long as she did exactly what he demanded, her family would live. His voice haunted her, and in her nightmares, his features contorted into the hellish creature that no one knew. She couldn't fight him. His power and intelligence far surpassed hers, and she didn't know who sided with him. If she dared to take a person into confidence, that person might be on his payroll. Or they might end up dead. As she considered those at the ranch, she wondered who was against her father and who supported him.

Humiliation for what she'd done last night made her physically ill. The rantings and pleadings were one thing. Prancing naked in front of Victor and throwing a shoe at him made her despise herself. He'd take a bullet for her, and this is how she repaid him? Her behavior only reinforced what the demon always said. *You're worthless, Lindsay. Stupid and good for nothing except what a woman can offer.*

She craved death, but she craved life more.

She pulled out a notebook from beneath her bed. Composing songs helped to ease her fears. The words and the melodies that poured from her heart brought a sense of peace to her shattered world. The last time she wrote a song, her mother had found the notebook and played the music on the piano. She thought Lindsay had copied it from a songwriter, even tried to find the recording as a gift. Mom claimed it was beautiful and expressed surprise that Lindsay enjoyed country music. She almost told Mom then, but why pursue a dream with no future?

Today she wanted to stroll across the ranch and recapture those little-girl moments before her world collapsed. A song danced across her mind, and she wished she had her guitar. That would make the perfect escape without drugs.

Grasping her pen, she opened to a blank page. If she began a song by first writing about her passion for the piece, then the lyrics and the music became more focused. Only country music touched her heart, because it mirrored a slice of life that offered honesty and real emotions.

A knock on the door reminded her Meghan was on duty. Lindsay wanted to trust her, but not Ash. He could be one of them. At times she thought Meghan could be working for her father's enemy too. But those thoughts diminished each time they were together. Dad had hand-selected Meghan, and the knowledge gave her hope.

"I'm busy. Had a rough night. But I'm sure you've heard."

"I need to talk to you. It's important." The urgency in Meghan's voice alarmed her. *Could something have happened to Mom, Dad, or Kelli?*

She tucked her notebook under the bed. "Come in, but I'm warning you. I'm not in the mood for questions."

Lindsay knew she looked horrible. The mirror had revealed cavernous pits beneath her eyes, and her pale skin would rival a corpse's. The shambles in her room matched what had gone through her mind in the wee hours of the morning. The frenzied thoughts were still there.

She wasn't insane. She was terrified.

Meghan opened the door and smiled. "Sorry about your bad night. This won't take any longer than necessary."

"Sounds like you want answers I'm not willing to give." Lindsay considered a few more colorful words to describe how she felt about being grilled but changed her mind. She wanted to leave that aspect of her life behind.

"More of an FYI." Meghan leaned against the door. "I hear we're going riding at nine thirty."

"Is Chip coming along?"

Meghan shook her head. "No, you're stuck with me and Ash. However, Chip is a looker and charming, too. But he's off-limits."

"Most things in this prison are banned for me. I can look, but I can't touch. Walk, but not too far. Dream . . . Never mind." Was Meghan for real? Lindsay pulled her thoughts into check. She was a fool to trust anyone.

"I have three things to tell you."

"Have you been saving them until my psyche could handle the stress? Because if you have, now is not the right time."

Meghan opened the blinds, and the sunlight blazed in like a spotlight on a movie set. "I've kept a few things from you. Important things, but I think you can handle them."

She drew in a breath and caught Meghan's gaze. Desperation had made her vulnerable. Or could Meghan be an answer to a frantic call for help?

Meghan pulled a chair to the bedside. "If what I'm about to tell you is too difficult, then let me know and I'll stop."

"Fair enough." Lindsay heard the sincerity in Meghan's voice.

"The first item on my list is that a bomb was planted in your car."

Her pulse quickened. "Anyone hurt?"

"One person killed. Another wounded. Both were residents of your apartment building. The latter will make a full recovery."

"Any arrests?"

"Not yet, but authorities are working on it."

Lindsay closed her eyes. The demon had grown bolder. "I should be surprised, but I'm not."

"Can you tell me anything that would help us bring these people to justice?"

"No. Haven't a clue. Must be the drug guys." Grief for those affected by the demon cut through her heart. What was he so desperate for that he'd resorted to murder? Her thoughts spun. She'd kill him herself if she had the chance. Maybe the answer lay there. "Do you have the names of those who . . . got in the way of the bomb?"

"If your father agrees, I'll pass it on. But I'm sure that was handled."

"Tell him it's important. I'd like to send a note or flowers or something."

Meghan nodded. "I will. The next item is about an armed man who tried to access your parents' home. He was shot and killed before agents could question him."

Lindsay swallowed the acid rising in her throat. "What do you know about him?"

"He was a member of a drug cartel in Colombia."

Lindsay stared at Meghan, hoping she hid the terror. Where else had his power spread?

"What do you know, Lindsay? Please. These people must be stopped."

"Nothing. The situation is scary. Seems to be getting worse."

"I agree. The third item on my list is about your father—"

Lindsay whipped her attention to Meghan. "He's all right, isn't he? Don't tell me something has happened to him."

Meghan touched her shoulder. "He's fine. As of 9 a.m. eastern time, he was sworn in as president of the United States. President Claredon has resigned due to poor health."

She held her breath. The cancer must have spread. *Does this mean Dad is safe or in more danger than before?* "So Daddy is now officially the president of the United States. I'm sure he's happy, but how sad for President Claredon. His wife is a strong woman, but this has to be . . . hard." She could easily slip into her infamous sarcasm, but she wasn't really that callous. "The president has battled cancer for a long time. Sorry he's losing the fight. The country will see Daddy do a fine job. They'll vote him in next November."

"Another reason for you to cooperate with us. We need to bring in those who've threatened you, your parents, and bombed your car. Lindsay, we desperately need your help in finding who is behind this."

She stiffened. "I can't help you. It's too dangerous. Besides, the Secret Service has the technology to find those responsible."

"I know you're afraid."

"You don't know a thing about it, and I am not going to endanger my parents' lives."

"They are already in danger. Use your head. A bomb and a man with a gun. How much worse does it have to get?" Control seemed to lace Meghan's words.

Lindsay wished she had the same strength. Then she could stand up to him. "You're asking the impossible."

"I agree those involved with the investigation will eventually find the person or persons involved. But why risk another life? I've seen your caring heart, Lindsay. You can't deny it."

Lindsay blinked back the tears. Not even Dave or Carla had gotten this close to the person who lived inside her, the person she longed to be. "Daddy shouldn't have called the hospital when I slit my wrist. That would have solved the problem."

"So dying instead of telling the truth makes sense?"

Lindsay trembled and dug her fingernails into her palms. "I'm the one who's fried her brains, remember? I'm not rational or logical. Nothing I could ever say would be admissible in a court of law. Some fancy lawyer would pull out my records, cite my mental instability, and the case would be dropped."

"Sounds like you've given it a lot of thought."

"Whatever." She'd said too much. The nightmares and the resulting panic had shaken loose what sense she had left.

"You're using your addiction as a crutch."

"It's safer there, Meghan. If you'll leave me alone, I'd like to dress and grab some coffee before we ride."

For a brief second, sadness spread over Meghan's face. Lindsay had caused it, just like she'd hurt anyone who had ever expressed caring. Maybe if she pushed hard and long enough, they'd all go away.

# CHAPTER 21

ASH QUESTIONED THE LOGIC of allowing Lindsay to ride after her traumatic night, but obviously Dave welcomed the diversion. Ash planned to go despite his lack of equestrian skills. The last time he'd ridden took him back about twenty-nine years, when he was six. His parents had taken him to a carnival and plopped him on a pony. He'd fallen off and had no desire to repeat the incident. Meghan had already shown him up on too many occasions, and it was time he demonstrated an SAIC's abilities. But he'd rather face a half-dozen armed terrorists than fall off a horse in front of the onlooking agents, Chip, Ethan, and Lindsay. He should have attached velcro to the seat of his jeans.

He glanced at a crystal-blue sky. Already the heat was reaching excruciating temperatures. Maybe Dave would think the day too warm for Lindsay's health and well-being.

Chip led two horses from the stables and handed the reins to Ash. "You and Bob's mounts are next. I'd like to come along if you don't mind."

"I'd love it. I'm ready for a good run." Lindsay flirted over her shoulder. Definitely on stage. "Did I hear you playing a guitar last night and singing a Kenny Chesney song?"

Chip grinned. "You did. He's one of my favorites." He nodded at the terrier. "Named this little fella after him."

Lindsay patted the dog. "You were fabulous. I thought I was listening to a CD."

Chip had fallen for her whole setup. "Thanks. I played for Meghan."

Lindsay pouted. "But not me? I'm jealous, Chip."

He laughed. "You need the Secret Service's permission for a concert. I'm only a ranch hand, not the leading source of entertainment."

Lindsay flashed her blue eyes at Ash. "Aren't you a country music fan?"

"Don't think so." Ash played through the scenario. Chip puzzled him. The doubts about him lingered like a taste of stale coffee. "But I don't mind a little diversion from the heat and dust."

"We'll make it happen soon. Excuse me while I get the other horses. They're saddled and ready to go." Chip tipped his hat at Ash. "It's going to be a scorcher, and the sooner we ride, the better."

Ethan followed him toward the stables. "And I'll get your horse, Son, so these folks aren't delayed."

Ash sensed Meghan studying him. Did she know he was . . . an inexperienced rider?

"Didn't know you were a horse lover."

"Of course. Isn't every man?" *Watch it, buddy, or you'll eat your words—literally.*

Meghan lifted her saddle's stirrups and pulled on the wide leather strap that slipped under the horse's belly.

"Don't you trust Chip to tighten the girth?" Lindsay wiped beads of perspiration from her forehead.

"Remember, I used to barrel race, and I always check the girth." Meghan finished and lifted the stirrup on Lindsay's saddle.

Chip led two more horses from the stables. "Meghan, I saddled that horse for Lindsay myself."

"Old habits are hard to break, but if you'd recheck the girth, I'd feel better."

"Paranoid, or is this part of your job?" Chip's tone ebbed toward irritation.

"Both. Took a couple of nasty spills when I was younger. Broke an ankle once."

Chip handed the reins to Ash and Bob, then turned his attention to Lindsay's horse. He swore. "What's going on here? The girth's been slit."

Meghan examined it. "And you'd didn't see this before?"

Chip shook his head. "I swear, when I saddled this horse, it was secure." He peered at the slashed girth. "That's fresh, and it's not quite all the way through." His gaze bored into Ash's. "Take a look for yourself. It would have broken in no time."

Lindsay stepped back. "I—I could have taken a bad fall."

"Right." Chip appeared as angry as Ash felt.

Whoever had sabotaged Lindsay's horse was on the ranch.

"Who was with you this morning?" Ash wanted to grab him by the throat and shake the truth out of him.

"Only me." Ethan's voice rose.

"Dad, I can defend myself. After I saddled the horses for Meghan and Lindsay, I left them tied out here while I walked back for a bottle of water. At the time, I didn't know who else would be riding."

Chip's set jaw and open stance gave no indication of lying, unless he was a master at concealing the truth. Ash examined the girth. For now, he needed Chip to believe he wasn't under suspicion. "I'd like for you to stay here and help me work through this. You could make my job easier."

"Be glad to." Chip's voice held skepticism.

"Bob, Meghan, I want Wade riding with you." Meghan hurried to the house to find Wade, who'd been on the phone with his pregnant wife.

This had gotten too close on Ash's watch, and he intended to find out who had set up Lindsay for a fall. And why.

★ ★ ★

With her hand resting on her SIG, Meghan kept track of every bird that flew, every trace of movement in the pasture, and every hint of a breeze. Wade had his binoculars glued to his eyes, and she and Bob flanked each side of Lindsay, wondering if someone watched them with deadly malice. Even their protectee swung her gaze from side to side.

Six agents staked out the Dancin' Dust, and someone had played havoc with Lindsay's saddle. If he'd gotten away with this trick, what would happen next?

Meghan's conversation with Lindsay replayed in her mind. How could she get her protectee to open up? Whatever she knew was bigger than a disgruntled drug dealer. The crimes of late were connected, including the cut girth. A gut reaction told her someone had bullied a mentally unstable young woman and threatened her. What she didn't understand was why. The fear in Lindsay's eyes said it would take lots of persuasion—and trust.

Later she'd discuss it with the team. Lindsay believed her parents were a target if she revealed any information. And that had proved true. Meghan's hunches had paid off in the past, and she had a few reservations about a couple of those walking the Dancin' Dust. But without proof, she'd keep her eyes open and her mouth shut.

# CHAPTER 22

Ash had walked into the stable twice in search of any clues about who had sabotaged Lindsay's saddle. Chip watched, fuming as well, but saying nothing.

"In the house. I have a few questions." Ash charged his words like a Harley on steroids. He'd get to the bottom of who'd threatened Lindsay's life, beginning now.

Chip opened his mouth, then clamped it shut. "I'll go, and I'll answer your questions. I don't have anything to hide." He stomped past Ash toward the ranch house. At the porch steps, he turned to face Ash nose to nose, his features stone hard. "Nothing about you intimidates me. I've met worse in boardrooms."

"You haven't been up against a Secret Service agent whose protectee's life has been threatened."

Chip didn't budge. "If I had anything to do with what just happened, then now is the time I'd be begging for mercy, right?"

"Don't cross me."

"You need to understand when a man says he's innocent."

"Inside." Ash would like to do a little old-fashioned grilling and persuade him to confess.

Lindsay. His responsibility. No one would hurt her as long as he breathed.

Once they entered the house, Pepper stepped from the hall

leading to the operation room, armed with the vacuum. Ash caught her glare. "Go pick tomatoes or something."

"I beg your pardon." She lifted her chin.

"Pepper, this is not a time to make me angry. The cleaning can wait."

"Go ahead." Chip stepped between her and Ash. "This is between the SAIC and me." He walked inside the operation room with Ash behind him.

To think the snake thought he was in charge. Fat chance. "Sit down."

Chip didn't budge. "I prefer to stand, unless we're talking across the table like two civilized men."

Ash noted the confidence in the man's eyes. Not a single twitch of treachery in his body. "All right." He pulled out a chair, and Chip did the same.

"Are you bringing out the waterboarding?"

Ash chuckled. "Depends on how quickly I could get you to a toilet."

"Try something else. Like figuring out how someone cut the girth while I grabbed a bottle of water and the rest of you were still inside the house? How many minutes do you think elapsed?"

Ash had met Chip's kind before. Thought they had all the answers when they were hiding the truth. But he didn't look like he was lying. And he made sense. "I want to know why you slit the girth on Lindsay's saddle."

"You can stop the Homeland Security tactics, A2Z." Chip leaned over the table. "Use your head. Why would I do it when I'd be the only suspect?"

"Because you're cocky enough to think you'd get away with it. So let's get to the root of the problem. Who are you taking orders from?"

"Are you deaf? Better yet, do you have a polygraph in your briefcase?"

"I don't think it's necessary."

"Find one. Because I'm telling the truth."

"All right. If you didn't try to hurt Lindsay, then who did?" Ash settled back in his chair. He could break this guy.

"No clue. But we could time how long it would have taken for it to happen."

Ash didn't want to admit that Chip had a good suggestion. "Let's do it."

They walked outside, where Pepper stood on the porch with her arms crossed. Ash nodded at her. "You can have your domain back."

"How generous. Remind me not to poison you."

At times, he'd given her reason to kill him. But why didn't people understand Lindsay's safety hailed as his first priority? National security came next, and his team slid into third.

"The horses were tied here at the gate." Chip pointed to the post that led into the corral. "Time me while I get a bottle of water."

Ash looked at his watch.

"Do you want one?"

Ash glared at him. "You might poison me."

Chip's brow raised. "It's a thought. But I'm not vindictive like Pepper."

Ash studied his watch. "Go."

Chip disappeared into the stables. Either the man was innocent or he'd planned the perfect storm. Ash considered the seriousness of potentially harming the daughter of the president of the United States, especially with the threats on her life. Not on his watch.

He'd call Warrington, but the man had pressures that Ash had no clue about, and finding who stood behind the car bombing, untraceable e-mails, and a drug runner who'd attempted entry into the new president's home consumed Warrington's attention.

For that matter, the president spent each morning learning about enemy activities, world conflicts, the state of the economy, military requests, and how he should respond to sundry problems and issues. The strength needed to lead this country would depress the strongest of men. Ash couldn't risk barging into the Shield's day through Warrington with something that could be nothing more than an accident or poor judgment.

He took a deep breath to clear his head. He'd send an e-mail to Warrington when he finished investigating what happened. Tomorrow additional agents would arrive, and crews would begin installing security upgrades appropriate for the president's daughter. Ash might rest a little easier then—but not until the stalker sat behind bars.

Someone had tried to kill the Shield in Atlanta. Could that have been an isolated incident, or was it somehow connected to the unsolved crimes of late? Meghan claimed Lindsay knew the force behind her personal threats, and fear of the culprit kept her quiet. Ash had discounted the theory because he thought Lindsay's brains were fried. Too often, she couldn't tell reality from hallucinations. But what if Lindsay had the answers? She'd worked hard under Dave's care. Appeared happier . . . except for her unwillingness to talk about the crimes. Why would someone want her dead?

Chip walked toward him carrying a bottle of water. "I took the same path as before. Got the water and took a look at the new colt. How long?"

"One minute, twenty seconds."

"Long enough to cut the girth."

"Did you see anyone before or after saddling the horses?"

Chip shook his head. "My mind was on other things."

"Like what?"

Chip glanced toward the pasture, then back. "Agent Meghan Connors. She's enough to make me think about returning to the corporate world."

Ash tried to ignore the green snake of jealousy weaving through him. "That's a discussion you need to have with her."

"And ignore that you're interested in her too?"

Ash liked this guy even less. "Let's get back to the issue facing you."

"Us, A2Z. You have a job to do, and someone tried to eliminate your protectee. She could have broken her neck. I don't appreciate being accused of a crime I didn't commit."

Ash didn't need a reminder. "We didn't look for footprints outside the stables."

"All right. Do you want my shoe size? I doubt we'll find a single thing. Whoever did this is smart enough not to leave evidence."

Chip irritated him more each passing minute. The man had led a department of statisticians in Dallas, but not here.

Two hours later when the riders returned, Ash still didn't have any idea who'd sliced the girth. But he hadn't tossed aside the idea that Chip could be involved. The department-head-turned-rancher irritated him, and to think he was interested in Meghan. She wouldn't waste a single moment with him. Her intelligence put his to shame.

But worse yet, if Chip played an honest hand, who among them walked with a killer?

# CHAPTER 23

MEGHAN WOKE from a deep sleep, every nerve alert. She listened and heard nothing. The green numbers on her nightstand clock illuminated 2:15. What had wakened her? When she was a child, her father said Satan did his best work in the wee hours of the morning, and if she wakened, then she needed to pray.

She blinked and glimpsed out the window at the star-studded sky. No sound or strange smells, just her body on alert.

Something touched her left cheek, and she brushed it off and rolled from the bed, grabbing her SIG on the way up. No one stood in the shadows. No one human anyway. Her gut feeling to be leery rose from the soles of her feet. She flipped on the overhead light.

About six inches from where she'd laid her head, a scorpion crept across her pillow—a striped-bark variety. Nasty. A true demon. Snatching one of her boots, she scooted the stinging devil from her pillow and crushed it. Good thing she always carried an EpiPen. Her reaction to a scorpion sting could have deadly implications—like an anaphylactic shock. Not a way she wanted to end her career.

She searched the ceiling above her bed, betting a month's salary that whoever had renovated the house had not nailed wire mesh across the air duct. First thing in the morning, she'd see that job was done. The local pest control would need to be called, and a work order written to add caulking and weather stripping. She cringed at the thought of involving more civilians in Secret Service business. Maybe Chip or Ethan could handle it.

The clock read 2:35, and she was wide awake. Glancing at what remained of the scorpion, she realized any hours left to sleep would be spent feeling invisible creatures crawling all over her body. Maybe she could get a little rest in the recliner downstairs. She reached for the quilt and sheet, shaking each one to make sure no more surprises awaited her. If Lindsay found one of these, she'd be in hysterics. Ash would probably unload his SIG on it.

Seemed odd that a man like Scottard Burnette, who grew up in Texas, would forget to take precautions against scorpions. Then again, when she'd checked the attic, the alarm system had contained faulty wiring, and she'd determined more than once that the remodeling contractor had skimped in other areas.

For certain, the first thing she needed was fresh air.

★ ★ ★

Ash threw back the sheet and swung his legs over the bed. No point lying there when he couldn't sleep. Especially when his mind raced about the threats made on Lindsay's life, the incident with her horse today, and the crimes committed in DC with no explanation. The slit girth baffled him. Not only had it been done under his nose, but the culprit walked among them. Never had the Secret Service looked so inept. On his watch.

The source had to be someone who had access to all that was going on at the Dancin' Dust and DC. But who? And why go to so much trouble over an addict with a history of lies and manipulation? What did that person have to gain? If Ash could figure out the motive, he could turn his mind toward thinking like the stalker.

Meghan said Lindsay was scared and knew more about the crimes than she claimed. He'd been over this before, and nothing came to mind but doubts about Lindsay's mental state. She'd always been paranoid. Of course, her behavior could be a manifestation of the withdrawal symptoms. He hoped she hadn't ruined her life, but neither did he want to think a member of his team was responsible.

Now that the nation had a new president, the urgency to find who'd initiated the crimes increased to mammoth proportions. A mastermind fueled the scheme, and if Ash gave in to his nagging feelings—a pounding in the back of his skull—he realized the problems went deeper than a drug dealer who hadn't been paid. Whoever had challenged the US government had sophisticated technology at their fingertips.

He walked to the dresser, listening to every creak in the wooden floor. Reminders. Always the reminders of how he'd failed in the past. He flipped open his laptop, and the screen flashed to life. Perspiration dampened his forehead, and his hands shook like an old man's. He rubbed them vigorously until a semblance of control allowed him to type in the address for the Secret Service secure site. Then his screen name and password.

The screen morphed into footage from seven years ago. Faces appeared on the screen, the same ones who stalked his nightmares. . . .

Agents Annette Hamilton, Joel Scott, and Ash were working undercover to arrest an LA gang leader by the name of Guerrero. The three agents had worked for two months on a counterfeit and drug ring and were finally ready to bring in the gang. The deal going down had police backup, and the agents were ready to celebrate.

Three of Guerrero's gang members stood behind him. Each one's chest was tattooed with a machete dripping blood. In the middle of the swap, Guerrero cocked his head, and the other three pulled out .357 Magnums. Joel attempted to reason with them until backup arrived. Annette's hand slipped inside her shirt. Ash hesitated, thinking Guerrero could be talked down. An instant later, a firefight broke out. Annette took two bullets, in the leg and back, that paralyzed her for life. Ash took two bullets to the shoulder, and Joel lay dead in a pool of blood. Ash blamed Annette for reaching for her weapon. LA police shot the three gang members, and Guerrero went to prison. But Joel was gone.

The truth hit Ash harder each time he viewed the scene. His hesitation was what killed Joel and wounded Annette. Never again on his watch. Never again. He exited the site, closed the lid, and stretched tired neck muscles. Nothing took away the nightmares.

God had given him a second chance to prove his worth, to keep those who led this country and their loved ones safe from jerks who had their own selfish agendas. That was his purpose. Each time he stopped a potential assassin, he redeemed his mistake. When he heard his nickname, he worked harder.

Redeem himself.

Protect others.

Keep his eyes and ears open to potential danger.

He blew out a sigh filled with regret, mostly about himself. His record sparkled with glowing commendations in the line of duty. No one complained about his job performance, and he had the potential of stepping into the presidential team. If he could stop telling himself he wasn't to blame for Joel's death, then maybe he'd believe it.

Slipping into his running shorts, T-shirt, and tennis shoes, he made his way down the stairs, stopping to greet Victor, who kept vigil outside Lindsay's door. His old friend knew about the nightmares and what caused them, but he never mentioned the incident.

Ash stepped outside and slumped into a rocker. Sweat dripped from his temples, more from guilt than the heat.

Meghan's face entered his tortured mind. He admired her, respected her. They were in line for the same coveted position. The self-condemnation of the past warred with a generous portion of admiration for her. More than admiration, and in such a short time.

Loneliness crept inside and took root like a vicious weed.

He swore never to have a woman on his team again, always blaming Annette. But he knew who was responsible, and it wasn't a woman agent. Had he claimed the lie for so long that he believed it? Why was it so hard for him to face the truth?

Meghan knew her stuff and was rightfully a strong contender to serve on the presidential team. He licked his dry lips. He needed that promotion for more reasons than he dared to count. His soul needed cleansing.

His organized future held no complications until Meghan entered the picture, messing with his mind and threatening to take residence in his heart.

So why couldn't he stop thinking about her?

The door behind him opened, and there stood the object of his most recent dilemma.

# CHAPTER 24

"MORNING." Ash gave Meghan a quick look, then motioned to the rocker beside him. Even in the shadows, she took his breath away. "Have a seat. However, there's a bad wind from the north, giving 'fresh country air' a whole new twist."

She laughed and sat beside him. "Can't sleep or taking an early run?"

"Both. I sent Rick inside to get a little rest until I decide what I'm going to do."

"I might join you on a run. That would throw off Chip's schedule."

Remembering Chip's words about his interest in Meghan sliced through him. The resident statistician had no idea what it would take to make a woman of her caliber happy. "What are you doing up at this hour?"

She huffed. "Sure you want to know?"

"I asked. Got a hunch about something?"

"Sort of. But nothing about the problems surrounding Lindsay. I was aroused from my slumber with a scorpion crawling across my face."

His attention whipped her way. "You're kidding."

"Wish I were."

"You weren't stung, were you?" Her file indicated an extreme reaction to bee stings. "Does your allergic reaction to bees include scorpions?"

"I've never been stung to know for sure. But it's off limits as far as I'm concerned."

"What did you do?"

"What every special agent would do. I rolled out of bed and grabbed my SIG, flipped on the light, and there he was." She stood and walked to the edge of the porch. "He met his maker."

Ash chuckled. An image of Meghan blowing a scorpion into a million pieces bannered across his mind.

"Very funny."

"How did it get into your room?"

"I think this one crawled through the air duct. Doesn't look like there's any wire mesh covering it." She sighed. "Anyway, I made a list of what needs to be done to ensure none of us has any unwelcome nightly visitors. I can only imagine how Lindsay would handle one of those creatures." She shrugged. "Anyway, this needs to be handled tomorrow for everyone's safety. But I'm too keyed up to go back to sleep."

"Will we need to call an exterminator?"

"Possibly. My guess is the Leonards can handle it. Maybe we can put Pepper on scorpion detail. She could sprinkle jalapeños around the attic."

"Good call."

"How soon will we be flooded with agents?" The light, citrusy scent coming from Meghan sure beat the scents floating downwind.

"0600. Now that Lindsay is a priority, we'll get the best that's available."

"I'll feel better when everything is in place. I'd feel even better if DC found who was causing all the havoc."

The nearness of her distracted him, causing his mind to whirl with thoughts better left alone. The light from a high mount on the stable caused her face to glisten, almost sparkle. He pushed himself away from the rocker and walked to the porch steps. Being that close to her messed with his head. *Think, Ash. You're the agent in charge.*

"I'm surprised you're not married. Most women agents don't last long. They find an agent who wants understanding, and then they're married and raising babies."

She joined him and stretched. "I'm not one of them, Ash. I'm in the Secret Service for the long haul. But I was engaged for about two months. Not to an agent."

He'd probably offended her, but he'd only voiced what she already knew. "My guess is you scared him off."

"Maybe I did. He couldn't handle my commitment to my job. Gave me a choice."

"If he loved you, then your job shouldn't have mattered." Why had he made such a stupid remark?

"My thoughts exactly. And you? Do you have a special someone?"

"Not with the schedule I keep."

He should walk away, ignore the tension that kept his heart captive. He frowned on agents fraternizing. Interfered with their responsibilities. Although it wasn't against the rule book, it was against his personal code. But that didn't diminish Meghan's intoxicating presence, the way her red-gold hair fell past her shoulders and curled against her chest. He envisioned the depth of her brown eyes and the lashes veiling them as though she held the secrets to unlock a man's mind.

"This isn't fair, you know." His thoughts were uttered before he could stop them.

She turned to face him, his downfall. "What isn't?"

"You," he whispered, "are the one agent who goes against everything I hold in high regard."

"Is that so bad? My skills are good, Ash. You can trust me to do my job."

"Oh, I do. No problem there."

Shoving aside logic and protocol, he gathered her into his arms and kissed her.

# CHAPTER 25

LINDSAY KNEW ABANDONMENT was her biggest issue. She lay awake listening, thinking, wondering. The old fears mixed with the new ones, creating more horror than she'd ever experienced. Daddy was now president, an honor he'd always wanted and one he deserved. He and Mom had dirtied their hands and risked their lives in Uganda to help children. Mom had nearly died from malaria and would battle its effects the rest of her life. Although Lindsay didn't fully appreciate or understand their sacrifice, most of the American people acted as though President Hall and the First Lady were saints. They had accomplished good and courageous feats, while Lindsay had waited at the boarding school for a phone call or a letter. That part hurt so very much. Their relationship would never be good. Chances were she'd die before true reconciliation ever began.

She'd seen her parents' love for her in the hospital when she'd tried to kill herself. All those years she believed neither of them cared, not realizing they didn't want to endanger her and Kelli in the disease-infested jungles. She rationalized their absence by convincing herself they didn't want her. Being sober had its pitfalls because the truth injected a poison that had no antidote.

It took getting clean and hours with Dave Sanchez to see how stupid she'd been. He'd helped her to see beyond her personal pain to circumstances that demonstrated Mom and Dad's love for her—not disgust, as she'd been told in the past. Kelli must have accepted their parents' role in saving the children of the world, because she was following in their footsteps by representing clients who could not afford legal counsel.

If only she could stay clean and have a life of meaning. But she'd thrown in with the devil, and he demanded payment.

Who worked with him? If she'd been hurt or killed today as a result of the sliced girth, evidence would show it wasn't an accident. She thought about each one of the agents on Ash's team and Chip and Ethan and Pepper. No one appeared to be on his payroll. But the demon responsible had once appeared to be her friend too.

She gasped and sat up in bed. Meghan. Yes, that made sense. How like him to have planted a woman agent to make sure Lindsay only talked to her. She thought Daddy had selected her, but maybe not. Was there a way to find out?

But Meghan had held her during the hallucinations. The agent listened to her rantings, made her laugh.

How sad if Meghan was no more than a commodity.

# CHAPTER 26

"WHY DID YOU DO THAT?" Meghan dug her fingernails into her palms to keep from smacking Ash's face.

"I don't know. It happened." Ash stiffened, his voice dangerously low. "You, Special Agent Connors, didn't fight it."

"And you, SAIC Zinders, had no right to take advantage of me."

"Take advantage of you? Give me a break. What was I supposed to do with you standing there dressed like—?"

He had to be kidding. "What? I'm in appropriate running gear. No cleavage, and my shorts are knee length."

"Please. You know exactly what I mean."

"Oh, so I lured you?"

"As I said, you didn't stop me."

Why had she gotten herself into this argument? Why . . . why was she so angry? At this rate, every agent on the ranch would hear them.

She had ended the kiss, but not soon enough. "Do I need to remind A2Z of your rules?"

"I know my own standards." His condescending tone had her bordering on completely losing her temper.

Then she remembered Rick was out there on his shift. "If you don't lower your voice, everyone will hear."

"No one's around but those blasted bugs."

"And Rick."

He blew out a sigh. She'd like to think kissing her had disoriented him, but fat chance.

"What about the Leonards?"

"Oh, so you wouldn't want Chip knowing what happened?"

Had he lost his mind? "What are you talking about?"

"Not a thing, Agent Connors. I suppose you're going to file a sexual harassment charge against me?"

"I could, and it would stand because of your reputation as a woman-hater. I'd simply add womanizer to the list." Meghan stepped back and studied him.

*Cool down. Evaluate the situation. Was his kiss so bad?* No matter that he'd made her furious. Meghan took several breaths to calm herself. "No. I'm not filing anything. I regret what happened, so maybe my anger is self-directed. I should have pushed you away."

He raked his fingers through his hair. "Hey, I'm sorry. We're alone. The chemistry was there . . . at least on my part." He stepped down from the porch, and she recognized his professional stance in the darkness. "Let's forget it ever happened. Hit Delete. We're under a ton of stress trying to figure out who's after Lindsay. And this desolation is the pits."

He wanted her to forget his kiss? Forget the touch of his lips on hers? Was he that mechanical? Did he think chemistry did its work in test tubes with hypothetical formulas, not on a front porch in the moonlight?

"Meghan, I'm sorry. It won't happen again. I'm just stressed."

"Sure. And I exploded." However, when she considered how he attributed his kiss to relieving stress, she wanted to smack the smug look off his face—again.

"What do you say we take a run?"

A run? Emotions were flaring like fireworks on the Fourth of July, and he wanted to run? Oh, why not. Then she'd take a cold shower.

# CHAPTER 27

THE ATTIC DOOR in the upstairs hall slammed shut. Ash handed Chip a towel to wipe the sweat from his face, while animosity flared from every square inch of the rancher.

"I'm telling you the truth." Chip frowned. "Every air duct is securely covered with wire, except the one above Meghan's room. Caulking's in place, and the attic is tighter than a drum."

"Why her room?" Ash wasn't believing this. He wanted answers now.

Chip moistened his lips. "How would I know? I'm paid to help keep this ranch running, not play errand boy for the Secret Service. Why don't you crawl up there in 110 degrees and look for scorpions with a black light? You could use your night goggles. And by the way, they are smart enough to avoid any areas over 100 degrees, which means they're smarter than I am. If the house had a problem, they'd be dropping into the kitchen or laundry or bathrooms looking for water."

"I'm trying to clarify how this happened." One more time, he faced the possibility of someone at the Dancin' Dust working for the other side.

"Then talk to the scorpions. They're nocturnal and forage at night."

"What did you mean by that remark?" Did Chip see him and Meghan early this morning? That's the last thing he needed.

"Any way you want to take it. You've already accused and convicted me of a crime I didn't commit, so fire away."

Ash should back off, but his temper was edging toward a cliff. "Did you put out any poison?"

Chip scowled, his fists clenched at his sides. "I hauled a full bag up there, and it's now empty."

"Did you double-check your work above Meghan's room?"

"She's the only reason I crawled into that inferno. If you continue to dish out much more, Special Agent Zinders, I'm going to be laying my fists into you. An agent on this ranch has brought out the good ol' boy in me."

"Do you know who you're talking to?"

Chip stared at him. "If you'd offer a little respect to the other people around here, maybe you'd get some in return."

He was probably right, but that didn't stop him from wanting to explode. "Thank you for taking care of the problem. Since I have no experience with scorpions, is there anything else you'd recommend?"

"We have a barn cat. Possibly another one would help. My dad claims chickens keep them away."

"Do you know where we can get those?"

"I'll find out and have Wade make the travel arrangements for me." Chip fired back his response. "Do you need the source of a cat and a few chickens in writing?"

"You bet I do." Ash turned and walked downstairs to the operation room. Why did Meghan's room have the scorpion problem when she would have a potentially life-threatening reaction to an insect sting? He didn't believe in coincidences.

The operation door was open, ensuring the agents had heard the upstairs shouting. Victor pecked away at the keyboard while Wade labored over a layout of the ranch for the security cameras. Neither man spoke, and why should they? For too long he'd made a point of being a pain in the rear, so no agent would ever be killed or wounded because of him. What thanks had he gotten in return?

Standing in front of the window, he looked out at the patio where Lindsay and Meghan appeared engaged in a conversation. Meghan's shift had barely begun, and even with no sleep, she looked amazing. Scratch that last thought. She looked good for an agent without much sleep. Meghan had gotten further with Lindsay in a few weeks than he had in four years. The agent was a professional, and she respected Lindsay.

Chip was right, and Ash was tired of alienating himself from others. In rare moments, he showed the side of him that he used to be. But the old Ash had allowed his best friend to get killed. These were his friends, his team members. He felt as responsible for them as he did for Lindsay.

"You don't have to carry it all." Victor's voice rose slightly over the steady clicking of the keyboard.

"Yes, I do. I don't have a choice."

★ ★ ★

After supper that night, Meghan slid into an ergonomically correct chair and reached inside her laptop case for a layout of the house. Exhaustion had settled in her bones, and sand had invaded her eyes. She wanted to crawl into bed but not yet. Glancing at the clock, she mentally checked herself out at 2100 and no later—if she made it until then. Until last night, she'd managed four hours of sleep for the past five days, and now her body demanded a deposit to cover the deficit.

Before the next few days were over, this property would resemble a compound. The exterior doors and windows were to be wired to detect those attempting to get in and a certain young lady from getting out. Meghan questioned whether the latter was necessary. Lindsay had shown progress. But did she still view the ranch as a prison? How tragic that the young woman needed protection from her own willful ways.

Feeling herself slipping into a sleep zone, she scooted back from the table and walked outside onto the front lawn, green and perfectly manicured, courtesy of Ethan and Chip. To the left of the lawn, an ancient oak tree spread its gnarled branches in every direction as though daring an intruder to step near the house. How tempting to curl up beneath the old tree and let the troubles of her life slip away.

Meghan shook her head, realizing the lack of sleep had caused her thoughts to drift. As long as daylight stretched across the horizon, the work around her continued. Since dawn vehicles had poured through the gate bringing equipment and specialists. The county sheriff had been informed about Lindsay's strategic position and the need to keep her whereabouts secret. Jean-clad agents covered the grounds like ants at a picnic. Rovers posted in jeeps and trucks would stop anyone jumping the fences, and the mounted cameras brought in a good feed. By the time the security plan was implemented, cameras, thermal imagers, and other up-to-date technology would be in place.

"I'm wondering how long it would take to string barbed wire along the property lining the road?"

At the sound of Ash's voice, Meghan cringed. She'd avoided him all day, and now he'd singled her out. "With the other security measures soon to be in place, is that precaution necessary?"

"Since those who threatened her haven't been arrested, I'd say twenty-foot-high barbed wire wouldn't be enough. Call me a daddy grizzly."

The image fit. She studied the cameras mounted at the gates, silently questioning their position—anything to keep her attention from Ash. He made her nervous. He caused her to shiver in ninety-five-degree temps, and her lips still tasted his kiss. The one she'd claimed she didn't want. "What did Warrington say about barbed wire?"

"Never asked. He'd say it was over the top. Is the alarm system working?"

"Hopefully tomorrow." She prepared herself for his complaint.

"Good. I saw you looking at the cameras. We're close to having the electronic motion sensors and the infrared high-definition day-light cameras in place. Wish we could expedite the installation."

"We're still out of the media's eye."

"For now."

She refused to look at him, fighting her irresponsible attraction. "When do we find out if we're being replaced?"

"Soon. Look, Meghan, I'm sorry a—"

"We deleted it, remember?"

"Wish it were that easy. I feel like a jerk." His attention moved to the front gate. "I am a jerk."

Grasping an ounce of strength, she faced him. "It's over. Done. I don't want to talk about it again."

"Just wanted to make sure you're okay." He spoke in a whisper.

Did he think the trees were listening? The man confused and frustrated her. "When I need a doctor or a shrink, I'll let you know. In the meantime, I have work to do. You have work to do."

He stepped back.

Meghan blew out a sigh. "I'm sorry. Just tired." She started to add she hadn't slept well for several days but decided Ash could survive without her personal information.

"Why don't you call it a day?"

"I still have a few things to do."

He chuckled. "Now you sound like me."

*Not so sure that was a compliment.* "I make a list every day of what I need to accomplish, and today's isn't completed."

"Meghan."

The familiar chill bumps rose, and her face became flushed. "Yes, sir."

"The name's Ash. I'm not good at this, but could we be friends?"

"I suppose."

"Thanks. I'll leave you alone to your thoughts." He took a few steps toward the front gate, then whirled around. "You're messing with my mind. Not sure how to handle it."

She certainly didn't know how to respond to that comment.

# CHAPTER 28

SUNDAY EVENING OF FATHER'S DAY, Meghan gathered with the team, Dave and Carla, and Lindsay around a long table on the patio for supper. Pepper flipped hamburgers on the grill, with the option of jalapeño or plain. She'd spent the afternoon in Ethan's garden, and the table displayed mounds of fresh vegetables. Maybe their cook was mellowing. The group looked more like friends ready to enjoy a barbecue than Secret Service agents keeping an eye on their protectee. The pool sparkled, but no one ventured toward its tepid waters. They were all celebrating the completion of the security detail.

Chip walked toward the group, wearing a smile that would rival a model on a New York runway. With his guitar slung over his shoulder, he reminded Meghan of his promised concert.

"Where's your dad?" Rick glanced up from the far end of the table, where he was reading something.

"He's going to church. Said we could save him a burger. Without jalapeños."

A chuckle rose from the group, but Pepper silenced them with a glare. "Too bad if I forget about the corn and burn it. Worse yet, if I forget the carrot cake."

"I'm not complaining." Ash sounded like a little boy. "She made me a special burger."

"I like the peppers." Rick turned his attention back to the paper before him.

"What are you doing?" Ash tossed a radish at him.

So A2Z had chosen to act like a human today. If Meghan were honest with herself, she'd admit he'd displayed likable traits before.

"Working on something for my daughter." Rick grinned and tossed back the radish. Normally the broad-shouldered man had little to say.

A sparkle lit Ash's eyes. "Why don't we believe you?"

He leaned back. All eyes were on him. "It's serious business when it concerns my daughter."

"Which one?"

"The sixteen-year-old."

Ash moved to Rick's end of the table and snatched the piece of paper. He read it and howled. "This is a note from some guy."

"Exactly. I'm analyzing his handwriting." He tapped his pen on the edge of the table. "She isn't dating this guy. Period."

Meghan knew a little about handwriting but not enough to jump into the conversation.

Ash nodded. "Yeah, look at how large he writes. He thinks a lot about himself . . . and his possessions. Probably selfish. I bet he's motivated by his own lusts."

Moans filled the air.

"And look how hard he pressed on the paper. Is he strong or determined to coax your baby girl into doing something she shouldn't?"

Rick snatched the paper. "I already told you she isn't dating him. He killed any thought of that when he wrote this note and allowed me to tear into his psychological makeup. The boy can prey on someone else."

"Better call her." Ash patted him on the back. "I'm not an expert in analyzing handwriting, but I wouldn't want him around my daughter."

"Hey." Wade stood. "Today's Father's Day, and I haven't gotten a call."

Pepper lifted a platter of burgers from the side of the grill to the table. "What about a text?"

Wade pulled out his phone. "I muted it when I went on duty." He checked his phone. "My own stupid fault. They called, and I missed it."

"Better return it." Ash laughed. "I won't let anyone eat your burger."

Wade sprinted to the other side of the pool. Great family man. Great guy, just like all of them. Meghan glanced up and met Ash's gaze. Instead of diverting her attention, he smiled.

She returned the gesture. So he wanted to be friends. . . .

"Did you guys call your families?" Ash lifted his glass of iced tea. "Better do so before we eat."

Meghan wished her father were alive so she could send her love. "What about you, Ash? Did you call home?"

He nodded. "I did."

"You have a father?" Only Victor could get by with that question.

"I do. The rumors I came from the planet Krypton are unfounded."

Victor took a very rare burger from Pepper. "The one I heard indicated something about a rock."

"Very funny. There's a reason why you always pull the grave-yard shift."

Meghan wanted to study Ash but feared he'd discover her try-ing to read him. Such a complex man. She thought he hid a few things. Maybe someday she'd discover what those things were.

Earlier Lindsay asked Meghan for permission to text her dad about Father's Day. Their protectee did care about her family, despite her own words to the contrary.

After they ate and helped Pepper take the leftovers and dishes inside, the camaraderie continued.

"Ready for a Texas-style concert?" Chip pulled his chair away from the table.

"I am." Lindsay flashed him a smile and pulled Chesney into

her lap. The terrier snuggled up to her like a long-lost friend. "Why don't you sit closer to me?"

"No, thanks. I need room." Chip must need to concentrate. The Dancin' Dust had enough problems without Lindsay zooming in on him, especially with the suspicion surrounding the ranch hand's questionable actions.

He played a few chords, then broke into a tune made famous by Keith Urban, followed by another song by Kenny Chesney. Lindsay clapped and asked for more. Three songs later, Chip set his guitar on a lounge chair and pulled a bottle of water from the ice chest.

"Mind if I take a look at your guitar?" Lindsay's soft voice didn't give any man much of a chance to refuse.

"Not at all. Do you play?"

"A little."

Meghan just learned something new. She'd wondered why Lindsay kept her nails short, and now she knew the reason.

"Thanks. Mine is under my bed at my apartment. If I'd known I was headed for a vacation, I'd have packed it."

Chip handed her his guitar. "Now it's your turn."

Lindsay didn't hesitate. She sat on the edge of a patio chair and began to strum a familiar tune.

"Isn't that an old Reba song?" Chip leaned in closer. "'Fancy'?"

"It is. One of my favorites."

"Can you sing it?" His gentle voice coaxed a smile from Lindsay. "I've seen Reba perform live. Always a great show."

"Me too." Without looking up, she played and sang the tune that caused Reba fans to go wild. When she finished, the entire group clapped.

"You are good." Meghan emphasized the last word, and she hadn't stretched the truth.

"Better than good," Chip said. "You have a set of lungs, girl."

Lindsay held out his guitar. "Thanks."

"Keep it," Chip said. "We all need another song."

"Really?" She blushed—the first Meghan had seen. Lindsay glanced from Chip to Meghan, then to Ash.

"I don't know who Reba is, but I like the music." Ash eased back in his chair.

"What was I thinking singing a song from someone you don't know?" Lindsay looked genuinely happy.

Meghan hoped she saw more of this side of their protectee. "I want to hear more too. Makes me want to send a recording to a music company."

Lindsay shrugged. "I think you're all deaf, but I do have a few favorites. Do you like Carrie Underwood?"

Chip whistled. "I've died and gone to heaven."

Without waiting for another response, Lindsay began a Carrie Underwood song. Lindsay had a unique style all her own, fresh and filled with passion.

When she finished and gave Chip his guitar, he asked her about voice training and the make of her guitar. "What other talents are you hiding from us?"

"None." She tilted her head. "You've heard the only one. I like to play and sing, and I do write a song occasionally."

"Stop it, right there." Meghan waved. "I want an original." How much could she encourage Lindsay without scaring her off?

"But I'm not very good. Really."

"Let your friendly Secret Service agents decide your talent," Meghan said.

"And your local ranch hand." Chip's voice caused a hush from the others.

Lindsay hesitated, her eyes void of any signs of drugs or alcohol. She sang about a small-town girl who left for the city and all it offered. But she broke a boy's heart. The girl realized she'd made a mistake but was afraid to go home. She missed the boy and the love they'd once shared. When Lindsay finished, she returned the guitar to Chip and thanked him again.

"Anytime, Lindsay. Maybe we can try a duet someday soon. I bet your parents love to hear you play and sing."

Lindsay's gaze settled on Chip, obviously uncomfortable. "I don't think either of them knows I own a guitar. It's not as though they're interested."

"Lindsay, I've heard you before, and you're talented." Ash picked up a Diet Coke from the ice chest. "Many a night I listened to you compose songs. Every one of them was a keeper."

Admiration for Ash lifted a notch. His comment was exactly what Lindsay needed. Tonight, Meghan had found plenty of good things about Ash.

Lindsay blushed again, clearly flustered. "Thanks. I guess I'm ready to go inside. Dave has probably been jotting down questions for our session." Glancing around, she smiled. "I haven't had such a good time in years. Thanks to all of you for making tonight wonderful. And happy Father's Day to those of you with kids." She grinned at Ash. "Superman didn't crawl out from under a rock."

Meghan settled into the lounge chair and processed what had happened this evening. She refused to think about Ash. That went nowhere, and right now she was furious for allowing him to creep into her heart. He wanted to be friends after he'd kissed her and blamed it on stress? She needed to concentrate on Lindsay. Her musical ability ranked above a casual interest to a possible career. She had the face of a blue-eyed, blonde angel and a unique low-range voice. Her lyrics touched the heart of country music and perhaps the heart of Lindsay Hall.

Meghan allowed another thought to swirl and float around her mind. Songwriters often developed their lyrics from personal experiences. How strong was the possibility that Lindsay might have revealed who was behind the crimes in her songwriting?

# CHAPTER 29

MONDAY MORNING, Meghan and Lindsay enjoyed breakfast poolside. Lindsay was unusually quiet, and Meghan felt certain it had to do with the previous evening. When Meghan mentioned her music, Lindsay told her—with a few expletives—not to bring it up again. How sad for this talented young woman to open her heart to something other than drugs and rebellion, only to feel as though she shouldn't have exposed her gift.

The morning drifted to afternoon in silence. Lindsay swam laps, and her body language shouted apprehension. Fear of what? Certainly not her music. Had she sobered enough to rethink her danger?

A few of the agents were sitting around the patio when Wade announced that at 1600 his wife had given birth to a baby son. He regretted not being there for his birth, but he'd have two weeks with his family soon. Between phone calls with his wife and family and being the recipient of many pictures, Wade was one proud daddy.

"Congratulations." Lindsay wrapped a towel around herself and asked to see the baby's picture. Wade handed her his phone. "He looks huge."

"Eight and a half pounds. His sister barely weighed six. I think I have a linebacker."

Bob took a long look at the baby's picture. "He has football hands."

Meghan did her share of admiring. "Does he have a name?"

"Not yet. We're still talking." Wade must have grown a foot since the day before. "I'll let you know as soon as we decide. My wife's tossed out a name, and I tossed out another, but I'm leaving it to her. She did all the work. Right now, I need a run. Like ADD on steroids." Wade looked at the sky. "It's a little hot yet, but I can handle the temps. Can't seem to come down from being a new daddy." He gestured toward the pool. "I might have to cool off once I'm back."

"Enjoy," Meghan said. "Then you can tell us what the rest of your family has to say about the new baby."

Wade disappeared into the house and returned shortly thereafter. He waved and jogged toward the driveway. Chip joined him, a common occurrence between the two men.

"He's lucky to have a family." Lindsay's remark revealed another need, one Meghan hoped she soon realized.

"One day, we'll all have a houseful of kids." Ash walked to the pool's edge, holding a can of Diet Coke. He dipped his fingers into the water. "Feels like bath water. We should celebrate Wade's son in style."

Bob propped his feet onto a chair. "I'm always hungry, and Pepper's a darn good cook. Reminds me of my mom."

"At least I've gotten her to put the hot stuff on the side. Smells like French-fried shrimp inside."

"The batter is loaded with pepper," Victor said. "Another night of peanut butter and jelly for you."

Lindsay joined Ash at the pool's edge. "How about letting me have a drink of your Diet Coke?"

"I don't think pop is on Dave's list." He dangled the can in front of her.

"Agent Zinders, you might have changed for the better since getting here, but you're still selfish. Dave will never know."

"You're right." He handed her the can. "I couldn't exist on what he's having you eat and drink."

She toasted him and laughed. A real laugh. Maybe Lindsay had worked through whatever plagued her this morning. Meghan prayed this upward trend for Lindsay would stay. Maybe—just maybe—she could convince the girl to share her songs. Even better if she shared what she knew about the stalker.

"I'm going in to talk to Pepper." Ash headed for the door. "See if I still have the charm. Who knows? She might fix me shrimp without the heartburn."

"Hey, Ash, I suggest you have me sweet-talk her." Victor hurried to the door and blocked him. "You haven't seen charm until I step into action. You think I'm good on a skateboard? Watch this."

"I've seen your suave techniques. Worthless. I'll handle Pepper."

Kids. They were acting like kids. This side of Ash brought to the surface feelings Meghan wanted to deny. Inappropriate. Against Ash's personal rule book. Tell that to her heart.

★ ★ ★

Ash found Pepper in the kitchen. She dropped breaded shrimp, one by one, into hot oil. It sizzled, and the enticing aroma made his mouth water. An evening of Rolaids didn't register on his to-do list.

"Sure smells good in here." He reached inside the fridge for another Diet Coke since Lindsay had kept his.

"Do you like shrimp?" She took a sip of Dr Pepper, a habit while she cooked, since he'd eliminated the wine.

"I sure do."

"This is my shrimp diablo. Scottard and his family love it."

Ash plastered on a smile. It would be hotter than blazes. "Any chance of getting mine plain?"

She smiled and pointed to a plate with a small mound of shrimp. "That's the weenie platter. Suit you?"

"For sure. Why the concession lately? Is it my irresistible personality?"

She waved a pair of tongs. "You've started acting human."

He chuckled. "I'll try to keep it up. How—?" His radio beeped, and his attention focused on the caller, stationed somewhere on the property.

"Agent down."

Ash's senses flew into action, with the report pouring through his ears. He rushed onto the patio, where the protective team hovered over Lindsay, escorting her inside. "Hurry!" Agents moved inside, toward the living area and the hard room. "Meghan, you're with me. The rest of you keep the perimeter secure."

She drew her weapon and fixed her eyes on the panoramic view around them.

Ash needed more information from the agent who made the report. "What happened?"

"Wade was shot while he and Chip were running."

"How is he?"

"Gone. Three of us are at the site—a mile and a half east of the front gate."

"What about Chip?"

"We have him right here. He's shaken but okay."

"Call an ambulance. I'm on my way." He raced to the gate with Meghan keeping pace. Every agent on the ranch scurried into position. Every weapon ready to fire. But quiet met him, with only the sound of grasshoppers pounding in his ears.

Chip, the resident statistician, was all right, while an agent lay dead. Ash knew who was behind the shooting. Too many coincidences. Heat added moisture to his skin and dripped down the sides of his face. Anger burned his cheeks as much as the temperatures.

Not Wade. Good man. Excellent agent. New baby, too. Hadn't even named him. Chip had to be behind this, and Ash intended to pull a confession out of him. He got away with setting up an accident for Lindsay, but not murder. Adrenaline forced speed into his legs, and the physical exertion helped curb his frenzied emotions.

Now was the time to gather information and do what he did best.

At the site of the shooting, the three agents stood with Chip, and one agent knelt beside Wade's body on the dirt road.

Meghan dropped to the ground beside Wade. She studied his forehead and the exit wound. "Looks like a Remington 700."

Ash joined her. "Keep talking."

"Speculation here. But the shooter is no amateur." She peered up at him. "Trained sniper. Possibly from the military. Looks like he positioned himself about 850 yards south of here."

Ash pointed to two agents, and they hurried off in that direction. He stood, his gaze focused on Chip. The man's eyebrows were drawn together, and his slightly parted lips revealed his fear. Was that fear of what he'd witnessed or what Ash might do? Chip shifted from one leg to the other.

"Chip, what happened out here?"

His shook his head. "I don't know for sure." His gaze met Ash's. "My friend's dead, and I have a right to know what's going on."

Ash seized him by the neck of his T-shirt. "We have the right to know who killed our agent."

Chip's jaw clenched, and he lifted his chin.

"Listen, Mr. Back-to-the-Ranch Statistician, someone just didn't sit out here and wait for a Secret Service agent to jog by. That sniper had inside information and knew when to squeeze the trigger."

"I don't know anything about it." Chip's voice rose.

"Give me one reason to believe you aren't behind this."

Chip struggled under Ash's hold, and two agents gripped his arms. "Okay. I'll tell you what happened. But I'm ready to take a polygraph or whatever's out there to prove my innocence."

Ash took a breath. "I've heard that before. Don't leave out a thing."

"How about having your men take their hands off me?"

Ash nodded. If Chip tried anything, they'd fill him full of holes. The first bullet would be from Ash's SIG.

"We were jogging about two miles from here. We turned around and headed back. Wade fell, and I thought he stumbled.

Then I heard a sharp, quick crack like the sound of a pencil breaking. When I checked on him, he didn't respond. So I turned him over, and that's when I saw blood seeping from his head."

"What did you do then?"

"I felt for a pulse. When I didn't get a reading, I snatched up his radio and contacted the first man who answered. I've had first aid and CPR, so I administered it to see if I could resuscitate him. But I think he was already dead."

Ash turned to the agent who'd radioed him about Wade. "Can you back up any of this?"

"Some of it. He was kneeling on the road beside Wade giving CPR when we arrived."

"Escort Chip to the house. Have Bob get a full statement. I want his quarters thoroughly searched. Confiscate any computers or cell phones." Ash looked at Meghan, whose attention focused on the area south of them. The terrain was hilly and rocky, the perfect area for a sniper to hide.

Who'd ordered the execution? And why? Did Lindsay know who stood behind the shooting? Fury raced through him. She wasn't close enough to Wade to confide in him, which made Ash wonder if he'd discovered something. Questioning her had to be done whether Dave approved or not.

Maybe the sniper wanted to show he could take out an agent. Or was Wade's death supposed to scare Lindsay into taking some kind of action or keeping quiet? Speculation and nothing concrete.

Ash turned his gaze back to Chip. He didn't trust him. Neither did he believe a single man instigated the bombing in DC, the threats, or Wade's death. Time to get this guy off the Dancin' Dust until they had answers.

This was bigger than anything he'd ever faced.

Ash understood this wasn't the work of just an inside man but a sophisticated operation, bigger than any of them could conceive. The thought had taunted him before. Now it had substance. Drugs didn't make sense. Could that be a cover-up for the real focus? But what?

# CHAPTER 30

ASH TOOK THE CALL from President Hall in the operation room and assured him Lindsay was unharmed but shaken in the aftermath of Wade's death. They'd removed her from the hard room but limited her to inside the house. "What do you have on the sniper?" The grief was obvious in his voice.

"Not a trace of evidence at this time. But the local sheriff's department is assisting us in combing the area."

"Ash, I don't understand the crimes here and at the ranch. With all of our technology, why can't we find who's behind this? My office received a call right after the shooting. Traced it to a deserted office here in DC."

"Did the caller give a reason or make demands?"

"It came through on my personal cell phone—muffled. Said it wouldn't be the last assassination. He also said the one responsible for Wade's death knew why, and that person was to blame. Warrington is handling the trace."

"Mr. President, we'll find who's behind this."

"I know I can count on all of you. Please, I'd like to talk to my daughter."

Ash walked back into the living area where Dave sat with Lindsay. She'd vomited after learning the news about Wade. "Your father wants to talk to you."

She reached for the phone. Her lips quivered. "Daddy, are you all right?"

Odd that she'd ask her father the same question he'd posed about her. The concern in her voice confirmed that she'd made progress in her rehabilitation, more than any other time in the past. Meghan claimed Lindsay was withholding information about the crimes. Then why didn't she speak up?

Lindsay reached for a tissue. "Be careful. You're president now, and the country needs you and Mom." She sobbed. "I'm glad Uncle Scottard is there with you too."

Ash had never heard her sound so caring. Getting off drugs had made a big difference and in such a short time. Dave and Carla's methods must be working, or maybe Lindsay had made the decision to put the drugs behind her.

"Daddy, now that you're president, I'd like to keep the same agents who are here with me now."

She nodded as she listened to his response.

"I . . . love you too." Lindsay handed the phone back to Ash and swiped at her tears.

He took the phone and smiled at her, silently giving his approval, whether it meant anything or not.

The president coughed, sentiment again clear in his voice. "I'll make the call to Wade's wife. She deserves to hear from me that her husband died in the line of duty. Did I hear she gave birth to their second child earlier today?"

"Yes, sir. It was a boy." Ash remembered Wade's excitement . . . and the baby hadn't been named.

"Take care of my Lindsay. I'm sure you heard her request to keep the rest of the team together."

"Yes, sir. I'm assuming you'll want her moved as soon as possible."

"I'm discussing that now with Scottard and Warrington. You'll get a call back in a few minutes."

While he waited, Ash went over the preliminary report

regarding Wade's murder. Anger burned hot again. How many times had he told himself nothing would happen on his watch? In the rocky terrain surrounding the Dancin' Dust, a sniper had fired and gotten away. No sign of him anywhere. Ash had failed, just like he'd done with Joel seven years ago.

Restlessness worked its way through him, and he walked to a back bedroom where Bob was questioning Chip. Ash observed the suspect, who had a habit of being in the wrong place at the wrong time, with no alibi. His face had broken out in red splotches, and his voice shook. Eyebrows raised. Still claimed he didn't know anything about the shooting until Wade fell. Chip wept. Not a sign of someone in bed with killers, but he could be a good actor. The guitar-pickin' statistician was about to face another interrogation when Bob finished. He'd be wearing handcuffs for a long time.

Ash's phone rang, and he snatched it up. Warrington. He walked through the house and outside to the patio.

"We've reached a decision. Lindsay is going to stay at the ranch."

Shock sent his head pounding. "Sir, do you think that's wise?"

"Moving her is exactly what the killer would expect. He made a point to get as close to the ranch as possible and kill one of our own, and then phone the president's office to brag. Ten more agents are on their way. No one working there leaves until this is solved. A plan is in motion."

"I don't trust Chip Leonard. I sent my reservations about him in an e-mail when Lindsay's girth was sliced. I think he set Wade up for a sniper."

A hummingbird lit on a flowering bush. Another bird called in the distance. The Dancin' Dust was not a sanctuary.

"I've made arrangements to have him picked up. Looks like he knows something about what's going on."

"I know the ranch has the latest security, but—"

"Lindsay stays there."

"Would you reconsider? She—"

"Zinders, the decision has been made. I appreciate your persistence, but let those who understand a criminal's mind handle this."

"Yes, sir." He clenched his fist.

*What kind of plan was that? A plan to get Lindsay killed?*

★ ★ ★

Two hours later, Meghan blew her nose and shook off the sorrow tearing at her heart. All agents understood death might be the ultimate price to pay for their protectee's protection. But she'd not processed the extreme nature of her commitment.

A sniper's bullet.

Wade's new baby son.

A widow.

How much worse could it get?

While Dave counseled Lindsay, Meghan needed air. She stepped out into the cooling evening temperatures—to grab control of her emotions and to pray for Wade's family. She glanced at Bob, who had taken Chip outside for questioning. Perhaps a change of scenery would open his mind. Chip had to know more than what he was stating. Too many coincidences. Ash had grilled him earlier, and Chip's story stayed intact. More Secret Service agents were on their way to pick him up. In her opinion, the vehicle couldn't get there fast enough.

Her gaze swept to the far end of the pool. Ash's back was to her, and he seemed to stare out at the pasture dotted with horses and a jeep keeping vigil. He'd known Wade much longer than she had, and he might need to talk. His often-repeated words of "Not on my watch" told her he had much going on in his head.

She walked to his side. His arms were crossed, and his features were stone hard. Although he didn't acknowledge her, she stayed, not sensing animosity.

"How long have you known Wade?"

"Four years. Four good years." No signs of emotion touched his face.

"His family too?"

"I'm his daughter's godfather. Hope I can attend the funeral."

She chose to say nothing. Let him take the lead. Sometimes silence offered more consolation than questions.

He turned to her. "Is this a first for you?"

"I've never lost a fellow agent like this. I'm angry, hurting for his family . . . and feeling responsible in some ridiculous way." She swallowed a mixture of sympathy and regret. "Wade was murdered on the day of his son's birth. He didn't step in front of Lindsay to stop a bullet or try to prevent a kidnapping or anything that makes sense." She wanted to say more, but she'd come to help Ash.

"I understand. A sniper pulled the trigger. Trained killers don't feel. It was a job. Something to collect a paycheck." He blinked, and she quickly averted her gaze. "This isn't the first time I've lost an agent."

"I imagine that makes it feel even worse."

"Surfaces bad memories and deepens resolve."

His nickname of A2Z made sense. "I'm really sorry."

"Thanks. Looks like the rest of us will stay on Lindsay's detail."

"I gathered that from listening to her phone chat with the president."

"And no one receives any time off until further notice."

She'd been fine with the mandate, but the other agents had talked about needing a break.

"After talking to Warrington, other things make me wonder if those in DC are working in Lindsay's best interest."

"In what way?"

"She's staying on the ranch. The consensus is the killer expects her to be moved, and the security is tight here. We'll get ten more agents tomorrow."

Why? She couldn't support DC's thinking. "That does sound strange."

"I'm sure it has to do with keeping the media in the dark about her location . . . and the priority of the security updates already in place. They should be here anytime to take Chip into custody."

"Does he know?"

"Not yet. Ethan will have a tough time with this."

"Can I talk to Chip?"

His whole body turned to her. "Why? Do you think he's innocent?"

"I'd rather approach him as a friend. See if he lets something slip. He did indicate an attraction to me."

"Go ahead. I'd love for him to hang himself."

# CHAPTER 31

MEGHAN CONSIDERED removing Chip's handcuffs, but he was a smart man and would see right through her ruse. Hostility burned in his eyes. Not at all like yesterday evening, when everyone laughed and teased, and he and Lindsay had entertained them.

She smiled, hoping to calm him. "I don't know why you're again suspected of ruining our operation here."

He stiffened. "I was innocent then, and I'm innocent now. Someone has set me up to take the fall, which means whoever is responsible will continue." He leaned forward. "I'm in handcuffs, while someone is planning the next move."

She slid into a chair across from him. "Tell me about your afternoon with Wade. I don't want to believe you're involved, but the evidence is stacked against you."

"Wade and I were friends. It happened so fast. Incredible." He shrugged. "Horrible."

"All it takes is a split second to end a person's life."

"What bothers me is I thought Wade had stumbled. I even teased him about it. What was I thinking? I thought snipers existed overseas, Mexico, or in big city crime, not in rural West Texas." Chip kept his gaze focused on her. He didn't pause in his speech or show any of the other signs of deceit.

"I'm sorry you had to witness it."

"I won't forget it either. Wade was an exceptional guy. New baby and all. Now that little boy will never know his dad. While we were running, he talked about taking him fishing, watching football games together. He laughed about his little girl's antics and was excited about going home in a couple of weeks to see his family. When this is over, I'm going to Ohio. Tell his wife how much he cared for them." He paused, all the while holding her gaze. "A2Z suggested I consult an attorney. Can't do that with these cuffs, and my dad can't get close enough for me to give him a name."

"We're only doing our job. Ash is taking precautions because you look like a person of interest."

"Yeah, but I don't appreciate his tactics. He didn't say one word about Wade. Strictly business." Chip's words rippled with sarcasm. "If that's what it takes to be a part of the Secret Service, then I'm glad I shovel horse manure."

Meghan formed her words carefully. "Do you suspect anyone on this ranch of committing the crimes?"

He shook his head. "If I did, I'd be shouting his name."

"I have another question for you. Did you plant the scorpion in my room, or do you know who did—even as a joke?"

"No, Meghan. At one time I was interested in you. But no more. I don't like being used." He took a breath. "I've been thinking about the scorpion incident. The loose wire above the duct in your bedroom was the only spot in the whole house that was not secure."

"I thought you said the wire was missing, not loose."

"It had been pried on two sides."

"Don't you find that unusual?"

"Which is why I'm bringing it up again. Maybe the contractor forgot to nail it down when the remodeling was done. Maybe I'm being paranoid. Maybe I'm a little scared too. I'm not used to having a friend murdered right beside me. Worse yet, I'm not used to being blamed for crimes I haven't committed."

Chip needed to be long gone from the Dancin' Dust. If he was innocent, then the truth would surface, and he'd be exonerated. Lindsay should be moved too. Keeping her here risked her life—and possibly those who guarded her. How many agents did Warrington have to lose before he realized an investigation needed to be launched internally? Meghan rubbed the chill bumps on her arms. Not sure she could voice the thought of someone within the Secret Service betraying them. Thinking about the downside of her assignment only blocked her from using the skills she'd been taught to keep her protectee safe.

*Get past Wade's death, Meghan. You have a job to do.*

She turned her attention to Chip. Later on tonight, he'd be gone, and Ethan wouldn't handle that well. Chip's account of the loose wire mesh in the attic bothered her. She'd run this past Ash. Better to have him grumble about her mentioning something trite than to find out later that it fit into the bewildering scheme.

"You have fond memories here, or you wouldn't have returned to help your dad."

"I do. Most folks don't understand my love of horses and the outdoors."

"I do a little, but not to your extent. I bet your mom loved to hear you sing and play."

"She did the best she could."

"What do you mean?"

"Mom was deaf. She felt the music through the soles of her feet, and she read lips." He offered a grim smile. "She clapped in perfect time. Even danced with Dad."

Meghan's heart sped. "Did she teach you how to read lips too?"

"She did." He quieted, as though remembering. "I wanted to be a part of her silent world, and reading lips helped me accomplish it. We used to sign back and forth to each other too."

"You must have loved her very much."

"I did. I was one of those kids who didn't rebel, so arguments were few in our household." He took a breath. "When we did disagree, it was a silent argument."

She smiled, but her insides twisted. Chip read lips. She'd seen him looking through binoculars around the ranch. He knew every word the agents said. Had he sold them out?

# CHAPTER 32

MEGHAN STUDIED the tormented look on Ethan's face as Chip was escorted to a Secret Service SUV. Three agents had arrived to transport him for further questioning.

"Dad, I want you to know I have no idea who shot Wade."

Ash opened the vehicle's door and Chip, with his hands cuffed behind his back, slid into the backseat.

"Dad, Mr. Burnette will get this cleared up, and I'll be back in time for church on Wednesday night."

Although Ethan's clenched fists indicated his anger, a tear trickled down his weathered cheek.

Chip's face could have been etched in stone. "I'll take any test they have to prove my innocence. I don't have anything to hide."

"This is not right." Ethan choked back his words. "I want to call Mr. Burnette and get this settled."

Ash closed the door and turned to Ethan. "Sir, we understand your feelings—"

"No, you don't. You have no idea what it's like to see your son hauled away like a criminal. Chip had nothing to do with Wade's murder or slicing that girth. Y'all are looking for a scapegoat. Someone is sabotaging your assignment here, but it isn't my son."

"Ethan—"

"It's Mr. Leonard to you." He watched the vehicle turn around and drive through the front gate.

Meghan saw the agony in the older man's green eyes, an intensity that she'd seen in father and son. Chip might be involved with this, but not Ethan. "I'm sorry," she said.

"I know you didn't have a thing to do with this. You're a good girl, and you saw the goodness in my son."

But she was one of the agents who thought he might be involved. "They need to find out who's responsible for Wade's murder. Then he can come back."

"And that will happen tomorrow. Zinders, I want to make a call."

Ash handed him his personal cell, and Ethan punched in a number. "Don't any of you fancy Secret Service agents leave. I want you to hear this."

Meghan didn't move. Neither did Ash nor Bob.

"Mr. Burnette, this is Ethan Leonard. We have a problem at the Dancin' Dust, and I'd like for you to speak to the president about it. Yes, sir, I can hold." Ethan glared at Ash and Bob. "I'm not surprised at this kind of treatment from A2Z, but Bob, you came across as a good man, just like Wade." He lifted his chin. "Yes, the problem here is Chip's been taken by the Secret Service as a suspect in Wade Enders's murder." Ethan listened, his eyes glistening.

Meghan saw the respect in Ash's face for Ethan, but she wasn't surprised.

"You think having him taken from his home in handcuffs is merely procedure? Harsh treatment, don't you think? My boy has a clean record." Ethan's face reddened. "That's all I ask. If you can speed the process and get him back on the ranch, I'd appreciate it." He snapped the phone shut and drew in a ragged breath. "Mr. Burnette's going to talk to the president about what's been done to Chip."

"I'm sure the Secret Service in conjunction with the White House will expedite matters." Ash stepped toward Ethan. "You and I have had our problems. What I'd like for you to understand is Lindsay's not just here to regain her health. She's been threatened."

Ethan's eyes narrowed. "And you think Chip is part of that too?"

"Sir, it's our job to keep Lindsay safe, and that means dealing with anything and everything suspicious. What would you do if Chip was threatened? Wouldn't you want every precaution taken to ensure his safety?"

*Well said, Ash.* Meghan would have been hard pressed to form such a sympathetic and honest reply.

Ethan shook his head. "This has all gotten too complicated for me. I'd just like for all of you to leave and give me back my son."

"We'd all like that, Mr. Leonard. Hopefully we can oblige you soon. Your home has been disrupted, and a horrible crime's been committed."

Ethan eyed Ash for several moments. "But my son didn't commit it, and Mr. Burnette believes in his innocence too." He walked into the stables.

Meghan turned to Bob and Ash. "Do you think Ethan is a part of a conspiracy?"

Bob rubbed his massive hands. "When I was a kid growing up in New Orleans, I discovered many a father who had no clue what his kids were doing. When the authorities picked them up, the fathers took the word of their kids. Every time." He looked toward the stables. "I'd say Ethan would believe in Chip's innocence no matter what comes out of this. The man lost his wife, and Chip is all he has left. His son is his hope for a legacy. No man wants to consider his own flesh and blood capable of murder."

"I agree with you." Meghan pressed her fingers into her aching neck muscles. Another long day, where thoughts and suspicions had bombarded her mind. She glanced at Ash. "What do you think?"

Ash hesitated, as though pondering her question. "I think until we have the killer in custody, all of us have to assume Chip's involved and Ethan is aware of it. If any of us look away for one second, Lindsay or one of us could be dead. You've heard me say enough about no one going down on my watch. Well, it happened today. No one knows better than I do what that means.

I suspect anyone who looks at me cross-eyed. Wade is the second good friend I've lost, and I have no qualms over how a confession is obtained from Chip, Ethan, or whoever else might have the answers." His narrowed gaze revealed his pain. "Being termed A2Z helps me get the job done. I trust all of you will come to me with anything and everything that might be related to solving Wade's killing and ensuring Lindsay's safety."

★ ★ ★

While Bob and Meghan filled in for Ash and Wade's shift, Ash stayed close to the computer. He anticipated e-mails to arrive for Lindsay, and he hoped the powers in DC changed their minds about not moving her. Caution rode with him. Here on the Dancin' Dust, Lindsay and those who protected her were in danger. Couldn't the president and Scottard see that? And how had Warrington been convinced that the ranch was the best place for her? For the first time, Ash realized how much he cared for Lindsay. He'd lost Wade, and he refused to give up Lindsay or anyone else to an assailant.

The agents swapped tales about Wade until after ten o'clock. Ash listened, adding a comment here and there. His mind continued to spin with memories . . . and why someone had gunned down an agent.

Once the other agents disappeared, he stepped out into the darkness to see Meghan. Ash needed to relieve her so she could get some rest. But he doubted any of them would sleep tonight.

Remembering the last time they were alone in the dark gave him pause, especially in his emotionally spent condition. He refused to take advantage of her grief to ease his own anguish. "Need some company?"

"Sounds good. I have a few things I'd like to discuss." She sounded weary. When she finished what she had to say, he'd insist she take a break.

Beneath the black veil of night, Meghan stared out at the

surroundings through night-vision binoculars. A professional who didn't take her work lightly.

Ash processed her earlier statements about Chip. First the loose wire over the air duct in her bedroom. But he could have lied. What interested Ash was Chip's admittance to reading lips, reinforcing his belief that the guy wasn't on their side. A mole to report their conversations and actions.

Anger sliced through his stomach and burned the back of his throat. "Bob didn't get a thing out of Chip today. He aced every question."

"Strange, since it looks like he's in the middle of the crimes. He could have been well trained, but his past doesn't indicate a military background."

"What about Ethan?" Ash honestly wanted her thoughts. "Do you think he's involved? I know you formed a good relationship with him."

"Actually I doubt it. He's a different breed from Chip—God-and-country sort of guy. Sure would like to know the kind of company Chip kept in Dallas."

"We're on that. Chip could be taking a paycheck that would more than compensate what he left behind in the corporate world. If he's guilty, Warrington will find out."

Meghan lowered her binoculars. "Can we talk about the information we have regarding the happenings here and in DC? I keep thinking we're missing something that's right in front of our noses. I'm sick about Wade, and I'm angry enough to be persistent until the killer is found." Her soft voice gave her a fresh appeal, innocence in an odd sort of way. Ash knew better. Behind those brown eyes smoldered intelligence and calculating skill. Another reason he liked her. Another reason he'd kissed her in the wee hours of the morning. Perhaps she had more insight after successfully working her way into Lindsay's confidence.

Her question to Ash surfaced. "Do you think today is linked to a drug cartel? Because I think it's something on a much bigger scale."

He believed the same, but he wasn't ready to share his thoughts. "I'm listening."

"We've already discussed the possibility of a cartel that had an agenda of mammoth proportions. I've considered organized crime stemming from one of President Hall's opponents or even enemies overseas. But to be honest, my intuition tells me the crimes between DC and the Dancin' Dust are connected, and it will get worse before it gets better. The longer it takes us to find who's responsible, the bolder the actions."

He liked the way her mind worked. Whether he agreed with her theories or not. "What about how thick Chip could be involved?"

"Not sure there. Until tonight, I didn't suspect him of anything. But he pretty much nailed his coffin closed with his admittance to reading lips."

"Tried, convicted, and judged, huh?" Ash studied her.

"He might not have pulled the trigger, but I bet he knows who did. I'm sure of it."

"Or do you want to have it solved so you can sleep better tonight?"

She stiffened. "Maybe. I've never been the type to condemn without evidence, but this is different. As crazy as it sounds, I don't want to think it's Chip . . . for Ethan's sake."

Meghan had taken this personally. Ash recognized the signs. The problem was he felt the same way. "It all goes back to the same questions we've asked ourselves all day. Why would someone hire a sniper to kill an agent assigned to the president's daughter? A daughter who has been trouble for this administration since Hall took office. Could this be about loyalty to Jackson Hall? Is that what the caller meant today?"

"Do you mean someone wants to eliminate Lindsay so the president can accomplish his goals and keep his opponents and the media out of his business?"

"Possibly. I'm sure Lindsay's demise has been on a few politicians' minds."

"Ash, think about it. Lindsay's an embarrassment, not a global problem."

"Some view her position differently. You and I have heard the comments that President Hall can't run the country effectively if he can't control his daughter. Makes me wonder what angle DC is taking in bringing this to a close."

"You could ask Warrington." Again, her soft voice did things to him that he welcomed and shoved away at the same time.

"I'm not in the elite circle." His voice sounded harsher than he intended.

"But you need to be. You're the detail man, and I think you're blaming yourself for the whole situation."

The fact she was right made him angrier. "Since when did you become a shrink?"

"I've been taking lessons from Dave."

His thoughts swung back to Joel's death and his vow to keep those around him safe from sociopaths with their own agenda. "You have no idea the ground you're stepping on."

"Wade's death was not your fault."

Did Meghan know about the counterfeit job, how he hesitated and killed his best friend?

"It's our job to keep our protectee safe. We all know the risks." He threw more anger and frustration into his words.

"Then act like it."

Adrenaline pumped through his veins. "Just what do you mean? Wade and I worked together for four years. Now he's gone, and I have no clue who pulled the trigger."

"Don't you think whoever is orchestrating this will eventually make a few mistakes?" She stuck her finger into his chest. "You're the SAIC, not God. Blaming yourself is not part of the equation. Just do your job. Keep the rest of us agents in line and focus on keeping Lindsay safe."

He clutched her fingers, but she kept her gaze leveled at him. If he could just see her face in the darkness.

"You're good at what you do, Ash. You're levelheaded, and you have the ability to think like the enemy."

"Thanks." He released her fingers. She was defusing him, and he didn't know whether to blow off more steam . . . or kiss her again.

"Still want to punch me?" A smile played into her words.

"Not exactly."

"Are you ready to talk about Wade?"

"I think so." He turned from her. She was good for him in more ways than he could calculate. She was tough when the situation called for it and tender when he needed a woman's touch. He took a deep breath. "One more thing about Chip. Another angle for us to consider. So many things point to him that I wonder if he's really a part of the master plan. However, the obvious could be a ploy to throw us off. In any event, Chip's now in the hands of the Secret Service."

"That's the A2Z I know."

"I'm afraid you know me better than I find comfortable."

She laughed, and the sound filled the night air, easing the sorrow. "Is that so bad?"

"I'm thinking it might be. Time will tell."

"You asked if we could be friends, and I gave a flippant answer. What I want to say is I *am* your friend, Ash. I respect your position and the way you care for Lindsay and the rest of us."

He wanted to draw her into his arms and speak those emotions buried in his heart. But not yet. Maybe not ever.

# CHAPTER 33

LINDSAY COULDN'T BRING HERSELF to eat, drink, take mounds of supplements, or consent to counseling today. Dave wanted her to get some sunshine, but all she could think about was Wade's murder. Alone in her room, she attempted to nap. But her mind continued to spin.

Wade—good and kind Wade with the new baby son—had been murdered. She'd seen pictures of his lovely wife and adorable three-year-old daughter.

The Secret Service had Chip in custody. Could he really be working with the demon? Chip had been sweet, seemed to be interested in her music. But her demon knew how to be convincing. After all, he'd pretended to care for her in the beginning.

If only she weren't clean and sober. Then she could forget the past and what the future held for too many people. What frightened her the most was that the demon had become more evil, as if he'd ever had a shred of integrity. People were dead. A bomb. A threat on Daddy's life, and a possible attempt on her own life. If she could figure out what he really wanted, maybe she could devise a plan to stop him. He hadn't wanted Daddy to be president, so what next?

Not quite two weeks ago, she believed suicide was the solution. But she'd been high then. Now she understood staying alive might be the leverage to stop him—and why he might want her dead too.

He'd have something for her to do soon. As in the past, she'd refuse. Then he'd go into his bargaining mode, then his threatening mode, before she finally gave in. What could he want from her this time?

Lindsay punched her pillow. He could arrange for Daddy's death. She wished she knew what he'd gain if that happened. Politics . . . she'd start paying more attention. Maybe learn to think like him. Tears slipped over her cheeks. He said she wasn't smart, that nothing she could do would stop him. She wanted to believe he'd lied then too.

Lindsay searched deep inside for someone she could trust. Someone who could help bring him to justice. Not just a sympathetic ear. But a person who would believe her story, a drug addict's account of a terrible conspiracy.

*But who?* echoed through the chambers of her heart. If she couldn't find someone to confide in soon, she'd find a way to kill the demon—before he found a way to kill her father.

# CHAPTER 34

ASH STUDIED THE CALENDAR on his computer. Ten days had passed since Chip had been escorted off the ranch. The media hadn't learned about Wade's death, due to his family's agreeing to a private funeral. Lindsay's whereabouts would remain a secret. Another agent was assigned to her protective team, a man by the name of Trey Phillips, a veteran agent. Likable. Didn't say much.

The Dancin' Dust had grown quiet, giving Ash time to analyze Wade's murder and develop a possible link to the threats made on Lindsay. Perhaps he'd spent too much time twisting the facts inside and out, because neither he nor the Secret Service had found any clues to help solve the unsettling crimes. At least no clues were revealed to him. Frustrating. Fearful, as though another crime would erupt at any moment. He expected it. Could feel it in the pit of his stomach.

Meghan entered the room carrying a guitar case.

He shifted his attention her way, his heart taking a nosedive. That situation had worsened too. He was drawn to Meghan like a magnet, rather ironic since they sat at opposite poles. "You got it."

"I did. I'll have to thank Victor for filling in while I drove to town to pick it up."

"Glad you're back safe."

"Ash, you can't follow your team around like an old mother

hen. If a sniper manages to take another one of us out, there's not a thing you can do."

But his feelings went deeper for Meghan, far deeper than he wanted to admit even to himself. "It's my job."

She leaned the guitar against the bookcase. "You're not our daddy."

He chuckled. "I get the message. Should we take this to Lindsay? I'm hoping she'll play for us on the Fourth."

"You had a great idea about purchasing this for her. She's going to be thrilled."

"Hope so. I've never been known as the Santa Claus type."

"So you've turned over a new page in the life of A2Z."

"Hey, watch it. You're only supposed to call me that behind my back."

She smiled. "You're a great SAIC, and I'm honored to be on your team. How's that?"

He knew why there'd been a change in him, but he couldn't let her find out. After all, he'd been the one to spout so many negative things about women agents and his personal code of conduct.

"Are you ready, Santa? Not sure where Lindsay is. I left her watching *The Egg and I*."

"Can you believe her? I ordered more of those old classic movies this morning. This time she requested Cary Grant, Henry Fonda, and John Wayne. Yesterday I mailed back a couple with Spencer Tracy and Katharine Hepburn." He picked up the guitar. "When she's not watching old movies, she's glued to the news. Heard her talking about her father's peace summit."

"I think you're beginning to like her."

"After four years, I guess I should. Honestly, clean and sober, she's great. Good sense of humor. Intelligent. And full of surprises. Yesterday she asked if I could find some books about World War II."

Meghan planted her hands on her hips and grinned.

"What's so funny?" Oh, he liked the way she looked.

"You. What started out as an effort on our part to help Lindsay work through Wade's death has helped all of us."

"Maybe I should go back to my grumpy self."

"I like the friendly, detailed guy."

He could get lost in those brown eyes, but not today. "Let's find Lindsay and deliver her guitar." He paused. "Have you discovered anything in her song lyrics to help us?"

"She refuses to share them, which makes me think something is hidden there."

Ash opened the door. "We'll keep working on securing her confidence. Follow me, Agent Connors. I think our protectee is in the game room."

They found Lindsay absorbed in *Sense and Sensibility*.

At the sight of them, her eyes widened. "What do you have?"

She reminded Ash of a child. Too bad the president couldn't see her fresh and full of life.

"We thought you might like a guitar. Victor did the research on the best country brands. Bob and Rick got you to tell them what models you preferred. Trey knows somebody who knows somebody who owns a guitar store. I ordered it, and Meghan picked it up."

Lindsay bit her lip, and her eyes misted. "Thanks. Oh, thanks so very much."

Ash started to hand it to her, but she reached up and hugged him. "I'm so sorry for all the trouble I've caused. I'm trying. I really am. But some things are impossible to change."

# CHAPTER 35

IN THE EARLY MORNING of the Fourth of July, Meghan jogged into the third mile, always mindful of the sniper who'd killed Wade. Her weapon accomplished nothing when a sniper could be hidden yards from where she ran. As soon as she showered, she wanted to talk to Ash and any of the other agents who'd listen. Something wasn't right.

America's birthday. Meghan loved this holiday—red, white, and blue. The love of friends and family. The smell of grilled hot dogs and hamburgers and mounds of potato salad. Homemade ice cream on a slice of hot apple pie and fireworks that lit a night sky. So why did she sense today could have an unhappy ending? A nagging pain at the base of her skull sent a message to her brain to be on alert.

Her thoughts came in sound bites.

Terrorists from around the world would love to make an impact on the US today.

Homeland Security had been vigilant for weeks.

Those behind Lindsay's threats hadn't been apprehended.

Wade's murderer remained at large.

However, the Dancin' Dust and DC had been quiet since Chip's arrest. He hadn't given the Secret Service any information, and he'd taken a polygraph and passed. The latter meant nothing since there were those who knew how to beat it.

Frustration charged through her body—and a heavy dose of fear.

Fear made her wary.

What was Lindsay hiding?

In the past, she'd kept her intuitions to herself. But history had proved these were God-given warnings, feelings of apprehension that paralleled her faith. She denied belief in the paranormal, but she did hold stock in God's supernatural. Let Ash take her thoughts and do whatever he wished. She owed them to Lindsay and her team.

Heading toward the front entrance to the Dancin' Dust, she waved at the agent posted there and Ash, who toasted her with a huge mug of coffee. Soon she recognized his favorite cup with the words *Coffee, Creative Lighter Fluid* written on the side. As strong as he drank his coffee, she wouldn't light a match near it.

"Good morning, Meghan. Sure glad I run before dawn. I can handle only so much sweat." Ash reached up onto a fence post and handed her an icy bottle of water.

Odd . . . Chip used to have one ready for her when she finished her run. "Perspiration." She managed between breaths. "Women don't sweat."

"Uh, maybe I should take your picture."

She took a long drink. "Very funny." He didn't use to tease. Lately she wondered if he felt some of the same attraction. Lord, have mercy on them if he did. For sure they'd destroy each other—two type A personalities who were in line for the same promotion.

"Can we talk on the way to the house?" The seriousness in his tone propelled her back to her apprehension about today.

"Sure." She glanced toward the stables. Ethan had mentioned last night about wanting to talk to her, but they could chat later on today. "I have something I'd like to run by you too."

They fell into step toward the ranch house. "You go first."

She toyed with how to preface her feelings. "Did Lindsay have a good night?"

"As far as I know."

"Everything all right in DC?"

"Again, as far as I know. What's up?" She sensed him studying her.

"I have a bad feeling about today."

"That's understandable, considering it's the Fourth. Is this a woman's intuition thing?"

*Great.* "As a matter of fact, it is."

"Keep it in reserve. I have a favor."

How dare he discount her.

"Meghan?"

"Yes. What's the favor?"

"The president and First Lady would like to see Lindsay."

"Isn't that Dave's job?"

Ash stopped in the driveway and frowned.

"Oh, I get it. Dave asked her, and she refused. So now the job goes to me."

"You sure are cute when you're mad."

What would he try next? "That might have worked on your kid sister or your girlfriend in college, but not me. Do your own dirty work."

"Lindsay prefers you over any of us."

Meghan met his gaze. "I'm trying to earn her trust so she'll make good choices, not coerce her into doing something she isn't ready to do."

"This is the president's request."

She swallowed her exasperation. "I understand. But Lindsay's fragile."

"Now you sound like Dave."

"In that respect, he's right. Okay. I'll talk to her. But I'm going to preface it with 'I know Dave's already approached you about seeing your parents.'"

They continued in silence.

"You're a stubborn woman."

"Thank you. Would you keep an eye out for anything out of the ordinary?"

He chuckled. "I can do that. How about breakfast on the patio?"

"Sounds like we're at a resort. The other agents might talk."

"They already are."

★ ★ ★

Ash waited on the porch with his third cup of coffee, two slices of crisp bacon, and two pancakes oozing with maple syrup—and no jalapeños. Pepper had bowls of blueberries and strawberries to commemorate the holiday. Normally, pancakes were his favorite breakfast.

But regret filled him for flirting with Meghan. How many agents had seen his irresponsible behavior? The long days with nothing to do but monitor the latest in DC and try to figure out who was behind the crimes had caused him to ramp up his personal Richter scale. He took a gulp of coffee and nearly choked. The Richter scale belonged to the earthquake that had rocked his heart.

"Ash, are you all right?"

Meghan had a habit of showing up at the most inopportune times. But he'd invited her. "Sure."

She slid into a chair with a cup of coffee in one hand and a plate with a pancake topped with strawberries and blueberries in the other.

"Haven't backed out of talking to Lindsay, have you?"

"No." She pointed to his cup. "Does that ever get washed?"

He grinned. "And ruin my flawless reputation?"

She grimaced. "Don't let Dave get hold of it." She took a sip of her own coffee. "I know this is a holiday, and it's business as usual for us, and I can't help but think, or rather hope, the shady happenings with Lindsay are over, but—"

"We're back to the women's intuition thing, and you've got a feeling about today."

"Yes."

"Okay, since you're going to talk to Lindsay about a visit from the president and Alexa, I'll keep my eyes open."

★ ★ ★

Meghan realized she'd hit a brick wall with Lindsay.

"I'm not ready to see Dad or Mom." Lindsay's quiet voice shook with vehemence. "I gave Dave my answer last night, and nothing's changed." She picked up the TV remote and resumed a segment of news.

Meghan reflected on her earlier words to Ash. She was right. Asking Lindsay to agree to a visit from the president and the First Lady invited fireworks of another kind. "I'm only asking to see if you'd thought about it."

"I didn't destroy all my brain cells. I do know how to speak."

"Okay. Topic ended. What do you want to do today?"

Lindsay scowled. "Just like every other day."

"When's the last time you baked chocolate chip cookies?"

Lindsay flashed her an incredulous look. "Never. I was thinking more along the line of a party with plenty of drugs and booze."

"You don't want that." What had brought Lindsay to such lows?

"Maybe you and Dave should shift roles." Lindsay muted the TV. "This morning I'd do anything for a drink or a hit of coke. Sell my soul if that's what it took. My life is a hellhole. Being stuck on this godforsaken dirt ranch. Chained to Secret Service agents. Can't text or talk to my friends. None of that is my idea of living. Daddy should have left me alone."

"Oh, you can commit suicide when you're free to leave here. But then Wade would have died for nothing."

"Aren't you a bit dramatic? Putting his life on the line was his job."

"Aren't you a bit callous?"

"Walk in my shoes."

"Take your pity party somewhere else, Lindsay. You cared about Wade, and you grieved his death like the rest of us."

Lindsay's face paled. She opened her mouth, then closed it. A moment later she resumed the news.

Meghan debated challenging the already-disgruntled young woman. "He's going to eventually get your father. What will it take for you to fight back?"

The news flashed about an airliner from New York to San Francisco having to make a forced landing. Twelve passengers had been hospitalized. Lindsay gasped. *Why did that upset her?*

"Murder is not all he's capable of," Lindsay said.

"Then help us stop him."

"You don't understand," Lindsay whispered. "It's out of my hands."

Pepper walked into the game room. "Excuse me, Meghan, but have you seen Ethan this morning?"

"No. Why?"

"Don't you find it strange that he's not out and about?"

"Ash is in the operation room. Why don't you ask him? He was outside early too."

"I did. He hasn't seen him either. That's not like Ethan. He's always up by four thirty and in the stables pampering the horses."

A shiver raced through Meghan—the premonition from earlier in the day hit her hard.

# CHAPTER 36

ASH KNOCKED ON THE BACK DOOR of Ethan's home. Fresh white paint. He recalled Ethan working on it a few days ago. Said he wanted it looking good when Chip came home.

When Ethan didn't respond after the third knock, Ash called out for him and turned the knob. The door opened.

"Ethan, are you here? We're a little worried about you."

Ash pulled his SIG and wound his way through the living area to a hallway that he remembered led to two bedrooms.

"Ethan?"

Both bedrooms were empty. Beds made. He walked back to the living area and then the kitchen. There, on the floor beside the table, Ethan lay on his side, dressed in his typical light blue shirt and overalls. A huge bruise covered the left side of his face and eye. Chesney sat beside him.

Ash felt the man's neck for a pulse but found nothing. "Ah, Ethan, what happened to you?"

He slipped his cell from his pocket and phoned for an ambulance. Ash hated this. Hated it.

★ ★ ★

Meghan stood beside Bob with Lindsay between them and watched the ambulance leave the front gate of the Dancin' Dust. Her stomach whirled with Ethan's death, the devastation Chip would feel when he received word, and how Lindsay must be feeling.

Bob nodded and stepped away. No doubt he understood Lindsay might need to talk. Meghan swallowed her own grief. Ethan always had a witty comment, even if the recipient didn't want to hear it. Dying alone seemed wrong, but he was now free of pain and in the company of Jesus. In truth, he hadn't been alone when his heart ceased beating.

Chesney trotted over to Lindsay, and she scooped the terrier into her arms. She buried her face in his soft fur. "I'll take care of this little guy. Ethan and Chip loved him."

"That's sweet of you." Meghan patted the dog's head. She cringed. A gnawing feeling refused to back off. Ethan had wanted to talk to her last night, and she'd asked him if it could wait until morning so she could call her mom.

She remembered he'd nibbled at the corner of his mouth. "One more day won't make much difference."

"We can talk now. I can call my mom tomorrow since it's a holiday."

He shook his head. "Listen, Meggie, your mother is far more important than this old man."

"I'll call her right now and come by when I'm finished."

"You know, I'm a little tired. I think I'll turn in early so I can be ready to celebrate the Fourth. Who knows? Maybe the Secret Service will turn Chip loose. I was mad at most of the agents, but I've forgiven them. Don't have much choice."

That was the last time she'd spoken with Ethan. He must have been feeling the forewarning of the heart attack then. What had he wanted to talk about? Probably Chip.

"I liked him." Lindsay's soft voice brought Meghan to where she should be—focused on her protectee.

"Me too. He had a sense of humor and wit that reminded me of my grandfather."

"He always told me I was pretty." She held the dog close.

"When you and I walked through the stables and admired the horses, he'd point out little things about them. As though they were his kids."

"He called me Meggie. Hadn't been called that since I was a kid."

"Chip told me neither of them had family left. But I bet people from all over the county will come to his funeral."

"Probably so. Wade used to take him to town and church. He said everyone there knew Ethan and loved him."

Lindsay smiled and whisked away a tear. "I'm tired of the deaths. I know Ethan's was natural, but it's too soon after Wade. Poor Chip. He must be miserable."

Would this draw out a confession from Chip? "Maybe you could write a song about Ethan."

"I think I will. Might help how awful I feel. Dave and Carla suggested I write a song too. You know, Meghan, the Dancin' Dust is cursed. Sometimes I don't think any of us will ever leave alive."

"Oh yes, we will. The situation's hard right now, but it's only a matter of time."

Lindsay tilted her head. "I don't think I'll ever be able to go back to DC."

"Dave will give you the tools to fight the addictions."

Lindsay turned and stared at the house. "Those who want me out of the picture haven't given up. They're just dragging their feet to scare me."

"Drug dealers are the lowlifes of the earth. They'll be caught."

Lindsay walked toward the house.

Meghan couldn't let her leave without some reassurance. "We're on your side."

Lindsay faced her. "Do you believe in demons?"

What did she mean? "I believe in a power stronger than demons."

"Then you'd better be calling on it."

# CHAPTER 37

ASH GLANCED AT HIS TEAM, Lindsay, Dave, and Carla gathered on the patio, like so many other nights. But tonight there were no sounds of laughter or teasing. Quiet. Ethan's confirmed heart attack had destroyed any thought of celebration. Earlier Meghan volunteered to feed and water the horses until Scottard Burnette replaced Ethan. The ranch could not operate on its own.

Chesney sat at Lindsay's feet, seemingly comfortable with the young woman. She'd attached herself to the terrier, and Ash supposed the dog was both a distraction and a comfort.

Pepper continued to bring out one tempting dish after another, each one with a card that read "spicy" or "weenie," and she had the grill hot for steaks. She took the award for being a trouper, rallying her talents to help them get through the evening.

"Since none of us are in a party mood, we could pay tribute to Ethan." Ash chose honesty. "I'll miss him. He was wise and lived his faith."

Bob cleared his throat. "Ethan was a bigger-than-life kind of guy. I think his passing today salutes who he was and what he stood for. Our country's founders and their principles were ingrained in him. If that's cheesy, then too bad."

"I envied his simple lifestyle." Lindsay's admittance came as a surprise to Ash. The cleaner she got, the more he respected her. "He said he believed in me. Called me Lindy Lou."

"Scottard Burnette called earlier," Ash said. "He's grieving Ethan's death. Plans to be here for the funeral on Thursday. Chip will attend too. The Dancin' Dust will be a busy place."

"I don't imagine I'll be going to the funeral." Lindsay's voice had suddenly taken a cold turn. "No point in sending whoever's after me an invitation."

"I understand. You can visit with Mr. Burnette afterward. He said he was looking forward to seeing you."

Lindsay stiffened. "He can look all he wants. I'll be in my room with the door locked."

★ ★ ★

Thursday at 1300, Meghan stood on the front porch and watched the extended-cab pickup drive through the gate of the Dancin' Dust with Scottard Burnette, Ash, and Victor. The three had attended Ethan's funeral and were returning for lunch.

Pepper had been scurrying about making sure she had Mr. Burnette's favorite shrimp diablo. She'd even persuaded the new ranch hand, Luke Skinner, to help her pick and shuck corn. Luke worked hard with little to say and lived in the area. He'd been employed by Mr. Burnette in the past.

Meghan's attention rested on the helicopter pad. The moment Burnette landed this morning, Lindsay had headed to her room.

"Tell him I'm sick." Her statement seemed skewed with her remarks earlier in the week. Instead of refusing to see him, she voiced an excuse.

One day Meghan intended to find out why Lindsay rejected the love of those who cared for her the most.

Mr. Burnette entered the house and greeted each person, giving Pepper a hug. He turned to Dave and shook his hand. "Is my Lindsay-girl still feeling bad?"

"I'm afraid so, sir."

"Surely she's not so ill that she can't see her Uncle Scottard?"

"Unfortunately, she's in bed, sir. Some days are good, and some are more traumatic. Withdrawals can be devastating, and she's grieving Ethan's death."

Dave was stretching the truth for Lindsay's sake. She must have given him a good reason not to see the press secretary.

"Does she still have hallucinations? The president is deeply concerned about those."

Dave nodded. "They're not as recurring."

Mr. Burnette stared at the staircase. "I think I'll just go on upstairs and knock on her door. If she's awake, I'm sure she'll see me."

Meghan started to protest, but Dave seemed to have the matter under control.

"I doubt it, sir."

Mr. Burnette snapped his attention to Dave. "Why's that?"

The tension could have been cut with a machete.

"She feels that it would be unfair to see you before she has an opportunity to have reconciliation with her parents."

"This is my ranch."

"And the president said I was in charge of her rehabilitation."

*Good going, Dave. Stand up for your principles.*

Mr. Burnette's eyes widened, and he poked his glasses onto his nose. His face reddened. "That's a step in the right direction for Lindsay. Not sure when the last time was that she thought about someone other than herself. So she must be making progress."

"Definitely. The treatment has made great strides."

"I've read your last report to the president, but I had difficulty believing you were getting through to her. Riding horses. Reading. Watching old movies. Taking an interest in news. It's a miracle." He reached out to shake Dave's hand again. "Congratulations. I just wish I'd heard the good news directly from her. More of a celebration instead of Ethan's funeral."

"We all wish that, sir."

"Ethan will be sorely missed. Knew every square inch of this land. I'd like to get Chip back here as soon as possible. He isn't any more involved with the drug dealer out to get Lindsay or the one who murdered Wade than I am. Until I can get Chip back on the Dancin' Dust, Luke will do an excellent job. Ethan introduced him to me a couple of years ago. Still, it's not the same. Never will be." He took a deep breath and smiled at Meghan. "I hope your role has been pleasant."

"It has, sir."

He chuckled. "How many times has she slapped you?"

Meghan didn't find his comment appropriate, but she kept her sentiments to herself. "None, sir." He shook his head. "Maybe I need some of those vitamins and fresh country air. You know, Agent Connors, I asked Ash on the way back from the funeral if he was keeping his hands to himself. Being stuck out here day after day with a pretty woman like you would drive me crazy. The nights here can be long and lonely." He laughed again.

Heat rose up Meghan's neck and face. The Dancin' Dust may be Burnette's ranch, and he might feel relaxed in his own home, but he needed a few manners. Beginning now. Not that she hadn't heard those types of remarks before, but she expected more professionalism from a high government official.

"Excuse me, sir. I need to relieve Bob so he has an opportunity to say hello to you." She forced a smile and walked past him to the stairway. Meghan caught Ash's attention, and he lifted his chin. For a moment, fury swept across his features.

*Thank you, Ash.*

Was Scottard Burnette's rude behavior typical when he wasn't with the president?

"I need to talk to my Pepper. Best cook this side of the Mason-Dixon Line."

As if on cue, she stepped into the living area. "I have lunch ready, but if you'd like to have a word with me first, I'm available."

Burnette walked across the room and embraced her again. "Do you have my favorite peach pudding pie for dessert?"

"I do."

"Shall we break into the liquor cabinet and give Ethan the send-off he deserves?"

Pepper's laughter rang throughout the room. "Sounds like a great idea."

Meghan clenched her jaw to keep from expressing how she felt about Burnette going against the president's orders by consuming alcohol while Lindsay was at the ranch. At least she was upstairs. She glanced at Ash, whose face held the same disgust as her own.

For that matter, Ethan Leonard didn't drink.

# CHAPTER 38

ASH STOOD NEAR THE HELIPAD and waved at Burnette. Once the helicopter took flight, he walked back to the house.

His first mission was to apologize to Meghan. Burnette's derogatory remark about her had angered him while driving back from the funeral, but he never thought the president's press secretary would repeat it. Ash should have said something then. In the past, Burnette had been in the presence of the president, and his impeccable manners were one of the things Ash had admired. Until today.

Pepper lingered with them, her spiked, white hair glistening in the sun. "Wonderful man. I'm proud to be working for him. Plus he likes my cooking."

"I still think he has a cast-iron stomach."

"You're just not a good ol' boy from the South. Now, I have a mess to clean up." She hurried on ahead.

Ash glanced at his watch. He turned his attention to Victor, Rick, and Trey. "I need to talk to Meghan before I meet with you in the operation room. Victor, would you check on the latest in DC? I won't be long."

Once inside, Ash made his way up the stairs. He'd realized something this afternoon that had emotionally toppled him. Not sure if he knew what to do about it, but the awareness, the understanding, scared him. He needed time to think about what this meant to his well-oiled, detailed life and his career.

When he didn't find Meghan outside Lindsay's room, he knocked on the door. "Meghan, this is Ash. Do you have a minute?"

The lock clicked from behind the door. Lindsay had been serious about avoiding Burnette. In Ash's opinion, her absence from lunch was a good thing, considering the patronizing attitude Burnette had toward their protectee—and the alcohol. He and Pepper were the only ones who indulged. The door opened, and the female agent who had upset his world smiled.

"Yes?"

"Can I talk to you for a few minutes?" He saw the hallway was empty. "Out here is fine."

She closed the door behind her and faced him. She'd changed from business dress to jeans and a light green top that looked really great with her red hair. Everything about her looked exceptional.

"I want to apologize for what Burnette said to you."

She pressed her lips—lips he remembered kissing. "It's not the first time a comment like that has been made about a female agent."

"Well, I don't approve."

She tilted her head as though trying to figure him out. "But you don't believe in women agents."

Now how did he get out of this one? "I basically don't. But you're a part of my team, and therein lies the difference. You're a good agent, professional 100 percent."

"Thank you, and I appreciate the apology. Although it wasn't needed."

He swallowed, wishing his feelings would find a comfortable place to light. "I don't think you or Lindsay got any lunch."

"We didn't, and we're both starved."

"The coast is clear, so you'd better grab some food before Pepper puts it all away."

With her head still tilted, she laughed softly. "You know, Ash, you're a decent guy, despite all the stories about you."

"Don't repeat that. I like the tough-guy reputation."

She touched his arm, and Lindsay's bedroom door opened. Meghan whipped back her hand.

"Watch it, you two. I saw that. Want to hear my predictions?"

"Absolutely not," Meghan said. "Hey, Lindsay, let's go get something to eat."

Lindsay giggled, but neither Ash nor Meghan joined in.

Downstairs, Ash entered the operation room, shaking off his response to Meghan's touch. He needed to focus on updating himself with the happenings in DC. He slid into a chair and typed in his password. He turned to Victor.

"Note anything out of the ordinary?"

"Media are questioning how the new president will be able to handle domestic affairs and continue his work with foreign policy, especially with the October Middle East Peace Summit."

"Good question. He was committed to bringing Arab countries and the Western world to the peace table. Any word from the White House?"

"Not yet. But with Burnette here for the funeral, kinda hard to make a statement."

Ash clicked into Lindsay's personal e-mail, a daily habit. Nothing suspicious had been sent to her account for days—that is, nothing he couldn't trace for legitimacy.

But today was different.

> Hey, Lindsay,
>
> I've missed you at the parties, and you're not keeping in touch with your friends. Just in case you've forgotten, I know your location. Did you think I was kidding before? Too bad about the murdered agent. But I wanted you to see that I'm serious. I need to talk to you before something else happens to another one of those prized Secret Service agents assigned to you. You know how to contact me.

Ash studied the message. This one, like the others, didn't have the typical twenties-crowd lingo. An attempt here and there, but the sender probably wasn't her age, or English was a second language. The drug cartel had decided to come out of their hole again. He sent a tracer and waited. Another e-mail came in for her.

Hey, Lindsay,

The Secret Service and all of their buds can look all they want, but they won't find me.

Give in and let's get together. We could have as much fun as in the old days. Glad to hear you're not saddled with Ash, the ass, like in DC. So a woman has taken his spot. She's a looker. Could go for her myself, but I like your body curled up next to mine. When can I see you? You don't need e-mail to get in touch.

Ash noted neither e-mail could be traced. "Looks like our stalker is on the loose again."

Victor frowned. "Another e-mail?"

"Two, and he's getting bolder. Take a look at this. What do you think?" Ash slowly rose to his feet and stared out at the pool while Victor evaluated the message.

The writer said Lindsay didn't need e-mail to contact him. Did she have a phone stashed away? If not, that meant someone at the Dancin' Dust had direct contact with the stalker.

When Ash sent a response, the message came back undeliverable.

# CHAPTER 39

LINDSAY USED THE MANY HOURS of the next week to read, watch her treasured classic movies, horseback ride, walk, and write the songs of her heart. No longer did she worry about someone criticizing her words or the melody, because those around her supported her. Some of the agents did so out of duty, but others like Meghan, Victor, Bob, and Ash were genuine. She could see it in their eyes. Almost like family—the family she'd always wanted.

Cravings for alcohol and cocaine haunted her, but she found the longer she stayed with Dave's treatment plan, the easier it became. She desperately wanted to stay clean, but the demon might have other plans. For certain, the last few years had her dangling from marionette strings.

Just when she felt courageous enough to escape the nightmare, the memories emerged along with the threats. What she knew trapped her more than the four walls that supposedly kept her predators away.

Last night, as she lay in bed, she thought again about the impact of her death and realized that if she were dead, nothing would stop him. But now people were dying as the demon grew more audacious. Lindsay smiled at her word choice. Reading had increased her vocabulary. In fact, she enjoyed learning. Once, her sister, Kelli, told her intelligence was why she often became depressed.

"You think too much." Kelli had spoken those words with a hint of teasing, but Lindsay had seen through it.

The two were walking along a parklike setting at boarding school. Kelli was fifteen and Lindsay was twelve. "What do you mean?"

"You're too smart. I work for my grades, and you never study."

"It's boring. Besides, who cares?"

"If you don't believe Mom and Dad do, which is a lie, then do it for yourself. You could skip a grade with no problem at all."

Lindsay giggled to cover her heartache. "There's no point when no one cares."

"Someday you'll see how wrong you are."

The next Saturday night, Lindsay smoked her first joint. She hungered for anything to replace her parents' lack of love.

"Lindsay, didn't you hear me? I just bought Boardwalk."

Her attention flew to the middle-aged woman with shoulder-length graying hair. "I'd rather play poker. This game lasts forever."

A smile tugged at the corners of Carla's mouth. "What kind of poker?"

"Texas hold 'em."

"You'll lose. I'm the poker queen." Carla reached into her purse and presented a pack of cards.

Lindsay laughed. "You carry a poker deck in your purse?"

Carla wiggled her shoulders. "You betcha. I worked my way through nursing school by playing poker. What are we betting?"

She glanced around the room. "I have no money. Hey, Pepper has a huge bag of flavored jelly beans in the pantry."

"Oh, sweet treats. That would work."

Lindsay feigned shock. "Carla, what would Dave say?"

"We're betting them, not eating them—as far as he's concerned." Her eyes twinkled. Why hadn't Lindsay seen this side of her before?

"You're on. But the popcorn ones are my favorite."

Carla leaned closer. "I like the jalapeño. But don't tell A2Z. He'd kick me off the ranch."

"Our secret."

Lindsay watched Carla, the matron nurse, shuffle the cards like a pro. "You look like a blackjack dealer."

Carla lifted a brow. "I've done that too."

Lindsay scrutinized her with new interest. "What else have you done?"

She continued to shuffle, the riffling sound filling the room. "A cocktail waitress before I danced in a topless bar. Then I learned how to play poker."

Lindsay couldn't stop the laughter. This middle-aged, plump woman had danced topless? "You what?"

"Lindsay, I'm sorry to interrupt your therapeutic session with Carla, but I have a call for you."

She spun to see Meghan, who peered at the deck of cards. "It's Scottard Burnette."

She didn't want to talk to him. Reminders . . . all reminders. "Can you tell him I'm busy?"

"Right. I see the poker cards."

"Busted." Carla's response was funny, despite the sickening feeling in the pit of Lindsay's stomach.

"Please tell him I'm in a counseling session."

Meghan gave him Lindsay's answer. "He says it's important. Has to do with your father."

Lindsay held her breath and reached for the phone. She was tucked away here and not causing any problems. What else did he want? "Hi, Uncle Scottard."

"How's my Lindsay?"

Acid rose in her throat, her familiar response to Burnette's prodding. "Following the rules. Taking my supplements."

"Wonderful. I missed you at Ethan's funeral. Hope you're feeling better."

She cringed. "Depends on the day."

"I'm so proud of you. Your father is anxious to see you, and I told him it would be soon. Right?"

"Yes. Soon."

"I'd like for you to walk outside where Agent Connors cannot hear our conversation."

She obeyed, begging for any deity to stop the whirlwind of terror that this man caused. "I'm on the front porch."

"Walk out into the yard, near the large tree."

Again she did as he bid. "I'm here."

"While I was at the Dancin' Dust, I hid a treat for you."

Lindsay's mouth went dry. "That's not necessary."

"Yes, it is. It's what keeps you alive. It's the candy that helps you cope with your pitiful life. Worthless, too, I may add. You'll find my gift in a locked tack box in the stable. The one labeled with my name. The key is on the peg in the stall of the horse you normally ride."

She pressed her lips to keep from screaming. The nightmare had begun again.

"I have some great news."

Dread inched across her heart and crashed into her senses. She closed her eyes and willed it all to disappear.

"Lindsay, don't you want to hear the news?"

"Not really."

"Your father has appointed me vice president. He doesn't have time to continue his work with foreign policy, and the Middle East Peace Summit in October is top priority for him."

"I'm sure you'll do a wonderful job."

"Oh, do I hear sarcasm? I expect your full support. Of course, my new role requires Congress's approval. But I don't think I have any worries."

*Does Dad have any idea what this appointment could mean?* "I don't imagine I'll be scheduling a Barry Knight interview about your new position."

He chuckled. "That's not on the agenda."

"I intend to stay clean and sober."

"But I have another surprise for you. There's a key to the liquor cabinet just for you. The Dancin' Dust must be driving you crazy."

"I told you I'm finished with drugs and alcohol."

He laughed, and the sound terrified her. "Not as long as you're taking orders from me. The key is in the kitchen, in the back of the silverware drawer."

"Why? You've been nominated as vice president. What else do you want?"

"That's my business."

"Can't you simply stop with your demands?"

"Not yet. I have plans. A little celebration is in order, don't you think? Take care, Lindsay. I hope you understand the weight of the country is on your shoulders."

How could she forget?

# CHAPTER 40

AFTER HER SHIFT on Saturday afternoon, Meghan walked through the stables, missing Ethan and the lightheartedness he'd offered to their remote location. She remembered his teasing, his love, his charm. Luke was a diligent worker but not a conversationalist.

Burnette had indicated Chip would be joining them soon. Now that the former press secretary was vice president, referred to as Copilot, he'd probably get the job done. Both Houses had affirmed his nomination, despite the opposing party's majority in the Senate. Most of the voters rallied behind President Hall, and although he was taking cautious steps, national opinion gave his approval rating in the midsixties. Media were furious, but only the political extremists were listening.

"Mind if I join you?"

Meghan turned to Ash, a smile whipping at the corners of her mouth. Heaven help her, but her heart had plummeted with this man, and if she was reading his body language correctly, he had the same problem. But she'd not mention the situation. After all, he held the title of SAIC.

"Company sounds good. Just missing Ethan."

"Me too. A good man. Warrington just called. Couldn't find a thing to connect Chip to Wade's murder or any of the other crimes of late. He'll be back here in a few days."

"The VP must have gotten his way." Burnette's discourteous remark still stung, and her respect for him had diminished. She considered he'd just buried a friend, and grief asserted itself in sundry ways. But his remarks and behavior were unprofessional.

"Let's hope Chip changes his mind and heads back to Dallas. His presence could be to Lindsay's detriment."

"Is she having a session with Dave?"

Ash nodded. "And not a good one. Heard a few words from her that I haven't been privy to in a long time."

"She's been in a bad mood for a couple of days." Meghan could trace her switch to the day Vice President Burnette called. "Earlier in the week she talked about mending the relationship with her parents."

"Must be tough with the realization she'll never be free of the desire for drugs."

"True. But sometimes God takes away addictions."

"You don't talk much about your faith."

She laughed. "It's not a subject that normally comes up when securing a protectee. However, prayers should be a part of protocol."

"I'm right with you. Makes me wonder what people do without God."

"They're miserable."

Another nuance about A2Z. *Lord, do You know where my heart is leading?*

"I have a question." He glanced about. "Are we alone?"

Surely this wasn't about the two of them. If so, she might run. She rubbed her clammy palms. "Yes. Luke is out riding."

"What I'm about to say is complicated."

Meghan's heart stepped out of her comfort zone. "Are you sure I'm the right person to talk to?"

He stopped to pat a chestnut gelding. "You're not naive, Meghan. You know what I'm about to say . . . or ask."

"The VPPD?" Maybe Warrington had offered him the position.

"Do I have to spell it out? Because you're making this hard for a man who is accustomed to dealing with fact, detail, procedure—not feelings."

"I think I understand." She whispered her response as if someone might hear.

"This requires a simple yes or no. From there, I'll have the information needed to take the next step."

She blinked. Did he analyze everything in his life? If he wanted to discuss a possible relationship, he probably had a spreadsheet in his pocket charting the pros and cons.

"I'd like to tell you why I've had an aversion to women in the Secret Service."

Relief flooded through her. "I've wondered what brought you to that decision."

Perspiration beaded his forehead. The stable was warm, but the intensity on his face topped the thermometer. "Once I've finished with my story, then I'll ask you the yes-or-no question."

Could she please have a break? "I'm listening."

"Since we spoke about faith, what I'm about to say is more of a confession. Something I hope can stay between us."

"Absolutely." *Oh, Ash, just get on with it.*

He swallowed hard, as though he might change his mind. "Seven years ago, while working counterfeit in LA, I was working undercover with two other agents involving drugs and gang warfare."

Bob had mentioned something about an incident seven years ago. *This must be difficult for him . . . more than difficult.*

"One of the agents was my best friend, more like a brother to me. The other agent was a woman. During the deal, things went south. When the gang pulled weapons, the woman agent reached for hers. Fire broke out. My friend lay dead. The woman critically wounded. I was shot too." He took a deep breath. "I blamed Annette. Watched the footage repeatedly. Still do. But the truth of the matter is I hesitated. Joel's death and Annette's permanent paralysis were my fault."

The emotion in his voice made her want to touch him, console him in some way. "You can't blame yourself for what happened to them."

"Oh yes, I can." Bitterness wove through his words. "I vowed that day no one would ever die on my watch again."

Wade. Now she understood why he despised Chip. "Ash, you're wrong. You aren't responsible for your friends' deaths or the woman's injury."

"But here we are bringing Chip back onto the scene."

"I see why you feel this way, except I don't agree with your shouldering the burden."

"It's also why Lindsay's safety is my top priority, and my agents are . . . well, they're very important to me."

"I understand." He had to be A2Z. His life focused on performance. How very sad. "I'm going to pray you find peace with your past. If God doesn't hold the situation against you, then neither should you."

He gave her a grim smile. "I figured you'd say something along those lines. On good days, I can form all the arguments about dealing with it. On bad days, I crucify myself all over again. Anyway, I appreciate your listening."

"Thank you for having the confidence in me to share your story. We all have our closet memories."

"You too?"

"Oh yeah. But not today."

"One hard-luck accounting is enough." His smile faded. "Which brings me to my question."

She wasn't any more ready to hear his next words than when their conversation began, but she'd do her best. Her cell phone rang. She slipped it from her belt and noted the caller ID. Mom. They'd just talked two nights ago. Her head pounded while she forced away a gnawing fear. "Hi, Mom. Everything okay?"

"I'm afraid not." Mom choked on a sob. "Shelley's gone."

"You mean she left the rehab?"

"Yes. Sometime yesterday morning. They called and said she'd signed herself out. The director tried to talk her out of it. Said Shelley was crying, but they couldn't convince her to stay."

Ash must have detected her need for privacy, for he left the stables.

"Mom, let's not think the worst. Has she called? Have you contacted any of her friends?"

"It's too late. The police found her body behind a sleazy hotel. Overdose."

# CHAPTER 41

MEGHAN SNAPPED HER PHONE shut and replaced it on her belt. Her thoughts seemed paralyzed by the devastation, not that she hadn't lived with this possibility for years, but she'd always believed Shelley would one day be able to walk away from the drugs.

A wasted life.

"Bad news?" Ash stood before her. Odd she hadn't seen him walk back inside the stables.

She took a deep breath to steady the sadness threatening to envelop her. "My sister was found dead. Overdose. She left the latest rehab. . . . Police found her body."

"I'm really sorry. No wonder you've taken such a personal interest in Lindsay."

"And another reason why the president wanted me on her protective detail. Looks like another piece of why I'm on this team just slid into place."

"It all makes sense."

"I . . ." She swallowed a sob. "In working with Shelley, I became acquainted with other addicts. I learned how they could manipulate. Saw the desperation when they did whatever it took to get to the next fix. Saw the withdrawal symptoms—" She stopped and walked from the stables, away from the dim light. The tears wanted to flow, but not until she was alone.

"Hey, there's no need to talk about this."

"But I need to. I wanted so much for my sister, just like I do for Lindsay." She took a deep breath. Control. "I need to rent a car and drive to Abilene tomorrow after my shift."

"I'll make the arrangements. Do you want more time to spend with your family?"

"No. I'm okay." She forced herself to look at him. "It's important for me to spend every moment I can with Lindsay. I don't want her to end up the same way."

"I understand. You've done wonders with her. Right now, I'm going to leave you alone. Don't worry about Warrington. I'll take care of the arrangements."

"Thanks." She remembered his question. "You wanted to ask me something."

He waved her off. "Unimportant. We can talk after you get back."

She watched him walk toward the front gate. He still wasn't satisfied with the position of the security camera. His attention to detail may have earned him his A2Z nickname and the bottom rung of a popularity ladder, but in truth he'd saved people's lives.

Keeping Shelley alive had been her goal too. But Meghan had failed. She hadn't been able to convince her sister that fleeing her problems in a state of euphoria didn't make them go away. Meghan touched her mouth to silence the audible grief. Their poor mother. She'd believed Meghan had the means to help Shelley fight the addiction. Every time she got strung out and needed help, Mom contacted Meghan for advice . . . and money . . . and whatever else was needed.

Meghan had let Mom down twice in the past few months.

★ ★ ★

Ash turned to observe Meghan, who had walked to the fence overlooking the pasture. She stared at the grove of trees and the winding creek, but Ash knew her thoughts weren't about nature. He believed she blamed herself, and he knew that feeling. He wanted to comfort her, but he held back. Why? If his heart had found a home in hers, why couldn't he be the support she needed in her time of distress?

So many complications. Caring for Meghan muddied his career, while it also made him feel fresh and alive.

After checking the security camera and assuring himself it was in the proper place, he walked back to the house. Grabbing a can of Diet Coke, he saw Dave had kept Lindsay past their normal counseling time. She no longer shouted like a drunken sailor, so maybe he'd made progress. While he waited, he walked to the operation room, where Victor studied something on his computer.

"Victor, heads up. Meghan's sister was found dead of an overdose."

His eyes widened. "I didn't know she had a sister."

"Neither did I. Anyway, she'll be leaving tomorrow after her shift. Thought you should know."

"Yeah. Thanks." He shook his head. "No wonder she goes over and beyond what's necessary with Lindsay."

"Right. Answers a lot of questions." Ash sat in front of his computer and checked e-mail. Startling news drew him into Warrington's message. "Finally. Listen to this from Warrington: 'We've made an arrest regarding the threats on your protectee. One of the e-mails was traced to a computer in the possession of a twenty-five-year-old illegal from Colombia, Carlos Vargas. He was living in an apartment in Maryland. Found a large stash of cocaine and street drugs. Fifty K in cash. No previous record. Claimed he worked alone. Denies knowing Jorge Ramos. Thought you'd want to know. We'll get to the bottom of this soon.'"

Ash eased back in his chair, relief spreading to his fingertips. Meghan would want to know the new development. Vargas's arrest lifted some of the pressure from all of them. With a little interrogation, the man would tell the Secret Service what they needed to initiate other arrests.

"I've got to head back to my shift in a few minutes. Will you make sure Meghan sees this update?"

"Sure thing. I wonder how many others are working with this guy."

"Hard to say. But this is a beginning." Ash logged on to Lindsay's e-mail, always checking for a lead. Although a man was in custody, habits were hard to break. A message popped up. Ash scanned it and pounded his fist on the table. *Why can't these guys leave her alone?*

Victor glanced up. "What's up?"

"Here's another message to Lindsay. 'Guess you heard an arrest was made. Bet the Secret Service thinks you're tucked away safe, and we'll never find you. Wrong, little lady. Your instructions will come soon, and in the meantime, you'll learn we mean business. When I tell you I want to meet with you, I'm serious. There's a bar about eight miles from the Dancin' Dust. What do you say?'"

"Whoa." Victor scooted back his chair.

"My thoughts too. Alert the rest of the team. I don't like the sound of this one."

# CHAPTER 42

ASH THANKED VICTOR for volunteering to take his shift so he could monitor any updates from DC. But as the evening edged toward sundown, the likelihood of Vargas's offering information decreased. Again the latest e-mail couldn't be traced.

Ash found Meghan alone in the living area. So sad. He captured her gaze. "It's been a long day for you."

Her shoulders lifted and fell. "If you don't need me, I'd like to take a walk."

"Do you want some company? Victor told me to get lost for another hour, and I have my phone if Warrington calls. I can listen to whatever you have to say." He paused. "You did it for me."

Meghan nodded. "I'd like that. The area on the other side of the creek near the grove of live oaks is pleasant. Serene. And this time of day it's cooler there." She offered a sad smile. "I'll take a flashlight in case the sun sets before we get back."

He grinned. "Deal." And if she needed a shoulder to cry on, he could do that, too.

After Ash informed Bob and Trey the two of them would be away from the house for a while, they walked beyond the barn into the pasture toward the creek.

"Burnette has a good eye for horses." She motioned toward three horses near the fence. "We had a couple of good quarter horses when we were kids, but not like these. I loved ranch life, the freedom, fresh air, and quiet. The Dancin' Dust reminds me of home. And of Shelley."

"You and your sister spent a lot of time together?"

"We did. Dad believed horses kept us out of trouble. Worked for me." Meghan stared out over the pasture. "Shelley was my foster sister. My parents tried to adopt her, but her mother showed up enough times to keep Shelley stuck in the legal system, as though spending a few hours with Shelley made her a mother. That's why she's not listed in my file."

"I heard you tell Bob your parents kept foster children over the years."

"It was an important part of our life—a way for Dad and Mom to share our faith."

"Wasn't it hard to say good-bye when they left?"

"Painfully so."

"Can't imagine anything worse than becoming attached to someone, then losing them."

"Losing my dad was worse."

Ash wanted her to tell the story. He knew the man had been shot. Let her voice all the things tearing at her heart.

"I know my records state a drunk killed him. Dad tried to stop a friend from driving drunk, and he pulled a gun. That was my dad. Always wanting to help."

"Like you."

She stuffed her hands into her jeans pockets. "Oh, I can be pretty selfish."

"Don't think so. Your record shows your sacrifices, and I've seen all you've given to Lindsay and the team since you've been here."

"Thanks, considering—"

"How I felt about having you on my team?"

She laughed lightly. "Ah, exactly."

Meghan had changed the way he looked at life . . . and his future. "So how did your sister handle your father's death?"

"Dad was her hero, and his death hit her harder than Mom or

I realized. She withdrew into an emotional cave. Counseling didn't help. We both had our moments of rebellion. Not sure what to do without Dad. She turned to drinking. Then to pot. Her senior year she straightened up and made plans to attend Texas A&M, where I'd already completed three years. Shelley wanted to be a psychologist. Said she needed to help kids like her who'd been knocked hard by abandonment issues. Then she got mixed up with the wrong crowd, and the problems started again. She didn't make it past her sophomore year. We tried one rehab after another. I actually thought she was making progress this time." Silence hung between them. "There were times I gave up. Told her so. This last time, I told her I was finished. The bank of Meghan had officially closed. She had to fight the battle. So, now you've heard my closet confession."

He understood what stalked her. Ash turned to a bird with gray feathers, its sound not matching its looks.

"That's a mockingbird." She watched it rise into the evening sky. "Sort of like how I feel. Anyway, Shelley was gorgeous. At least she used to be before the drugs took over."

"Like Lindsay?"

"So much like Lindsay that at times I want to shake some sense into her. To me, keeping our protectee safe also means keeping her healthy." She glanced at him. "I believe in my job, Ash. Every aspect of it."

"It shows," he whispered. "Between you and Dave, Lindsay is making strides to build a new life." They continued walking, and he didn't care if they walked until midnight. "Were you able to keep in contact with Shelley?"

"Every chance I got. Mom and I paid for rehabs and counseling. But she didn't really want to get clean. To Shelley, her life held no meaning. She and Dad were extremely close. He encouraged her to go on to school and seek out God's purpose for her life. After his death, the only thing that mattered to Shelley was escaping into drugs. This last rehab was her idea. She came to me and pleaded for help. Said she was ready to leave it all behind and make sure when she saw Dad again that he'd be proud. We believed her, especially when she went to church with Mom."

"How's your mom doing?"

"I talked to her again a few minutes ago. The funeral is Tuesday. She's okay. Told me not to give up on our protectee. She doesn't know the extent of her issues, just what she's heard from the media."

"Do you mind discussing Lindsay?" Ash had deliberated her circumstances since he was assigned to her. He'd never found the answers, but he wanted them.

"Not at all. If you haven't figured it out by now, I'm invested in her. More now than before."

"Do you think she wants to change?"

"Most of the time, I think she does. But as I've said before, a fear stronger than an overdose is twisting inside her. Although she is responding to Dave and we see a huge improvement, I'm concerned it's for the wrong reasons. Cooperation means she gets to go home. On the other hand, is the source of her nightmares in DC? If so, going home is a setup for suicide."

"You've claimed she's afraid. Explain that to me."

"The way she leans so close to the truth, then backs off. I'm convinced she's covering something so deep that she can't get out. But I need proof. I wish she'd understand we want the best for her, not simply to babysit her until she has the freedom to resume her old lifestyle."

"So you think the music, the reading, and the other interests are a cover-up?"

"I think they're diversions. Here she has the opportunity to explore interests that she hasn't time for in DC." Meghan lifted her chin. "I think this is less about who was selling her drugs and more about something far worse. The bombing pointed in that direction, Wade's death, the e-mails. Even the scorpion on my pillow."

Ash thought she stretched her last comment. "Are you serious? Scorpions are a part of the habitat here."

"Then why was the wire mesh removed from the air duct in my room and the others were intact? Think about it—I'm the only female agent, and President Hall asked me to help his daughter find purpose in her life. And I bet I'm the only agent highly allergic to bee stings."

Irritation hammered against his head. "I trust all the agents on my team."

"But, Ash, whoever is causing the problems has our trust."

He shook his head. "Chip? Ethan's dead."

"I have no one to pinpoint, only the inkling that the answer is closer to us than we could ever imagine."

Was this about a woman's intuition again? "I can't go along with your supposition. Everything points to drugs and Lindsay's history."

"Even Wade's death?"

They stopped beneath a live oak. In the distance, the fiery sun played its last tribute to the day. He took a deep breath. "My suspicions run on logic. I've run backgrounds on every agent here, looking for a hole. We have cutting-edge software, and still we can't trace every e-mail or find out who's behind it."

"My mind has worked through a dozen scenarios. And I have an idea."

Ash studied her. "Your sister's been found dead, and your mind is working on finding who's responsible for all the chaos here and in DC?"

"I have to. If I dwell on Shelley, I'll fall apart." She swiped at a tear. "The best way I can pay tribute to my sister is to help Lindsay find her way back. I know we're protectors, not crime solvers, but I believe part of the problem is here."

"All right. What's your idea?"

"Think about what I'm proposing while I'm gone. This last e-mail was hostile. But what he wanted was for Lindsay to meet him at a local bar. My guess, it's a dive where only good ol' boys and their girlfriends hang out. I'm Lindsay's size, and we have similar features. I want a wig, blue contacts, and a set of clothes. Let me play the part and beat this jerk at his own game."

She was nuts if she thought he'd agree. "No way would I permit that. It's too dangerous."

"I can handle myself. But I wouldn't want anyone else to know what I was doing."

"Are you sure you're not simply reacting to Shelley's death?"

"I'm motivated by what's happened. But I've been thinking about a way to draw them into the open for a long time."

He grasped the challenge in her voice. "Meghan, I—"

"Please, think about it."

But he wouldn't. The idea of risking her life in a foolhardy effort to pose as Lindsay sickened him.

# CHAPTER 43

IN THE EARLY HOURS of Tuesday morning, Ash realized how much he missed Meghan. The ranch was quiet. Nothing new in DC, and no more e-mails to Lindsay. So he waited and wondered.

Waited for DC to find the stalker.

Waited for DC to find who'd bombed Lindsay's car and killed one person and hurt another.

Waited for DC to find the sniper who'd murdered Wade.

Waited for Meghan to return to the ranch.

Wondered when President Hall would make a decision about who would be on his PPD.

Wondered if the goal of his career was really worth being in competition with Meghan.

Wondered if someone he trusted had betrayed them into the hands of an unseen enemy.

And although he'd taken a double shift to cover for Meghan since she'd left and he should be sleeping, his mind refused to cease whirling with thoughts about everything in his life.

At 0400, Ash tore back the sheet and walked to the window in his room. He'd never have peace, and he'd surely never have a life with Meghan until his world stopped crashing in on him. He'd almost asked her if they could work at a relationship, but the news about her sister's death took a lead. Reality held him captive. As long as he kept the past locked away, the two of them were doomed.

Glancing at his laptop on the dresser, he shook his head. This time he had no intention of watching the footage of Joel's death. He was finished with the guilt and shame of blaming Annette for his own failure to perform. He had an appointment with destiny—and as dramatic as it sounded, that was exactly how he felt.

He remembered Ethan talking about Chip one day having a come-to-Jesus meeting. At the time, it sounded ridiculous. Now it made sense.

Ash needed to either face the past and deal with it or give up and stay in his miserable shell. In a way, he reminded himself of Lindsay, cowering under fear.

"All right, God," he whispered. "Bring it on."

He shivered in the shadows, wishing his utterances hadn't made it all so real. The competitive part of him sought to challenge God. Losing Joel was unfair, so he took on the role of A2Z and thrived on what it meant to be detail oriented. But it hadn't cured the sleepless nights and the way he kept people at a distance.

Ash couldn't control his destiny any more than any other poor human being on the face of the planet. Should he pick up his Bible and read until his eyes blurred and he wept like a child? Granted, humility had never been his trademark.

Did he need to simply sit in the dark and wait for an audible voice to tell him he was forgiven?

Breathing in deeply, he recalled something his grandmother used to say: "To be forgiven, one must forgive."

If he wanted true release from what happened to Joel and Annette, then he had to forgive himself. He could almost hear the swish of the revolving door that had kept him in the cycle for too long.

The memories would always be with him, but they didn't have to rule him.

At 0600, he picked up his phone and called Annette Hamilton. On the third ring, her husband answered.

"Tim, this is Ash Zinders. I apologize for the early hour, but I'd like to speak to Annette."

"Can't it wait until a civilized hour?"

Tim Hamilton despised Ash, and he had good reason. Perhaps the call was too selfish. He'd let Tim set the stage. "It's important, or I wouldn't be bothering you."

"All right."

A few moments later, Annette answered. "This had better be good, Ash. You aren't one of my favorite people."

"I had that coming. Look, Annette, call it soul-searching or a need to clear my conscience, but I want to ask your forgiveness for what happened in LA. I blamed you when I was the one who got you shot and Joel killed. I hesitated. My fault."

"What?" He heard the incredulous tone in her groggy voice.

"I'm asking if you will forgive me for blaming you."

"You're asking a lot, considering I took the heat, and now my life is spent in a wheelchair."

"You're right."

"Have you gotten religion?"

"Guess so."

"You sorry—" She swore. "I'm not making it easy on your conscience. Go light a dozen candles or see a priest." Annette hung up.

Ash snapped the phone closed. Odd, her words had not stung his soul. He'd done his part. That's all he could do.

And the peace filling him felt good. Real good.

★ ★ ★

Meghan stood at Shelley's graveside, her arm wrapped around Mom's waist. Only a few flowers remained, the special sunflowers Shelley treasured. The other plants and arrangements were to be delivered to the elderly in their church. Shelley would have wanted it that way. She loved the older generation, and when she was sober, she volunteered at nursing homes.

Mom trembled, sorrow wracking her body. Those who had attended the graveside service were gone or had already driven to the luncheon at church.

"How often have we spoken about this very thing?" Mom reached for another tissue in her purse.

"Many times. We thought we were prepared, didn't we?" Meghan kissed her mother's cheek.

"Shelley didn't have the strength to fight the addiction. She needed your father."

They all missed him, but Meghan didn't feel talking about him would help her mother work through Shelley's death.

"Oh, sweetheart, how cruel of me." She leaned her head on Meghan's shoulder. "You tried so hard."

"We both did. I wish I could have talked to her before she left the rehab. Maybe I could have gotten her to continue with the program."

"Don't do that to yourself. The what-ifs will eat you alive. What I don't understand is that the last conversation Shelley and I had was positive. She thanked me for not deserting her. She wanted to talk to you personally and thank you too."

Shelley often made claims, but she simply didn't have the strength to follow through. "We'll never know, Mom."

"But I felt so encouraged after our conversation."

Meghan remembered Dad's death and Mom's regrets of not always supporting him in his work to help others. "Let's go on to church and get through this day."

Mom nodded and blew her nose. They walked toward Meghan's car. "Tell me about Lindsay Hall. Is she doing better?"

She could only say so much about her protectee. "She's doing very well. Honestly she's a talented young woman. Intelligent, too."

"I'm glad, but I wondered about all the nasty things the news say about her."

"I can't tell you about my work, since she's the president's daughter."

"But I'm your mother, and what you tell me doesn't go anywhere. I pray for her every day . . . just like I did our Shelley."

"And like our Shelley, Lindsay must make the proper choices if she's going to have a fulfilling life. I know she can. I encourage her at every opportune moment."

"Unhappiness leads to coping mechanisms that have the potential to kill us."

"You're so right. Keep praying for her. I'm not sure how long she will be at the current location, and I'm afraid what will happen when she regains her freedom."

"I understand. She has a piece of your heart."

"She does." Meghan opened the car door for her mother, then took one more fleeting look at the grave. Once she seated herself and started the engine, she felt Mom studying her. "What are you thinking? Something I need to know about Shelley?"

"My concern is you. Are you doing okay with the cancelled engagement?"

"I am." She thought of Ash and how he'd come to mean more to her in a short time than the man she'd once agreed to marry.

"It must be lonely working with a team of men."

"We're all friends, and we get along fine." She'd like to tell Mom about Wade's death, Lindsay's stalker, and her suspicions about someone at the ranch betraying them, but that was classified information.

"What are you not telling me?"

Meghan smiled and drove toward the church. She doubted if either of them felt like eating. "Why do you think I'm keeping something from you?"

"You're my daughter. I know you."

She could reveal a little of the turmoil keeping her awake at night. "Remember the time Dad went to the pound and brought home the dog that didn't like women?"

"Chuckie? How could I forget? You girls wanted to make friends, and he snapped at you every chance he got. Me too."

"Remember how Shelley gave up, but I kept trying to find ways to befriend him?"

"Oh yes. I begged your dad to get rid of the dog, especially after he bit you twice."

"But I eventually won him over."

"Tenacity is one of your strengths."

"I just wondered if you remembered."

Mom touched her arm. "Oh, Meghan, do you have a Chuckie?"

Tears filled her eyes. "I'm afraid so."

"Is he an agent?"

Meghan nodded. "Don't say a word. I know I said I'd never consider another agent because we'd destroy each other with our commitment to our careers."

"Maybe you should have told that to your heart."

# CHAPTER 44

TUESDAY AFTERNOON, while Lindsay watched a movie, Ash read the headlines on his BlackBerry. He inwardly moaned.

*President Hall and Vice President Burnette Clash over Foreign Policy.*

Ash fumed. The Shield had worked hard to organize the Middle East Peace Summit. His plans had the potential to put the United States back into the forefront as a world power who orchestrated peace with Arab countries. Ash had heard the rumblings about the president and vice president hotly debating the peace summit and current foreign policy. According to the news release, Vice President Burnette refused to take the president's place at the peace talks. The article continued with news claiming Vice President Burnette had met with Speaker of the House Randolph in an effort to cancel the peace summit's agenda. At this point, the president and the vice president were taking three days at Camp David to settle their differences.

President Hall had to be questioning his choice of VP, even if the two men were lifelong friends. Didn't the president know how Burnette felt about crucial issues before he nominated him? Political allies didn't conceal their views, unless another agenda was in place. Of course, if they didn't come to an agreement, the president might yank his daughter off the Dancin' Dust.

Ash weighed the two men's personalities. Until recently, Burnette seemed content in the background. But since attaining his VP status, he'd become vocal about the current administration, and he'd been seen with Speaker of the House Randolph, who strongly opposed many of President Hall's foreign and domestic policies. The *New York Times* claimed Randolph planned to toss his hat into the ring for the presidential election. If that were true, where would that place Burnette?

The muddy political waters seemed to dredge up opposition against President Hall on a daily basis. The more he worked at unifying the country, the more the media criticized him.

Ash's radio buzzed. "We have four TV networks at the front gate. Looks like the sharks have arrived. An RV for each alphabet station."

"Let 'em get a taste of dirt in this heat. They won't get near Lindsay."

★ ★ ★

By the time Meghan arrived at the gate of the Dancin' Dust on Tuesday night, the area was lit up like a camp revival. So the media had found Lindsay. Who'd leaked the information? Since the ranch belonged to the vice president, that may have been a logical place to search. For nearly five weeks, Lindsay had been tucked away without anyone taking notice. Now, not only were the media leeches looking for a pic or an interview, but the ones who'd been stalking her were alert. Meghan scanned the crowd, searching for signs of someone who might have a bullet with Lindsay's name on it.

As Meghan pulled up to the gate, reporters pushed their way toward her car like flies on cow patties. She ignored the heckles and questions and lowered her window for the agent who manned the gate.

"When did the uninvited guests arrive?"

"This afternoon."

"If I'd known we were having a party, I'd have brought sweet tea."

His grin spread from one cheekbone to the other. "I hear the temps will be around 105 tomorrow. That should be interesting, especially from those who're used to air-conditioned offices."

The agent's remark sounded like something Ash would say. She'd missed him, and after the chat with her mother earlier today, she'd allowed her feelings to sink into her heart. He'd changed so much in his attitude toward her, but a softening and an appreciation for women agents didn't mean their relationship would work. The fear of searing her heart again made her wary.

Ash Zinders, A2Z, the most unlikely man she could ever fall for. Stubborn. Opinionated. A stickler for detail. But that was only the surface. Beneath his rule-book facade was a man capable of great compassion. After he'd confessed his guilt in the death of his friend and how he'd blamed a female agent, his gruffness and prejudice made sense. She hoped someday he was able to deal with the truth.

What had he wanted to ask her? The last time they were together, she sensed he wanted to talk about the two of them. The thought had petrified her. But not now. Logic told her the assignment on the Dancin' Dust needed to be completed before either of them considered the future.

Meghan parked the rental, pulled out her small carry-on, and walked to the back porch. Ash sat on a rocker, his rugged features illuminated by the porch light.

"Are you waiting for me?" She poured lightness into her voice. No doubt he was fuming over the reporters at the front gate.

"Maybe. Not exactly. But it's good to see you." He joined her at the bottom step, then lifted her carry-on to the porch. "Want to sit and talk for a few minutes?"

Unusual request. "Sure. I saw the party. Do you have any idea who tipped them off?"

"I've speculated on that since they showed up. Maybe Chip found a way to alert the media before he was returned. Or the reporters got smart, considering the ranch is owned by the VP. Anyway, Bob's filling in for me until I get a call."

While the creak of the rockers matched the mood of the southern skies, she also heard the weariness in his voice. "What else is going on?"

"Another untraceable e-mail."

She'd hoped Vargas had been behind all the calls or could have told the SS who was paying him off. "Every time they find one player, another turns up."

"Looks that way. Hey, I'm unloading on you after a funeral. How's your mother?"

"Okay. Mom's tough. She has a strong support system through her church. They won't abandon her."

"What about you?"

She smiled. "I'm all right. Guess I'm more determined to help Lindsay."

"I figured so. She's been asking for you."

"I've been wondering about her. Has she been behaving herself with reporters ready to snap her picture?"

"Oddly enough, she's been withdrawn." He cleared his throat. "I wanted to tell you something. Especially since you heard my . . . confession. So I was waiting for you."

She studied his face—the face she'd longed to see since leaving her mother. "I'm listening."

"I took care of things. Even called Annette and apologized."

The stress of the funeral and Ash's news caused her to swallow hard. "Wonderful. How do you feel?"

"Relieved." He chuckled. "Do you suppose Warrington will believe I've eased up on my attitude toward women agents?"

"Probably not."

He sobered, and she wondered what else was on his mind. "The days were lonely while you were gone."

Meghan's heart did a flip. Had she heard correctly? "That's sweet of you."

He leaned closer. "I don't have a sweet bone in me. But I can try to be a decent guy."

"The other agents will appreciate the change." She gripped the sides of the rocker. "Is this a confession or a promise?"

"How about both? And I'm referring to you." His whisper blended with the insects' chorus.

"Ash, do you know what you're saying?"

He stiffened. Maybe she had heard wrong. Her emotions had been worn thin today.

"I do. Been thinking about it since you left." He caught her gaze and refused to let go. "Some things about me—my analytical nature, my concern for those on my team, Lindsay—won't ever change. It's who I am. I'm dripping in responsibility and perfectionism. Can you handle that?"

What could she say? With the critical issues surrounding this assignment, the threats to Lindsay's life, and her struggle with drugs and alcohol, how could they discuss a relationship? Meghan wanted to see if she and Ash had a chance for happiness, but she feared it just the same. "Have you thought about how we might kill each other? I mean we're both so stubborn, independent, competitive . . ."

He touched her arm. "I like the challenge."

"What about your rule book?"

"I rewrote a few paragraphs."

She attempted to slow her pulse, while everything about her was conscious of his hand on her tingling flesh. "What about the promotion?"

"The Shield will choose the agent best suited for the job."

She leaned back against the rocker and stared out into the dark pasture—black except for agents guarding the ranch. "I wish I had night goggles."

"Why?"

"So I could see where this is going."

"Impossible. But we can take it slow. See if it works. Pray about it."

He was saying all the right things. She didn't want to think their remote location might be why he'd approached her. Her feelings were deep, and they'd be the same if their assignment were in the middle of DC.

"Meghan—" he cupped her chin and turned her face to his gaze—"don't you think I've turned this situation inside out? The joke's on me. A2Z is admitting he needs a woman in his life. Can you give me a chance?"

She wanted to. A lump rose in her throat. Now was not the time to cry. She felt vulnerable enough without adding tears to the mix. She needed time to think about Ash's words. Today had been filled with too much emotion for her to make a logical decision.

The door slammed behind her, and her attention flew to whoever had caught them . . . talking.

"Hey, Victor." Ash's hand slipped from her chin, and he scooted back into his chair.

"Hi, Victor." Meghan wanted to wipe the smirk off his cute little face.

"Thought I'd get some fresh air. But I see I'm interrupting. Must be a serious development." Victor grinned at Meghan. "Pepper said you were back. Thought I'd check for myself."

"I am." She stood. "Guess I'll put my things away and say hi to Lindsay."

"Don't let me break up a cozy conversation."

"Very funny." Ash's dry tone didn't miss Meghan.

How many years had it been since she'd sensed heat flooding her neck and face?

"Must be hotter out here than I thought." Victor shrugged. "Both of you are red-faced."

"No one's laughing." Ash's tone lowered.

"You're right. Looks like I need to step back inside."

Meghan reached for her carry-on. "And to think I missed you, Victor."

He laughed, but she refused to linger and fall prey to another of his comments.

"Seriously, I'm sorry about your sister." Victor opened the door. "Good to have you back. Lindsay's watching one of her classic movies, but I don't think she's paying attention. About an hour ago, she had a good cry. Dave couldn't get a thing out of her."

"I'll check on her now."

Meghan's mind and heart seemed to be filled with more than she could handle.

# CHAPTER 45

MEGHAN EASED ONTO THE SOFA beside Lindsay. "What are we watching tonight?"

"*Adam's Rib*, Katharine Hepburn and Spencer Tracy." She didn't make eye contact with Meghan. "It's one of my favorites."

"You say that about every Hepburn and Tracy film."

Lindsay turned to her and smiled. "I guess I do. I've never seen so many movies in my life. But it helps pass the hours." Her shoulders slumped, and she paused the movie. "I'm sorry about your sister. Didn't know about her death until you left."

"Thank you. How have you been?"

"Sad. Worried."

"Can I help?"

Lindsay sighed. "I sound selfish after what you've just gone through. Dave's tried. So did Carla. But my problems go far deeper than any of you could reach."

"Have you tried God?"

"I'm sorry. The God thing isn't for me."

Meghan tossed around what she could say at this point. Shelley had resented mentions of faith too. "I've been praying for you."

"Now it's my turn to thank you. What's . . . what's going to change now that the media have found us?"

"I have no idea."

"Do you know anything more about my dad's meeting at Camp David with Uncle Scottard?"

"I'm blank there, too."

"I heard the Middle East Peace Summit may be postponed until January. But I never believe what I hear on the news."

Smart girl. "Once I learn something, I'll let you know."

"I missed you." Lindsay resumed the movie. Her face looked like a mask of emotional battle scars. And her response to the president and VP's disagreement was natural. Perhaps Lindsay simply needed more time to fight the dark cloud of depression. She'd been clean for over five weeks, and they'd all be at the Dancin' Dust for at least five more. Lots of hours for Lindsay to work through the problems tormenting her life.

If only Shelley had stayed at the rehab . . .

Today had been difficult. Memories of Shelley and all the efforts made to help her shake the drugs had stalked Meghan all the way back from Abilene. Seeing Lindsay struggle for coping skills with similar issues was tough. Then Ash's request.

Her cell phone rang. No ID registered. Probably a wrong number, but she answered it anyway.

"Shelley's death was no accident," a man's muffled voice said.

Meghan sensed the blood draining from her face. "What do you mean?"

"Lindsay is poison to all of you."

The call disconnected.

★ ★ ★

Still sitting on the back porch, Ash analyzed every word he'd spoken to Meghan, regretting Victor's interruption before he could get an answer. His cell rang, and he noted it was Warrington.

"We don't know who tipped off the media about your protectee's location, but we think it was simply by deduction."

"I figured that. Only a matter of time."

"Any problems?"

"Not any more than expected. The agents have the situation in hand."

"The president doesn't want to move her. He still feels the ranch is the safest place to keep her from the drug dealers."

"And what about Carlos Vargas?"

"Nothing at this point. His boss is our concern."

"Unless he is the boss."

"Doubt it. Not smart enough."

Why couldn't Warrington tell him what was really going on? "I understand this is all about power and how much damage the drug cartel can do to the president. But what else can you tell me?"

"Not yet, Ash. Another item on my list is the vice president has requested Victor and Bob for his protective team. However, the president wants them to remain on their current assignment until Lindsay's stalkers are found and she's healthy enough to return to DC.

"One more thing: per instructions of the president, Chip Leonard will be escorted to the Dancin' Dust in the morning. He's clean, and I'm sending you the report. The VP needs him running the ranch. Luke Skinner will continue on a part-time basis, Monday through Friday, 0800 to 1500, driving in and out as before."

"Yes, sir."

"Just do your job."

He replaced his phone as Meghan stepped onto the porch. Her pale face instantly alarmed him. "What's wrong?"

"Just got a call. A muffled voice told me Shelley's death was no accident. Said Lindsay was poison to all of us." She leaned against the door. "He hung up before I could ask any questions."

A hoax? Ash couldn't discard it. "I'll get somebody on it right away."

"Really? I think the problem's right here. Who else knew about Shelley?"

# CHAPTER 46

FRIDAY MORNING, Lindsay watched Chip train a colt to lead in the corral. With the colt against the fence, he snapped a rope onto the left strap of the halter and urged the animal to walk alongside him. Now and then she heard Chip softly praise the animal. A lot of parents could do well by watching him.

Meghan stood beside her, offering little conversation. Lindsay appreciated the way the agent seemed to sense when she was deep into her own thoughts and didn't try to invade her privacy.

Lindsay waved at Chip. "Good morning."

He ignored her. This was his third day back on the Dancin' Dust, and they'd yet to talk. He was angry, and she supposed he had every right to avoid her. He'd been accused of being an accomplice to murder, and his father had died of a heart attack. Given the same circumstances, she'd be high and staying high.

Ever since Burnette had told her about the drugs in his tack box and the key to the liquor cabinet, she'd been determined to stay away from the stables. Despite the terror of what was happening around her, she valued being clean. She refused to sink to the drug-addicted level like before. But what choice did she have?

She studied Chip. Did he know what lay inside the tack box? If he worked for Burnette, wouldn't he be quick to befriend her?

Other than the depression and restlessness of coming down from the drugs, she was stronger, felt more alive. Her body no longer ached, and the horrendous headaches had eased. Maybe Dave's methods weren't so radical after all. The incredulous amount of supplements were working, and she'd begun to enjoy her twice-a-day smoothies. While it all lasted.

Wrestling with reality had its drawbacks. If she dwelled on it for very long, the blackness grew in its severity. She wondered about her father and Burnette at Camp David. What did Burnette really want? Had he been the one to tip off the media? So many questions and no answers.

Perhaps she understood just enough to keep her frightened. Lindsay slowly walked to the house and Meghan joined her. Pepper had her raspberry smoothie ready on the kitchen counter. Taking a long drink, she wished life's problems could be solved as easily as taking vitamins. The nation needed to be detoxed.

She set her glass on the counter and rubbed the chill bumps on her arms. The A/C in the house had been turned down to accommodate the hot-blooded male agents. But if she were honest, the ice cubes bumping into her veins had more to do with Burnette than the temperature setting inside the house.

Two and a half years ago, she realized he'd fed her full of lies and deception. And when she threatened to tell her father, he countered with a threat to kill her parents and Kelli. For a while she tried to figure out why. When nothing solid surfaced, she realized the only way to protect her family was to follow orders.

Here on the Dancin' Dust, with her hours free of friends who used her and all the wasted time spent in activities that only hurt herself and others, the thought of freeing herself from Burnette and possibly saving others emerged again. Ironic, considering where she was held prisoner. If only she could trust someone enough to tell them the truth. Maybe someone smarter who could figure out how to stop him.

Tears brimmed her eyes, and she took another gulp of her smoothie to counter the overwhelming helplessness. With the lucidity that walked beside her each day, she wanted to believe she could make a difference. Were her aspirations a fairy tale?

The relationship between her and her parents could never be mended, but she had to try to keep them alive. And sweet Kelli had so much to offer the world.

Meghan had revealed much about her life before becoming a Secret Service agent. Teenage rebellion headed the list. But she'd survived. Then her sister died of an overdose. Like Lindsay's family, Meghan professed to be a Christian. Although Lindsay had no use for a God who allowed monsters like Scottard Burnette to roam, she held no ill thoughts for those who chose to believe.

She watched Meghan, who reached inside the fridge for a bottle of water. Maybe the agent could be trusted. She'd never appeared like a woman who could be bought.

"Has my father called lately?"

Meghan smiled. "Every morning before he's briefed for the day."

How long would the man who held the most important job in the country stay alive? Could she do anything to stop the downward spiral?

# CHAPTER 47

Lindsay glanced at the clock: 2:35. Wide awake, she walked to the window. Outside, armed agents protected her. Inside, agents would give their lives for her, not because they valued or respected her, but because they were committed to their role. How meaningless when they didn't know who stalked the Dancin' Dust. Who gave the orders. Who controlled so many people.

Today, while viewing Chip at the corral and deliberating why he avoided her, she saw he had the courage to stand in the middle of a horrible situation. Pushing aside the thought of his possibly working for the demon, she thought about Chip Leonard as a person. His father was gone. His reputation was marred. And yet he chose to return to the Dancin' Dust and face those who, in her opinion, had destroyed his life. That took guts. Something she longed to have. She attempted it once and lost. So she curled up into a ball and became a pitiful drug addict who bowed to the one who'd started it all.

Granted, the reasons for the broken ties with her parents seemed irreparable, and her actions had embarrassed Kelli. But she didn't want any of them hurt or worse. So did she fight and hope they stayed safe? She sensed he'd kill them no matter what she promised to do. Perhaps that's what being off drugs for six weeks did to a person. But she'd been in this position before and cowered.

What she needed was proof that she could take to Meghan. Yes,

Meghan. She feared Ash might be a part of the scheme. After all, he'd been a part of her life for over four years. If only she could get on a computer and check out a few things. But that was a useless thought.

She had to try before time ran out. Taking a deep breath, she opened the door. Victor sat on a chair outside her door. His attention flashed to her.

"Victor, I need to talk to Meghan. It's important." She willed her heart to slow down.

He nodded slowly and reached inside his pocket for his cell phone.

"Please, would you just get her? I don't want anyone to know. It's private, a woman thing."

He glanced toward Meghan's bedroom door.

"She's just down the hall," Lindsay said. "Have her come to my room."

"Are you sick?" Victor peered at her. "You look pale."

"I'm okay." She took another breath. "I'm so sorry about Wade. I wish I'd taken the time to tell him how much I appreciate him— all of you. And I'm sorry for the many times I've abused you."

He offered a grim smile. "All of us are committed to our jobs, and that means protecting you. They'll find whoever killed Wade and stop the drug dealer."

Lindsay wanted to say more, but emotion stopped her. In the past, she'd treated those who would give their lives for her with contempt—cursing, physical abuse. Shame filled her. The drugs and alcohol had masked the guilt, and she often longed for the escape again. Maybe Burnette was right. She was stupid, and her parents had never wanted her. Lindsay stiffened. Did she have the courage to do the right thing?

A few minutes later, a knock at the door told her Meghan had arrived. She invited the agent into her room and willed herself to tell the story, part of it anyway.

"Victor said you wanted to talk." Without makeup, Meghan looked Lindsay's age.

Lindsay nodded. "I'd like to go outside, if you don't mind. Away from the house and anyone who might hear what I have to say."

"Let's go."

Once the two had walked onto the back porch, Lindsay breathed a little easier. The house or even the pool area could be bugged. "Let's walk to the corral, where we can talk privately."

Once there, she anchored her hands on the gate, thinking again about Chip's stubborn stand. The difference being he might not have anything to hide. Whereas she did.

"I need to tell you a few things about what's going on—the threats made on my life and probably Wade's death. Meghan, I have to be able to trust you."

"You know you can. I've wanted to help you from the beginning."

"Which is why I'm talking to you now. This involves more than a vengeful drug dealer." She shrugged. "I wish all of this was that simple."

"I'm listening. Do we need to have Ash here?"

Lindsay sensed panic taking momentum. "I'm afraid of him. He could be one of them."

Meghan didn't offer opposition. "I'm sure this is hard."

She nodded and glanced about to ensure they were alone. "You were given my history at the start of this assignment—about getting kicked out of boarding school four years ago."

"Yes, I remember reading that."

"I was a kid who looked for ways to get attention from my parents. So I smoked pot and deliberately got caught. I wasn't addicted to anything then." She couldn't look at Meghan, not when her past actions had nearly destroyed her father's aspirations. "One of my father's friends came to see me under the pretense of helping me clean up my act for the good of Dad's political career. Instead he faked sympathy, reinforcing what I believed about my parents and confirming my fears that they didn't care about me.

He told me I was a nuisance, an embarrassment." Lindsay stopped. Dare she continue?

"I'm listening, Lindsay. I'm not going to judge you by anything you tell me."

Lindsay tried to ignore a sinking feeling in the pit of her stomach. "I was miserable, and he gave me pills to help me cope. He said they would help me feel better. He said he loved me even if my parents didn't. I swallowed every word."

Meghan stiffened. "Are you telling me one of your father's friends got you hooked on drugs?"

"Yes."

"Who is it? The president needs to know."

"It's much more complicated. Since being here, I've tried to figure out a way to stop him, but each time I think I can go to my dad, a tragedy occurs. Like the bombing. And Wade."

"Lindsay, help me understand."

"The man is a liar and a killer. He'll stop at nothing to accomplish his agenda." She shrugged. "I don't even know what he really wants."

"Who would do this to you and your father?"

Lindsay couldn't breathe his name yet. There were agents patrolling the area, and one of them might be reporting to Burnette. Rick strolled beyond the pool, but he could have a listening device. "I'm not sure of the whys, but right from the beginning he set out to discredit Dad's name. That's where I came in. In exchange for drugs, I did what he told me. I no longer cared about myself or what I was doing. All I could think about was how much I hated my parents for what they'd done to me, and how much I wanted them to suffer. The drugs and alcohol allowed me an escape."

"What's changed your mind?"

Lindsay drew in a breath. "I'm afraid Dad is going to be assassinated."

"Why haven't you told anyone about this? Tell me who is the one responsible."

"He told me no one would ever believe me because of my history. I have so many issues with my parents, but having them killed is not on the list."

Meghan touched her shoulder. "I can't help you unless you tell me who is committing these atrocities."

Lindsay took a deep breath. She trembled. "Scottard Burnette." Either Meghan believed her or not.

Seconds ticked by.

Meghan stared out into the darkness. "Thank you for entrusting me with this." She whispered the words as though she had to come to terms about the corruptness of the vice president of the United States. "I don't know what to say, except Ash needs to hear this."

"Please. I'm afraid he's working for him."

"Not Ash. He's dedicated to the Secret Service and you. Plus he's committed to the Lord, like your father."

"But someone here is feeding dear old Uncle Scottard information." She spit the words, remembering the many times she had to fake their affection. She considered her next thought, but she'd come this far. "I've wondered if the house is bugged."

"More of a reason to confide in Ash."

Lindsay turned to Meghan. "And you believe I'm telling the truth? You're not going to wake Dave and have me diagnosed as insane?"

"Not at all."

"What about my history, Meghan. Is he right? Because if he is, there's nothing I can do to help protect my family."

"You're doing what is best for your family's safety and yours." Meghan lifted her cell and punched in Ash's number on speed dial. "Ash, I need to speak to you outside. Lindsay and I are at the corral. Come alone. Please don't tell any of the others."

# CHAPTER 48

EARLY SATURDAY MORNING, shortly before 0430, Meghan descended the stairs after making sure Lindsay was calm and back in her room. The second time their protectee revealed her story about VP Burnette, she cried. Meghan realized Lindsay didn't trust Ash, but he'd comforted her in a way that had soothed her apprehensions. Hopefully Lindsay would be able to sleep with the realization she no longer carried the burden alone. Although the secret unlocking the tragedies in DC and on the Dancin' Dust might be more than the two agents could handle.

Meghan needed to talk to Ash and sort out what they'd heard and what steps should be taken. Knowing his habits, she found him in the operation room. He looked like he'd gotten as little sleep as she had after listening to what Lindsay had to say.

He must have sensed her presence, because he smiled, and her insides melted. Why hadn't some woman snatched him up? She needed this assignment finished for more than one reason.

"Are you still processing?" She hoped her words were obscure enough to keep her message private. If the house was bugged, their conversations needed to be guarded.

"I am. No conclusions yet."

"How about a walk? We can brainstorm together."

Shortly thereafter, the two walked toward the front gate under the veil of darkness, their voices low, both carrying fresh mugs of steaming coffee.

"Do you think she was telling the truth?" Ash said.

Meghan was about to ask the same of him. "My intuition tells me she was. At least I've got the pounding in the back of my skull that usually indicates my intuition is right. She repeated the same story to you as she did to me. Nothing changed. She's clean and coherent. If what she told us is true, then it certainly answers a ton of questions."

He chuckled. "My instincts tell me this is the real deal—a feeling in the pit of my stomach."

"Maybe we need to take out stock in Tylenol and Rolaids."

"Either that or plant ourselves in a shrink's office."

"What does he hope to gain from this?"

"Maybe he has a self-interest project. Some type of legislation he'd like to have passed. But that doesn't make any sense. Lindsay has no political influence with her father. Seriously, we need more proof than Lindsay's story."

"But how do we find it? If this is true, the road ahead is deadly." Meghan wished they had hours to talk through the implications of the vice president of the United States committing treason.

"We have to catch him in the act, which sounds like an impossibility. Then I have to consider that all those on his payroll may not know who's calling the shots."

"Are you going to contact Warrington?" She glanced his way, but he hadn't clenched his jaw to indicate he'd made a decision. "Or are you thinking he's part of it?"

"Blunt, aren't you?"

"He's blown off our concerns about Lindsay."

"But he has to take his orders too." Ash sighed. "Warrington's always been a man of integrity."

Meghan gazed at the grounds, seemingly quiet and peaceful, while agents monitored everything that moved and breathed. Her doubts about Warrington surfaced. "A conspiracy of this magnitude has money and power behind it. We're nothing compared to that. Easy to squash. Have you started an investigation on Burnette?"

"You know I have. Only been an hour, but I've begun to put a few pieces together. Once I have a little time to work on it, I'd like to discuss him with you."

"I've been thinking about a few things too." In the darkness, she felt more at ease to speak her mind, but not about Warrington. Not yet. "Remember the scorpion incident?"

"I've thought the same thing. Burnette had access to your files, which means he knew about your reaction to bee stings." He paused. "He suggested your bedroom. Said it allowed you close proximity to Lindsay. But who removed the wire?"

She massaged her neck muscles. "I wish I knew. And there's more. Burnette knows the president wanted me protecting Lindsay to gain her confidence and to help her stay off drugs. Burnette could have feared she might tell me the truth. And my guess is he knew about Shelley, whether he had anything to do with her death or not." She steadied her thoughts. "I don't think he was involved with my sister's overdose. That doesn't make sense. More like he used it to try to scare me."

"I think his call after the funeral indicates he might think Lindsay already told you about him. Was an autopsy performed on your sister?"

"No. Thought about it, but why put Mom through the ordeal?"

They walked a few more feet. Meghan questioned Burnette's motives and who might have thrown in with him.

"Burnette agreed with me that women had no place in the Secret Service," Ash said. "He told the president that your presence on the team would be a mistake."

"Imagine the damage we could have done to his scheme if we'd been friends from the beginning."

"Agents extraordinaire." He chuckled, no doubt to help alleviate some of the bewildering aspects of Lindsay's story. "I've chased away a few female agents in my time. It took one beautiful agent who is as stubborn as I am to change my tune."

"Don't forget it either."

In the dim light, he flashed her a grin that would melt an iceberg. "Look at the situation this way. If we were still at odds and Lindsay caved in with the truth, I would have discarded the whole crazy story."

"And Burnette had no real worries with Carla because Lindsay resents any mother figure. So he's using everything he knows to not only discredit Lindsay and keep her terrified, but to ensure we fail. Someone here is working against us." The idea of someone they trusted betraying them sickened her. Chip had insisted upon it too.

"Warrington told me Burnette has requested Victor and Bob for his VPPD."

She moaned. "Oh, Ash, I can't believe either one of them would stoop that low."

"Neither can I. But a plan succeeds when all the players know their part. Lindsay's story stays right here until we have proof about Burnette's involvement."

"I agree. Lindsay reminded me that Burnette is allowed to speak to her at will. He's been using those times to increase his threats. During a recent call, he told her where to find a stash of drugs. If she's right, then her story is solid."

"Has she used them?"

"She says not. I'd like to think our prayers had a hand in keeping her clean and urging her to tell us what's going on."

"I'm sure Burnette hasn't figured the hand of God into his plan. After the way he talked about you the day of Ethan's funeral and his insistence on having a few drinks, my respect for him dropped to the bottom."

"I wanted to smack his face. Actually I was stunned at his lack of professionalism. According to Lindsay, that's the day he hid the drugs."

"I don't suppose she told you where to find them."

"In a tack box in the stables."

Ash stopped on the driveway. "I remember he wanted to walk there alone—to remember Ethan working with the horses."

Meghan's blood pressure zipped up. "Shall we see what's inside his tack box?"

They walked toward the stables, the sun rising in the eastern sky. "Chip won't be happy with us poking around in his domain."

"Do you think he's in on this too?"

"I don't think so. Let's see how this plays out."

Meghan waved at Chip leading a saddled horse outside for an early morning ride. After telling him good morning and hearing nothing in return, she and Ash entered the stables. There, on a peg inside the stable of the horse Lindsay often rode, was a key. Meghan slipped it into her hand.

"Halfway there." Ash's whisper validated the truth of Lindsay's words. "I wonder where we can find Burnette's tack box? It's supposed to have his name on it."

They searched the stables and found nothing. Frustration inched through her, leading the way for Lindsay's story to be merely another drug addict's way of getting attention. "I'll ask Chip. He's more apt to talk to me than you."

"You're prettier."

"Thanks, but I'm on the opposite side."

Ash waited while she strolled outside to find Chip. If ever she needed to use her feminine wiles, it was now. In the early morning sunlight, he tightened the girth on his horse. Memories of another loose girth scrolled across her mind. He caught sight of her and scowled.

"I need to find the vice president's tack box."

"What for?" His response would have frightened a rattler.

"He lost a watch and thinks it might be there. I think the tack box has his name on it."

Chip adjusted the saddle and glared at her. "Give me one reason why I should help you?"

Bitterness met her gaze. "I can't, Chip. You have far too many reasons to despise all of us. And in your circumstances, I'd feel the same. I'm only passing on what the vice president requested. I have the key, but I can't find the box in the stables."

He patted the horse. Chip had more issues with the Secret Service than she cared to address.

"I moved the tack box into my living quarters. Dad made the box and took a lot of pride in his workmanship." He swallowed. "Do I need to borrow your phone so I can call Burnette about this intrusion on his property?"

"That's up to you, but he did tell me where to find the key." Meghan forced a smile. "I'm only following orders."

He wrapped the reins around a fence post. "I'll bring the box around. Unless you pull a gun, I prefer not to have you in my home." Animosity laced his words.

"Thanks. I appreciate it."

Moments ticked by, and she prayed Chip didn't have a cell phone to call Burnette. He'd been patted down when he returned, but Burnette could have found a way to ensure they had contact.

Ash must have gotten tired of waiting, because he joined her outside.

"Chip went after the tack box. He had it in his quarters."

Ash nodded. Just when she'd given up, Chip walked around the side of the stables carrying the box.

He set it on the ground with a thud. "I put this in Dad's room for safekeeping when I returned from my Secret Service–inspired vacation. Burnette called me on Bob's phone on Tuesday. Said no one was to have the tack box unless the person had a key. So I guess that's you."

Perhaps Chip might be innocent, or he could simply be following orders. For that matter, Bob fell under the same scrutiny.

"I want to see you open it. Make sure you don't take anything but his watch. I'm still on Mr. Burnette's payroll."

Meghan's heart plummeted. What did that mean? She dropped

to her knees, turned the box toward her and away from Chip, then inserted the key. The padlock opened. Holding her breath, she lifted the lid. It held a saddle blanket, a studded bridle that cost more than most horses, and a halter. Beneath the blanket lay a framed Marine photograph. When she pulled the photograph into her arms, she spotted a yellowed, folded newspaper with the headline "Lt. Kyle Burnette Hangs Himself in Prison Cell." Burnette's son. She'd forgotten the incident. When she touched the newspaper, she noted something beneath it. Slipping her hand under the paper, she felt a plastic bag and a powdery substance. Without looking, she knew the contents.

Lindsay had been telling the truth.

# CHAPTER 49

FROM THE LOOK on Meghan's face, Ash realized she'd found the drugs, and she needed to get the evidence out of the tack box. "Thanks for helping us, Chip. I'll make sure the vice president knows about your cooperation."

"Just finish up here so I can go about my business."

"We didn't have a chance to talk at the funeral, but your dad was a good man. Every time I had a question about the ranch or his garden, he turned it into a teaching moment." That part about Ethan was true.

"He died before his time."

"I agree." Ash reached out to shake Chip's hand. He trusted the stat man about as much as he trusted Burnette, but Meghan needed time before Chip noted what she was doing. "He even explained to me the differences in the flowering bushes. Told me to stay away from the oleanders."

Chip narrowed his gaze. "They're poisonous, like a few other things around here."

Meghan brushed her hands. "I can't find the watch. He must have lost it in the house."

Ash lifted the heavy box and handed it to Chip. "Thanks again."

On the way back to the house, Meghan handed Ash the bag, and he stuffed it into the waistband of his jogging shorts and pulled his T-shirt over it. "Do you want to get this confirmed? Looks like coke to me."

"I will, and I'll keep it for now. We'd better hope Chip doesn't notify Burnette."

"We might end up like Wade."

Anxiety assaulted him. "I want to talk about this later on, maybe while Dave and Lindsay are in a counseling session."

"What do we tell Lindsay?"

"That we found the coke. You're good for her, Meghan. Without her trust in you, this situation would have grown worse."

They'd nearly reached the back porch, and Ash had no intentions of discussing Burnette so close to the house. "I'm going to be worthless today. No sleep and a million things to do."

"Me too."

"That gives me an idea."

She tossed him a puzzled look. "Which is?"

"A way to cover up what we're doing."

"I don't understand."

"What I've been wanting to do since the night of the scorpion." He took their coffee mugs and set them on the porch step.

She laughed. "People will talk."

He wrapped his arms around her. "That gives us an alibi when we sneak off."

"Hmm, smart man."

"We'll need lots of excuses. Give them much to talk about." The desire to kiss her clouded his normal logic.

"Maybe we should start now." His lips descended on hers, tasting, taking, giving. Meghan slipped her arms around his neck. "This is even better than the first time."

"By the time this assignment is finished, we'll be pros." Her whisper prompted him to pull her closer.

When the kiss was over, he found it difficult to focus. But he needed to continue his research on Burnette and look for a bug. "I have a few things to do in the operation room."

Their foreheads touched. "Do you need any help?"

"As long as you promise not to be a distraction. Shall we refill our coffee cups? I need a shot of caffeine before a cold shower." He kissed the tip of her nose. "We make a good team."

In the kitchen, Ash greeted Pepper, also an early riser. She was sprinkling cinnamon over freshly rolled-out dough. His stomach growled. Working all night had a tendency to make a man hungry.

In the operation room, Meghan closed the door behind them. Ash bent to examine every inch of the heavy table. She checked the small one where they served coffee.

"Has the Middle East Peace Summit been officially postponed to January?" She climbed onto a chair to search the chandelier.

"Not officially, but it probably will. Vice President Burnette hasn't had much of an opportunity to review what the president has put together."

"My guess is they worked out something at Camp David. The president values diplomacy, and the peace talks are important to him." Meghan stepped to the floor and shook her head.

Ash pointed her to the bookshelf, while he searched the chairs. If a bug existed, they'd find it. Meghan worked fast. Oh, how he appreciated her.

"How long do you think we'll be here with Lindsay?" she said.

"Other rehabs have been at least three months. One in Utah lasted six."

"I think she's doing well."

"Tonight she was acting strange. Makes me wonder if she has a stash." He glanced up and smiled at her.

"We could ask Dave. He recognizes the signs." By now, Meghan had lifted out a half dozen books with no luck.

Ash finished the fourth chair, four more to inspect. "Do you suppose anyone suspects us?"

"Are you kidding? The great A2Z sneaking off with a woman agent?"

"Very funny. I'll remember that, you insatiable woman."

Meghan flirted over her shoulder. "Your fault."

He examined the ceiling. Why hadn't he checked there first? He reached for a small penlight on the table.

"Have you heard from Wade's family?" Meghan pulled out another armful of books.

"No. I'll visit them when this assignment is over."

"Can I come along?"

"I'll consider it. You'll have to behave yourself between now and then."

"Honestly, the late nights are killing me."

"Are you telling me I'm not worth it?" He shone the light around the air duct frame. He'd unscrew it, but the noise would alert whoever might be listening.

"Not exactly. But it would have been courteous if the president had allowed us to have four weeks on and two weeks off."

"I agree. Day after day on this ranch is making me crazy—except for the time with you."

Ash spotted a small round device that looked like a watch battery in the lower left-hand corner of the air duct. He gestured to Meghan. For now, it would stay in place, and they'd use Burnette's bug to their advantage.

"I need to get a shower before breakfast." Meghan replaced the book in her hand.

"First I need a kiss. It's a long time before I can do this again." He gave her a celebratory kiss. "This ranch is not so bad after all."

"Except when you and I can't steal away outside."

"Not so sure I can wait until tonight." He glanced around them, looking for something he might have missed.

"I don't suggest letting the rest of the team observe our . . ."

"Affection? Remember I'm the agent who despises women in the Secret Service."

"Have I successfully changed your mind?"

"Let me show you."

# CHAPTER 50

LINDSAY SLEPT HARD, and when she did waken, her first thoughts were what she'd told Meghan and Ash. Had she made a terrible mistake? The news. She had to find out if Dad and Mom were okay. If Burnette had found out what she'd done and killed her parents, the media would be reporting the tragedy on every network.

She hit the power button on the TV remote in her room. Soaps and game shows lit the screen. News networks were busy as usual with a steady stream of bad situations all around the world. But nothing about the president and First Lady. Lindsay leaned back against the pillow. She had done the right thing. Meghan and Ash would find a way to stop Burnette. She wasn't alone.

But one of the agents had to be working for Burnette. How else could a sniper have known when Wade and Chip ran? Could it be Chip? She didn't think so.

*I'm stronger than this. I won't give in to the bullying.* She tossed back the blanket and headed for the shower. Breakfast, counseling, reading, the pool, horseback riding, and smoothies filled with supplements. A thought occurred to her. She could act like she'd found the drugs. That would appease Burnette. Make him think she was following orders. But first she needed to toss the idea by Meghan.

*I am stronger.*

*I can do this.*

A twinge of emotion swept through her. For a moment, she wondered what it would be like to be part of a real family. Burnette had told her they didn't care. Lindsay shook her head. If she lived through this, she'd talk to Dave about the past. She couldn't think of a single reason why they'd left her in the boarding school during her birthday or the summer between her freshman and sophomore years. Two weeks at Christmas, two weeks for spring break—if she was lucky—and a few weeks during the summer. Why? She gave up making excuses for them when she was twelve. But learning the truth might push her into addictive behavior again.

# CHAPTER 51

EARLY MONDAY, Meghan and Ash stepped onto the back porch and faced the still darkness of predawn. She treasured this time of day. Running together in the early hours gave them time to not only talk about their common problems but to also get to know each other better. He wanted her to meet his parents, and she wanted him to meet her mother. They shared green as their favorite color. He opened presents on Christmas Eve, and she opened hers on Christmas Day. He liked to water-ski. She preferred snow. Once the assignment was over, she'd miss this.

They broke into a slow jog toward the front gate. She dreaded this small section of the five-mile run. Even at this hour, four reporters lurked outside their RVs, looking for a new story about Lindsay Hall.

"Do you ever feel like we're goldfish in a big sea of sharks?" Meghan studied a familiar figure on the other side of the gate, a balding man who had a foul mouth.

"I think some of them would sink their teeth into both of us for info about Lindsay."

"And they say we're ruthless. A few are respectful. But not many. Maybe this will be the one morning they'll leave us alone."

"Don't count on it. It's all about having their name in print."

The gate opened, and the agent nodded a good-morning. The

bald reporter at the gate stood in front of them. "What's going on today?"

Meghan and Ash swerved around him. She scanned the area for the figure who might not fit in with the rest, the one who'd try to slip through the gate and gain information about Lindsay. She understood Ash did the same.

"Is Lindsay sober?" The same man's persistence was like sandpaper against her nerves.

"When is the vice president making an appearance?" came another voice. "Doesn't the president care enough about his daughter to visit her? Or has he written her off?"

"Has he decided to keep her here until she learns how to keep her mouth shut?" This came from the obnoxious bald man.

Meghan and Ash jogged past the RVs.

A sharp sting to her shoulder caused her to gasp. She touched the wound and felt the blood oozing down her arm.

"Meghan, what's wrong?" Ash's whisper broke through the pain.

She stopped in the middle of the road and walked back to the reporter.

"Meghan?" She ignored him. Something inside her was close to snapping.

"Which one of you threw a rock at me?"

The reporter from the gate chuckled, his bald head glowing under the light mounted above them. "Got your attention, didn't it? Of course it was an accident."

Ash appeared beside her, but she didn't need rescuing. The events of the last six weeks had left her restless . . . and angry. "Do you have any idea what you've done?"

"I want to know if the president intends to keep his daughter here until she learns to behave herself." He reached for another rock.

"And you think throwing a rock at a Secret Service agent will get you an answer?"

He smirked and turned to look at who might be watching. "Not my fault you got in the way."

The rock danced back and forth in his hands. A camera flashed. This incident would hit the front page of every newspaper, TV, and radio coast to coast.

*Calm down, Meghan. Sharks are flesh eaters, and he's only living up to his pitiful, innate responses to life.*

"Hey." The man pointed to Ash. "You can't talk? You let a woman speak for you? Ah, I bet you and the lady are sharing a bed."

She counted to five, but when another camera flashed, her resolve slid to her toes.

"Ignore him, Meghan." Ash's words failed to calm her.

"I got a hundred bucks for the first one who gives me a few answers so the public can read what's happening out here."

Meghan wiped the blood streaming past her elbow and walked to the man, never taking her eyes off his face. She had all the control she needed. "If you ever throw a rock at me again, you'll regret it." Wiping her bloody hand on the front of his golf shirt, she smiled. "Excuse me; my bloody hand got in the way of your shirt. Send me the cleaning bill." She whirled around and resumed her run.

Several feet from the scene, she realized her actions had dropped below the professional level. "I'm sorry, Ash. I shouldn't have touched him. Now my face and his bloody shirt will be all over the news."

"Don't worry about it. I wanted to flatten him when I saw the blood. You handled it better than I would."

"That doesn't make me feel any better. But I like your chivalry."

"Thank you, ma'am. And remind me not to ever make you mad."

She wiped the blood trickling to her wrist. The rock had cut deep.

"Meghan, let's head back so I can look at your arm."

"And give that bald weasel the satisfaction of knowing he

stopped me? I'd bleed out first." She forced a laugh, but her response to the injury nibbled at her conscience. "How can we get rid of those guys?"

"Drain the pool."

"I'd like to pull the plug on them and Burnette." Her anger rose again.

"Yeah, but the VP seems to have the president in the palm of his hand."

Like the reporter's rock. "Do you ever wonder or hope Warrington and the president are getting wise to him?"

"All the time. If the president suspected Burnette had anything to do with Lindsay's addiction, he'd be behind bars. Unfortunately the VP is the prez's blind spot."

"I wish I knew how to have a private audience with him. But Burnette would stop or deny everything. It's all back to finding the proof we need."

"I want Lindsay off this ranch." Ash's determination frosted his words. "But I don't have the clout to get it done. Everything I've tried has backfired."

"That doesn't mean we quit."

"I can't figure out what Burnette is waiting on. The next election? See if the Speaker of the House seeks the nomination? Or is he planning an assassination, in which case he won't need Lindsay? You know he's not sending the e-mails and texts. Too smart for that."

"I'm not giving up on finding a way to talk to the president."

"Uh, I realized your backbone at the gate."

"Don't forget it either. I wonder if he'll be waiting for me now that he's had time to think about his bloodied shirt."

"Probably. Guys like him feed off confrontation and—"

"I know, Ash. He'll be back for more. It'll take more than a stone for me to lose it this time."

Her shoulder continued to sting the next two miles and then back to the ranch. Talking about Burnette's treachery with no solution depressed her. Compound the situation with the pain in her shoulder, and she wanted to go back to bed. Burnette would hear about today and gloat.

Up ahead a small group of reporters swarmed the gate.

"How's the shoulder?" Ash said.

"Needs to be cleaned. Still bleeding."

"Do you think it needs stitches?" His concern touched her.

"It wasn't a bullet." She huffed. "Then I'd have unloaded on him."

They were forced to stop by the balding man, who stood in the way of the gate.

"Sir, please move." Ash's voice held a deadly tone.

"Not sure I know how."

Ash pulled his radio clipped to his running shorts. "I need two agents at the gate immediately. Also call the sheriff. I have a reporter here who assaulted an agent."

"All right. You made your point." The man backed away.

"Too late." Ash replaced his radio. "I want your name and who you work for."

"My employer is none of your business."

"Suit yourself. Doesn't stop the charges. And you might want to call your lawyer."

Meghan bit back a grin. Having A2Z on an agent's side felt good.

# CHAPTER 52

MID-MORNING, while Dave engaged Lindsay for a counseling session, Ash stepped outside to find Meghan. The heat nearly stole his breath, or was it the gravity of what he'd learned about Burnette?

She waved from the garden. Crazy woman, she held two tomatoes. As he drew closer to her, he laughed.

"What's so funny?"

"Your freckles match the tomatoes."

"The last person who said that ended up with a bloody nose."

"A reporter?"

She handed him a tomato. "Good save. Fifth grade church camp."

"Why am I not surprised? Where do you suggest we eat these, Miss Fiery Redhead? Remember we're supposed to look cozy."

"Cozy?" She laughed. "Yeah. Rick told me at breakfast to be careful, that you had a reputation."

He raised a brow. "What did you tell him?"

"That I was using you to make a point."

He hoped not. He was in too deep.

She wiggled her nose, looking much too cute. "Ash, I have to tell them something. If we're going to be an item, I need to deny it as though no one has noticed." She paused. "I have a favorite spot to eat our tomatoes, and I have a knife and two napkins."

"Is it the oak tree in the front?"

"Yes, sir."

They walked around the house. This morning, he hadn't been ready to talk about it. Now he had much to tell her and little time. Worse yet, his answers complicated the situation.

"I have questions about Burnette," she said. "And we haven't had a spare moment to discuss the bug."

"What do you know about him?"

"A little. I'd forgotten about his son's suicide until I saw the photograph of Kyle in his officer's uniform and then read the newspaper headlines."

Ash looked to see if anyone was watching. They needed to appear like two people enjoying each other's company. "His death occurred a year before Burnette's appointment as press secretary."

"I remember his son's court-martial. The world watched to see if Kyle would be convicted of killing civilians in Afghanistan."

"I never thought there was enough evidence. Especially when the defense claimed the civilians were armed and fired at his men first."

"But he was still sentenced to twenty years at Leavenworth— which never happened because he committed suicide." She glanced at him. "How do you get over something like that?"

"I'm thinking he didn't."

They sat beneath the tree, but he had no appetite for the tomato. He focused on the court-martial, searching his memory bank for details about the case.

"Ash, I'm now remembering Burnette's wife appeared on national networks and protested their son's conviction."

"She left him before the sentencing. I still remember her interview on *The Barry Knight Show* in which she blamed US foreign policy, claiming our priorities were centered on looking good in the eyes of the world. She maintained we handled terrorists with kid gloves while our country's sons were killed defending our freedoms."

Meghan stared at the reporters at the front gate. "If Burnette held the same views, then he had motivation to get even, seek change in foreign policy . . . which would explain the recent disagreement between him and the president. But I don't recall his reaction to his son's conviction and suicide."

"He maintained a stoic front during the trial. Refused to give a statement. Said he wanted to put the tragedy behind him." Ash's thoughts wove Lindsay's story with Burnette's past. "With his son dead and his wife gone, he had nothing to lose. I wonder if he voiced how he felt about his son's court-martial to President Hall."

"Lindsay might have an answer, but I doubt it. Doesn't seem like the kind of conversation he would have while filling her with lies and drugs."

Ash considered how Burnette could have deceived the president. "Maybe Burnette convinced his old friend that he'd put the past behind him."

"And Burnette keeps his emotions in check while in public."

"However, we saw a different side of him at Ethan's funeral. Inappropriate remarks don't make a man a killer. But providing drugs and threatening the lives of others is a different story."

"And now he's the vice president." Meghan's face hardened. "Lindsay's concerned he's planning an assassination. With President Hall out of the picture, Burnette would really be a dangerous power."

"If I piece together why Wade was killed, I bet he learned something about Burnette or who's betraying us here. If this blows up in our faces, we could be tried for treason. But I can't ignore it."

Meghan sighed. "Neither one of us would make the presidential team."

"We might find ourselves slinging burgers on a chain gang."

"So what do you suggest?"

"I think it's up to us to track down the truth. Lindsay is right about one thing—who can we trust?"

She rubbed her arms in the heat. "I have more questions for her. Oh, she asked me this morning about acting like she was using again."

"Good for her. We have to act fast before Burnette finds out we've been in his tack box."

"I've been thinking about that too. Remember I wanted to pose as Lindsay to see if we could draw out who's been sending her e-mails?"

"Meghan, that's even more dangerous than before."

"The stakes are higher. Someone lower on the totem pole might be willing to plea-bargain. Respond to that e-mail. It may be untraceable, but that doesn't mean someone's not monitoring it. Say Lindsay's willing. State she's using or drinking again. In fact, let's buy a phone and send it from there. Burnette might think she's found a way to make contact with the outside world."

"I can't allow you to do this." Ash studied Meghan. She had his heart, and he'd do anything to protect her.

"Ash, please. If you have a better way to trap him, then let me hear it."

He didn't have another plan. And that's what scared him the most.

★ ★ ★

Late morning, Meghan and Lindsay jogged far enough from the pasture gate to keep the agents happy and the reporters at bay. They snapped a few pics, but Lindsay knew how to keep her face from view.

"If you'd get up in the morning when I do, we could avoid this afternoon heat."

"Dream on. I used to come in at that hour, and now you're suggesting I climb out of bed then."

"Just a suggestion. Ash and I run before dawn."

Lindsay laughed. "Ash has an agenda."

"And your meaning?"

"He is so into you that it's almost gagging."

Good. Their act was working, but they weren't feigning a thing. "I thought we hid it from the others."

"Bob and Victor think it's hilarious, since he's supposed to be the woman hater."

Bob and Victor were to be on Burnette's VPPD. The thought of either of them being behind Wade's murder turned her stomach. "I'll try to do a better job of sneaking off."

Lindsay laughed again. "I could teach you a few things, if you're interested." They waved at an agent in a jeep. "I don't know how Burnette finagled the drug-dealer hoax, but there is no truth in it. I've always paid my way." Lindsay slowed to a jog. "This heat zaps my energy." She kept her voice low, obviously suspecting anyone and everyone.

"Does the name Medellín Cartel mean anything to you?"

"No. I'm assuming it's a drug cartel."

Meghan brought her jog to a walk. Lindsay couldn't talk and run. "The man arrested in connection with the original threat has ties to the Medellín Cartel."

"Burnette has to buy his stash somewhere."

Meghan had toyed with asking Lindsay about helping them since she proposed her idea to Ash earlier in the day. "How far are you willing to go to help us bring Burnette to justice?"

"What do you mean? I'm in too deep to back out."

Meghan took a cleansing breath. She hadn't expected Lindsay to cooperate this easily. "The guy who's been sending you e-mails wants to meet at a bar near here. I'm going for the gold. I want to pose as you and trap the jerk. So I need to borrow something from your closet and pick up a wig."

"Not sure if that's fun or dangerous."

Ash had mentioned the dangerous part more than once. "It's my job to keep you safe."

"But I thought an agent would step in line of a bullet, not pose as the protectee."

"I believe in doing whatever it takes to catch those who have threatened your life and the lives of others."

"Okay. We're probably the same size, but I don't have a thing here that you could wear. But we could do a little role play so you'd sound like Lindsay Hall. Teach you the walk and the come-on."

Meghan sensed the thrill of adrenaline begin to roll through her veins.

# CHAPTER 53

Ash and Bob sat on the front porch rocking like two old men while Lindsay and Meghan strolled about a hundred fifty feet in front of them. He didn't know the ex-linebacker from the New Orleans Saints well, but his record was spotless. Had he been bought?

"Tell me how a guy who has made millions in football gives up fame and fortune to be a Secret Service agent?"

"Stats, Ash. When I looked at the guys who retired and walked with a cane or had their knees replaced, I realized the glory, big bucks, and stadium cheers didn't amount to anything if I had to force myself out of bed each morning."

Ash chuckled. "So you substituted shoulder pads for a Kevlar?"

"Got to keep the excitement going."

"How did you like your assignment with Bush Sr.?"

Bob grinned. "Great guy. A lot of wisdom. Age is slowing him a bit, but he still has the vitality and enthusiasm that we all remember from his earlier days. Barbara Bush is a true lady. She might not tell you what you want to hear, but she makes you like her just the same."

"Do you miss the city?"

"Of course. This is boring." He frowned. "And depressing. We're stuck out here in the middle of nowhere, and in six weeks' time, an agent is murdered, a good man keels over from a heart attack, and a suspect is returned to work the ranch."

"Not what you thought, huh?"

Bob frowned. "I'm an agent. I do whatever it takes. But I'd like to know what's going on. Why hasn't Wade's murder been solved?"

"They say drug dealers are involved with connections to a cartel in Colombia."

"Then force the ones in custody to talk." Bob's language didn't fit a man being paid by a killer. "I could handle it."

The answers Ash needed still weren't coming. "Do you think the new president is to blame?"

"I don't know. He's a good politician. A good man. But I don't agree with his foreign policy. He wants to shake hands and make friends with the ones who'd rather see us all dead."

"Sounds like you agree with the VP."

"I do. At least he has the guts to stand up for what he believes instead of being a yes-boy and directing the Middle East Peace Summit."

"I thought the president and the VP came to an agreement. Makes me wonder if foreign policy will be a big issue in the next election."

"Speaker of the House Randolph may toss his hat in the ring yet. He and Burnette share the same views on public policy. Politics is beyond me." Bob shrugged. "But my guess is the party will stand behind Hall unless something major happens."

★ ★ ★

Monday evening, Meghan and Lindsay walked through the stables. They stopped to admire the new colt that Chip had named Strait. Meghan sorted through how she felt about Chip's avoidance. His behavior had potentially thrown him into the same pot as Burnette. However, she hadn't discarded his innocence.

Last night she'd sent an e-mail to the guy who'd used intimidation to get Lindsay to meet with him. He'd quickly responded: Friday at 10, Silver Spur.

Meghan patted the colt and noted Chip worked outside with one of the horses. "Has Chip made any attempt to be friends?"

"Not at all." Lindsay looked his way. "I thought he was a nice guy, but he blames all of us for what's happened. Not that I blame him."

"Can I ask you a favor?"

Lindsay planted her hands on her hips. "After I teach you how to get a guy, how to dress, and the latest makeup tips, you still want a favor?"

"I do."

"Bring it on."

"Try to get Chip to warm up to you. Then ask if you can borrow his truck."

Lindsay lifted her chin. "You do trust me."

Meghan nodded. "I believe you're a smart young woman who cares for others far more deeply than anyone ever realized. I believe you have a purpose in this world, and you can win the game against drugs and alcohol."

She swiped at a tear. "Thanks. It's hard. I wake up in the morning wanting a drink. And when Pepper makes Mexican food, I want a margarita so bad. Will it haunt me forever?" The sincerity in Lindsay's eyes said more than all the smoothies and nutrients that Dave could pump into her body.

"I honestly don't have an answer."

Lindsay nodded. "My own fault."

"Try God."

"Not yet. Maybe someday." Lindsay gave her a grin.

*Such a pretty girl—a girl with a big burden.*

# CHAPTER 54

LINDSAY THOUGHT how much she wanted to please Meghan, and asking Chip to borrow his truck was at the top of the list. Kelli would like the agent. They had strength to deal with stress and not allow others to destroy them. How strange that helping someone could make her feel good about herself. She'd play this role and help stop Burnette. "I'll not fail you."

Meghan gave her a thumbs-up. "You're on. He's close enough to hear your every word."

Lindsay squared her shoulders. This would be her finest performance. "Just leave me alone." The familiar line was reminiscent of the days when she hated the world. "All you care about is making sure Daddy and his new administration forget about me. I want away from here, away from everyone telling me what to do and when to do it. I'm clean and sober. Can't anyone trust me to stay that way?" She whirled around and stomped out of the stables, heading in Chip's direction.

Meghan followed. "Where are you going?"

"To talk to someone who isn't on the government's payroll."

"Dave and Carla are in the house. Do you want to talk to them?"

"No, please. I need a life." Lindsay walked toward Chip, who'd turned to take note of the commotion. "Lindsay, let's talk about this."

"No. I can't talk about anything." Until two days ago, her words were true.

"All right. I'll give you a little space." Meghan backed up several feet.

Lindsay swung her attention to Chip. "Please, don't put me in the same box with the agents. I had nothing to do with what happened to you."

Chip continued to brush the horse. Anger swept his handsome face, an emotion she understood when her world shattered.

She leaned against the corral fence. A collection of memories swirled about Burnette. This was her chance to stop him. "I thought you might go back to your old job in Dallas." She felt bad for deceiving him, considering how much she liked him before Wade's death . . . unless he was part of Burnette's team.

He shook his head. "Returning to my old job sounded like a great way to leave the past behind. But this is where I learned to feel good about myself. This is where Dad and I grew close again. He loved living here and working with horses, and so did I."

"Burnette didn't persuade you?"

Chip shrugged. "He asked me to return for Dad's sake, and I wasn't sure what to do."

She recalled how Burnette could manipulate people, play on their emotions. "The good thing is we won't be here forever."

"True. I can make a decision then. But it's lonesome here."

"Isn't there a bar within a few miles? The Silver Spur?"

He nodded. "A honky-tonk. Weekend two-steppin' with good ol' boys and their girlfriends. I did a few gigs there."

Lindsay sensed the longing of a good time without the paybacks of a tousle in bed or a hangover. "I'd love to go—get away from this place."

He shrugged. "I'd love to take you. We could sing and play together."

"That would be fun." And it would. She longed for a life in the country and all that meant.

He started to brush the mare again. "When this is over, it's a date."

"What if I could find a way to sneak off?"

He shook his head. "No, pretty lady. I'm not doing anything to upset these agents. Dealing with Burnette is hard enough."

"I thought you liked him."

"Nope. He only signs my paycheck. My dad thought he hung the moon."

She tilted her head curiously. "Not sure I understand."

He laughed. "Means he highly respected him. Could do no wrong."

*Good thing Ethan didn't know the real Burnette.* "Oh, I get it."

"I've lost my ideals about our government."

"Me too. Mind if I watch you work?"

"How about a swap? You can watch me sweat if you'll bring out your guitar later on tonight."

Lindsay's heart sped away. *Oh, Chip, please be free of Burnette. I like you. I really do.*

Back in her room, Lindsay picked up her guitar and strummed her latest song, a tribute to Ethan, who held more wisdom in the palm of his hand than a roomful of PhDs. Not that education or a career choice molded a person. But an attitude of the heart. There was another line. She walked across the room for her notebook.

What was Burnette planning for the clandestine meeting at the Silver Spur? Had he used her up and needed to get rid of her? Except he wouldn't be eliminating Lindsay Hall; he'd be pulling the trigger on Meghan.

# CHAPTER 55

TUESDAY MORNING, Ash drove Burnette's truck east into downtown Austin to a specialty shopping area that was supposed to have most of what he needed. His mission had more than one stop in the area, but he estimated about an hour to complete his errands before stopping by the Austin Police Department with Burnette's bag of cocaine.

First on his agenda was to buy the clothes Meghan needed on Friday night. She'd given him a list of her sizes and showed him online what the items looked like. This shouldn't take long.

After parking the truck, he entered the glittery shop called a boutique and was met by a tall brunette.

"How can I help you today?" If her smile had been an Olympic sport, she'd have taken all the medals.

"I'm looking for a few items for a friend." He pulled the list from his jeans pocket and handed it to her.

She gestured to the back of the boutique. "We received a new shipment of jeans yesterday. I'm sure we'll find just the right pair for your friend. Our selection is at its peak."

*Piece of cake.*

Thirty minutes later, Ash contemplated how he planned to lecture Lindsay and Meghan on their choice of attire. This was a country bar, not an international event. How did President Hall keep Lindsay in clothes? Thank goodness Meghan had her own jewelry, or he'd be physically sick. Whatever happened to JC Penney? Meghan had better keep these clothes clean because next Monday he planned to return all of them.

"And does your friend have a suitable bra for the top you've selected?" The sales girl leaned over the counter. She must have thought he was stupid.

"I'm sure she does, and I don't have her size." He was not going there.

"Let's take a look anyway."

Like a lamb led to slaughter, he followed her to the intimate section. This area needed temperature control—much too hot. Then he realized the customers must try on the underthings and needed warmer temps.

She held up a pair of red panties. "We suggest this type of panty to wear with our jeans. Doesn't show a line. I'm sure this will fit her."

Another $49.95.

He hadn't budgeted for a belt either. The cow that supplied the leather must have eaten caviar and drank champagne.

At the truck, he placed the bags in the extended cab. His lecture to those who awaited his return had grown to sermon proportions. And he hadn't visited Nordstrom's for the boots nor the wig shop yet.

His stomach growled, but he couldn't afford a hamburger and fries. He leaned his head on the steering wheel and saw the gas tank registered near empty.

After filling the truck, he made a stop at Walmart for a bag of chips and a liter of Diet Coke and several of their bags to stuff his purchases into. No one at the ranch must suspect what he'd done. But his pale face might be an indication.

The assignment from Meghan and Lindsay had taken more time than he planned. He'd be late returning to the ranch. Glancing at his watch, he headed toward the Barton Creek Square mall.

Today had been over and beyond the call of duty. Good thing

he liked Lindsay. Better yet that he loved Meghan. If they were ever to marry, she'd have to keep working to buy clothes. His credit card company had already phoned him to authorize the boots purchase. Why were wigs so expensive?

His last stop brought him to the downtown police station.

Hours later, he drove through the front gate, still reeling from what he'd learned about the bag of coke confiscated from Burnette's tack box. A reporter snapped his picture, but Ash kept his eyes on the driveway leading to the house. His findings sealed Burnette's depravity. All of Ash's doubts about how far the VP would go to ensure his agenda had vanished.

Could Lindsay handle this latest twist? A nagging thought told him her fragile emotions might spin in the wrong direction. She'd shown considerable strength and a willingness to help bring Burnette to justice. But Ash also sensed she viewed this as a diversion from the boredom of the ranch.

He parked the truck in the four-car garage, wishing Meghan were free to carry in the goods. The other agents were talking about the love-struck couple, which is what they needed to cover their investigation. But if those men caught him with these purchases, the teasing would never end. For now he'd store the Walmart bags in the truck, then sneak them to Meghan later.

He greeted Pepper in the kitchen. She was cleaning vegetables, including jalapeños. His stomach would never be the same.

"Hey, beautiful, have you seen Meghan?"

Pepper lifted a brow, causing her spiked, white hair to lift even higher. "Oh, the man's in love."

"With you?"

"Think again, A2Z. The man who had my heart is gone, and no one can replace him." Her words were light, but he heard the longing.

"Guess I'll have to find another woman to ease my aching heart."

She dried her hands and opened the fridge. Handing him a

Diet Coke, she narrowed her eyes. "This is the best I can do. You might think you're hiding this affair with Meghan, but we all know about it. You should have taken lessons on how to hide your personal life."

He pretended shock. "All I asked is if you knew where I could find her."

"Hopeless." She picked up a small paring knife and a cucumber. "I heard Lindsay say she wanted to take a swim. If you wait by the pool, I'm sure they'll be out shortly."

He grinned and toasted her with the pop can.

Within a few minutes, Meghan and Lindsay were poolside.

"You two can talk. I'm cooling off." Lindsay giggled. "Did you enjoy shopping?" Before he could scowl, she dived in.

Meghan eased onto a patio chair beside him. "Where are your purchases?"

"In the truck. Considering they cost me half of Fort Knox, I thought you could help me bring them in later."

She picked up a bottle of water. "I'm excited to see my outfit."

"I'm sure you are. Good thing you're one of my favorite people."

"I thought about warning you. Lindsay does have expensive taste. I'll pay for the wig and clothes."

"Can't we return them?"

She bit her lip in an obvious attempt to keep from laughing. "That's not ethical. I'll pay my way."

The red in her hair sparkled golden highlights in the sun, and he softened a little. "We'll talk about it after Friday night. How about eBay?"

She frowned. "I might want to keep them. What else did you learn?"

He took a long drink from his Diet Coke. "We have more ammunition."

"How's that?" She held up a finger. "Remind me later to discuss the details about Friday night's escapade."

He nodded. "I had the bag of coke evaluated. Found out it's pure cocaine."

Meghan took a deep breath and focused on Lindsay swimming laps. "Snorting coke that hasn't been stepped on would have taken care of Burnette's problem. No one would have a clue what happened other than that she overdosed."

"Can I talk you out of Friday night?"

"I told you I'd pay for all of it."

"This is not about money, and you know it. This is a setup to get you killed, not Lindsay. Burnette is on to us."

"Have you forgotten I'm a crack shot?"

"Don't they check for guns at the entrance?"

She shrugged, but it didn't ease his trepidation. "They check IDs for age, not to see if you're packing. This is rural Texas."

"I want you to forget the whole thing."

"Can't talk me out of it. You've just reinforced how quickly we need to stop Burnette before another person is hurt or killed."

# CHAPTER 56

AFTER SUPPER, Meghan invited Lindsay to see Ash's purchases. She had yet to open the bags, and the excitement had nearly driven her crazy. Nothing like new clothes and the love of a good man to make a girl happy.

"Can you imagine the horror on the salesgirl's face if she knew he'd put this merchandise in Walmart bags?" Lindsay lifted the jeans and nodded her approval.

"I wish I could have watched it all." Meghan pulled out a sleeveless, green knit top that dipped to a low cowl neck—a little too low.

"Great color for your hair." Lindsay held it up. "Good choice."

"Definitely top of the line." Meghan laughed. "What in the world?" Her whispers caused another laugh. The red panties were totally unexpected. Whoever had waited on Ash had led him around by the nose. Her cheeks flushed warm at the thought of pulling out the panties in front of him.

"Those weren't on the list. I know the brand, absolutely necessary for no panty line." Lindsay tilted her head and peeked into the bag. "Making sure nothing else is tucked inside."

"Uh, let's hope not." Meghan slipped the panties back into the bag and lifted the lid off the boot box. "Whoa. These I like."

"Me too. Glad we wear the same size. The heel's not quite as high as I like, but they complete the outfit. Glad he found black ones." She stood back. "You'd think we were girlfriends."

297

Meghan smiled. "Difference is you'd look better in this than I will."

"Don't think so. Ash will notice, trust me." Lindsay picked up the last bag containing the wig. "Try it on, Meghan. I'm anxious to see if you can pull this off."

So was Meghan. Although the smoky bar would hide their differences, she needed to look like her protectee. After slipping the blonde wig over her red hair, she arranged it. "Stand beside me at the mirror."

The resemblance startled both of them. Lindsay shivered. "By the time you add makeup, you could fool Burnette."

"That's the idea." Meghan removed the wig and set it on her dresser.

"What you're doing for me is risky. Burnette is sending some-one after me, and you'll be the target."

Meghan reached inside the closet for hangers. She wasn't going to debate who the target really was. "This is what I choose to do. I can handle myself."

"You'll have a gun?"

Meghan grinned. "Yes. It'll be inside the waist of my jeans."

"What about martial arts?"

"I can fight with the best of them. Don't worry about me. We need evidence to take to your father. Proof that Burnette is behind a conspiracy against him and the country."

Lindsay swallowed hard. "Do you have any idea why?"

Meghan toyed with what to say. If Lindsay had access to a computer, she could search online and draw the same conclusions. "We think he's seeking revenge for what happened to his son."

"The suicide over the court-martial." Lindsay sat on the bed. "Dad told me Burnette was using me as a surrogate child because he'd lost his own." She shrugged. "Burnette must have fed Dad one lie after another. I know I got the whole buffet."

"When this is all over and he's on trial, will you testify?"

"Yes. Although I realize his defense attorney will discredit me in every way possible, I can handle it as long . . ." Her blue eyes watered. "As long as I know you'll be there. If I can look out into the courtroom and see your face, I'll do whatever it takes."

"I wouldn't abandon you."

"There are days I want a drink, when I can taste it. Feel it trickling down my throat. And some days I want to get high and stay there forever. But if I were free of him, I think I could be strong."

Should she tell Lindsay the truth? "When you're tempted to get high, remember this: the coke Burnette hid for you was pure."

Lindsay paled. "No one would have ever known."

Meghan touched her arm. "You can beat this."

Lindsay swiped beneath her eye. "Keep telling me that, and one day I'll believe it." She sighed. "Someday I want to have an intelligent conversation without crying."

"One day you'll be helping other people fight their demons."

Lindsay stared at her through watery eyes. "I hope so. I really do." She shook her head. "All right, what about earrings, bracelets, rings, and a necklace that drops into—"

"I've got it all. Except wheels. Did you make any progress with Chip?"

"I believe so. We talked, which is more progress than before."

"If he saw me dressed like this at night, I don't think he could tell the difference."

"I'll do my best. He's pretty much a stickler for the rules. I'll ask him tomorrow afternoon. I think he's riding in the morning."

# CHAPTER 57

LINDSAY SPOTTED CHIP several yards from where he normally worked with the horses. Today he was training a cow horse for competition. In the last few days, she'd come to realize the hours he spent training Burnette's horses were a way of working through his grief. Sounded like a better option than drinking and snorting coke. The thought of Burnette's attempt to kill her with the same drug he'd once introduced her to made her even more determined to stop him.

She climbed over the fence, noting Ash and Trey were not far behind. Ash understood she needed alone time with Chip and would keep Trey at a distance.

"Hey, he looks good." Lindsay's words brought a grin from Chip.

"We're getting there. His stops are good. But his spins aren't."

"Shows how much I know. When do you plan to compete?"

"In the fall. Burnette sometimes shows up, but now that he's the vice president, I doubt if he has the time."

Lindsay hoped he was in jail before the weekend. "I have a favor."

He rode up to her. "You want to ride?"

"No." She smiled, wishing she had time to invest in a relationship with Chip. "I want to get away for a few hours Friday night. A girlfriend is meeting me at the Silver Spur."

"Ash and Trey are taking you to a bar?"

"No. They don't exactly know about it."

Chip grimaced. "Lindsay, I won't take you. Can't imagine the trouble I'd be in."

"I wouldn't expect you to, and I'm not going to drink. Just see my friend. But could I borrow your truck?"

"It's a manual transmission."

Lindsay moaned. "I have no clue how to drive one of those." The words were out before she remembered Meghan would be driving it.

"Sorry."

"I hate being cooped up here. One hour. That's all I want."

Chip dismounted. "I have a car."

"I've never seen it."

"It's parked in the garage with Mr. Burnette's truck."

She tilted her head. "The Mustang? Could I borrow it?"

"I don't know. If you started drinking and then got into an accident, I'd—"

"I'm not drinking."

"But you have a drinking problem."

"Chip, this isn't about sneaking off to party." This was about ending Burnette's reign of terror.

"And you think you can sneak off the ranch without those agents finding out?"

She nodded and waited.

"I don't think you can pull it off." He reached inside his pocket. "I have the keys to my Mustang." He shook his head and dropped them back inside his pocket. "I'm probably being really stupid here, but I'll go with you. I have to know you'll be all right. You've come a long way in your sobriety, and I'd hate to see you ruin it in one night."

Lindsay blinked back the emotion. Chip acted as though he really cared, and she was starting to care for him. Lying to him didn't build trust. She should know. And yet she had to persuade him to let her go alone to the Silver Spur.

"Lindsay, if you want to see your friend, I'll take you."

She didn't have any idea how this would work. She hoped, oh how she hoped, he wasn't helping Burnette. Perhaps Meghan and Ash could devise a solution. "Okay. I'll be at the garage Friday night at nine thirty."

Burnette had to be stopped . . . soon.

# CHAPTER 58

THURSDAY MORNING, Meghan and Ash jogged in silence. The threat was still there for a sniper to pull the trigger, but she didn't believe lightning struck twice in the same place. However, the weasel reporter was always waiting for them at the gate.

Meghan's thoughts bubbled to the surface. "I've been thinking about our problem."

"Too bad we're in the dark. When you're concentrating on something, your freckles deepen."

"Were you the class clown?"

"Nope. I was the class nerd."

"The studious type?"

"You got it. The oldest of three. Ultraresponsible."

"I see. So did you go into law to ensure the world became a better place to live?"

"You are too good, Agent Connors. Pair that assumption with a Christian who couldn't seem to get past the rules, and that's me."

"That *was* you. Past tense. Right?"

"You bet. My spiritual awakening while you attended your sister's funeral has me on an uphill climb."

She sighed. Her heart had dipped into admitting her love, while his heart climbed closer to God.

"You had a question?"

His comment brought her back to the topic pressing her mind. "Did Kyle Burnette have a wife?"

"Yes. She was in the Marines too."

"Any kids?"

"I don't think so. If Burnette had grandchildren, he'd be spending all his spare time with them."

"True. And nothing in the house indicates children visiting. Okay, nix that."

"But you have me thinking, Meghan. We can't exclude anything."

His use of *we* gave her a warm feeling, one she couldn't deny. "Okay. What happened to his wife?"

Ash turned to Meghan. "I have no idea, but we need to find out."

He did it again with the *we*. The implication now gave her chills. *Focus, Meghan. Later, after Burnette is brought to justice, you can explore your feelings for Ash.*

"I wonder if Chip could give us any information," Ash said. "He'd know if Burnette's daughter-in-law ever visited here."

"He'd have to think it came from Burnette. And don't forget, I'm using his car tomorrow night."

"I wonder how he'd feel about his boss if he knew about the cocaine in the tack box."

"That's edgy." Meghan didn't want her plans tomorrow night ruined.

"Isn't edgy what we do best? I mean, our job description is Secret Service, and we're acting like a couple of FBI agents."

"Oh, spare me. Don't even put me on the same team." Any other time, Meghan would laugh. But nothing was funny about what they'd uncovered. "The FBI thinks they're the best out there, so we're out to prove them wrong. After all, are they even working on this?"

"I'm sure they are. Should we both approach Chip, or do you want to handle it alone?"

Meghan wrestled with the whole idea. "He'll be inside the stables starting his morning routine when we pass. Look, I think he cares for Lindsay, and she likes him. I've noticed that when she's around him, she's more mature, confident."

"Hadn't noted a possible romance. Must be a woman thing. For both their sakes, he'd better be innocent. But if you think we can get his cooperation based on his feelings for Lindsay, then let's reveal just enough to get a few questions answered. I'll go with you."

"Either he's working on an Academy Award or he's ignorant of Burnette's scheme. No more analyzing the situation?"

He frowned, but she knew he was faking it. "You do try my patience. But as soon as we're done, I'm going to see what I can find out about Kyle's wife."

"And make me wait until I have a break to find out what you've learned?"

He nodded, and they rounded the bend in the road before the front gate—and the sharks. "The possibilities have my head spinning. We both know Burnette isn't working alone."

"Don't let your head explode, A2Z."

He sucked in a gasp. "You've referred to my alias! I thought we'd gone beyond condescending nicknames."

"Oops. Guess I let my guard down."

"Between you and me, I like it. Fits my persona. But if you ever breathe a word of that, I'll have to—"

"Kiss me?"

He chuckled. "Not exactly. But I could be bought."

They kept their gazes away from the sharks searching for blood. Meghan had fallen for one of their tricks. Never again.

The half-mile stretch to the house filled her with anticipation, not for finishing the run, but for the outcome of talking to Chip.

They entered the stables and found Chip in Strait's stall. He ignored them, but that was about to change.

"Chip, we'd like to talk to you. Won't take long." Ash's tone was calm, even.

His eyes never left the colt. "Got another tack box to open?"

"We'd like to tell you what we found in that box."

"Not interested."

"What if we told you it concerned Lindsay?"

"Maybe."

"Would you take a walk with us away from the stables?"

In the shadows, Meghan saw a flash of anger. "You can talk to me right here."

Meghan stole a glance at Ash, then concentrated on convincing Chip of their sincerity. "This isn't a conversation we'd like for anyone else to hear. In fact, if Lindsay were awake, we'd have her join us."

"Then wait until she's up."

"Every minute that passes increases her chances of being killed." Meghan's words caused him to snap to attention.

Chip opened the stall. "Okay. But I'm not in the mood for a pack of lies."

"I'm going to let Ash explain the tack box and its contents. Either you're for us and protecting Lindsay, or you're working for the other side. We're taking a chance, and I hope we're not wrong." She punched her last two words. For sure, if he was in any way aligned with Burnette, she'd kill him herself.

Beyond the garden, the three watched the gray sky break into faint light.

"I'm ready, Ash. Don't waste my time."

"All right, I'll get right to the point. Did anyone else have a key to Burnette's tack box?"

"Not to my knowledge."

"Have you heard from Burnette?"

Chip stiffened. "How would I? You've taken everything that could link me to the outside world."

"I had to ask. Part of my job."

"So why mention the tack box? It's back in my dad's bedroom."

"Meghan found a bag of cocaine in the bottom of it."

"Now you're telling me Burnette uses coke? Get real." He hesitated. "Or are you saying someone planted it?"

"We're wondering if someone else could have a key."

"Makes sense. Planting drugs in the vice president's personal effects diminishes his position." He looked at Ash, then Meghan. "What does this have to do with Lindsay?"

Meghan took a deep breath. "If someone can plant cocaine in the VP's tack box, then he can get to her, too."

"I don't know a thing about this. I'm willing to help Lindsay, even if I can't stand the agents guarding her."

"I'm sure you've had your fill of disruptions—and tragedies. I imagine the VP's guests are usually quiet."

"Barely know they're here."

"Does his daughter-in-law visit often?"

"Erin?"

Bingo. Meghan might have found something useful after all. "I've lost track of where she lives."

"Ask her father-in-law."

"Doesn't matter. We're just concerned about the key to the tack box." Ash reached out to shake his hand, and Chip took it. "Thanks for your help. We'd appreciate it if you'd keep all of this to yourself."

"You got it. Hey, Erin was here a few days before you arrived."

Meghan's insides danced. "Was the vice president with her?"

"No, she left before Pepper got here."

"Did Ethan cook her a fabulous dinner? I remember what he did for me."

"No. She spent the afternoon in the house and drove off right after sunup."

★ ★ ★

Ash watched the clock, anticipating Meghan's arrival during Lindsay's counseling session. What had Erin Burnette been doing prior to the Secret Service's arrival? Could Speaker of the House Randolph be involved in the plot too? How many others had fallen under Burnette's spell?

When Meghan entered the operation room, the two grabbed sandwiches and drinks before heading outside. This time they walked toward the front gate. Midway, he felt safe to relay his findings.

"What did you find out?" Meghan's breathless question caused him to tingle.

Oh, he did have it bad for her. She occupied too many of his thoughts, caused him to think about things like permanence. A family. Kids. "Hair-raising stuff."

"Ash, what did you find out about Erin Burnette?"

He studied her, noting the intelligence in her brown eyes. "With what Chip told us today, I strongly suspect she's working with her father-in-law. But we need proof."

"Tell me more."

"Erin did her stint in the Marines. Sharpshooter in Afghanistan. Returned home about two years ago."

"Where is she living?"

"Idaho. Elementary schoolteacher."

"Most teachers take the summer off, and the extra hours provide an opportunity for other things." He watched her ponder the information. He loved this woman's mind.

"Can we find out if she has close friends?"

"That means someone needs to go there. Someone we can trust."

She released a deep sigh. "Who? We have no clue who's involved, and it's not safe for Lindsay if either of us request any time off."

He felt the same dead-end emotions. "We're stuck here until we can find someone who's willing to risk a sniper's bullet."

# CHAPTER 59

LINDSAY ATTEMPTED TO CONCENTRATE on the counseling session, but all she could think about was Meghan's dangerous mission for the following night.

"You've made tremendous progress." Dave's words of praise were sincere. But unless Meghan and Ash could stop Burnette, more people would die. "What's wrong? You should be glowing."

"I'm working hard." She hesitated, moistening her lips as though the wetness would help find the words to blanket the truth. "Getting back into the real world will be a strain on my sobriety."

"You aren't going back yet. We have lots of ground to cover first."

She nodded. "My parents. My sister. Many things I haven't told you."

"You've never told me what you're afraid of." He studied her, as though he already knew the truth.

What if Dave worked for Burnette too? She trusted her counselor, and then she didn't. Dave admitted her parents had interviewed him extensively. So had Burnette, which meant the demon had time to offer the psychologist a larger fee to follow his agenda.

"Lindsay, you can trust me."

Could she? Maybe not. "I'm afraid of sinking back into the life that got me into this mess." That much was true.

"We'll keep talking about the tools to help you. When you're released, we can meet every day. But you'll have to do your part."

She needed to tell him some of the truth, the reality of a recovering addict. "I know to stay away from old friends and make new ones. Avoid party situations and find other productive means of filling my time."

"That's a textbook answer, but it'll do for now. You've already discovered new interests."

"They aren't new, just covered up."

"Your parents are churchgoers. What do you think?"

"Faith is something I've not found credible."

"I don't either, but others find belief in a deity comforting, reassuring."

Chip believed in God, and they'd discussed what it meant to follow Christ. She'd look into the whole thing more for him than her parents. Sad, but admittedly true.

Sometimes she hated that others took care of her while she floated from one scheduled event to another.

"Who found you, Dave? My parents or Uncle Scottard?"

"The president and First Lady. Your uncle wanted another psychologist."

Hope crept inside. "How did my parents interview you?"

He laughed. "They must have had a hundred questions, and a copy of every case I'd treated."

"And what is your success rate in helping addicts stay clean?"

He sat back, obviously surprised at her question. "75 percent."

"How many fell under the category of coke and alcohol?"

He hesitated. "Both addictions? About 30 percent."

"I'm a tough one. Do you think I can make it?"

"When it comes to the bottom line, it's all up to you. However, you understand the process."

She nodded. Now to move on, to have something to report to Meghan and Ash. "What did Uncle Scottard have to say?"

Dave rubbed his hands. "He wanted to know how much freedom you'd have on the ranch. If I permitted you to take long walks alone, like a stroll through the stables or along the creek."

"What did you tell him?"

He smiled. "You're asking strange questions today. I told him walks were encouraged, but you had to be accompanied by an agent. The only time an agent might not be present was during intense counseling. Even then I assumed one would be close by."

Lindsay touched his arm. "Thank you, Dave. You've always been honest with me, and I appreciate it. The future looks better for me than the past, but every day will be hard if I'm to conquer the drugs."

She hoped the future held promise. Thinking otherwise could drive her back to old habits.

# CHAPTER 60

FRIDAY NIGHT, Meghan put the finishing touches on her makeup—a few more layers and colors than she normally applied. Actually, a lot more. She took a long, admiring look at her reflection. Her budget didn't include these name brands, and she'd never owned clothes this expensive. But she liked the green knit top, sleek-fitting jeans, boots, and jewelry. Blinking, she added eyedrops to the blue contacts.

Picking up the highlighted blonde wig, she slipped it into a Walmart bag and positioned her SIG into the back of her jeans. If a cowboy wanted to dance, she'd have to refuse. Excitement brewed right below the surface of caution. Tonight's rendezvous had the potential to end Burnette's power play.

Lindsay planned to stay in her room tonight, which made Victor's job easier, since Ash had asked him to work a double. Victor Lee possessed all the outward traits of a loyal agent. For that matter, so did Bob. Heaven help them if either man had thrown in with Burnette.

Ash planned to follow her to the Silver Spur. The problem was Chip. He thought he was accompanying Lindsay to the bar. But she and Ash had worked out that hitch.

*Let the games begin.* Meghan opened her bedroom door. She walked to the stairway that led to the family room, where Bob, Victor, and Rick played cards with Carla.

Carla saw her first. "Where are you going?"

"Out for a little while."

Bob startled. "Does Ash know?"

"He's about to."

Victor whistled. "Looks like you have a date."

"I do."

"With who?" Bob clenched his jaw. So he was loyal to Ash.

"Chip."

Victor slowly nodded. "I see what you're doing. Good luck."

Bob rubbed his jaw. "Be careful, Meghan."

"I will."

"You look real good." Victor walked her to the door. "Ash does know, doesn't he?"

"Maybe." She understood Victor and Bob could be dealing her a deadly hand.

Outside Ash was nowhere in sight. At the garage, she opened the door and groped around in the dark until she found the Mustang. If Chip had kept his word to Lindsay, he'd be waiting inside. The moment the light from the car door illuminated his features, Chip stepped out.

"What's this all about?" Anger creased his features.

Meghan slid onto the seat and shut the door. "Don't blame Lindsay. She's only trying to help us find Wade's killer. She's upset about deceiving you."

"And you still think it's me?"

"If I did, I wouldn't allow you to spend so much time with her. I need transportation to the Silver Spur."

"Why didn't you ask?"

"Would you have agreed?"

Silence ruled for several seconds. "So you want a ride. That's it?"

"Yes."

He got back into the car.

"Thanks, Chip. We want Wade's murder solved and the stalker

found who's been threatening Lindsay. I'd like to think it might happen tonight."

"I feel like I'm living in a nightmare."

He backed the car out and headed to the road, where an agent manned the gate. Chip rolled down his window, and the agent peered inside.

"Evenin', Agent Connors, Chip."

"Hey, we'll be back later." She flashed him a smile.

Once they were on the road, she pulled the wig from the bag and positioned it in place.

"You're impersonating Lindsay." His words were flat. "Setting somebody up?"

"I am. I have another favor."

"Why am I not surprised?"

"I need your car. Ash will pick you up in a few minutes."

"Oh, why not. Never thought I'd be in a mess like this."

"I hope you're not involved."

"The only thing I'm guilty of is falling for a girl with history— including addictions."

She hoped he didn't live to regret losing his heart. "For what it's worth, I think she really likes you." Her cell rang, and she snatched it up while noting the headlights in the side mirror.

"I'm right behind you," Ash said.

"We'll pull over at the next crossroad." She glanced at Chip, and he nodded.

"Do you have the bug?"

Annoyance swept through her. "I'm an agent, Ash."

"All right. Have to check on my girl."

She grinned despite her irritation. "Are you trying to defuse me?"

"Worked, didn't it?"

The Mustang stopped, and Chip unbuckled his seat belt. "Be careful."

"I will. Thanks." She exited the car and rounded to the driver's side, while Chip got into Burnette's truck with Ash. How ironic that Burnette was helping them nail his own coffin.

★  ★  ★

Ash noted Chip's stiffened body. The man had more than one reason to be angry. Yet in the past few days, Ash had changed his mind about him. He sensed a good man, one who'd not participate in a murder. Time to get closer and see what happened.

"I can't apologize for doing my job." He chose to reveal more information. "What would you do if you were committed to protecting Lindsay's life?"

Chip sighed. "I'd do whatever it took to make sure she was safe."

"Now you know where Meghan and I stand."

"I could use more honesty. I'm not, nor have I ever been, the bad guy."

"I'm banking on those words." Ash wanted to dig deeper about Ethan, a suspicion that refused to let go. "Did your dad have a heart condition?"

"No. His checkups were always good. No elevated blood pressure. Cholesterol levels fell within the norms, and heart disease isn't in our family. My grandpa lived to be ninety-eight." He stared out into the dark night. "I don't know why the doctor didn't detect a heart problem. I thought about an autopsy, but I was grieving and angry at the time."

The nibbling at Ash's mind continued. "How well did your dad know the vice president?"

"They were good friends, and Mr. Burnette trusted him with his prize animals. Dad knew him long before I did."

"Before his son committed suicide?"

"Before Kyle was born."

"Do you know if your dad and the vice president talked about his son's death?"

"I'm sure of it. Mr. Burnette spent a couple of months at the ranch afterward. Dad said he shed buckets of tears."

"Did the VP spend much time here later on?"

"Yes. His wife left him during the trial, and he preferred the solitude of the ranch. What are you driving at?"

The idea Ethan had been murdered pounded at his brain. "Chip, I'd like to have an autopsy done on your dad."

Chip's gaze flew to Ash. "Why? Do you think one of the agents had something to do with Dad's death? Wade's murder? Lindsay's stalking?"

"I don't know, but I'd sure like to find out. Chip, you're a smart man. You could be working against us, but I don't think so."

"Do you need blood to prove it?" Bitterness dripped from his tongue.

"Let's hope not. Do you play chess?"

"A little. Dad and I used to bring out the board now and then. Why?"

"I'm just wondering if you're a pawn. Now I need to know the rest of the players." Ash pulled up next to a fence line at the Dancin' Dust. "Once you jump the fence, an agent will escort you back home."

"All right. Get the autopsy done. I want to know how my dad died."

# CHAPTER 61

MEGHAN SENSED EXCITEMENT kicking into gear when the flashing lights of the Silver Spur came into view. Trucks, motorcycles, and a few cars filled the parking lot, and the moment she opened the car door, honky-tonk music met her ears. She'd added a few miles since she'd been to a smoky dive. This time she wasn't searching for Shelley.

A curved bar swung to her left, crowded with cowboys and cowgirls who mingled at tables and perched on bar stools. A live band tuned their instruments. The lead singer held a fiddle, two men played guitars, and a woman sat at the drums. Two overhead beams spotlighted the scuffed wooden dance floor. Her gaze swept the place, wondering if her blind date watched her. An empty stool looked like the best place to wait.

She ordered a Sprite and observed the goings-on. The band hit a two-step and couples moved to the dance floor. She declined an offer . . . and observed.

A broad-shouldered man, typical of the jean-clad crowd, stood beside her. "The band's better than usual."

"I wouldn't know."

"That's because you haven't been here before."

*Good.* "Do you always notice the first-timers?"

"Only the pretty ones." He leaned on the bar beside her. "You're drinking Sprite?"

"I am." She studied his face. Good-looking. Scruffy beard. Too much cheap cologne.

"Don't you want to loosen up?"

"I'm plenty loose right now."

"Wanna dance?"

"I'm waiting on someone."

"Lucky man."

"I'll decide later."

He straightened. "If he doesn't show, I'll be close by. Don't wait too long. I have my regulars."

This wasn't the right guy.

By midnight, four cowboys had asked her to dance, and two had bought her another Sprite. She headed to the ladies' room and then to the car. A couple leaned against a truck and kissed. Two guys smoked and laughed. Looked like all the action was inside, but none of what she hoped to find. Ash sat parked at the rear of the parking lot. What a wasted night, and he'd spent a ton on her clothes. Maybe when Lindsay's stalker had been found, he'd take her two-steppin', and she'd show him how the West was really won.

She started the Mustang and let the air conditioning cool her discontent before she phoned Ash. "Sorry. Our guy didn't show."

"We took a chance. No big deal."

Except what Ash had spent on clothes. "Do you think he got tipped off?"

"Who knows? Could be someone at the ranch figured us out."

"What do you think about Chip?"

"Either he's a good impersonator, or he's legit. Look, you drive on back. I'm going to hang around a little while. See if anyone follows you."

"I'll pay you for these clothes."

"Would you stop that? I think it was worth the view."

She laughed and pulled out of the parking lot, spitting gravel and spinning tires. Hmm. She wondered what Chip's Mustang would do on the open road. Four miles later, she noted headlights barreling behind her. Easing over, she hoped he wasn't a drunk. When he didn't pass, she sped up. So did the truck.

"Ash, I got a pickup on my rear. He's doing seventy."

"I'm on my way. No one left here."

Meghan pressed the accelerator past seventy-five. "He's doing eighty."

"I don't like this. I'm hurrying."

If the driver meant to eliminate her, he'd be firing shots. Ahead she spotted a short bridge. No point alarming Ash. She urged the Mustang faster and approached the bridge. The truck stayed on her tail. So he had a game plan. *Lord, I could use a little help here.* The truck slammed into her as she entered the bridge. She struggled to keep the car on the road. The truck pounded her, like a fire-breathing monster that refused to give up, causing the Mustang to crash into the concrete bridge. The car flipped, sending it midair and into blackness.

★ ★ ★

Ash heard sounds of a crash. He pressed the accelerator to the floorboard, hoping she'd not been hurt.

"Meghan! What's going on?" When he didn't hear a response, he called for her again.

Racing down the road, he looked for taillights to gauge what had happened to the Mustang. He neared the bridge. About fifteen feet of the concrete embankment had crumbled. Slamming on his brakes, he swerved the truck onto the right side of the bridge just past the impact. Grabbing his flashlight and SIG, he slid down the hill. The Mustang lay wheels up in a dry creek bed.

He snapped open his phone. "Victor, someone ran Meghan off the road. The car flipped off a bridge. Call an ambulance. We're about four miles west of the ranch. Stay where you are. This could be a ploy to nab Lindsay." Snapping it shut, he made his way to the driver's side.

*Not on my watch. Not on my watch. Not Meghan.*

The flashlight illuminated her body slumped over the steering wheel. Blood trickled down her face. "Meghan, are you all right?"

He yanked on the car door, but it wouldn't budge. Hurrying to the other side, he kicked in the window and opened the door. "Meghan."

He crawled in and felt for a pulse. She was alive. He released the seat belt, debating whether to pull her out or wait for the paramedics. "Talk to me." When she didn't answer, he carefully lifted her body from the wreckage.

A slight moan escaped her lips. He kissed her while tears blurred his vision. "Hold on, baby. Help's coming." Why hadn't he told her he loved her? "If you can hear me, I love you."

The sound of a siren filled the night air. How long had he held her? Ash had no idea if the emergency vehicle was the sheriff or an ambulance, but she needed help.

*God, please. Not Meghan.*

# CHAPTER 62

LINDSAY WOKE SHORTLY after one thirty in the morning, her TV blaring with an old movie she'd seen before. Meghan should be here by now, and Lindsay wanted to know if the stalker had been found. Her heart sped at the thought of a man naming Burnette as the one who'd ordered Wade's death and stalked her, bombed her car and killed another person. He might even be behind the attempt on her father's life in Atlanta. She slipped into a pair of running shorts and a T-shirt and opened her bedroom door. Victor and Bob stood by the stair railing.

"Hey, guys. Is Meghan back yet?"

Lines creased Bob's brow.

"What's the matter?" She glanced from one agent to the other. "Where's Meghan?"

"I'll get Dave." Bob walked the hallway. "He's downstairs."

A sickening dread spread through her. A need for air compounded with lightheadedness assaulted her, a sensation she recognized as a panic attack. She breathed in and out just like Dave had taught her. Meghan had to be all right. She'd risked her life to help bring Burnette to justice. She focused on Victor. "Is she alive? Just tell me that."

"Yes."

"How bad? What happened to her?"

"I don't know the details."

Lindsay descended the stairs, willing her heart to stop its rapid beating. Dave met her at the landing. This was her fault. All her fault. "I have to know about Meghan. I know it's bad, but Victor won't tell me a thing."

Dave took both her hands. "She was in a car accident—"

"The Silver Spur is only nine miles down the road." Her breathing grew more rapid, and she trembled.

"Take a deep breath, Lindsay. Look at me."

Her gaze darted everywhere but at him. She couldn't help it. Meghan was hurt, and she had to be in horrible condition from the looks on everyone's faces.

"Lindsay." His sharp voice captured her attention, and she looked into his kind face. "Breathe in and out slowly."

"Will you tell me about Meghan?"

"I will as soon as you calm yourself."

Several moments later, he led her to the sofa in the family room. She sat there, conscious of others watching her. She wanted to be strong. Hated the weakness. "I'm okay. I want to know about Meghan . . . and the car accident."

"We don't know anything yet. An ambulance has taken her to the hospital."

"Thank you." Her voice quivered. "I want to wait here for word." She glanced around. "Is Ash with her?"

"Yes. He'll phone us from the hospital." She'd grown to appreciate Dave's soothing voice.

The back door opened, and Chip walked in. His flushed face revealed his concern. "I heard the news from one of the agents. Any updates?"

"Nothing yet." Bob shook his hand. "We appreciate your concern."

Had the agents begun to believe in his innocence?

"I figured she'd gone solo." Chip's gaze softened. "Lindsay, you okay?"

She nodded. "It's my fault, and I know it."

He crossed the room and knelt in front of her. "It's Meghan's and these agents' job to protect you. Don't blame yourself."

"I lied to get your car."

"It's okay. I understand, and given the same circumstances, I'd have done the same."

"If I hadn't angered the wrong people, none of this would have happened. First the bombing, then Wade, and now Meghan. Why can't the cops or the Secret Service or someone find these guys?" She knew the answer. *Tell them. . . . Tell them. . . .*

But no one would believe the vice president of the United States murdered people. Meghan tried to help, and look what happened. They'd be after Ash, too.

Chip had been with both agents tonight, but she had no idea for how long. "Ash shouldn't be alone at the hospital."

"The sheriff's with him. I stopped in to tell you that I'm heading there now. Someone needs to be with Ash." He threw his attention at Victor.

"Sounds like a great idea, since none of us can leave. Sorry about your car."

"It can be replaced. And thanks. I'm leaving in the next few minutes." He took Lindsay's hand and gave it a gentle squeeze. "I know you can't take calls, but I'll be thinking about you."

Lindsay saw in the depths of his green eyes what she'd never seen in a man before. It both welcomed and frightened her. "Meghan and Ash are Christians. They'd want us to pray for them."

Chip held her hands. "Sounds like an Ethan Leonard quote. I don't have a direct line to God, but we can try."

# CHAPTER 63

MEGHAN'S BODY THROBBED from her head to her toes, as though she'd been beaten and left to die. She prayed for strength to endure the agony tearing through her. Why hadn't someone given her a pain shot? For the first time in her life, she understood why Shelley, Lindsay, and countless others chose drugs to alleviate physical and mental torment.

"Meghan?"

*Ash.* She should summon courage, not let him see her like this.

"If you're awake, squeeze my hand."

She hadn't been aware of her hand in his, only the intense pain. She forced herself to move both hands, not sure where his enveloped hers.

"Good girl."

Ash's voice sounded warm, gentle. She wanted to see him, but her eyes refused to open. How had this happened? Now she remembered. A truck had pushed her over a bridge as she drove back from the Silver Spur. Fire shot through her lower abdomen and caused her to cry out. Enough of this.

She struggled to open her eyes, though a cloud covered her vision. She saw images but nothing recognizable.

"I quit." Had she spoken the words as she intended, or were they mere thoughts that she couldn't communicate?

"I don't blame you."

He'd heard, and he understood. "Can't do this . . . any . . . more."

"Of course."

"You—" This time the pain rippled up and down her right leg—"win."

His lips brushed across the top of her hand. "No, sweetheart. You're the winner."

She wanted to say more, to tell him she'd resign from Lindsay's protective detail as soon as she could hold a pen. Lindsay wasn't safe with her. Meghan didn't have the ability to keep Burnette and his people away. She gasped with the throbbing in her body.

"Miss Connors, you have a morphine pump. All you have to do is squeeze it when you are uncomfortable. Here, I'll show you." A woman's voice broke through Meghan's thoughts. She placed a rubber bulb into her hand and helped her squeeze it. "You can't overdose. Use it. There's no reason for you to suffer. No reason for you to be a hero."

If only she had the strength to tell the woman that she could never be a hero. Her role as Lindsay Hall's protector was over. She'd failed. She couldn't even drive without getting run off the road.

"Will she sleep?" Ash's words soothed her. He must be disappointed in her disgusting performance.

"Probably so. And that's what we want."

A warm sensation spread through her, bringing with it relief, and she slipped into peaceful darkness.

★ ★ ★

Later that day, Ash studied the battered, serene face of the woman he'd once wanted to despise. Now he loved her, ached for what she was going through. He steadied himself while talking to Warrington.

Where once selfishness ruled in the guise of purpose, now passion and love breathed life into his rock-hard heart. Meghan brought back the dreams of a little boy who played with Hot Wheels and believed a frog belonged in his pocket. A little boy with five smooth stones who trusted that the Goliaths of his life would always be defeated. How one woman could make him feel protective when she had the skills to protect him was baffling.

Ash glanced around Meghan's hospital room, seeing and smelling the roses he'd sent to her. Her eyes were closed, yet he knew she was listening to his every word to Warrington.

"Ash, do you really think an autopsy is necessary for Ethan Leonard? I mean, he was an old man who worked himself to death."

Ash's jaw clenched. "I think it's critical. The man didn't have any health issues. No heart problems in his family, and you know what's been going on here."

"Who do you suspect?"

He wasn't going to tell him what he knew about Burnette until he had more leverage. Neither was he going to toss out a name without proof. "I can't say yet. But I'll have a name or names to you soon."

"Are you saying an agent is involved in a conspiracy? Come on. They're dedicated guys."

"Think about it. If Ethan didn't die of natural causes, then Chip's clear of any involvement. Then we have a real problem." Ash wanted to confide in him about Burnette, but not until he knew Warrington could be trusted.

"True. I didn't feel comfortable about having him returned to the ranch. The VP created more problems when we removed him than I care to name. Said no one but a Leonard could handle his horses."

"So you'll order the autopsy?"

Warrington paused. "All right."

"Thanks, and I appreciate your putting a rush on it."

"Keep your eyes open. This mess keeps getting worse. How's Agent Connors doing?"

Ash smiled at the woman he loved. "She's trying to get released today, but that's not happening. Said she could recover from a concussion at the Dancin' Dust."

"I'll save my lecture for when she recovers. Can't believe she didn't break anything. She's a tough gal."

"And a dynamite agent."

"Oh? What changed your mind about her?"

"Eight weeks on a remote ranch in West Texas."

"You've just cracked your image."

"I know. The Secret Service will never be the same."

Warrington chuckled. "I'll be back with you as soon as I have the autopsy report."

Ash turned off his phone and leaned over to plant a kiss on Meghan's lips. "You have become a habit."

"Addiction?"

"The good kind." He took her hand into his, remembering his first view of the wreckage. "You scared me."

She smiled through swollen lips. Her right eye had turned a deep purple and a bruise swept across her cheek. "I was lucky. I ache all over, but looking at you, having you right here beside me is all the medicine I need."

"I prayed hard from the moment I saw where the car had gone off the bridge to when the doctor said you were one lucky lady."

"That's God."

"Yeah. For sure."

She studied him. "You haven't been back to the ranch."

"Oh, you noticed my shirt? Didn't want to leave my lady. Two agents have replaced us for now."

"I'll be back on duty tomorrow."

"Right."

She frowned. "My memory is zilch. Nothing after hitting the bridge."

"Good, considering."

She nodded. "I remember pain."

"Do you remember quitting?"

Her brown eyes widened. "You're kidding." She bit her lip. "I remember dreaming about it."

"Does that mean you've changed your mind?"

A tear slipped from her eye, and he dabbed it with his finger. "How can I give up on Lindsay? Or bringing him to justice?"

"That's my girl."

"I wish I could remember something that would help find who pushed me over the bridge. I'd go after him myself."

He chuckled. "I believe you would. Makes me feel sorry for the scorpion you found in your bed. But I promise you, his days are numbered. Chip stayed with me until eight this morning. Once you woke, he drove back to the ranch. Told me the agents, Dave, Carla, and Lindsay prayed for you. And if you can believe this, it was Lindsay's idea."

She squeezed her eyes shut, but he saw another tear. "She's going to make it, Ash. I feel it."

"Hope so. Chip and I talked, and I believe he's innocent of any crimes. He also told me that he didn't see any skid marks on the bridge."

"Have the authorities found anything?"

"Not yet." Ash wished he had something positive to report.

"The autopsy will tell us a lot. But I wish we could have obtained one without bringing Warrington into it."

He nodded. "No choice. If Warrington is involved . . ." The implications were more than he wanted to consider at the moment.

"We're both dead."

Ash smoothed back the hair from her forehead. "Not us. We're super agents."

"I think you've been using my morphine pump. Can I see what I look like?"

He wanted to prolong that aspect of her recovery. "Vanity is not a positive attribute."

She closed her eyes. "I'm leaving in a few hours, which means

I'll get a good look in the car. I'd much prefer to see how others will see me, so I can be prepared. It's not Halloween yet."

He grimaced. "Close. On the way back to the ranch, you can take a peek in the rearview mirror. And the earliest you'll be released is tomorrow."

"Can I always expect the truth from you?"

"You can."

"And you're not holding back on me? I don't have a broken nose or missing front teeth?"

"No, baby, you're beautiful except for a few shades of blue and purple."

"Thank you. I'm going back to sleep."

He'd promised himself he'd tell her of his feelings when she awakened. "I have to tell you something."

"I'm listening."

His phone rang again, and the caller had priority. "Yes, Mr. President."

"I'm calling to check on Agent Connors. Warrington is keeping me informed, but I wanted her to know how much I appreciate what she attempted to do last night."

"Thank you, sir. She's resting."

"Don't bother her. Please tell her I'm behind her all the way. We will bring an end to these tragedies. On a personal note, Dave's reports are glowing, and I know much of Lindsay's progress is attributed to Agent Connors's encouragement."

"I will. Thank you." The phone disconnected.

"Wow. I feel important." Sleep threatened to overcome her. "What . . . what did you want to tell me?"

He leaned over the bed. "I love you, Meghan Connors. Not sure how it happened, but I realized it when I pulled you out of Chip's Mustang."

Her eyes flew open, and a smile spread from one bruise to another. "I dreamed you were carrying me and told me those very words."

"You weren't dreaming."

"I love you too. What an unlikely pair. We—"

He touched her lips. "Get some sleep. We can talk later."

Watching her sleep peacefully calmed him. Raking his fingers through his hair, he wished they had answers. Burnette's plan ticked away, and Ash had no idea when it would explode next. Who had sold out to him? Each time he considered a member of his team, he pulled a blank. Burnette requested Victor and Bob, but these were trustworthy men. Dave had no contact with Burnette, but they could be corresponding in secret. Then again, Burnette could have Dave earmarked for the next hit.

Every person at the Dancin' Dust could be linked to Burnette. Ash had watched their body language, listened to what they said, followed them. Who could it be?

Then a thought occurred to him. A consideration so ridiculous that at first he tossed it aside. His sleep-deprived mind must be affecting his logic. But it made sense. The autopsy report had the potential to add another player to the chess game. He thought Chip was a pawn, used for whatever purpose Burnette needed. The knight danced two steps in his comfort zone and took one step into the unknown, and that was who Ash wanted to nail.

He fretted about taking Meghan back to the ranch tomorrow. In her vulnerable condition, someone might try to hurt her . . . again.

# CHAPTER 64

MONDAY AFTERNOON, Lindsay scribbled the line of a song she'd spent the past two days perfecting. The tune danced through her head, but the words were another matter. Her premise was to show how wildflowers were like people's lives, blooming for a season. But the idea refused to translate on paper.

Maybe a song about her fragile feelings for Chip deserved her energy and passion. She pressed her journal to her heart, much like how she used to hold her teddy bear, relishing its softness. Not that she wanted immaturity in her writing, but an appreciation for what made life worth living.

Chip . . . Being with him urged her to be a better person. To stay clean and honest. She could laugh with him and relax. Perhaps that's what she valued the most about him. No pretense. No fear of being used. Some girls dreamed of a handsome prince. Lindsay longed for a simple man who understood her need to be close to nature, the earth, and animals. She smiled. This was the Lindsay she kept tucked away. Until she met Chip.

She lay the journal in her lap, opened to a clean page, and began again. A knock on her door interrupted her musings.

"Lindsay, Vice President Burnette would like to talk to you." Ash's voice held no emotion. While here at the Dancin' Dust, she'd learned how his impassive tone was really an invitation for her to make a decision.

"Please tell him I'm busy." She picked up her pen.

"He says it's urgent."

Burnette's requests were always urgent and greedy and selfish. She hesitated. If she didn't take his call, he'd make sure someone was hurt or killed.

"I'll talk to him." She slid from the bed and opened the bedroom door. Ash's face was grim. The thought of putting the call on speaker crossed her mind, but Burnette would be furious. Ash closed the door behind him, but she hoped he listened.

"Hi, Uncle Scottard."

"Is my girl doing well?"

The sound of his voice sickened her. "I'm not your girl."

He chuckled, and she shivered. "Agent Connors had a nasty accident. So sorry to hear she nearly died. But you shouldn't be surprised."

She moistened her lips. "What do you want?"

"Is Ash near you?"

"No. I'm in my room. He's in the hall."

"I want to know why you haven't been into the liquor cabinet or my other gift. Dave's reports about your progress upset me."

"I'm not drinking or using. I'm clean and sober, and I intend to stay that way."

"Upsetting me is not a wise choice. Think about Agent Connors."

Her knees weakened. She hated him, the old desperation sinking into her soul. "Please do not call me anymore. I've been your puppet long enough."

"And you will continue to do whatever I say. Now get that liquor cabinet open, and I want you to find Chip and get the coke from my tack box."

The coke that would kill her? She disconnected the call. Tossing the cell phone on the bed, she fought the rising hysteria.

"Ash. Ash, help me." The door flew open, and she walked into his arms. "Make him stop. Please, make him stop."

"Soon it will be over." His whisper failed to comfort her.

The phone rang, but neither she nor Ash made an effort to answer it.

# CHAPTER 65

LATELY ASH DREADED answering the phone. Especially when Burnette had made demands on Lindsay, like earlier today. The VP had cursed for thirty seconds when Lindsay refused his second and third calls.

Near dusk on Monday evening, Warrington called Ash.

"Yes, sir."

"Do you have time to answer a few questions?"

"Sure." Had he and Meghan's investigation been discovered?

"The VP has a complaint about you. Claims you and Agent Connors refuse him access to Lindsay when he calls."

What a stretch of the truth. "I have no idea what he's talking about. I've never refused his calls. Lindsay might choose not to talk to him. But that's her decision."

"The VP claimed you'd use Lindsay as an excuse. He wants you to put her through to him regardless of her willingness to speak to him."

What was this all about? "Sir, forcing my protectee to take a call is not my job."

"Ash, I agree. If the request hadn't come from the VP, I wouldn't have wasted my time or yours."

"Has the president been notified of the VP's ridiculous accusation?"

"He will be. I'll get back to you after I brief him. He's been tied up all day."

"Anything else, sir?"

"Bear with me, Ash. I see light."

Was Warrington merely indicating disapproval of Burnette's request? Or could he be on the same track as Ash and Meghan? Being the Lone Ranger and Tonto had its downfalls.

★ ★ ★

After breakfast on Tuesday morning, Meghan had forty-five minutes before her shift. She refused to shirk her responsibilities, though Victor had volunteered to work for her until she was at 100 percent. A walk along the creek sounded like a good way to be as close to tranquility as possible. However, Ash would be furious when he learned about it, as though she'd keel over with a headache. The whole chaotic situation of attempting to prove Burnette's guilt had kept her awake at night and her stomach swirling during the day. The headaches since her accident hadn't helped either.

Faith was an issue, and she recognized her own failings in that department. Everything in her professional and personal life had bottomed out—deaths, disappointments, betrayals. No point in drudging through the mud with any of it. She desperately needed answers, and she knew God had them. Why couldn't He send an e-mail outlining what she should do next? Right now, a burning bush would suit her. Everything she and Ash had done to stop Burnette had ended in disaster.

Her dad once said God only used failures. She'd put that quote to the test.

What concerned her most was that an evil man appeared to be winning the battle. Lindsay's fragile emotions could cave at any time. People were dead.

"Meghan."

She whirled around to see Ash walking toward her. The lines in his forehead indicated something else had gone wrong.

"We have a problem."

"I figured so by the look on your face. What is it this time?"

"The reporter who harassed us at the gate?"

How could she forget with the media feasting on her photo, smearing blood over his shirt. "What's he done now?"

"He was found about ten minutes ago with his throat cut."

Her heart plummeted. "I suppose his death looks like one of us did it."

"Of course. We threatened him."

"How did Burnette manage this?"

"He's hired professionals, Meghan. We've known his capabilities for a long time. Warrington told me yesterday that Burnette's complaining that we don't put his calls through to Lindsay."

She stretched her neck to ease the hammering against her skull. "So what are we to do now? Is Burnette rewriting the Secret Service's code?"

"It was more of an FYI thing. Makes me wonder if Warrington might be getting wise to him."

"In the meantime there's only two of us. How can we continue to fight him and keep Lindsay and her father alive?"

"We've got to find a way to get an audience with the president."

"Would Lindsay agree?"

"She has to."

# CHAPTER 66

Lindsay couldn't bear to see the disappointment in Meghan's eyes. "I can't talk to Dad about Burnette. He believes every word the man says." Hopelessness laced her fears. "My history destroys anything coming from my mouth."

Meghan stopped in the driveway leading to the gate. Her face was a mass of bruises, and yet she insisted upon doing her job. "You don't know that for sure. Your father loves you."

"Don't manipulate me. I've had enough of those tactics."

"I'm only trying to convince you that you're the only person who can get through to your father about his vice president."

"And I'm telling you I can't. Burnette would punish me by convincing Dad to make sure I stay here for the next year. How would you feel about spending months under Burnette's thumb?"

"Look what's happened up to this point. How many people are going to die before you realize you have the ability to stop him?"

She shook her head. "Leave me alone. I can't do it." Lindsay took a deep breath. She trembled at the memory. "I tried once, and Dad went straight to Burnette. Told him everything I said. Dad called my psychiatrist, and between the doctor and Uncle Scottard, I spent six months in a psych hospital. The diagnosis was a personality disorder. Dear Uncle Scottard told my parents and the psychiatrist that I confessed to hearing voices that urged me to kill them and myself. And oh, Uncle Scottard recommended the psychiatrist. He was an old friend."

Meghan's face softened. "Oh, Lindsay. I'm so sorry. I knew about the hospitalization and the diagnosis, but I should have figured out the rest."

"Now you have the scoop. I won't put myself through six months of sedation and therapy for a condition I don't have. At least here I have hope he might fall over from a heart attack or someone will put a bullet through his head." She wanted to help, but the memories of those six months were like an open wound. "You have to stop him, but I can't help you. Nothing I say can be used in a court of law."

Meghan stiffened. "One more time you've swallowed Burnette's lies."

"You're the trained professionals. I'm nothing but a drug addict."

"A recovering drug addict."

"No. Please, don't ask me again."

"What if Ash and I were with you when you talked to your father?"

"Haven't you heard a single word I've said? It isn't happening. I'm not crazy. I don't have a personality disorder. I'd rather be dead than subject myself to Burnette's fury." She shuddered. "The truth is the psychiatrist never diagnosed me with personality disorder. But Burnette convinced my dad that the likelihood was there."

"How much does Dave know?"

"He has my files. We've talked about it, but of course not about Burnette." Lindsay leaned forward. "Burnette has a hold on my dad stronger than blood ties. And I'm afraid it will be the death of him."

# CHAPTER 67

WEDNESDAY AFTERNOON, Ash scanned his e-mail, always look-ing for something that would pull together the case against Burnette. He'd gotten away with far too much, and his successes were bound to make him cocky. Ash didn't think Chip suspected Burnette, which was a good thing for now. Didn't need another man dead. But as close as Chip and Lindsay were getting, she might weaken and tell all. Ash tapped his pen on the table. Lindsay understood Burnette's mean streak, and she'd not knowingly endanger Chip's life.

An e-mail from Warrington flagged his attention. The autopsy report was attached. Ash clicked on the file.

The autopsy found "no gross evidence of myocardial infarc-tion." Ethan had not died of a heart attack. What Ash surmised now had validity but no proof. The pathologist indicated the final diagnosis would await review of the histologic sections—portions of various organs processed under microscopic exam. It helped to have a cousin who was a doctor to interpret medical terms. The testing could take up to six weeks, the toxicology aspect even lon-ger, but Warrington indicated he'd put a rush on all the testing, not just on the results. Ash typed back to Warrington that in the event Ethan was poisoned, he wanted to know the substance. A few moments later, he forwarded the report to Meghan.

Needing a break to allow the autopsy's findings to sink in, Ash walked out onto the back porch and gazed at the pool. Lindsay had swum earlier, but she'd appeared distracted—like the rest of them. Disappointment swept through him at the thought of Lindsay refusing to contact the president about Burnette. He couldn't blame her, but the only way they would get an audience with the president was through Lindsay. Fear wrapped around her as tightly as the drugs had imprisoned her. All thanks to Burnette's ability to control her with a single phone call.

Now a reporter lay dead. Granted Ash had little use for the foul-mouthed man who had nothing better to do than throw rocks at a woman, but he hadn't wanted the man dead. Warrington had already called and asked for statements from him and Meghan. One TV network had Ash and Meghan under arrest. Another called them "persons of interest." Burnette was behind it. But again, how could his treachery be proved?

"Ash."

He swung around at the sound of his name. Chip dripped in sweat. Like Ash felt.

"Do you have a few minutes? I have some information about the murdered reporter."

Chip might be an answer to prayer. "Let's hear it." Ash pointed to the bench on the other side of the pool. He still wondered where other listening devices might be hidden.

"You know I run at 0200. This morning on the way back through the gate, I saw someone enter that reporter's RV."

"Did you happen to see enough to identify him?"

"At the time, I thought it was a woman, because of the size." Chip anchored his hands on his hips. "Didn't think much about it until the man turned up dead."

Ash recalled the estimated time of death. He also pondered Chip's description of a small person . . . or Erin Burnette? "The coroner said he died around 0300."

"Which means I probably saw the killer enter his RV."

"Did you note anything else about the person?"

Chip drummed his fingers on his thigh. "The reporter glanced around a few times before closing the door behind him."

"Did he see you?"

"I don't think so. Pretty dark along the road."

"How was the person dressed?"

"Jeans. Black T-shirt."

"Would you be willing to tell the sheriff your story?"

"You know I would."

Ash shot a glance at the road. The sheriff had been there most of the day. He flipped open his cell phone and dialed his number.

# CHAPTER 68

"I CAN'T BELIEVE you've never baked chocolate chip cookies." Meghan pulled brown sugar from the pantry and set it beside the flour, salt, and vanilla. Pepper had given them permission to use the kitchen while she picked vegetables in the garden.

"My mother was either working with desperate people in Africa or playing the role of a politician's wife, and I spent most of my life in boarding schools. We didn't bake cookies."

Compassion flowed through Meghan. Time spent with her mother lived like a treasure in her heart. "What about Christmas?"

"Either someone gave us a fancy basket of cookies or Mom bought them."

"That changes today. Someday you'll have kids of your own, and you will be Queen Mom with a single batch of homemade chocolate chip cookies."

Lindsay shrugged. "If you insist. My culinary skills amount to mixing beer and liquor or punching a few buttons on a microwave. Oh, I can pour a mean bowl of cereal."

Meghan grimaced and stepped back into the pantry for parchment paper. "We're about to alter Lindsay Hall's history. We'll need two sticks of butter and two eggs. We should have gotten them out earlier."

"Why's that, Paula Deen?"

Meghan cocked a brow. "Oh, you know a chef."

"I've watched a lot of TV shows lately. So why should we have set out the butter and eggs?"

"Both need to be at room temperature."

Lindsay opened the fridge. "Do you suppose Chip likes chocolate chip cookies?"

Meghan laughed at the pun. "Every man does. I plan to make sure Ash and the team receive a ton of these. This recipe is supposed to make six dozen, but I like to make big cookies. So we'll have about four dozen. Ever heard the way to a man's heart is through his stomach?"

Lindsay waved a finger. "The way I heard it isn't repeatable. But I'm here to change my ways, so I'll learn to cook."

"You really like him, don't you?"

Lindsay blushed, and the response surprised Meghan. She had so much hope for her protectee.

"He's kind and gentle, and we share so much in common."

"Like what? Besides music." Meghan pulled a mixing bowl from the cupboard.

"A love for the country life. Horses . . . well, all kinds of animals. You'll laugh at this one."

"No, I won't. Bring it on."

"We like to be around older people."

Another delightful surprise. Tears brimmed Meghan's eyes, and she quickly blinked them away. Her job description placed a clamp on sentiment.

"Why are you getting emotional?"

"Thought I hid it."

Lindsay laughed. "You've got to work harder on your skills, Agent Connors. Why did my interest in the elderly bring on a few tears?"

"Because I've prayed for you and your recovery, and it's happening right before my eyes."

"When this is over, will you stay on with me?"

Meghan didn't want to mention the possible PPD assignment.

Leaving Lindsay would be difficult. The affection she felt was akin to a little sister, but Meghan would have to be careful and not let it cloud her judgment. "Let's set the butter on the back porch. It'll soften faster. Then we—" Her cell phone rang.

Caller ID registered Scottard Burnette. She glanced at Lindsay, who'd proceeded to unwrap a stick of butter and drop it into the mixing bowl.

"Yes, sir." Meghan detested addressing him with any respect.

"Good morning, Agent Connors. I need to talk to Lindsay."

She muted the phone. "The vice president would like to speak to you."

Lindsay's eyes flashed fire. "What about?"

Meghan resumed her call. "Lindsay would like to know what this is about."

"Kelli. That's all she needs to know."

Meghan communicated the information to her protectee. Lindsay turned ashen and took the phone.

"What's happened to Kelli?" She clenched her free hand. "Yes, I'm in the kitchen with Meghan. . . . When? . . . Is she in the hospital? . . . Why didn't Mom or Dad call?" Lindsay gasped, and her frantic gaze flew to Meghan. "I'll call Mom myself."

She stiffened, as Burnette obviously had more to say.

"You're a liar. I would have been contacted by now. Be glad I don't have a gun." Lindsay disconnected the call and handed the phone to Meghan. What had Burnette done now? "Please, would you get my mother on the phone. I need to talk to her immediately."

Meghan had both of Lindsay's parents on speed dial. "Do we need to talk first?"

"No. For once I can handle something on my own." She paced the kitchen. "Mom, this is Lindsay. . . . Good to talk to you too." Determination swept across her features. "Soon, Mom. Soon. Is Kelli all right?" Lindsay clenched her fist. "I had a bad dream about her and wanted to make sure she was okay." She continued to pace the floor while listening to her mother. "The dream scared me."

Lindsay caught Meghan's attention, and Meghan gave her a reassuring smile. From what she could tell, Lindsay had responded to Burnette in a manner that displayed her growing courage. But she also hoped nothing had happened to Kelli Hall.

Lindsay's face broke into a wide smile. "Thanks, Mom. Would you tell her I love her, and I'm getting better every day. Love you too. Give Dad my best." She returned the phone and gestured for Meghan to join her outside. The two walked to the oak tree. "Burnette is scum," Lindsay said.

"Tell me what happened."

Lindsay leaned against the tree and buried her face in her hands. "He told me Kelli's apartment building had caught fire, and she'd been taken to the hospital for smoke inhalation. He also said my disobedience was the cause."

"But your mother says Kelli is fine? Why would he lie about something like that?"

Lindsay sighed. "It's all part of his game. He wants me to know what he's capable of if I don't do what he wants."

Meghan's phone rang again. She knew without looking that it was Burnette.

"Answer it." Lindsay's tone emitted pure strength. "Better yet, let me."

"Are you sure?"

Lindsay hesitated. "You're right. If we give any indication you know what's going on, he'll target you again."

Meghan nodded. "Yes, sir." And she handed the phone to Lindsay.

She listened for a minute, visibly trembling. "I understand. All right. I'll do it." She turned the phone off and looked at Meghan. "Just like I said. His call was a warning. If I don't obey him, he'll do something to hurt my sister. I need help in figuring out how to deceive him."

"Depends on what it is." Meghan and Ash hadn't found a bug

in the kitchen, but that didn't mean there wasn't one planted. They couldn't talk there now.

"There's another key to the liquor cabinet in the silverware drawer. I want to open it and get a bottle."

Meghan held her breath. "I can't let you drink."

"No, but we can pour it down the drain in your bathroom. Put the empty bottle in my room and pretend I'm drunk. I'm sure there'll be vodka in the liquor cabinet. Won't be a smell, so I'm good with my vow to stay clean."

Lindsay was attempting to beat Burnette at his own game. "We'll need to hurry. Pepper will be inside soon to start lunch." She walked farther into the yard. "She's talking to Luke, but her basket doesn't look full."

"I have no idea how you can keep Dave from finding out the truth."

"I'll handle Dave. Ash will have to be told. If we had a key to your bedroom, we could lock you inside. Increase the drama."

"I have one. Courtesy of Uncle Scottard."

"Great. I'll get the bottle, and you head upstairs. We'll stage an argument."

Lindsay shook her head. "Hide the bottle in your room until later. I want to make these cookies first." She took a deep breath. "Burnette's not going to ruin my first cooking lesson."

She captured Meghan's gaze. "Days like this, I feel like I could do anything to stop him. But I know tomorrow I'll panic again."

# CHAPTER 69

"CARLA, YOU'VE HAD quite an impressive career." Ash needed to rule out Carla's role in Burnette's plan. They talked in the loft area usually reserved for Lindsay's counseling sessions.

The gray-haired woman, who looked like a grandmother of a dozen, tilted her head. "Are you talking about what I did before nursing school or after?"

"All of it."

She removed her orange and purple reading glasses. "I'm sure you have every little detail there. At one time, I dreamed of dancing as a showgirl in Vegas. That's where I met my first husband. Should have seen his drinking problem. Anyway, I could have made it in Vegas, but deep inside, I wanted to be a nurse." She grinned like a teen. "Financing my education was a blast."

Ash laughed. "I heard about it. What caused you to go into psychology?"

"All the weird people I met. Then I realized I was just as . . . unique." She laughed. "The difference came with a desire to help them over the hurdles of why they chose abusive behaviors instead of facing life square in the face."

Ash heard the shouts from the kitchen. What was going on? Sounded like the old Lindsay. She and Meghan were supposed to be making cookies. How could that have caused such a ruckus?

"I'm after my patient." Carla made it to the stairs before she finished her words.

Ash rushed after her. He smelled the tantalizing aroma of chocolate chip cookies, but it didn't match the fire brewing from one of the cooks.

"It was a stupid idea." Lindsay's tone took on a high pitch. He hadn't seen her like this since the first week at the ranch. "You're not my mother, Agent Connors, or my sister. Even they didn't try to teach me kitchen duty. Take a look; I'm not twelve, either."

Meghan's gaze bored into their protectee. "You did a fine job. The cookies taste great. I don't understand why you're angry."

Lindsay swept her hand across the countertop and sent a container of flour to the floor. "Clean that up, b—"

He remembered that Lindsay. "What's the problem here?"

Meghan lifted her chin. "I was trying to find out myself."

"Lindsay, what's wrong?" Carla stepped closer to Lindsay.

"Get away from me. All of you are worthless pieces of garbage. I'm tired of living in a fishbowl." Lindsay swore again. Could she have gotten hold of drugs? "Carla, don't you see what Meghan and the others are doing?"

"No, I have no clue."

"You're an idiot too. They want me to be a good girl—leave the drugs and booze alone. Learn to cook. Play board games. Watch old movies. Next thing it will be sewing lessons. I went along with this baking cookies thing to get Meghan off my back. But now I see what this is all about." She whirled around to shove a mug off the counter, but Meghan caught it.

"I'll get Dave," Carla said. "He's reading poolside."

"I'm not talking to him or anyone else." Lindsay hurried through the kitchen and up the stairs to her room. She slammed the door.

Lindsay had been doing so well, opening up to him and Meghan. What had happened to end her progress?

"Ash." Meghan's whisper grasped his attention. "It's all right. I'll tell you later. This is cool. Really."

But he wanted to know right now. "Where's Bob?"

"Outside, where he's supposed to be."

"Get him in here. You and I are going to take a little walk."

Meghan grinned. "Yes, sir."

Within a few minutes Ash and Meghan stood in the middle of an empty corral, where she told him what Lindsay had stated about her call with Burnette. "Obviously the VP doesn't think Lindsay can outsmart him."

"What she's doing takes guts. She's afraid for her family, and his stunts keep getting worse. I admit, I thought she'd spiraled in there."

"How much longer, Ash?"

He wished he had an answer, and yet he knew she didn't expect one. "Until we have all the evidence to prove to President Hall that his longtime friend has betrayed him."

She nodded. "Lindsay gave a convincing performance."

"She made a believer out of me. If the kitchen's bugged, then he'll have heard it all."

"The look on your face was priceless."

"Thanks. Tell her it was too bad I didn't have a tranquilizer gun."

"I will. Shall we continue our charade? How about tearing me apart on the back porch. That should take care of any possible traitors among us."

"You're enjoying this far too much." He tossed her a grin. "But I do know how to rip an agent apart."

"I promise not to cry."

"Okay. I suppose you two have more drama for us?"

"Sure thing. I'll get the empty vodka bottle from my room, and the two of us will battle it out. Once you take over my shift, we'll try to talk to her again. Then she'll lock her door."

"Not sure how I feel about that."

"Me either. There's nothing in her room to hurt her. I looked earlier. We could always tear down the door. Oh, she promised me she'd keep the door locked for no more than one hour."

"Can she fool Dave?"

"The idea is he'll be the only one she wants to talk to. This has got to work, Ash. If Burnette doesn't believe she's broken her sobriety, he'll bring out both barrels."

"Are you documenting all that's going on?"

Meghan nodded. "I know you are too. Having both versions will keep the truth flowing."

"Or look like a conspiracy against the vice president of the United States."

# CHAPTER 70

FRIDAY, JUST AFTER LUNCH, Ash contemplated Lindsay's charade the night before. She'd done a good job of displaying the old Lindsay. Even Dave and Carla appeared to believe her. Now for Burnette to hear about her drunken brawl and leave Lindsay alone. How long could all of this go on before the evidence was compiled against him?

Ash checked his e-mail and saw Warrington had sent him an attachment. The pathologist had completed all the testing. In short, Ethan had been poisoned by oleander, and there were two people on the ranch who could have accomplished this. One was Dave, who had a generous supply of herbs, and the other was their quirky cook. But Meghan had said Ethan wouldn't eat Pepper's cooking—too spicy for him. Dave? Ash didn't think so.

Ethan must have tripped onto information revealing the identity of who was working for Burnette. He probably approached the person and was poisoned before he could relay who'd been betraying them. Ethan's warning about the flowering bush repeated.

*Everything about the oleander bush is poison. Just stay away.*

Could Chip have any insight to what might have happened? Always questions. What did this new development mean for Lindsay and the president?

Ash powered off his computer. He needed to talk to Chip. On his way outside, he reached inside the fridge for a Diet Coke.

Pepper was nowhere in sight. Normally, this time of day she was busy in the kitchen.

Chip had a horse on a lead rope, urging it around the corral. Lindsay watched from the fence, and Meghan stood beside her. Ash wasn't so sure Meghan should be in the heat with her recent concussion, but she was a stubborn woman. She'd have to faint before giving in to resting. Bob watched from the shade, a smart man.

Ash joined Meghan. "How's my girl?" he whispered.

"I'm fine." Lindsay laughed. "Excuse me. You were referring to me, right? Is this a nomination for my Oscar performance last night?"

Ash tossed her a grin. "Was there any doubt?" The change in his protectee demonstrated the power of prayer and determination. He hadn't given up on her approaching the president with the truth about Burnette.

Ash also saw what was developing between Lindsay and Chip. Not sure if a relationship between the two would work. Chip had the strength, and Lindsay looked to him as a sort of father figure. Not exactly a textbook perfect match but not necessarily a bad one either. Then again, her maturity level had taken a big boost.

"I'm assuming you want to talk to me. Why else would you endure this heat?" Meghan still looked pale. She probably had a headache, to which she'd never admit. They were so much alike.

"Honestly, I need to talk to the main man in the center of the ring."

"This must be important." Meghan leaned against the fence. "Your eyebrows are giving you away."

He wanted to kiss her. "This won't take long. Hey, Chip. Can I see you for a few minutes?" The man released the lead rope and walked with Ash beyond the stables.

"More questions?"

Trusting Chip with the truth reminded Ash of the need to bring the ranch's secrets to light. "You know me pretty well. This is about your dad."

"The rest of the autopsy report?"

"Just got it. The findings aren't good, Chip. He was poisoned—oleander."

Chip's face flushed red. "My dad was murdered. I can't believe it. Who would dislike him enough to kill him? Unless . . ."

"What are you thinking? Because I have my own idea of who might have wanted him dead."

"I bet he learned more about who shot Wade, which means the person who killed him had to be an agent or a friend." Chip paused. "Before I accuse anyone, I want to hear your thoughts."

"Other than you, who did he trust on this ranch?"

"Pepper." He spat the word. The suspicion that had kept Ash awake at night had surfaced as truth. "She often brought him a glass of iced sweet tea in the evenings. Dad claimed no one could make it like she did. She could have boiled a few flower petals and added it to his tea." He punched his fist into his hand. "No one else could have done it. Dad ate our food, and one of us cooked it." He studied Ash's face. "If you don't have her arrested, I'll have to question her myself."

"I'm going to talk to her now. Get some answers. Get her off the ranch and into custody."

"Fat chance of that. She left about eight thirty."

Fury raced through him. Had Burnette tipped her off about the autopsy? "Any idea where she was going?"

"No. Only that she took Burnette's truck. Headed east."

The cameras at the front gate would have captured the footage, but she still had over two hours on them. Ash whipped out his phone and pressed in the county sheriff's number. "We have a murder suspect who left the ranch at approximately 0830 this morning, driving east. She's driving a black 250 Ford truck. Name is Pepper Davis. I'll call back in a few minutes with the license plate number." He snapped it shut and studied the anguish on Chip's face. "She won't get far."

"I thought her husband was a Secret Service agent."

"Yes; he retired and had a heart attack."

"How convenient."

Ash hadn't considered that aspect.

"Wait a minute." The force of Chip's tone demanded Ash's attention. "Who is she taking orders from?"

"We don't know. Look, I need to make a call to DC."

Chip waved a finger in front of Ash's face. "Not so fast. I've lost a friend and a father in this chaos. And I think I've put it together. The reason Wade's killer wasn't found and the reason my dad's dead is because the one calling the shots is a high-profile figure."

"Chip."

"Sorry, bud. I'm not a stupid redneck."

"I can't give you classified information." Ash needed to call Warrington and update him.

"Does Lindsay know? I bet she can make a few good guesses."

"I would like for—"

"Forget it. I'm finding the answers."

"You'll upset her."

"She's stronger than you give her credit for." He pressed his lips hard. "I bet it's Burnette. Lindsay hates him. Pepper and Dad swore by him."

"And you?"

"I thought he was manipulative."

"Chip, I'm asking you not to say anything to Lindsay about the autopsy report or anything we've just discussed. It could hinder her mental health."

Chip hesitated. "For how long?"

"Until we're able to talk to Pepper and evaluate what she says. Even then, Dave may need to talk to Lindsay first. She's been my protectee for over four years. I've got a stake in this too."

Chip drew in a deep breath, the range of anger and grief evident on his face. "All right. I need to wrap my brain around some of this and figure out why the VP of the United States—or anyone—would want Wade and Dad dead and what that has to do with Lindsay."

Ash nodded and left the stables. As soon as he'd walked beyond earshot, he had Warrington on the line and explained Pepper's disappearance.

"I'll add more firepower to the search," Warrington said. "If she's behind the crimes there, then we've got a start in drawing this to a close."

"You and I know this isn't about drugs." Ash realized he might be stepping off a cliff.

"But that's all we have been able to figure out so far."

"I imagine the VP will be upset about his cook potentially poisoning his number one man." A swirling hole of fury raced through him.

"Doesn't look good. Keep in touch. I want to know the moment she's found. I have a few questions of my own."

If the media got hold of the autopsy report, they would splatter it from sea to shining sea. The repercussion against the president and the party could be devastating. Ash was certain the VP had no concerns about his own reputation. Even with Pepper a prime suspect in the ranch killings, Burnette still held the winning hand. For that matter, Pepper probably wouldn't live through the day. That meant Victor, Bob, or Dave could take her place and would continue with Burnette's plans.

★ ★ ★

"To think I liked the woman." Meghan wanted to go after Pepper with her rifle and SIG.

Ash's jaw tensed. "Looks like she cooked more than three meals a day."

Answers crept into her many questions. "Do you realize she could have cut Lindsay's girth that day? I remember seeing her in the garden earlier. Worse yet, she could have poisoned all of us."

"Calm down. We're another step closer to bringing Burnette to justice."

Meghan concentrated on those techniques that shoved away emotion and centered on logic and reasoning. "Do you still think Warrington might be involved?"

"No clue. I tried to bait him, but he didn't bite."

"Is Dave telling Lindsay now?"

"He's waiting for you. She leans on you as much as she does Dave and Carla."

Meghan moistened her lips. "I'm on my way. I'd like to think this might be the incident that pushes Lindsay into calling the president. Ash, let's be real. Pepper will be dead before lunch. Burnette won't risk her trying to cut a deal."

Meghan wished she could see and hear the responses from the other agents when they learned about Pepper. More could be involved, and she was a fool if she chose to believe otherwise. She walked back to relieve Bob. The house was bugged but hopefully not the front porch. She prayed Lindsay would be able to keep her mind clear . . . and not fall apart. Or perhaps faking a breakdown might ease Burnette's mind that his plan was intact.

Dave, Carla, and Lindsay sat waiting for her. Dave's eyes revealed his concern and rightfully so. Lindsay's strength was about to be tested one more time.

Lindsay trembled. "Meghan, what's going on? It has to be serious for all of you to be here."

"Just something you need to know."

Lindsay's gaze darted from Meghan to Dave. "Is my dad okay?"

"Yes." Meghan eased beside her on the porch swing.

Lindsay grasped her hands. "I'm ready. Dave, I don't mean any disrespect, but please let Meghan tell me what's going on."

"No problem." He touched her knee. "You can handle this."

Meghan took her hand. "Ash received Ethan's autopsy report this morning. It shows our friend was poisoned by the plant he warned us all about."

"Oleander," Lindsay whispered.

"Yes."

"Who did it?"

"We're not sure."

Lindsay gripped Meghan's hand. "Ethan and Chip ate their own food." She gasped. "Oh no. Pepper brought him iced tea every night." She stood. "Where is she?"

"She left this morning. The authorities are looking for her."

# CHAPTER 71

ASH STARED OUT into the dark night, watching, listening, and always wondering if tonight Burnette planned to eliminate Lindsay. The day had been worse than stressful. Adrenaline had poured into every breath the moment he received the autopsy report indicating Ethan's cause of death. Pepper. How had he not seen through her deceit? Ash Zinders, A2Z, accuracy of 85 percent in detecting lies. Pepper had played a good game. For that matter, she'd even threatened to poison him.

In two more hours, when his shift ended, he'd check his e-mail again to see if Pepper had been found. But his gut feeling said she was either out of the country or dead. At 2330, his phone rang. Warrington.

"Found Pepper Davis east of Austin."

Ash's throat ran dry. "Did you get a confession?"

"She had a bullet in her head. Her car had been set on fire, but we got to it before it exploded."

Execution style. "What happens now?"

"I'm scheduled to talk to the president in the morning."

"Are we moving Lindsay?"

"That's up to the president. The VP still believes she's safest there. He claims his cook must have been working alone in some vendetta against Ethan Leonard, and that's why she left."

Ash attempted to push aside his anger, but the stupidity ringing through his ears shoved aside respect for his boss. "Is all of DC deaf and blind to what's happening here? I have three murders, and you think Lindsay is safest here?"

"Ash, you aren't stating anything I haven't voiced to the president. I'll—"

"Don't give me the 'I'll call you later' line. Lindsay may have had her moments that drove us all nuts, but someone is trying hard to kill her and those closest to her. You and I know it's someone connected to this ranch."

"I can't give the order to move her."

"I'm ready to move her on my own."

"Then what happens when you're followed and she ends up dead?"

Warrington had hit him in the face with the truth. "What would you do?"

"Don't trust anyone but Agent Connors. I'll get back to you as quickly as I can. Hold on. This is the president now."

Ash waited. However, patience had long since left his data bank. He prayed the president thought through what was happening at the Dancin' Dust and the futility of trusting Scottard Burnette.

"Ash, the president is talking to the First Lady and the vice president in the morning."

Ash wanted to throw his cell phone. If he knew of a safe place to hide Lindsay until this was over, he'd already be there.

When Rick took over Ash's shift, he saw no other way than to enlist Chip's help. And he needed that help tonight. Ash knocked on his door. He heard the TV blaring.

"Chip, got a minute? I'd like to talk to you."

Chip opened the door, and he motioned Ash inside. "How many times have we had these conversations?"

"Too many." Ash stepped inside and seated himself in front of the TV. When Chip reached to turn it off, Ash stopped him. "I don't want anyone overhearing our conversation."

"What do you need this time? I've opened a tack box, let you borrow my Mustang, answered vague questions in which you leave out pertinent information. And before that, I was accused of murder." He lifted a brow, indicating a hint of anger. "What's left, my blood?"

Ash wondered if after he told Chip the truth, he'd cooperate. "I had that coming and more. You deserve to know what's going on here."

"Humor me a moment. After all, I'm a stats man. Detail and problem-solving are my expertise."

Apprehension seized Ash. He was in this for broke, and Chip had already figured out much of this on his own. Warrington had told him not to trust anyone but Meghan, but he had to go on instinct. Chip had proved himself when Meghan had nearly been killed by one of Burnette's men. "Go ahead."

"You and Meghan are working separate of the team assigned to Lindsay. From my understanding, Secret Service agents protect key people, not solve murders. That tells me you two are working independent of Washington." He picked up a photo of Ethan, then replaced it. His body language was open. "So I asked myself, why? When Meghan was in the hospital, I had hours to think, and my mind hasn't shut down since." He rubbed his palms. "I began putting happenings and bits of conversations together. Things you, Meghan, and Lindsay said and didn't say." He studied Ash. "You haven't stopped me, so I must be on the right road."

Ash kept his emotions intact. "I'm listening. Keep going."

"You think Burnette's behind this. Tough position. Dangerous, too. He's the vice president. The president's longtime friend. Supposedly Lindsay's uncle and counselor. However, I know she despises him. You can't go to anyone else because you don't know who's wallowing in the mud with him. Neither can you leave to dig up the stuff you need to prove his guilt."

From Chip's smug look, Ash considered backing off, but curiosity drove him on. "Anything else?"

Chip's eyes narrowed. "Pepper may have poisoned my dad, but I want whoever ordered his death prosecuted. Wade was a friend, and I'll never forget his shooting. A dedicated woman nearly lost her life in this mess, all due to a mysterious killer, who obviously is not a spurned drug dealer. And Lindsay has her own share of problems without being chased by a stalker. I don't know the why, but I'm getting there." He scuffed the floor with his boot. "You asked me about Erin. She's one tough ex-Marine. Tell me I'm wrong."

"Maybe the Secret Service should recruit you."

He shook his head. "Been thinking about the FBI."

"Can't let you do that. We're rivals."

They laughed, and it eased the mounting tension. Ash had to trust him. He took a deep breath and told Chip the whole story.

"Pure coke?" Chip's body stiffened. "It keeps getting worse."

Ash nodded, studying him. Looking for signs of deceit. "I haven't taken you into my confidence to pass away the time."

"Figured that. What can I do?"

"You're not a trained professional. What I'm about to ask means you could be headed into a den of wolves."

"Let me decide that. I don't have much else to lose."

*Except Lindsay—and your life.* "I need to find out if Erin Burnette is conspiring with the VP."

"I'm all over it."

"Burnette won't want you leaving the ranch for a couple of days."

"I'll tell him I need to get away. The constraints you've put on me are more than I can handle right now."

"And you're sure? If Meghan and I go down with this, chances are you will too."

"I'll do it. Erin and I have talked a few times. I could attempt to look her up. If I find her, I'll ask her out. If she's nowhere around, then I'll knock on a few doors. She told me about living in a little town in central Idaho."

"I have the address inside."

"She claimed to teach third grade."

"I've confirmed that. How soon would you be ready to leave?"

"I'll call Burnette first thing in the morning and leave before noon. How long do you think it will take me?"

"How about three days or less? I'll get you a cell phone before you leave."

"Sounds good. Burnette's an early riser, so I'll be at the house around 0600 to place the call."

Ash reached to shake his hand. "You're a good man, Chip."

"Thanks. I tried to tell you that a long time ago. I want Lindsay safe."

Ash saw the glint of love in Chip's eyes at the mention of her name. "We all do."

# CHAPTER 72

Sunday at noon, Lindsay picked through her salad. Meghan sat beside her poolside, along with Dave and Carla. These people had done enough for her, and it was time she gave back. Lindsay mentally listed what Burnette had done since her arrival at the Dancin' Dust. He'd bombed her car, killing one person and hurting another. He'd arranged for Wade's murder. He'd attempted to eliminate Meghan—twice. He'd ordered Pepper executed, so she couldn't be questioned about Ethan's death. And those were only the things she knew. Ash or Dave would probably be next. Or Chip, because he'd befriended her. Or maybe her father.

*I'm the only one who can bring this to an end.*

She had to try, to hope Dad believed her instead of his friend, the man Dad referred to as the brother he'd never had. Where did that leave Lindsay? Was this a worthless pursuit? But she remembered the tears her father shed the night she tried to commit suicide.

*Make a stand. Do the only decent thing you've ever done.*

"I understand you're not hungry." Dave's gentle voice tugged at her thoughts. "But you need to eat."

"Thank you." She set the plate on a small table. "Carla, I appreciate your efforts in fixing lunch, but I can't eat right now."

"Would you like to lie down?" She felt Dave's gentle eyes on her.

Lindsay shoved aside the doubts and turned to Meghan. "Can I speak to you privately? I'd like to call my father. Maybe we could do this by your favorite tree?"

Meghan set aside her uneaten salad. "Let's go."

Once the two were beyond hearing distance, Lindsay chose her words. "I'm going to ask Dad to come to the ranch as soon as possible. I'm going to tell him the whole story. But I need you and Ash to help me put together the happenings in the order they occurred. With proof of Burnette's guilt, he'll see that this is not a fabrication."

"Are you ready for this?"

"I have to be. This mess keeps getting worse. I know Ash wanted more proof, but I don't know what his boss would do with it. I can only hope Dad believes me and accepts my story. You've always told me that truth eventually triumphs over lies. I . . . I have to try to stop Burnette. This will only get worse if I don't."

Meghan handed her the cell phone.

Lindsay's hand trembled, but she refused to retreat. This was war, and she had no intention of losing. Punching in her dad's number, she glanced at Meghan. "You, me, and Ash are the Three Musketeers."

Meghan nodded.

"Hi, Dad. I know you're busy, but I felt this was important."

"It's great to hear your voice. Let me excuse myself for a moment from this meeting." She heard him tell Scottard to continue without him. If only Dad understood what that meant. The implication caused her to shiver. "I'm back."

"Dad, I need to talk to you about something very important. Can you come here?"

"Sure." He paused. "I could get away early in the morning. Be there around eleven."

"Wonderful. Can you do me a favor? Come alone. I can talk to Mom at another time. I'd like for just us to spend the time together."

"All right. I'd like that."

"One more thing. Would you not tell Uncle Scottard? You can fill him in when you're back in DC. I want the honor of being the first to . . . tell you about some changes in me."

"This sounds serious."

"Daddy, it's about you and me and the past four years—even before that, if I'm honest. It's personal. I mean, tell Mom but no one else."

"I've heard so many good things about you from Dr. Sanchez."

"He knows his stuff, Dad. But Meghan, Ash, Carla, and the rest of the agents have helped me too."

"I'll see you in the morning. I'm looking forward to it."

"I love you, Dad."

"Oh, sweetheart, I love you too."

Lindsay swiped at a tear and handed the phone to Meghan. "He'll be here in the morning around eleven. Does that give us enough time to prepare what I need to say?"

"The timetable can be done in a few minutes. What needs to be said should come from your heart with the same passion you used when you told me about Burnette."

Lindsay's mind spun with doubt. "I'm afraid he won't believe me. Burnette is right about one thing. My history in telling the truth is not good."

"Don't try to psychoanalyze the situation. You are his daughter, and he loves you very much."

"There's no other way to end these tragedies. I have to tell Dad the truth."

# CHAPTER 73

ASH TURNED OFF THE TV. His shift had ended an hour ago, but he needed to unwind before going to bed. Bob had taken Chip to the Austin airport shortly before lunch, and Ash hoped he hadn't sent the man to his death. Ash had started out suspicious of Chip, but clearly his judgment of character lately had bottomed out. Scottard Burnette—a man who had the facade of a patriotic American and the heart of a murderer. Ash focused on the facts played out over the past seven years since Kyle Burnette's death. Burnette had motive and the ability to enlist others to help him.

Ash had begun to think of Chip as a pawn, but who held the roles of the other players? Pepper's actions made her look like a knight, two steps in familiar territory and one step outside of her realm to follow Burnette's orders. That made so much sense, since the knight could move before any of the other pieces. The bishop? Hard to say at this point. A bishop was equal in strength to a knight but was restricted to either a white space or a black . . . like in DC or just at the ranch. A rook could only move in a straight line. That could be a member of Ash's team. Didn't want to go there. Burnette needed Erin to do his dirty work, and that made her a queen. Burnette was definitely the king. Now to take out the chess pieces, nab the queen, and put the king in handcuffs. Not every chess piece was needed to take the king. One simply had to plan all the right moves.

Tonight, Lindsay had been quiet, unlike her puckish moods of late. She seemed disinterested in the movie, and she didn't want to discuss politics. Diving into Lindsay's emotions was Dave's job. But she had a huge undertaking in the morning. The fate of all their futures rested on the president's believing her story and the documented evidence sealing Burnette's guilt.

Ash also knew she was missing Chip, and he chose not to bring up the man who had swept her off her feet. The man who might be one more in an increasing line who had given their lives for her.

His cell rang, and he snatched it up. Chip. "Hey, been waiting to hear from you."

"Figured so. Before I tell you what I've found out, how's Lindsay?"

Ash grinned. "She's doing well. I think she might be missing you—a little, anyway."

"Wonderful. That girl is growing on me. But I'll be careful. I know the price paid for getting under the Secret Service's skin." He laughed.

"Ouch. For your sake, I didn't take that personal."

"As you can probably tell, I'm high on my investigation. I think Erin is in cahoots with Burnette. I didn't find her, and her neighbors weren't much help. Said she stayed to herself. An elderly man told me she has boyfriends. I told him I thought I was the only one. He told me to go find another girl. Erin had two other boyfriends, and they were rough looking. Then I talked to the manager of the apartment complex. Erin paid her rent until September. Told him she'd resigned from her teaching position and planned to travel over the summer. But she wasn't ready to give up her apartment. The clincher is she had her mail forwarded to Scottard Burnette in DC."

"You are good."

"That's why the FBI wants me. Maybe the CIA, too. Never can tell."

"We have first dibs, and don't forget it. Chip, this is great info."

*Now, how to prove she's working with Burnette?*

"Does this have anything to do with her stint in the Marines?"

"Expert marksmanship."

"Wade's sniper."

"I'm thinking that too. Be careful. Burnette's not stupid. I don't think he'd suspect you, but I'd like to keep you around."

"I'll be home tomorrow night."

"Good. The president will be here then."

"Who made the arrangements?"

"Lindsay asked him to visit."

"What about Burnette?"

"Just the president."

"Ash, are you telling me that Lindsay's going to tell her father about Burnette? She's been afraid to open up because of her past."

This guy was good for her. "You'd have to ask Lindsay."

"Which I can't, because I'm not on the list."

"You can ask her yourself tomorrow."

"Let's hope we can all celebrate."

Ash hoped so too. "You've done a great job, and when this is over, I know the president will give you a commendation."

Chip chuckled. "I may have to ask for Lindsay's hand instead."

"Are you serious?"

"Hmm. Maybe so. I know she's had her problems and her addictions. But sometimes those problems make us stronger people."

"Now you sound like your dad."

"That's why I'm the Chip."

"Be safe. I'll see you soon." Ash disconnected the call.

If Erin was involved with Burnette, she could have recruited a couple of her Marine buddies to help. If only Ash trusted Warrington. Then the right people could dig deeper.

★ ★ ★

Meghan stood at the helicopter pad, her heart beating nearly as fast as the whirling blades. Lindsay stood between her and Bob. She could almost feel her protectee's reservations. It amazed Meghan that a wise man like the president hadn't seen through Burnette. She prayed the hours ahead brought the president to the realization of what the VP had done.

Meghan and Ash had pieced enough together to know the death of Kyle Burnette and foreign policy were at the root of the situation. Speaker of the House Randolph could be involved—another chess piece, as Ash would say.

If the president failed to accept Lindsay's story and the proof from Meghan and Ash, this meeting had the potential of ruining her and Ash's career or even getting them killed. Worse yet, if this failed, Lindsay and her parents could be assassinated.

The president exited the helicopter and shook Ash's hand. The moment he glanced at Lindsay, she was in his arms. Meghan wondered how long it had been since the two had embraced. Father and daughter sobbed.

A few moments later, the president and Lindsay, arm in arm, strolled toward the house.

He kissed the top of her head. "My girl, my beautiful girl."

Meghan clothed herself in professionalism and prayed the reunion stayed intact.

Lindsay gazed into her father's face. "Thank you so much for coming. I can only imagine your schedule."

"This worked out fine. I have an excellent staff, and they know how to get in touch with me." He scanned the ranch, probably thinking of the last time he'd made this trek under much different circumstances.

"I wish you could stay a few days." Lindsay's voice quivered, but she seemed in control. "Better yet, I wish you and me and Mom could spend a few days together. Even Kelli."

"We'll make it happen."

"I want to leave here, but . . ."

"What?"

She smiled. "I think I'm more of a country girl than a city girl."

He laughed, a deep-throated sound. "That surprises me."

"I know. We have lots to catch up on. Carla has made lunch for us. Would you like to sit inside, maybe in the operation room?"

"An unusual place for us to talk, but that's fine with me."

"I'd like Ash and Meghan with us."

Again the president displayed his surprise.

"I have so much to say, and they've supported me. Poor Ash. I owe him as much of an apology as I do my family."

"And we're getting you off this ranch. Scottard thinks this is the safest place, but he's wrong. I've listened to his reasoning about this long enough."

Meghan looked away to keep from voicing the truth about the VP.

Carla had sandwiches prepared in the kitchen. The president and Lindsay filled their plates, but Meghan and Ash declined.

Meghan captured Lindsay's attention and smiled. *You can do this.*

After being seated at the table across from each other, President Hall took Lindsay's hand and asked God to bless the food. He thanked Him for the opportunity to spend time with his daughter.

Lindsay took a deep breath. "I've been reading the Bible. I have questions. Guess I'm exploring."

The president's eyes moistened. His reaction proved to Meghan that he was not only a great leader, compassionate and wise, but a man capable of deep love.

"Wonderful. I'm very pleased."

Lindsay took a small bite of her sandwich. "Before I begin, I want to say how deeply sorry I am for the past several years of screwups. Words are not enough, so I plan to show you my sincerity in the days ahead." She took a drink of her water and breathed in deeply. "I understand our relationship has been severely damaged by what I've done and said. Honestly, I still have questions about what happened during my growing-up years. So I'm hoping after I leave here, we can get involved in counseling. Possibly Dave, if he isn't sick of working with me."

"A prayer answered."

Tears flowed from Lindsay's eyes. "Daddy, I'm not an answered prayer. I'm an alcoholic and drug addict, and I still crave them. But I want to stay clean. No matter what. That's why I called you yesterday. I've hid the truth about many things, including the horrible crimes that have happened."

The president narrowed his gaze. "I get the impression that what you are about to say will help the authorities make arrests."

She nodded and took another sip of water. "Before I begin, I'd like for Ash to tell you what he found in this room and to present you with proof of what I'm about to say."

The president stared at Ash in obvious confusion.

"Mr. President, there is a bug in the air duct above us. Everything that has gone on in this room since the Secret Service arrived has been recorded. Even now. We decided to leave it there so whoever planted it would not realize we were on to him. Now, of course, the issue is moot."

"Is Warrington aware of this?"

"Not to my knowledge, sir." He handed the president a manila envelope. "The contents will back up much of what Lindsay is about to tell you."

The president pushed back his sandwich. Concern etched his features.

Lindsay watched her father's every move. *Good girl. Show your confidence.*

Yet Meghan held her breath.

"Do you remember when my rebellion skyrocketed, the summer I was fifteen?"

"I do."

"Back then, you wanted me to talk to Uncle Scottard. He'd lost his son, and you thought the diversion would help his grief."

The president nodded. Meghan observed him. His eye twitched. Did he suspect the truth?

"It didn't happen the way you were told. He told me I wasn't loved or wanted. Instead of helping me to work through those feelings, he confirmed them."

The president's eyes widened. "No, he—"

She held up her hand. "Let me finish, please. This is very hard because I know you respect him. But it has to be said." She looked at Meghan.

*You can do this, Lindsay.*

She pressed her lips and inhaled. "Who do you think gave me the grass once I was home from boarding school?"

The president rubbed his face.

"Yes, Daddy, Uncle Scottard. He did other things too."

His shoulders arched. "Did he ever assault you?"

"Not physically. Once I was home, he gave me pills. Said they'd make me feel better." Lindsay continued with her story, while the president's face hardened.

"Since I've been here, he's called and made threats. Even told me where to find coke. It was pure cocaine, Daddy. It would have killed me." Lindsay cited the torn wire mesh in Meghan's bedroom that permitted the scorpion to fall onto her pillow, Wade's murder, Meghan's near encounter with death, Pepper's role in killing Ethan, and the extra key to the liquor cabinet. Lindsay took a deep breath and let it out slowly.

The president paled. He stood and walked to the window overlooking the pool. "I can't believe this. He's . . . he's been like a brother to me since college days." He shook his head. "Warrington phoned me last night and said he had an urgent matter to discuss about Scottard. I assumed it was about moving you, that having you remain here was entirely too dangerous. I blew it off. Said I was too busy, and I'd already decided to take you back with me today." He turned to Lindsay. "If you leave the ranch, then Scottard loses control."

Lindsay stared at her father. "He said my history would discount anything I ever said to you. But he's gotten bolder. Meaner."

The president turned to his daughter. The color of his face

had changed to crimson. "He will pay for this." He picked up the manila envelope and reached for his phone.

As he flipped it open and punched in a number, the door flew open. Burnette stepped into the room. Glock in hand, he kicked the door shut. "Just how am I going to pay for this?"

# CHAPTER 74

ASH REACHED FOR HIS SIG and stepped into Burnette's line of fire just as Meghan took her position in front of Lindsay.

"Don't even try, Ash. I'll kill you both. Put your gun on the floor. Kick it toward me, and keep your hands high. By the way, this room is soundproof, and none of the agents waiting outside will hear a thing. Don't really need my silencer, but it comes in handy. Meghan, you too."

Ash and Meghan did as they were told.

Burnette kept his back to the wall with Ash and Meghan on either side of him. "Meghan, move away from Lindsay."

Neither Ash nor Meghan budged.

"Shall I open fire and see who goes down first?"

"Scottard, what's this about?" The president's soft voice from behind Ash stole Burnette's attention, but his gun did not waver. "Hey, we're friends. Let's talk about what's got you so worked up."

"A way to change our country. Make it strong again. I hate to do this, but I don't have a choice."

"There's always a better option than violence."

"Only when all else fails." Burnette's voice rose. "Ash, get out of the way."

Ash calculated his next move. Could he kick the gun out of Burnette's hand before it fired? But Burnette had a clear shot, and Ash would need to take a long stride to physically stop him. "You're a dead man, and you know it."

"Doesn't matter at this point. The good old USA has taken everything I ever had."

"Scottard, I thought you loved your country." Maybe the president could talk some sense into him. He'd been known to talk his way out of dangerous situations in Uganda.

"Once I did. Before I realized the US would rather throw its sons and daughters into a terrorist's path than look bad in the eyes of the world."

"Is this about the Middle East Peace Summit? We talked about foreign policy at Camp David. I thought we came to an agreement."

Burnette sneered. "You support your own views. You didn't listen to anything I had to say. You didn't have a son commit suicide after facing a humiliating court-martial for defending his men. It was all political. Nothing about truth or defending our nation. As president, I'm going to stop the stupidity of worrying about what Islamic countries think about us. I'll put legislation in place that shows the Middle East that the US is the most powerful country in the world."

"What kind of legislation? Help me understand, Scottard."

He waved his gun. "All Arab countries are our enemies. They're infiltrating our country. Getting into politics. Building their mosques. Destroying our economics with rising oil prices. Why can't you see it?"

"Scottard, I agree there are problems. Let's talk. I value your feedback."

"Talk? Kyle was my son, not yours. I'm going to put the US back on the globe."

How sanctimonious. Ash needed time for Burnette to lose concentration.

"I'm so sorry," the president said. "Kyle's death was a tragedy—"

"A tragedy?" Burnette's voice rose. He laughed, an insane sound that alarmed Ash. He needed Burnette to climb out of his anger, get him to brag.

"Found your bug," Ash said. "Smart move."

"Oh, you did?" Burnette didn't budge. "Thanks to Bob and Victor's very informative discussions, I heard about the president's little trip here. Learned a lot by listening in on what happened in this room."

"Why not let the president and Lindsay go? Then we can talk." Ash kept his tone even. "You make sense." His cell rang.

"Ignore the call."

"What if it's DC?"

"Answer it and be quick."

Tom Warrington's name read across the ID. "Yes, sir."

"I've got men within a mile of the ranch," Warrington said. "Got wind that the VP is there. Can you talk?"

"No, sir."

"Is the president in danger?"

"Affirmative." Ash kept his focus on Burnette.

Warrington swore. "Stall him."

"I'll call you later." Ash flipped the phone shut and slipped it into his shirt pocket.

"Get your hands back up. What did he want?" Burnette kept his Glock trained on Ash.

"Said the agents needed some time off. I'm to call him later."

"Oh, you'll have plenty of idle moments when I'm finished."

Ash offered a tight-lipped smile. "I'd like for just the two of us to work something out."

"Don't think so. This is Lindsay's fault. If she'd done what I told her, I wouldn't have to kill the president." His gaze narrowed. "Too bad the attempted shooting in Atlanta wasn't successful. Thanks, Connors, for eliminating the only witness."

"I'd like to understand what Lindsay didn't do for you?" At the sound of the president's voice, the lines across Burnette's forehead relaxed.

"Use the drugs. Let the media have an interview. Stick to her behavior from the past. Not one American would support you if she'd have obeyed me."

Ash feared Burnette's madness would move him to open fire. His attention had to be diverted so he could move closer.

"Did you have Wade killed too?" Meghan said.

If she could secure his attention long enough . . .

"He was getting a little suspicious. Started asking Pepper too many questions about her affiliation with me. Fortunately, his wife went into labor, which gave me time to figure out how to eliminate him." He waved his gun at Ash. "My bullets will go right through you and Jackson. Don't you see? All I need is a straight shot to end this."

"Did Erin do it?" Meghan grasped his attention but only long enough for Ash to inch closer.

"Bright girl. She saw what the government had done to Kyle. By the way, Erin did a fine job with your little sister. She didn't refuse a hit of coke and died in euphoric bliss."

*Stay calm, Meghan. We can do this.*

"What about Ethan?" Meghan's even tone plodded ahead.

"That's all Pepper. She was the best cook around. Smart gal, too, until she got a little too greedy. Wanted more money. Said she had a journal filled with incriminating evidence. Told me she had it when she left the ranch, but if she was telling the truth, it was destroyed in the fire. She realized Ethan was on to her and decided to brew him a little oleander tea."

"What if she kept a copy? What are you going to do then?" Meghan bored her gaze into Burnette's face.

"She wasn't smart enough to do that. Thought I was going to marry her. What a tramp." Burnette's hand trembled. "That's what happens to those who stand in my way. The way of our country's greater good."

Ash knew Meghan could take out Burnette if given the chance. But she'd have to get her gun first, and it was three feet from her right foot. Ash calculated the timing needed to snatch his SIG from the floor and bring down Burnette. All they needed was the right moment.

"I suppose when you're president, your wife will want to come back." Meghan tilted her head.

*Keep it up, Meghan.* He leaned forward while Burnette focused on Meghan.

"She will. Trust me. Once I'm the most powerful man in the country, she'll beg to come back."

"Will you let her?"

Burnette's head snapped back at Ash, as though he understood Meghan's diversion. She dove for her SIG and shouted for Lindsay to get down. Burnette whirled back to Meghan and took aim.

Ash pushed the president to the floor at the same time he reached for his gun.

"Not this time." Burnette turned his weapon back to Ash and fired, sending a bullet into Ash's arm.

That was all the opening Meghan needed, and she closed in with a shot to Burnette's heart.

It was finally over.

# CHAPTER 75

## Six Weeks Later

MEGHAN LINKED HER ARM into Ash's, mindful of the sling where Burnette's bullet had shattered a bone. She pointed to two riders heading their way. "I see them."

He looked around the Virginia countryside. "This farm is beautiful."

A few of the trees were dressed in shades of orange and gold. Rolling. Picturesque. "The red barn looks like it stepped out of a magazine."

"I agree—a real estate magazine with a fancy price."

She laughed. "Not like the Dancin' Dust."

They walked toward the white fence. "I admit it had a different kind of appeal. But I don't miss the scorching heat, the snakes, or the jalapeños." He kissed her cheek. "But there I found you."

"And changed your image."

"I'm still the detailed, pain-in-the-rear agent, except when I'm around you."

"Keep talking and you might dig yourself out of this."

"Would an 'I love you' help?"

She patted his arm, the one without the sling. How she loved this man. "Maybe if you were five and wanted a cookie."

"Oh, the next fifty to sixty years are going to be rough."

She frowned. "Is there no pity for me, A2Z?"

He moaned. "Maybe a little." The riders drew closer. "Hey, Chip and Lindsay look good."

"It's called love, and they're happy."

"I know the feeling."

So did she, like living in a fairy tale where she was a princess who'd found her prince.

The couple rode to the fence and dismounted. Ash reached out to shake Chip's hand, while Meghan hugged Lindsay.

"You have one beautiful piece of property." Ash whistled. "This city boy could do some serious R&R here."

Chip wrapped his arm around Lindsay. "Thanks. Far enough from DC to be comfortable and close enough to see my girl."

Lindsay flashed him a smile. "I couldn't believe he'd bought this place. Wait 'til you see the farmhouse. It's stunning." She turned to Meghan. "I understand you've been permanently assigned to me."

"I have. And Ash is now a part of the PPD."

"I'm so glad. Did Daddy tell you my plans?"

"He said you had some exciting news, but that was it."

"I have two years of school left, so I'm switching my major to music. I want to teach kids." She shrugged. "And whoever's interested."

"Wonderful." Meghan had wanted a beautiful life for Lindsay, and now it looked like she was on her way to achieving it.

Lindsay glanced at Chip. "We're getting married in a year. And we're working on plans to turn this farm into an equestrian rehabilitation center for stroke victims, as well as those of all ages who are physically and mentally challenged. We hope to incorporate music into the program."

"That is amazing," Meghan said. "I'm thrilled for you."

"Congratulations." Ash wrapped his arm around Meghan's waist. "I could get used to a place like this."

"Give yourself a few years, and I'll let you come visit." Chip chuckled.

"Ouch. But I might have to take you up on it."

Meghan couldn't remember being happier. She and Ash would always have their stubborn clashes, but they'd been talking to Dave about open communication.

"So when are you two tying the knot?" Chip said.

Meghan wanted to stand on her tiptoes and shout the news.

"We aren't waiting a year." Ash laughed. "New Year's Day in Abilene. Can you make it?"

Chip nodded. "We'll be there."

"Is the nightmare really over?" Lindsay leaned her head on Chip's shoulder. "Sometimes I wake in the middle of the night and wonder if Burnette might still be in charge."

Meghan hadn't been able to put Shelley's murder out of her mind either. She needed to forgive what had been done to her sister. "It takes realization that God is always in charge, and He will heal our hurts if we let Him."

"So many people were hurt by Burnette's insane ideals." Lindsay shook her head. "I think I'll always be on a campaign to make sure truth rises to the surface."

Meghan didn't want Lindsay to ever be afraid again. "The trials will begin soon. Erin has agreed to testify in exchange for lesser charges. But the important thing is Erin will face a judge and jury for her crimes. An electronic copy of Pepper's journal was found in her safe-deposit box that backed up everything about Burnette."

"What about Speaker of the House Randolph?" Lindsay glanced at Chip, worry lines indicating her concern.

"He hasn't been exonerated. Time will tell."

"Guess I don't trust anyone who was connected to Burnette," Lindsay said.

"Rightfully so." Meghan wanted the couple to put the past behind them. But that was impossible. One day at a time. "You two are one brave couple."

Chip pulled Lindsay closer to him. "We were desperate. Burnette had so many people fooled."

"When Warrington phoned me that morning in the operation

room with the president, I knew he'd put all the pieces together. I should have trusted him from the beginning. When Wade was killed and Burnette insisted you were safest at the ranch, Warrington began his own personal investigation."

"And you began assigning chess pieces to the whole thing." Meghan stared up into his handsome face, a face she'd never grow tired of.

"I was the pawn," Chip said.

Ash nodded. "Pepper became the knight. Erin the queen. Burnette the king. They all believed the end justified the means. But that's not how it works here. Our country has a system, a way to express opinions and possibly change policies without murder and coercion."

Meghan sighed. "When Burnette's son committed suicide and his wife left him, his grief and bitterness slowly turned to insanity. What began as a noble thought of changing US foreign policy became an obsession with deadly intent."

"He loved his country," Ash said. "Wanted to save her from terrorists."

Chip took a deep breath. "Our country has rallied since the conspiracy was exposed."

Meghan shook her head. "It could have created national distrust. But the media, despite how I feel about them most of the time, pulled the American people together, especially with Lindsay's willingness to tell her story."

"Reminds me of my dad—God, country, and the American tradition." Chip kissed the tip of Lindsay's nose. "Values the Leonard household will continue to uphold."

Meghan sensed Ash's gaze. Love swelled for his devotion, honesty, and faith.

"The Zinders household will uphold those same traditions." He smiled, the light of love ever strong in his eyes. This was only the beginning for them, and she couldn't wait to see what the journey from A to Z would hold.

# A Note from the Author

<small>Dear reader,</small>

Thank you for reading *Attracted to Fire*.

I believe an air of mystery surrounds the Secret Service. At times, I've wondered if a specific gene is necessary to fulfill the role. Certainly something in an agent's DNA must be required for the rigorous training.

"The vision of the United States Secret Service is to uphold the tradition of excellence in its investigative and protective mission through a dedicated, highly-trained, diverse, partner-oriented workforce that employs progressive technology and promotes professionalism."

What if I had chosen to be a Secret Service agent? What if I didn't like the person assigned to me? What if my protectee didn't like me? Would I take a bullet for that person? A hero's epitaph is still an epitaph. Yet there are many courageous men and women who are dedicated to protecting the lives of key political figures and foreign dignitaries. They understand and accept the challenge. I admire their sacrifice.

Meghan and Ash were united in their commitment to protect Lindsay Hall. Their job description demanded extreme concentration, precise marksmanship, and rigid physical endurance. Top of the list was the ability to step in front of a bullet.

I hope you enjoyed reading about the Secret Service and taking a glimpse into the unique lives of Special Agents Meghan Connors and Ash Zinders.

*DiAnn*

Expect an Adventure
DiAnn Mills
www.diannmills.com
www.facebook.com/diannmills

# About the Author

Award-winning author DiANN MILLS is a fiction writer who combines an adventuresome spirit with unforgettable characters to create action-packed novels. DiAnn's first book was published in 1998. She currently has more than fifty books in print, which have sold more than a million and a half copies.

Her titles have appeared on the CBA and ECPA bestseller lists and have won placements through the American Christian Fiction Writer's Book of the Year Awards from 2003 to 2008. DiAnn was also a Carol Award finalist in 2010. She received the Inspirational Reader's Choice award in 2005, 2007, and 2010 and was a Christy Award finalist in 2008 and a RITA Award finalist in 2010. In 2010, DiAnn won the Christy Award for *Breach of Trust*, the first book in her Call of Duty series. The second book in the series, *Sworn to Protect*, was a finalist for the 2011 Christy Award.

DiAnn is a founding board member for American Christian Fiction Writers and a member of Inspirational Writers Alive; Romance Writers of America's Faith, Hope and Love chapter; and the Advanced Writers and Speakers Association. She speaks to various groups and teaches writing workshops around the country. DiAnn is also the Craftsman mentor for the Jerry B. Jenkins Christian Writers Guild.

She and her husband live in sunny Houston, Texas.

# Discussion Questions

1. Meghan and Ash are at odds from the very beginning. What helps them work together as professionals, despite their personal differences? Could you have handled Ash's critical nature?

2. Lindsay has her own demons. How did you feel about her parents' determination not to give up on their daughter's addictive behaviors?

3. Every good man and leader wants a friend closer than a brother. In what ways does Scottard Burnette look out for Jackson Hall?

4. Dr. David Sanchez has a unique approach to helping Lindsay combat her addictions. How did you feel about his methods?

5. Ethan Leonard has his own philosophy about life. How does his son feel about his values?

6. Ash finally finds the courage to make restitution with the past. What did you think of the response he got? Have you ever had to make a difficult apology? How was your apology received? Have you ever been asked to forgive

someone for something you weren't sure you could forgive? How did you handle that?

7. Meghan's accident nearly kills her. How does it affect those around her?

8. Initially, did you trust Chip? Why or why not? If you began to trust him more as the story unfolded, what was it that made the difference?

9. Do you think President Hall and his wife share any of the blame for Lindsay's situation?

10. What do you think might have happened to Pepper's husband?

11. Scottard Burnette has lived with the anguish of his son's death and his wife's abandonment. What did you think of his rationale? Did you feel sorry for him? Why or why not?

12. Do you think Lindsay and her parents will ever have a loving and open relationship? Why or why not?

13. In your opinion, does the end ever justify the means? Discuss your reasoning, along with any examples from your own experience.

# CHAPTER 1

LIBRARIAN PAIGE ROGERS had survived more exciting days dodging bullets to protect her country. Given a choice, she'd rather be battling assassins than collecting overdue fines. For that matter, running down terrorists had a lot more appeal than running down lost books. Oh, the regrets of life—woven with guilt, get-over-its, and move-ons. But do-overs were impossible, and the adventures of her life were now shelved alphabetically under fiction.

*Time to reel in my pitiful attitude and get to work.* Paige stepped onto her front porch with what she needed for a full work-day at the library. Already, perspiration dotted her face, a reminder of the rising temperatures. Before locking the door behind her, she scanned the front yard and surveyed the opposite side of the dusty road, where chestnut-colored quarter horses grazed on sparse grass. Torrid heat and no rain, as though she stood on African soil. But here, nothing out of the ordinary drew her attention. Just the way she liked it. Needed it.

Sliding into her sporty yet fuel-efficient car, she felt for the Beretta Px4 under the seat. The past could rear its ugly head with-out warning. Boy Scouts might be prepared; Girl Scouts were trained. The radio blared out the twang of a guitar and the misery of a man who'd lost his sweetheart to a rodeo star. Paige laughed at the irony of it all.

She zipped down the road, her tires crunching the grasshoppers that littered the way before her. In the rearview mirror, she saw birds perched on a barbed wire fence and a few defiant wildflowers. They held on to their roots in the sun-baked dirt the way she clutched hope. The radio continued to croon out one tune after another all the way into the small town of Split Creek, Oklahoma, ten klicks from nowhere.

After parking her car in the designated spot in front of the library, Paige hoisted her tote bag onto her shoulder and grabbed a book about Oklahoma history and another by C. S. Lewis. The latter had kept her up all night, helping her make some sense out of the sordid events of her past. She scraped the grasshoppers from her shoes and onto the curb. The pests were everywhere this time of year. Reminded her of a few gadflies she'd been forced to trust overseas. She'd swept the crusty hoppers off her porch at home and the entrance to the library as she'd done with the shadow makers of the past. But nothing could wipe the nightmares from her internal hard drive.

Her gaze swept the quiet business district with an awareness of how life could change in the blink of an eye. A small landscaping of yellow marigolds and sapphire petunias stretched toward the sky in front of the newly renovated, one-hundred-year-old courthouse. Its high pillars supported a piece of local history . . . and the secrets of the best of families. Business owners unlocked their stores and exchanged morning greetings. Paige recognized most of the dated cars and dusty pickups, but a black Town Car with tinted glass and an Oklahoma license plate parked on the right side of the courthouse caught her attention.

Why would someone sporting a luxury car want to venture into Split Creek, population 1,500? The lazy little town didn't offer much more than a few antique stores, a small library, a beauty shop, Dixie's Donuts, a Piggly Wiggly, four churches—including one First Baptist and one South First Baptist, each at opposite ends of town, one First Methodist, and a holiness tabernacle right beside Denim's Restaurant. She wanted to believe it was an early visitor to the courthouse. Maybe someone lost. But those thoughts soon gave way to curiosity and a twist of suspicion.

With a smile intended to be more appealing than a Fourth of July storefront, she crossed the street to subtly investigate the out-of-place vehicle. Some habits never changed.

Junior Shafer, who owned and operated a nearby antique store, stooped to arrange his outside treasures. Actually, Paige rarely saw an antique on display, just junk and old Avon bottles. "Mornin', Mr. Shafer. Looks like another scorcher."

"Mornin'. Yep, this heat keeps the customers away." The balding man slowly stood and massaged his back. "Maybe I'll advertise free air-conditioning and folks will stop in."

"Whatever works." She stole a quick glance at the Town Car and memorized the license plate number. No driver. "Looks like you have a visitor." She pointed to the car.

Mr. Shafer narrowed his eyes and squinted. "Nah, that's probably Eleanor's son from Tulsa. He's helping her paint the beauty shop. She said he had a new car. The boy must be doing fine in the insurance business."

"Now that's a good son."

Mr. Shafer lifted his chin, then rubbed it. "Uh, you know, Paige . . . he ain't married."

"And I'm not looking." She'd never be in the market for a husband. Life had grown too complicated to consider such an undertaking, even if it did sound enticing.

"A pretty little lady like you should be tending to babies, not books."

"Ah, but books don't grow up or talk back."

He shook his head and unlocked his store.

"I have a slice of peach pie for you." Paige reached inside her tote bag and carefully brought out a plastic container. "I baked it around six this morning. It's fresh."

He turned back around. A slow grin spread from one generous ear to the other. "You're right. You don't need to go off and get married. I might not get my pies." He did his familiar shoulder jig. "Thank you, sweet girl." He reached for the pie with both hands as though it were the most precious thing he'd ever been offered.

The door squeaked open at Shear Perfection.

"Mornin', Eleanor," Mr. Shafer said. "I see your son's car. Glad he's helping you with the paintin'."

"That's not my son's." Miss Eleanor crossed the street, shielding her eyes from the steadily rising sun. "He isn't coming till the weekend."

Paige's nerve endings registered alert. "Won't that be wonderful for you?" She took another passing glance at the vehicle. "I wonder who's driving that fancy car? Too early for courthouse business."

"Somebody with money." Mr. Shafer lifted the plastic lid off the freshly baked pie and inhaled deeply. "Can't wait till lunch."

"Mercy, old man, you're already rounder than my dear-departed mama's potbelly stove." Eleanor's blue hair sparkled in the sunlight as though she'd added glitter to her hairspray.

"You're just jealous. If you weren't a diabetic, you'd be stealing my pie. Paige here knows how to keep a man happy."

One block down, a man carrying a camera emerged from between one of Mr. Shafer's many antique competitors and the barbershop. He lifted it as if to snap a picture of the barbershop. Paige swung her attention back to her friends. He could be the real thing. She hoped so and forced down any precursors of fear.

"What's he taking pictures of?" Eleanor paused. "I'm going to ask." Determination etched her wrinkled face. She squared her shoulders and marched toward the stranger as though she represented the whole town.

Good, Eleanor. I'll head back and let you do the recon work.

Eleanor and the stranger stood too far away for Paige to read their lips, but at least while the two talked, the man couldn't take pictures. A few moments later, the stranger laughed much too loud. Eleanor reached out and shook his hand, then walked back.

Paige focused on Mr. Shafer. She picked up a watering can leaning precariously against a rotted-bottom chair. "Is this a new addition?"

"Nah. It was inside. I just brought it out yesterday."

From the corner of her eye, she saw the stranger stare at them. Medium height. Narrow shoulders. Italian-cut clothes. Couldn't see the type of camera. The stranger walked their way, shoulders arched and rigid. Unless he was a pro, she'd have him sized up in thirty seconds, and then she'd go about her day—relieved.

Mr. Shafer lifted his gaze toward Eleanor. "Who's your friend?"

"Jason Stevens, a photographer looking for some homespun pictures about small towns in Oklahoma."

The way he's dressed? Paige's heart pounded. She replaced the watering can. "Did he say for what magazine?"

"Didn't ask. Why don't you? He wants to take a few shots of us standing in front of our businesses." Eleanor beckoned to Stevens. "Come on over and meet my friends. Paige here wonders what magazine you work for."

The man continued to smile—perfect teeth, perfect smile. "It's for a newspaper, the *Oklahoman*." He stuck out his hand. "Mornin', folks. I bet you'd like your picture in the magazine insert." His camera rested in the crook of his right hand, a new Nikon with fast lenses, perhaps a D90 or D200. No dents or sign of use. Who was this guy? He wasn't any more a photographer than Eleanor or Mr. Shafer.

Have you used that piece of equipment before today?

"Welcome to Split Creek," Paige said. "I'll pass on the picture, though. I'm not photogenic, but you have a beautiful day to photograph our town." She turned and started across the street to the library.

"Of course you're photogenic," Eleanor called. "No one wants to see a couple of old fuddy-duddies like us, but you'd make front-page news."

"You two are the center of attention. I'm the dull librarian." Paige continued to move rapidly across the street.

"Wait a minute," Stevens said.

"Sorry. I need to open the library."

"Come on back, sweet girl. There's no one waiting to get in," Mr. Shafer said.

She lifted her hand and waved backward. Guilt nipped at her heels for leaving them with Stevens, but she had more at stake than they did. "See you two later. Nice meeting you, Mr. Stevens."

She unlocked the old building that had once been a bank but now served as the town library. It oozed with character—beige and black marble floors, rich oaken walls, tall ceilings with intricately carved stone, and a huge crystal chandelier the size of a wagon wheel. The areas where tellers once met with customers now served as cozy reading nooks, and a huge, round, brass-trimmed vault—minus the door—held children's books. The windows still even had a few iron bars. If only the town had high-speed Internet access. They'd been promised that modernization for months.

For a precious moment, she relaxed and breathed in the sights and smells. Bless dear Andrew Carnegie for his vision to establish public libraries. Because of his philanthropy, Paige had a sanctuary. From the creaking sounds of antiquity to the timeworn smell of books and yellowed magazines, she had quiet companions that took her to the edge of experience but not the horror of reality.

In a small converted kitchen behind a vaulted door in the rear corner, Paige placed a peanut butter, bacon, and mayo sandwich in the fridge. Reaching down farther into her tote, she wrapped her fingers around a package of Reese's Pieces. Those she'd stash in her desk drawer. The rest of the peach pie sat on the backseat of her car. She'd retrieve it once Stevens moved down the street, preferably out of town.

If he worked for Daniel Keary, her life was about to change—and not for the better. She shook off the chills racing up her arms. I can handle whatever it is. Snatching up her tote bag, she closed the kitchen door behind her. With the election nearly three months away, Stevens could be one of Keary's men sent to make sure she still understood her boundaries. Regret took a stab at her heart, but there was nothing she could do about Keary's popularity. She'd tried and failed against a force too powerful for her at the time. But her prayers for truth continued.

Her sensible shoes clicked against the floor en route to the front window. Standing to the side, she peered out through the blinds to the sun-laden street for a glimpse of Stevens. He continued to take pictures. Mr. Shafer would most likely give him a tour of the town, beginning with his store and the history of every item strewn across it. The so-called photographer from the *Oklahoman* entered the antique shop.

*That'll bore him to tears and chase him out of town.*

Paige went through the morning ritual of checking the drop box for returned books, of which there were six. She changed the dates on the date-due stamps and stacked the books to be shelved in her arms. The seasoned citizens of Split Creek representing the local book club would arrive any minute, as regular as their morning's constitutional. For an hour and a half they'd discuss the merits of their current novel, everything from the characters to the plot. Today they couldn't storm the shores of the library too soon for Paige.

As if on cue, Miss Alma bustled through the door—her purse slung loosely from her shoulder, her foil-wrapped banana nut bread in one hand and two books in the other.

"Good morning, Miss Alma," Paige said. "Do you need some help?"

"No thanks. If I loosen my hold on one thing, everything else will fall."

A picture of PoliGrip hit Paige's mind. "Well, you're the first today."

Miss Betty sashayed in, a true Southern belle dressed in her Sunday best, complete with a pillbox hat. "Miss Paige, may I brew a pot of decaf coffee?" she asked.

"Yes, ma'am. It's waiting for you." Oh, how she loved these precious people.

Within moments the rest of Split Creek's Senior Book Club

arrived. Paige waved at Reverend Bateson, and as usual, Miss Eleanor and Mr. Shafer were bickering about something.

"At least we agree that Daniel Keary should be our next governor," Miss Eleanor said.

At the mention of that name, Paige thought she'd be physically ill. Keary was running on an Independent ticket, and she didn't care if a Democrat or a Republican pulled in the votes. Anyone but Keary.

"I have banana bread," Miss Alma said. "But don't be picking up a book with crumbs on your fingers."

"We know," several echoed.

Paige appreciated the comic relief. The rest of the members placed chairs in a circle beneath the massive chandelier while Paige checked in their books.

The library door opened again, and Jason Stevens walked in with his camera. The sight of him erased the pleasantries she'd been enjoying with the book club members. He made his way to the circulation desk and stood at the swinging door, trapping her inside.

Hadn't she just swept the bugs off the steps of the library?

"Since you won't let me take your picture outside, I thought I'd snap a few in here. Wow—" his gaze took in the expanse of the building—"this was a bank." His brilliant whites would have melted most women's resolve.

Paige approached the swinging door. "No pictures, please. They always turn out looking really bad."

"How about lunch?"

"Are you coming on to me?" Disgust curdled her insides.

He waved his free hand in front of his face. The man knew just when to utilize a dimple on his left cheek. "I'm simply looking for a story to go along with my photos. This library is charming, fascinating, and so are you."

Revulsion for the dimple-faced city boy had now moved into the fast lane. "Miss Alma, I'll help you arrange the chairs."

"Nonsense." Miss Alma shook her blue-gray head. "You help

this young man. Those old people can do something besides stand around and complain about their gout and bursitis."

Any other time, Paige would have laughed at the remark. But not today.

"Looks like they have everything under control." The low, seductive tone of Stevens's voice invited a slap in the face.

"I suggest you visit with a few other business owners for your newspaper's needs," she said.

"I'm very disappointed."

"You'll get over it."

"Can't we talk?" He leaned over the swinging door.

"You can leave, or I can call the sheriff. Your choice." She picked up the phone on her desk and met his gaze with a stare down.

"So much for sweet, small-town girls." He tossed her his best dejected look. Obviously he wasn't accustomed to the word no.

Her reflexes remained catlike thanks to tai chi workouts still done at home behind drawn curtains. With minimal effort, she could dislocate a shoulder or crash the kneecap of an opponent twice her weight. Such skills were not a part of the job description for most small-town USA librarians, but then again most of them didn't have a working knowledge of Korean, Angolan Portuguese, Swahili, and Russian. The ability to decipher codes, a mastery of disguise, and a knack for using a paper clip to open locks . . . not to mention a past that needed to stay buried. She had to resist the urge to toss Stevens out on his ear. Calm down.

"I'm sorry we don't have the book you wanted. I'm sure one of the branches in Oklahoma City can help you."

A silent challenge crested in his gray eyes, and she met it with her own defiance.

Stevens walked to the door and turned, carrying his camera the way patrons carried books. "Know what? This town would be a great place to hide out a CIA operative."